STANDING GROUND

A Matt Sheridan Novel - Book Three

Robert Cole

Carentan Publishing

Ebook ISBN: 979-8-9875410-4-3
Paperback ISBN: 979-8-9875410-5-0

CWO3 (Ret.) Frederick A. Custer Jr.
USMC / US Army
1940-2023

The world is a better place for having had him in it.

CONTENTS

CHAPTER 1

November 11, 5:41 am

The rocky coast of the Old Head of Kinsale was ominously dark under the light of what the ancient Celts called the Darkest Depths Moon. The entire family's hopes and dreams lie in building a life along this coastline, and Matt hoped the darkness of the rocks did not portend their future in Ireland.

After the stress of being forced to flee their new home off the coast of Maine, the last twelve days aboard the Irish Rover had been almost entirely uneventful. Despite the darkness of the coastline under the setting moon, the entire family was filled with eagerness and anticipation over their impending arrival in the harbor of Kinsale.

With the Old Head now off of their port side, Matt knew that the entrance to the River Bandon lay approximately five miles ahead on the southern coast of Ireland, with the harbor of Kinsale an additional two miles up the river. They would glide along with the rising tide into Kinsale Harbor at their current speed just after first light.

The trip across the Atlantic aboard the luxury super yacht had started full of excitement that had quickly turned into long stretches of boredom interspersed with violent bouts of seasickness. Only Stan, Liz, and Kim had proven immune to the evil hand of that sadistic monster, Poseidon—or whoever was responsible for the rolling swells of the Atlantic seas that ensured nothing could remain in one's stomach.

While most of the twenty-five passengers found their sea legs after the first few days, Derek and Amey had found the trip especially nauseating and had spent most of the voyage praying to the porcelain gods.

"Penny, for your thoughts," Clare asked, leaning into the darkened office where Matt now sat. The small office amidship on the owner's deck had become his sanctuary. Matt spent much of the day at this desk planning, strategizing, and making lists.

"Good morning," Matt replied. "Just sitting here going over the contingency list for arriving in Kinsale. One can never be too prepared."

"Spoken like a true Army Ranger," said his wife, leaning down to place a steaming mug of hot coffee in front of him while giving him a quick kiss and then taking a seat in the plush leather chair on the opposite side of the mahogany desk.

Despite calling the Irish Rover home for the last twelve days, Clare still hadn't become comfortable with the pure luxury of their surroundings. She had never imagined a scenario where she'd be sleeping in the owner's cabin of a 205-foot luxury mega yacht on a cross-Atlantic voyage. Then again, she'd also never imagined most of the things that had happened over the last two months: cataclysmic destruction of US cities by nuclear bombs, a smallpox pandemic that decimated 99% of the world's population, militarized biker gangs bent on killing her family, a second civil war, and a rogue American president that had dispatched a warship to capture her husband.

Given all that, life aboard the Irish Rover didn't seem so far-fetched.

"Are the kids awake? Was anyone else up already?" Matt

asked, taking a sip of his coffee.

Even in the dim light, his wife's beauty showed brightly, and he enjoyed savoring these moments. Her shoulder-length blond hair was pulled back in a ponytail and her eyes matched the deep brown of the mahogany desk.

"Kids are still asleep, hopefully for another half hour. Molly was in the galley making breakfast and said most people planned to get up at 6:00 to be ready to enter the river before 7:00 am. Are we still on track for that time?"

"Yeah, Stan says we're right on schedule. Dawn is about 7:15, so I've asked him to anchor us offshore but close enough that we can see details on land. We'll reel in the two smaller boats and take the Midnight Express to scout out the harbor as we discussed."

Clare looked at her husband while taking a sip of her coffee. She had always admired his ability to stay calm no matter the circumstances, but she could tell he was pretty excited about this morning's adventure. Their nuclear family of four had extended over the last eight weeks to include twenty-one additional people, and Matt and Clare felt the enormous weight of being responsible for their extended family's continued survival. Everyone had followed Matt's decision to head to Kinsale without hesitation; this morning, they would know if this had been the right decision.

"I have to admit," said Clare. "I'm looking forward to being back in Ireland. It's a place we've always enjoyed, and my fingers are crossed it's as lovely as it's always been. And honey, we're as prepared as we could be. Everyone knows their role, and you have thought through every possible scenario that could play out in the next few weeks. We're ready, Matt."

"I know we are," said Matt. "But there's always something we didn't think of. Always."

They both sipped their coffee in the darkened office,

enjoying the silence and each other's company, lost in their thoughts. As was customary throughout the voyage, peace and quiet never lasted very long. After a few minutes, they heard stirring in the salon area behind them, where a couple of the young adults had been sleeping on the sofas, followed by footsteps on the marble foyer outside their office.

Pete poked his head into the office doorway. "Hey Matt, everything still moving forward as we discussed last night?"

"Mornin', Pete. Yes, Stan should have us anchored just offshore the mouth of the River Bandon in about an hour," said Matt.

"Sounds good. Dave and I have everything we need already prepositioned in the garage. So once we drop anchor, we can open up the swim deck, reel in the Hinckley and Midnight Express, and load up. Everyone should be waking up now, and Molly has fixed one of her famous pancake breakfasts."

"Thanks, Pete. We'll be down to breakfast in just a few."

Pete nodded and headed back down the central staircase to the dining room, where breakfast would be served. Matt had known Pete for over twenty years, going back to their days as fraternity brothers at the University of Vermont, and Matt continued to be amazed at how much Pete still resembled Tom Cruise. While Stan captained the yacht, Pete had taken on the responsibility for the two smaller boats currently being towed behind the Irish Rover.

The first was a Hinckley 35—a 35-foot million-dollar yacht of the finest craftsmanship. The Hinckley was tied to a yoke at the stern of the Irish Rover and was towed approximately seventy meters behind the super yacht. Tied behind the Hinckley on a similar tow system was their 37-foot Midnight Express. This boat was the original tender that accompanied the Irish Rover when Matt and his group took possession of it in the harbor of Rockland, Maine.

The two were amazing boats in their own right, and Matt had selected the Midnight Express for their initial foray into the River Bandon and up to Kinsale Harbor. Not knowing what types of obstacles or enemies they might encounter, the open-bow configuration of the Midnight Express allowed for the emplacement of a crew-served machine gun. Additionally, the boat's three 350-horsepower outboard engines allowed it to cruise at up to 40 miles per hour with bursts of speed up to 70 miles per hour, a capability Matt hoped wouldn't be necessary but would welcome if it was.

"I'll go wake the kids up and meet you on the main deck," said Clare, getting up to depart the office. While everyone was looking forward to making landfall today, she recognized they were opening themselves to uncertainties that could bring considerable danger to her family. Her excitement was tempered with apprehension.

"Sounds good. I'll be down in a few," replied Matt, mentally rehearsing every potential contingency they might encounter this morning.

CHAPTER 2

November 11, 7:20 am

The emerald green hills of Ireland appeared gray in the morning dawn. Matt sat next to Pete on the pilot's bench seat of the Midnight Express, easily wide enough for three people, as they cruised north at about fifteen knots into the mouth of the River Bandon. Matt shivered in the cold morning air, glad he had opted for the heavier fleece underneath his full kit of plate carrier and load-carrying vest stuffed with 30-round magazines.

The river maintained a steady width of approximately 1/2 mile before turning sharply to the west in a hairpin turn two miles inland from the coast. Matt noted their position on the 20-inch Garmin marine chartplotter, one of two that sat side-by-side on the pilot's console. The hairpin turn in the river created a peninsula of land that reminded Matt of an awkwardly shaped nub of a piece to a jigsaw puzzle.

On the chartplotter, the nub was labeled James Fort, and Matt knew this was the remnants of a 17th-century fort built to defend the harbor in the aftermath of the Spanish siege of Kinsale in 1601. On the east side of the river, directly across from James Fort, was the much larger Charles Fort. Matt had visited the museum at Charles Fort several times, always admiring the panoramic vista from the massive stone bastions of the pentagonal fort that had been a British garrison for well over two hundred years before being abandoned in the 1920s.

On the near side of James Fort, fronting Charles Fort across the wide river, was a small sandy beach just over a hundred yards wide. Without being told, Pete edged the Midnight Express towards the beach along the west side of the river and slowly brought the boat to a halt about a hundred yards from shore. This was all part of their reconnaissance plan, and Matt turned to watch the next stage being put into action.

LT, or Brent as he was known to his parents, and Dave held a small drone in the open stern of the boat while Liz stood in front of them with a controller box in her hand. The gray plastic drone looked like an alien creature, with a rectangular-shaped body and four squat legs containing propellers. As Dave held it, the propeller blades came to life with a barely audible whirring noise. Matt watched as Liz flicked the controls, and suddenly, the drone shot upwards. A third-year midshipman at the Naval Academy when the cataclysm hit, Liz was the only one of the group familiar with operating a drone.

During the planning for this reconnaissance, Matt was leery of simply dashing into the mouth of Kinsale Harbor in the hopes that it was either abandoned or friendly. Not only could such boldness have devastating consequences for their family, but given all the resources at their disposal, it simply wasn't necessary. The picturesque seaside village of Kinsale lay just over 1/2 mile to their northwest, beyond the hill upon which James Fort sat. Given the minimal winds at dawn, the drone would be over the town in minutes and could safely broadcast real-time video, giving the team a birdseye view of Kinsale.

Matt was intimately familiar with Kinsale, having stayed there several times on trips to visit his sister-in-law Tracy's family, who all lived nearby. In fact, Matt's first trip to Ireland had been for his brother Donald's wedding right here in Kinsale.

Many factors contributed to Matt's selection of Kinsale for

their new home, not the least of which was his familiarity with the area and it being his brother's last known location before the cataclysm. The Republic of Ireland had a pre-Black Pox population of slightly under five million people and was a law-abiding nation with a very low percentage of gun ownership. County Cork, spanning the entire southwest coast of the island nation, was sparsely populated yet had a strong mix of vegetable, dairy, and livestock farms along with a robust fishing industry.

Ireland was also a destination Matt felt the US government would be least likely to follow them, hopefully assuming his family had fled either to Canada or the Caribbean. Twelve days prior, Matt and the family had been forced to feel Vinalhaven in the middle of the night after learning that the renegade President of what remained of the United States government had issued an arrest notice for both Matt and Stan in the desperate hope of gaining access to their supply of vaccine and the QuAI supercomputer. The US Navy was most likely to search for the Sheridans along the east coast of North America.

These factors made Ireland an ideal relocation destination for his family to establish a new life.

"We're coming up over the harbor now," said Liz, looking at the drone's iPhone display clipped into the control box.

Matt, Pete, and Dave crowded over her shoulders in an attempt to watch the live feed. Derek remained in the bow of the Midnight Express, scanning the shoreline with his binoculars, an M240B belt-fed machine gun resting on bipods at his feet. LT maintained a similar watch from the stern.

The dawn's early light had given way to the sun cresting the horizon to the east, providing enough visibility for them to see the harbor and the colorful buildings surrounding it. Liz raised the drone's height to about two hundred feet and positioned the camera for a panoramic view of the harbor. It was just as Matt remembered, minus the hustle and bustle of thousands of tourists walking and driving along the narrow streets of the 700-year-old town that had become known as the foodie capital of Ireland.

"Perfect, Liz," said Matt. "Keep flying due north into the mouth of the harbor. Just past the marina, do you see where that narrow peninsula juts in from the east side? Can you hover right there and give us a 360-degree view?"

"No problem." Liz's fingers twitched on the controls, and the drone flew steadily above the sailboats neatly parked between the wooden slips of the Kinsale Marina. The drone came to a hover, and Liz slowly panned the camera in a clockwise circle, starting in the west.

"Hold it right there, please."

Matt knew the camera faced due west along Pier Road, the main road that led north-south along the edge of the harbor, and watched as the camera slowly pivoted northward in a clockwise rotation. This anvil-shaped inlet at the head of the river's hairpin turn formed the basis of the town of Kinsale, which, over hundreds of years, had developed along the entire shore of the inlet. At the drone's 9 o'clock position, the west bank ran due north-south for about 1/4 mile and was filled with the colorful hotels and restaurants often seen in the postcards of Kinsale Harbor. Along the north, at 12 o'clock, Kinsale's old town evolved into a warren of narrow one-way streets and alleys home to dozens of art galleries and boutique shops interspersed every few doorways by a pub. Rotating to the east, between the 1 and 2 o'clock positions, the anvil-shaped portion of the harbor extended into a narrow inlet of water pointing due east. As the north coast of the River Bandon made its hairpin turn, right at the 3 o'clock position for the drone, a thin peninsula of land extended between the river and the inlet and contained a few rows of old, scenic houses in an area known as Scilly.

As the drone completed a full 360-degree circle, Matt asked

Liz to pause with the drone facing due west. He could see the gray and white stone facade of Actons Hotel, the small town park with the children's playground, and the row of restaurants, including the famed Fishy Fishy—Clare's favorite restaurant. The town looked precisely as it had the last time Matt had visited, except for one thing.

Nothing moved.

Not a single person could be seen.

Matt knew that people might still be asleep in bed as it was still early morning. However, what he was looking for and thankfully did not see were any signs of conflict or danger. There were no emergency vehicles, no barricades, no checkpoints. The town did not appear to have been damaged by fire or any other disaster. It simply appeared empty.

Movement at the edge of the screen caught everyone's attention, and without needing instruction, Liz pivoted the drone and used the camera to zoom in. A pack of a half-dozen dogs ambled through the park on their own, seeming to wander north toward the old town. The visibility of the video camera was so good that Matt could see the tracks the dogs created in the park's long grass covered in early morning dew.

"Place looks empty," said Pete.

"Yeah," agreed Matt. "Liz, could you reposition the drone to the east? Just over Scilly. I want to get a good look at that house on the end with the pier. That's our first choice for a landing spot."

"Sure thing." They all watched the video feed as Liz maneuvered the drone seventy meters to the east across the narrow width of the harbor's opening.

"Lower, please," directed Matt. "Maybe just twenty feet or so above the water."

The video picture descended so they could look straight at

a large, two-story Georgian house painted yellow and fronted by a manicured grass and crushed stone garden. The home and its adjacent barn, which Matt thought was likely a boat house given the large open doors that led down to a sloped stone ramp, was set back about thirty meters from the stone wall that formed the water's edge. Steps had been built in the stone wall that led down to a floating dock.

"Okay, looks good to me. What does everyone think?" Matt asked.

"Looks good to me, too. I can pull the Midnight Express right up, and we can dock her there," said Pete.

"Yeah," said Dave. "Place looks deserted. That landing spot puts us outside the town but on a peninsula where we'll see anyone coming our way. It's way better than docking at the main marina, which'll expose us to anyone in town."

"Okay," said Matt. "Liz, bring the drone back.

Once we have it on board, we'll head to Scilly." Matt and Pete took their seats back in front of the center console, and in a few minutes, they heard the faint, high-pitched whir of the approaching drone. Liz brought it slowly downward until it nested firmly in Dave's outstretched hands. Matt waited a few seconds more for them to stow the drone in its bag, then motioned for Pete to head out into the river.

Matt reached down and toggled the small microphone clipped to his vest below his neck. "Irish Rover, this is Matt. Empty Nest, over."

"Roger, Matt, we copy Empty Nest," replied Stan.

"Empty Nest" was the brevity code that meant no activity or threats had been seen during the drone flyover. As part of the planning for the mission, Matt had made a list of brevity codes that corresponded to segments of their reconnaissance trip. Given that they were using unsecured radio communications on standard frequencies, Matt didn't want anyone to use specific place names in case someone overheard.

Matt imagined Stan sitting on the bridge with Clare and others eagerly awaiting updates from Matt's team. Matt knew they could follow the Midnight Express' progress on the Irish Rover's radar system but would likely lose contact once they rounded the hairpin turn at James Fort due to the radar relying on line of sight. Stan, who had preceded Liz and his daughter, Juliet, at the Naval Academy, would likely be standing ramrod straight, staring out the bridge's windows, reminiscent of the Navy Captain he had been before forming the billion-dollar tech startup, QuAI. Matt joked that if they ever made a movie about this adventure, Tom Cruise would have to play Pete while a taller, Lethal Weapon-aged Danny Glover would be a perfect match for Stan.

"Proceeding to Sparrow now," said Matt. Sparrow was the code for the yellow house in Scilly. There were six other places with codenames along the harbor that Matt had identified as alternate landing sites should the large yellow house on Scilly not be the best.

"Roger, be safe," replied Stan.

CHAPTER 3

November 11, 7:46 am

Pete guided the Midnight Express into Kinsale's harbor, just above wake speed. The three outboard engines were almost silent, and all six on board kept a vigilant lookout as they approached the small floating dock. Despite the drone footage not displaying any threats, tensions were high amongst the crew.

Derek had the M240B propped up on its bipod legs on the boat's bow, ready to neutralize any threat should one appear. At the stern, LT scanned the houses along the Scilly harborfront while Liz used binoculars to scout any threats or signs of life on the opposite side of the harbor in the old town area of Kinsale. Dave sat on the cushioned seat in front of the center console, ready to assist Derek with the machine gun and scouting to their front. He was tasked with grabbing the bow line and jumping to the dock to secure the boat. Matt sat next to Pete, attempting to watch everything and everyone simultaneously.

Pete expertly maneuvered the boat alongside the floating dock, lightly flipping the engines in reverse to bring the boat to a halt as Dave stepped onto the dock and secured the bow line to a cleat. Liz tossed him the stern line, and he quickly secured the Midnight Express to the dock.

The peninsula of Scilly was a narrow finger of land sloping steeply down from the mainland hills for approximately five hundred meters. At slightly over a hundred meters in width, the Scilly High Road served as the peninsula's spine until it bisected Lower Road, which looped around the outer edges of the finger. A single row of large houses ringed the external side of Lower Road, each a large waterfront estate, the newest of which was more than two hundred years old. A warren of small homes and pubs had melded together on the inner side of Lower Road and up along the Scilly High Road. Most buildings were made of stone and timber, and some, such as the famed Spaniard Inn, traced their roots back to 1650 or earlier. Matt had downed plenty of pints of Murphy's in the Spaniard and felt very comfortable returning to this area.

"Okay, everyone. Keep your head on a swivel. Treat anyone we see as friendly until proven otherwise. Remember, we come in peace. We'll seem way more menacing to them than they will to us," said Matt as he climbed onto the dock.

Their previous few days before departing Vinalhaven had been filled with violence and gun battles against a totalitarian regime calling themselves The Base. This group, consisting mostly of criminals, degenerates, and savages that had survived the pandemic, was bent on forging a new Union of American States minus a Bill of Rights where slavery and rape were common practice. Matt's family had been forced to defend themselves and attack The Base several times, and Matt did not want his family's first experience in Ireland to be one of violent conflict.

They had been extremely fortunate during the 12-day voyage to have access to QuAI—the artificial intelligence supercomputer owned by Stan and Pete. While the computer system and its enormous data center were physically contained in an impenetrable vault built under a mountain in Charlottesville, Virginia, and operating under perpetual hydropower from an underground river, Stan had brought with him a portable version of QuAI that was capable of interfacing with the main datacenter using satellite communications. This allowed their group access to an incredible wealth of satellite imagery and sensor information on the town of Kinsale and the surrounding areas of County Cork.

With the boat firmly secured, all six of the team walked quickly across the dock and up the ancient stone steps carved directly into the stone retaining wall. At the top, Matt paused to take in the property's beauty. Named Raffeen House, the stately Georgian manor looked across an expanse of manicured lawn and crushed stone. While the lawn needed mowing, Matt could tell that the yard had once been immaculately maintained. Like many waterfront homes of its period, the front was oriented due south, facing the harbor, while the back door opened onto the narrow Lower Road behind it.

Matt watched as his team's choreographed and rehearsed movements played out before him. Pete and Derek moved to the southeast corner of the property next to the oversized stone boat house, where a wrought iron fence provided visibility down the Lower Road to the east. This vantage point allowed the two of them to cover any approaches from the east or the water and keep an eye on the Midnight Express.

Dave, LT, and Liz moved forward quickly towards the front entrance to the home, stacking up on the right side of the door in preparation for making entry. Giving Pete a thumbs up, Matt sprinted forward to catch up and take his position behind Liz at the back of the stack. Dave, a former US Army paratrooper whose post-military career in law enforcement included serving as a member of the NCIS SWAT team, was their designated breacher. He had a Halligan breaching tool in his hands and examined the door jamb for the best place to wedge the tempered steel pry bar.

"Hey, Dave," Matt said calmly, trying to lighten the

situation. Everyone was very keyed up, and while he wanted everyone to be cautious, he didn't want this to become a full-on assault unless the situation warranted it. "This is Ireland, man. Try the doorknob first."

Dave smiled and reach out to check the knob. Sure enough, the knob turned easily in his hand, and he pushed the door wide open.

"Hello!" Dave yelled into the home. "Anyone home? We mean you no harm." Dave paused and listened for a few moments, noting the silence. "Hello?" He yelled a final time. Silence.

Dave turned to make eye contact with Matt, who nodded toward the interior. Dave and LT moved quickly inside, followed immediately by Liz and Matt. While the house may be well over two hundred years old, Matt could tell it had recently been renovated to the highest standard. The floor was dark hardwood covered with modern rugs, while the walls were painted a stately gray. The furniture was modern and comfortable. A wide central hallway led straight to the back of the house, and a staircase led upward. To the right, Matt could see a large, formally furnished drawing room, and to the left was a combined kitchen and dining room. Leaving Liz in the hallway, Matt moved left into the kitchen to see Dave and LT clear the family room in the back left corner of the house.

"First floor clear," said Dave. "Seems empty to me, Matt. Just smells musty."

"Agreed," said Matt. "I'm guessing it was vacant before the Black Pox hit. Be careful clearing upstairs. Liz and I will wait here.

Five minutes later, Dave returned from upstairs. "All clear. Everything's empty. Beds are made, and closets only have a few clothes. My guess is that this is a vacation house, and the owners weren't here when the pandemic hit."

Matt nodded, reaching to toggle the microphone for the hand-held radio clipped to his vest. “Irish Rover, this is Matt. Sparrow is green. Repeat: Sparrow is green. Proceeding to Falcon.”

“Roger, Irish Rover copies Sparrow is green, proceeding to Falcon.”

Matt knew that the entire extended family, for that’s what their group had become, would breathe their first sigh of relief, knowing their first target had been clear. However, Matt also knew everyone would still be on edge as the next step, codenamed Falcon, entailed finding a vehicle and cruising through the streets of Kinsale. Matt wanted to ensure the town was clear or friendly before bringing their 205-foot superyacht into the harbor. If Matt had said “Ostrich,” those on the Irish Rover would know Matt had decided to explore the town on foot, likely due to some perceived threats. “Falcon” was their best-case scenario, and Matt hoped Kinsale was exactly what he had planned.

“LT, could you and Liz go check the boat house and see if maybe there’s a vehicle there? We need to find ourselves some wheels.”

“Sure thing, Matt,” said LT, heading for the front door with Liz in tow.

“If this place is a vacation home for someone in Dublin, I doubt they leave a car here. What do you think?” Matt asked Dave, the two of them now alone in the house. Married to Matt’s cousin Michelle, Dave had been one of Matt’s closest friends for years, and the reason Matt had selected Maine’s coastal island of Vinalhaven as their destination when living in Vermont became untenable. Dave’s family owned a cottage on Vinalhaven, and Dave’s prior military and law enforcement experience had proven invaluable to the family over the last month. Completely bald and standing only 5’7”, Dave was incredibly fit, strong, and not someone anyone would want to tangle with.

"Yeah, I agree," said Dave. "I think we just go along as planned and check the neighboring houses. Trying to hotwire a car is too much hassle, but someone will have a set of keys hanging on the wall or in a dish on the counter."

"Okay, let's go out and see if Pete has seen anything." They walked out the front door and across the lawn to where Pete and Derek stood. As they walked, LT and Liz came out of the boathouse, shaking their heads negatively.

Matt laid out a plan for all six grouped at the back of the yard. "Okay, we'll stay in groups of two. Dave and LT head north to check the homes on the backside of this house, while Liz and I will go east along Lower Road. When you find a suitable vehicle in the yard, check for keys in the car or, more likely, in the home where it's parked. Keep everyone updated on the radio. Pete and Derek, you hold down the fort here."

Everyone nodded, and there were no questions. Dave opened the latch on the wrought iron gate, and he and LT quickly moved up the narrow lane toward the back of the house and homes up on the hill. With Liz following close behind, Matt began walking down the Lower Road to the east.

The Lower Road was narrow, barely wide enough to allow a single car to pass. Matt had driven these streets before and remembered driving in Ireland required extreme alertness and patience. There was a reason Ireland joined Israel and Jamaica as the only three countries in the world where credit card companies would not offer vehicle damage insurance for rental cars. Drivers here often drove too fast for the conditions but were also extremely courteous when encountering each other on these narrow lanes and yielding to allow others to pass. As he and Liz walked down the lane, a waist-high stone wall separated the road from the harbor on their right, while several stone buildings crowded right up to the edge of the road, allowing no room for even a sidewalk.

The first building on the left had the words "The Spinnaker" painted in large blue letters along the front of the building. This had been a lively pub on Matt's first visit to the old country, but he knew it had closed down several years prior. Walking past, it appeared the pub had never reopened, and the small car park along its side was empty of vehicles. As they continued to walk, the view across the harbor to their right offered incredible views across to James Fort.

Just ahead on their left were two beautiful houses, built up on the side of the hill with large white-trimmed picture windows across the front to take advantage of the amazing view. The first home had a driveway wrapped around the backside of the house with no vehicles visible, but the second home had a large parking area in the front. Matt smiled when he noticed a small Toyota SUV and an Audi sedan parked in front. Matt's sister-in-law Tracy's father owned one of the larger Toyota dealerships in the area, about ten miles up the road in the town of Carrigaline, and this SUV bore the red and white sticker of his dealership, O'Riordan Toyota.

Liz also saw the vehicles, and they both quickened their pace up the bricked driveway. The sun had risen high enough to cast its warmth and push away the coldness of the morning. Matt reached for his radio to inform everyone of their find.

"This is Matt. We're about a hundred yards east on Lower Road. There's a house with two vehicles. We're going to clear the homes and look for keys."

"Roger," Pete replied immediately.

"Sounds good, Matt," answered Dave. "We just found a little Fiat pickup truck. LT has the keys, and we're seeing if it will start. FYI, the home had two bodies."

"Okay," said Matt. "If it starts, bring it down to the house where Pete and Derek are."

Matt motioned for Liz to move up to the side door of the

white house, where the two vehicles were parked. This was the entrance closest to the driveway and the one most likely used by the residents. Reaching out to twist the knob, Matt found the door locked.

Damn, Matt thought. *Dave has the Halligan tool.*

Matt looked closely at the small glass panes on the door and confirmed that the lock was a simple deadbolt. Liz stepped forward with her M4 in her hands, reversing the weapon to strike a quick blow against the window pane with the butt of the weapon.

"Wait!" Matt hissed, causing Liz to stop just before smashing the weapon into the window. Matt reached down to the side of the driveway where a row of bricks separated the driveway from the lawn and quickly pried out a single brick. "No sense risking breaking the butt of a weapon unnecessarily."

Matt handed Liz the brick and watched as she shattered the window pane closest to the deadbolt. She carefully picked out all the glass in the frame, then reached in and turned the deadbolt. The door opened easily.

The sickly stench of death quickly erased the salty tang of the harbor. This was a smell both Liz and Matt had become accustomed to, and it was not unexpected. The door opened into a mudroom off a large, modern kitchen, and Matt and Liz began clearing the house. They found the source of the smell in the upstairs master bedroom—a couple who had died of smallpox lying together in bed. It was impossible to determine their age from their state of decomposition.

Without a word, they closed the door to the bedroom and went back downstairs in search of car keys. Liz found them within seconds, sitting in a bowl on the counter by the door.

"Great find!" Matt said. "Now, let's see if these bad boys will start." Matt grabbed the Toyota key and headed straight for the

RAV4 parked outside the door. Clicking the button on the key fob to open the door, Matt was disheartened when he didn't hear the familiar chirp signaling an unlocked door.

"Shit!" He exclaimed. "Damn battery is likely dead. Try to unlock the Audi, Liz." He watched Liz click the unlock button several times on the sleek Audi key fob in her hand: silence and no flashing yellow lights on the front of either vehicle.

"That sucks," said Liz.

"Yeah. Yeah, it does."

The radio crackled with Dave's voice. "Matt, no joy. Battery's dead. We did find jumper cables in the garage, though. Please tell me your vehicle still has some juice."

"Ah, not at the moment," Matt replied into his radio mic. "But gimme two minutes. I have an idea."

Matt looked around the driveway and thought his plan would work. Luckily, the owners had combat parked both cars so they pointed down the steep driveway.

"What's the plan, Matt?" Liz asked.

"Have some faith, Liz. You're about to see some magic at work and learn something probably unknown to every American in your generation."

Liz looked at him skeptically. "Uh, yeah. Okay, Matt. I can't wait." Ever Pete's daughter, Liz's smile seemed to be mocking Matt, her dark-brown hair tied in a ponytail under a ragged Boston Red Sox hat and a look on her face that made Matt feel much older than his forty-two years.

Matt walked over to the RAV4 and used the key to unlock the door. As with most of the cars in Ireland, the RAV4 had a manual transmission. He put his rifle on the passenger seat and slid into the driver's seat. Pain shot up from his right kneecap as it banged forcefully against the steering column. He cursed silently as he reached for the lever that would adjust the seat rearward, allowing him to slide his 6'3" frame into the front seat. Putting the key in the ignition, Matt tried to start the car. As expected, the engine cranked slightly, but the battery didn't have enough juice to start it. Leaving the door open, he motioned for Liz to come towards him.

"Okay, here's what I need you to do, Liz. Get behind the vehicle and push with everything you've got when I say Go. We need to get this thing rolling down the driveway as fast as possible."

"For what? You're going to try to coast it over to the Raffeen House? Dave might have jumper cables, but we still need a charged battery."

"Oh, ye of little faith. Just watch and learn, Grasshopper. And push!"

Matt stood in the doorway as Liz moved to the vehicle's rear. He had already left the ignition in the On position and familiarized himself with the handbrake and gear shift, leaving the RAV4 in neutral.

"Ready?" Matt asked.

"Ready," replied Liz.

Matt reached in and released the parking brake. He could feel the wheels loosen as gravity pushed the vehicle downward. With one hand on the door frame and the other on the open door, Matt yelled, "Now! Run!" He pushed as hard as possible, and the RAV4 moved easier than anticipated. Its momentum began to pick up in several steps, and Matt was running beside the open car door. With a burst of speed, Matt pushed hard and then jumped into the passenger seat. "Keep pushing, Liz!"

The RAV4 rushed toward the bottom of the driveway as Matt pushed in the clutch pedal with his left foot and shifted into first gear. Matt heard Liz stop running behind him, and he let the SUV pick up speed as it neared the bottom of the driveway.

Wait for it. Wait for it.

Matt waited until the vehicle was almost at the bottom of the driveway, where he figured he had as much speed as he would get. Matt quickly popped his foot off the clutch with the car in first gear. The vehicle lurched and bucked for a quick second as the dashboard lit up and the vehicle's engine jumped to life. Matt quickly pushed down on the clutch and revved the engine several times, breathing life into a battery that had lain dormant for several months. He brought the vehicle to a stop along Lower Road, continuing to breathe life into the battery by revving the RPMs.

Liz ran up beside him, a bit out of breath from sprinting down the driveway. "How'd you do that?" She asked, a bit dumbfounded.

"Magic," replied Matt.

"No, seriously, Matt. How'd you do that?"

"Honestly, Liz, I have no idea the mechanics behind it. My dad showed me this when I was little, and our family car had a dead battery one winter. In college, I used to do this all the time when the battery froze on my little Nissan Sentra during the cold Vermont winters. Half the time, it was your Dad who was pushing. You can only do it with a standard transmission, but something about the speed and popping the clutch while in first gear allows you to bypass the battery and start the engine."

"Okay," said Liz, not sure what to say. "I guess you old people can teach us something new after all."

"For that, young lady, you get to walk back to the house." Matt put the RAV4 in gear and drove the hundred yards down Lower Road to the corner of Raffeen House, watching Liz trot along the road behind him. Matt reached down and toggled his radio mic. "Hey Dave, we got one started. Where are you?"

"Just up the hill behind Sparrow."

"Roger. Liz, go link up with Pete. I'll be back in a few minutes with both vehicles."

Matt drove around the back of the Raffeen House, juked around a narrow corner, and saw Dave standing at the base of a short driveway next to a small, neat house thirty meters up the hill. Matt pulled into the driveway adjacent to a small black pickup truck. It had a Fiat logo, but Matt was unfamiliar with the design as it was unlike pickup trucks in the United States. It had four doors, but the pickup bed seemed about half as long as a normal truck bed. LT had the hood already opened and a pair of jumper cables in hand.

In minutes, both vehicles were parked in the crushed stone yard of the Raffeen House, with their engines running.

CHAPTER 4

November 11, 12:17 pm

Stan expertly maneuvered the Irish Rover so that it came to a standstill alongside the long floating dock of the Kinsale Yacht Club. The dock consisted of a 100-meter-long central spine with four perpendicular docks of similar reach spaced evenly along its length. This arrangement allowed for over two hundred individual boat slips, about half of which were currently empty. The occupied slips were mostly filled with various-sized sailboats interspersed with some fishing boats and cabin cruisers. Most boats in the harbor were docked in slips, with maybe a dozen mooring balls floating in the harbor.

Matt and his team had driven around the streets of Kinsale for the previous few hours, noting the complete absence of everyone. It seemed as if everyone had simply disappeared into thin air until Matt had led the 2-vehicle convoy up onto the R605 road and past the small campus of the Kinsale Community Hospital. Cars stretched along the road, parked haphazardly in the grass and in shallow ditches. Matt and Dave got out quickly to check inside the walls of the hospital compound and were immediately assaulted by the smell of death. It was only necessary to venture a few yards past the entrance gate, where they could see several refrigeration containers and stacks of filled body bags. It was immediately clear that people had flocked to this location upon coming down with symptoms of the Black Pox, yet only their spirits had left the hospital grounds.

Matt stood on the dock next to Derek, watching as Pete and Dave piloted the Hinckley and Midnight Express along the same dock in front of the superyacht. They had gotten lucky in that the main spine of the dock had been cleared along the side facing the river, allowing for easy tie-up of all three of their vessels. Given the width of Kinsale Harbor, the end of the dock was only about fifty meters across the water to the stone wall of Raffeen House. They would still need to traverse by road about one kilometer around the harbor to transit between the yacht and the Scilly peninsula, but it would be quite easy to maintain visibility over the yacht from the Raffeen House.

Matt watched as Liz secured the lines of all boats to the dock while Kim and Dylan lowered the gangway from the Irish Rover. All of the Rover's nineteen remaining passengers were gathered on the main deck, waiting to step onto land for the first time in more than twelve days. Matt greeted, fist bumps, or hugged everyone as they disembarked, gesturing for them to continue down the dock to where LT waited on the concrete wharf. The November sun shined brightly on their arrival, and most everyone wore nothing but a fleece to ward off the autumn chill.

Everything was proceeding according to plan, and after needing to flee Vinalhaven in the middle of the night, it was important for Matt to provide his family with a sense of normalcy. Survival was not simply about staying alive; it was about creating a future for his children. Many of the planning sessions on the Irish Rover with his "adult council" focused on how best to build a new life in Ireland. The first step, Matt knew, was making everyone feel safe.

That feeling of safety started right now. Matt had instructed LT to escort everyone who had disembarked to the park across the street. Matt proceeded up the gangway, where only Stan,

Molly, and Clare remained onboard.

"Are we all set?" Matt asked.

"Yes, Matt," said Molly. "We've got everything packed up and ready to go. Dylan and Grace will help us carry things over to the park."

"Thanks, Molly. I think this will be just what we need." Molly, in her late sixties and the oldest member of their expanded family, had become their de facto grandmother despite being the actual grandmother of only Grace. Having run a successful farm while living next door to Matt's brother Donald's in Vermont, Molly had assumed control of the galley onboard the Irish Rover and had organized their meals for the entire voyage.

"Everyone is so excited to see Kinsale. Are you sure it's safe, Matt?" Clare asked.

"Yes. As sure as we can be, anyway. Some people must still be alive here, but in our drive today, we saw no sign of any violence. No checkpoints, active or abandoned. No bullet marks in any buildings, no smashed windows, and no burned stores. Kinsale simply looks like it was abandoned."

"Okay. That's a relief. Although it's sad to think that everyone here is also gone. Most people hoped that the Black Pox hadn't been as severe here."

"Yeah, I know. I hoped that as well. We'll know more when we explore inland, but I'm confident we're quite secure here. I've instructed everyone but LT and Derek to put away their gear and long guns. They can carry pistols, but I want the kids and the younger crowd to start feeling like things will return to normal."

"Well, I certainly think what we're bringing will help," added Molly. "Here comes Dylan and Grace, right on time." Love had sprouted when Matt and Molly weren't looking, and Matt's 18-year-old nephew and Molly's 24-year-old granddaughter had become an inseparable couple. Together, they carried a large wicker basket piled high with two soft-sided coolers.

Matt excused himself and walked quickly through the main salon and up to the owner's quarters, where he and Clare had been sleeping the last two weeks. He quickly stripped off his plate carrier and vest, leaving the Glock 19 holstered on his belt. He then reached into a large duffel bag and removed an item he thought would add to the family's afternoon.

Matt returned to the main deck and noticed everyone had already left the dock area, leaving Dave alone, sitting on a lawn chair, his M4 rifle resting across his knees. They had all agreed to always leave one armed sentry aboard the Irish Rover, and Dave had volunteered.

"You sure you're good staying here?" Matt asked. "I'm happy to pull the first watch."

"Nah, man. You go on up to the park. It's important. Pete's gonna relieve me in half an hour, so I won't miss much."

"Okay. Thanks, Dave. I'm so glad we have you and Michelle with us."

Matt could see everyone at the park about a hundred yards down the road and set off on foot to meet up. There was so much to do to make Kinsale their new home, but Matt also knew that taking some time to enjoy things was critical. Matt had decided they would spend at least the first week sleeping on the Irish Rover, which took away any pressure to set up housing quickly. He wanted to take his time and do things right from the beginning.

And that beginning was a picnic.

As Matt entered the park through an opening in the stone wall, he could see his two kids and several young adults playing on the swing set. Molly, Clare, and Marvi were laying out food items on one table while several others sat talking animatedly at another of the picnic tables.

"Hey, Dylan!" Matt shouted. "Heads up!" With that warning, Matt tossed the best spiral he could with the object he'd retrieved from a bag in his room—an NFL-regulation football. Dylan stood up and caught the ball effortlessly, prompting some of the assembled ladies to cheer.

"I'm open, Dylan! I'm open!" Matt's 11-year-old son Christopher yelled, launching himself off the swings to dash across the open grass of the small park. Dylan, who without the cataclysm would likely be playing quarterback for his high school football team right now, launched a high, floating spiral that Christopher sprinted to catch up with and receive into the cradle of his arms. Pretending to score a touchdown, Christopher spiked the ball on the ground and did his version of a touchdown dance.

Everyone in the park was all smiles. This was exactly what Matt had intended to accomplish. He could feel the tension of their escape from Maine and the cross-Atlantic voyage melting away as everyone finally began to relax.

CHAPTER 5

November 11, 7:43 pm

The adult council met in the interior dining room after an enjoyable afternoon of a picnic and some guided tours. Everyone ate their fill of Molly's delicious lunch, and at different points in the afternoon, both Matt and Dave had driven small groups around the main streets of Kinsale and over to Scilly and the Raffeen House. At no point did they see any indication of any violence that had occurred during the pandemic.

After the picnic, Matt, Dave, and Pete each led groups to walk around the town and check out the various shops, restaurants, and stores. The goal was not to scavenge but rather to identify what there was to scavenge and how difficult that would be. Between all recon groups, they had formed two basic conclusions. First, the town still had considerable supplies, especially canned goods at the various restaurants. Second, it appeared that there were at least some residents left alive in the area. They had identified several stores where the dust had formed and been recently disturbed, including the grocery store, pharmacy, and bookstore. Many of the doors to the shops had previously been forced open, but these intrusions had been done in such a manner as to minimize damage. Unlike the widespread looting they had witnessed in Vermont and Maine, whoever was taking items from the shops in Kinsale was doing so respectfully.

Everyone on the council had already been briefed about what they had found on their recon trips, and the focus of this meeting was for the informal leadership group of the nine oldest adults to formalize their priority of work now that they had a first-hand assessment of Kinsale.

"First, I'd like to thank Molly, Marvi, and Clare for organizing such a wonderful picnic this afternoon. Our goal was to make everyone feel like this could be their new home, and I think we accomplished that with flying colors," said Matt, starting the meeting. A round of clapping and verbal endorsements followed Matt's comment. "Clare and I have been here several times, as have Kelsey, Derek, and Dylan. I'd like to hear what the rest of you think now that you've seen the town."

"It's perfect, Matt. Just as described and in line with all the information we've reviewed from QuAI. The fact that there's no evidence of previous violence proves that the threat level is extremely low compared to what we were facing back in Maine." Kim's mention of violence made Matt think of the circumstances that had led Kim to join their family. A marine biologist at the famed Woods Hole Oceanographic Institute, Kim had been stranded in Rockland, Maine, with a group of MIT graduate students at the onset of the pandemic. Several of The Base's brutal barbarians had brutally attacked Kim and her group. While Matt had led a small team to rescue her, it was not before Kim and some of her students had been savagely beaten and raped. Since the attack, she had rarely left Matt's side, and despite the trauma of the incident, she had quickly become an invaluable member of the extended family.

"The threat level may be low, but not zero," added Dave.

"True," said Kim. "Maybe manageable is a better word."

"Exactly, Kim. Well put," said Dave. "I think with our capabilities and firepower, we have little to fear from the most likely threats in Ireland. However, we still don't know much about what's happened here, so we need to maintain a security posture that will allow us to respond to the unknown."

"I think that's a given," said Matt. "We've already discussed maintaining at least one sentry 24/7, and by sleeping on the boat for at least the next week, we should know a lot more about any threats in our environment. What other issues are different now that we've seen Kinsale?"

"The two things that concern me the most, Matt, are heating fuel and power," said Stan. "And my concern isn't so much for this winter but more for the long term. From what I've seen so far, most houses use oil furnaces for heat, with a few homes having wood-burning stoves. I've no doubt we'll be able to find the local heating oil company and figure out how to load a truck and deliver it to the houses we decide to occupy. That will get us through this winter - but what about next winter? And the one after that? At some point, like gasoline, the heating oil will lose its efficacy and won't burn. I don't believe we'll ever be able to refine oil, so that leaves us with a long-term heating problem on an island with very cold winters."

"Good point, Stan," agreed Matt. "Your second concern?"

"Electricity. We haven't ventured far from Kinsale, but I've yet to see a windmill, and I can't imagine solar farms would be very effective here. We know from QuAI that there are some wind farms about forty miles north of Cork City, but that's likely not a place that works well for us long term, as I believe we want to be near the coast. Again, we have the Irish Rover for power generation to keep QuAI going and our radios charged, but in the long term, if we want to build a new life here, we'll need to solve the power generation issue."

"We discussed this at length on the voyage over, Stan," said Kim. "I agree with you completely, but I don't think anything's changed from what we strategized on the way here. We knew Kinsale likely would be without power."

"I'm just bringing it up, Kim, as Matt asked for our thoughts," said Stan. "It's not a problem we need to solve this week, but it's something we're going to need to solve in the next six months."

"Agreed," said Matt, trying to keep the conversation on track. "We're going to have a lot of discussions about electricity in the coming days. Anything else anyone wants to add?"

"I feel like the food situation is quite good," said Molly. "We know we have over a six-month supply of food onboard the yacht, but from what Dave and Matt have seen, there's likely at least another year's worth of staples in Kinsale. We brought a significant seed bank with us, and from the pictures Matt took of some of the farms up on the hills above Kinsale, I think we likely should have no problem establishing a sustainable farm. I do think that getting a handle on livestock and farm animals should be a fairly high priority. If we can get a supply of sheep, cows, chickens, and pigs, we can add fresh meat and dairy to our diets to keep us nourished long term."

"I couldn't agree more," said Matt.

"I'm writing all this down, Matt," said Michelle, who had become their de facto record keeper throughout the journey. As a lawyer, she was extremely organized and kept great notes.

"Thanks, Michelle. And Molly, I know our original plan called for us to look at establishing a livestock farm during the second week on the ground, but I think, given the low-threat environment, we can move that up several days. Everyone agree?"

Everyone nodded affirmatively.

"So, looking at our current plan, we have three primary tasks tomorrow. First, we establish our motor pool, and we previously voted Pete as our transportation czar. We need to make sure we have a couple more boats and at least six to eight working vehicles, with fuel topped up for all of them. Right?"

"Right," said Pete. "I spent this afternoon checking things out. The marine fuel situation here at the marina is excellent, as they had the foresight to stabilize their fuel storage tanks. That covers the Hinckley and the Midnight Express, but the Irish Rover uses AGO, and we'll likely have to go to the port in Cork or Ringaskiddy for that. Matt and I also checked out the Top Oil petrol station up the hill on the R600 road. It had plenty of both gasoline and diesel fuel. We'll add a stabilizer to it tomorrow, and that location will likely serve as our filling station. Stan, what's our fuel situation on the Irish Rover."

"Well, the tanks were full with 140,000 liters in Rockland when the pandemic hit. Between the generator being on minimally for a month, plus our twelve-day voyage, we have just under 40,000 liters remaining. That's about six days' worth of travel or about 90 days' worth of full-time generator power."

"Okay, so Irish Rover AGO fuel is a priority, but something we can deal with in a week, right?" asked Pete.

"Yes, waiting a week won't make a difference as long as we're not planning another voyage. We have other things to do first that are more critical."

"Okay," said Pete. "So, as far as priority one tomorrow, we need to find eight suitable vehicles, get them started, up and running, and fueled. The first place I want to check is the road outside the hospital. The way those cars were parked haphazardly, with many double-parked, I'd bet a lot of people left their keys in the car. That will make things much easier than breaking into houses and finding keys. But we'll do that if we have to."

"Great, so that's our priority task tomorrow," said Matt. "Pete, you can have all of Kim's group plus Grace, Dylan, and Gianna to help you. And that brings us to our second priority for tomorrow—clearing enough houses on Scilly for all of us. Dave, Derek, LT, and I will do that starting first thing in the morning. We'll use a similar marking protocol as we did in Vinalhaven, but there are a dozen houses on the end of the peninsula surrounding Raffeen House that we need to clear. This will also give us much more info about what we have there for resources and living arrangements."

"And what's the third priority?" Clare asked.

"The third priority task is to start scouting farther outside of Kinsale. Tomorrow afternoon, I'd like to check out the airport as well as Carrigaline, the town about twenty kilometers away where Tracy's family is from. The next day, I want to get into Cork City, about thirty kilometers from here, just past the airport and Carrigaline. I suspect we'll encounter at least some people on that trip, so I want to be prepared."

"And what about after tomorrow?" Marvi asked. "Are we still planning to divide into teams like we discussed on the voyage?" Marvi was referring to the several lengthy strategy sessions that had taken place on the Irish Rover during the 12-day voyage, the last meeting of which had resulted in an agreement to divide the family into teams that would focus on specific tasks to be accomplished.

"I don't think anything's changed in that regard, Marvi," said Matt. "Unless you have a concern you'd like to bring up. Just like we did in Vinalhaven, once we settle in here, I think it makes sense for everyone to have a specific role supporting our long-term survival. And dividing into teams is the first step in that process."

As Stan's wife and Juliet's mother, Marvi was used to taking a back seat to others in her family. However, despite being married to one of the richest tech entrepreneurs in the world, Matt had always thought Marvi was the smartest of the couple. She had been a highly successful consultant and entrepreneur, having started and managed several Michelin-star restaurants. With the explosive success of Stan's company, QuAI, Marvi had spent the last few years focused on raising her family. Since joining forces in Vermont, Matt had come to rely heavily on Marvi and Clare to manage all aspects of the family dynamic while he focused on external threats.

Matt was first introduced to Stan and Marvi White more than a decade ago by Pete, who had worked closely with Stan in the Navy. The three couples had often vacationed together with their children. One of the fastest-rising officers in the Navy, Stan had taken early retirement to pursue his dream of starting a company focused on artificial intelligence. The result was QuAI, a company that had made the White's billionaires several times over.

In the aftermath of the cataclysm, with a person's net worth holding no value, Stan's supercomputer could quite possibly be the most valuable asset on earth. As one of the world's most advanced machine-learning supercomputers before the cataclysm, it now contained many of the secrets that had died along with 99% of the world's population.

CHAPTER 6

November 12, 12:13 pm

Matt took a tentative bite of his pasta and watched as Derek and LT also seemed to be forcing their meal down. It wasn't that they weren't hungry; it was more that they had left their appetites in one of the many houses they had cleared of bodies that morning in Scilly. Based on what he had seen, it was clear to Matt that the majority of people here in Ireland had simply crawled into their beds and succumbed to the Black Pox. In many cases, the last family member left a note for loved ones that detailed the horrors of caring for their spouse, children, parents, and sometimes extended family and friends. Reading the letters in each home, Matt gleaned that the government of Ireland had informed everyone that no vaccine was coming, the hospitals could not provide care, and the best course of action was simply to stay at home and pray for the best.

Some of the homes they had seen had rudimentary graves dug in the yard, but the pox hit so fast and hard that often all the household members came down with the disease simultaneously. The result was that, in most houses, people often died in their beds. Matt's instinct was to say that they had "died peacefully in their beds," but knew the end stages of smallpox brought anything but a peaceful death.

Matt and Dave, along with Derek and LT, had started

shortly after first light by breaching eleven houses on the Scilly peninsula's westernmost point. Eight of the homes had an unlocked door, but three required the breaking of panes of glass in a door to release the deadbolt lock and allow entry. Not coincidentally, those three homes had no deceased occupants. In the remaining eight homes, the team found between one and seven residents in each house that had succumbed to smallpox.

The first two hours had been spent searching the houses, but the last several hours had consisted of wrapping each of the bodies and carrying them respectfully out to the home's yard. Matt had yet to decide how he wanted to dispose of the bodies and wanted to speak to the group tonight after dinner. He hoped to find a tractor with a backhoe and put all the bodies in a mass grave. As they cleared out more and more of Kinsale, he knew a large burial ground would be required.

Matt twirled his fork in his pasta and contemplated forcing down another bite. He looked across the table at Dave, who had already wolfed down his meal and was scraping the dregs of sauce from the bottom of his bowl. Clearly, dead bodies had no impact on Dave's appetite.

"Hungry, huh?" Matt asked a bit facetiously.

"Hell yeah, man," said Dave. "Hauling all those bodies worked up my appetite."

"Seriously, Dave?" Derek asked. "The maggots and decomposing bodies didn't bother you?"

Dave looked up at Derek, unsure if Derek was serious with his question. "Nope. I mean, we wore gloves and masks, and I washed my hands. But I've seen a lot worse than dead bodies decomposing for two months. Don't get all squeamish on us now, brother. Eat up. You're going to need your energy."

Derek thought of replying but didn't know what to say. Just then, they heard a bunch of people on the gangway, and a minute later, Pete, Kim, and several others walked in and sat at the dining room table.

"Hey, guys! How was the vehicle hunt?" Matt asked.

"Excellent," said Pete. "We now have nine vehicles parked neatly on the road out front."

"That's fantastic," said Matt.

"Yeah. The one advantage of the world's end is that you can pretty much park wherever you want."

"Any problems getting cars? What kind were able to find?"

"It was surprisingly simple," replied Pete. "There were at least fifty vehicles parked in front of the small hospital up on the back side of town, and I'd say half or more had their keys still in the ignition. The biggest find, though, was a limo service company right downtown. They had a small car park with several Mercedes sedans and vans. We took the two vans but can easily return to get more if we want."

"Outstanding," said Matt. "Did you have to jump-start all of them? How about fuel?"

"Yeah, we found a few more sets of jumper cables, so that wasn't an issue. We also took all the vehicles up to the petrol station on the hill and filled everything up. The siphon pump we brought works great. We even got you a present."

"A present? I'm afraid to ask," said Matt, smiling.

"A low-mileage Porsche Cayenne SUV. We figured it would be a great car to conduct a recon. Easily fits four plus gear, has all-wheel drive, and is fast enough to get you out of any sticky situation."

"I love it," said Matt, his smile growing. "I can't wait to test drive it. We should..."

Everyone's radio barked simultaneously with Liz's voice, an octave higher than normal and excitement evident in her voice. "Matt, Dad, come quick. Someone's approaching on foot."

A look of shock passed across everyone's face, and Matt was the first to react physically by jumping up from his chair and dashing out of the dining room and down the yacht's interior stairway to the main deck. Pete, Dave, and Derek followed closely on his heels.

"Are you in danger, Liz?" Matt asked over the radio, intentionally keeping his voice calm. Matt had always known they would eventually encounter survivors in Ireland; he just hadn't expected it to be while eating lunch.

"No, Matt. It's a woman and a teenage girl. They don't appear armed and are crossing the street towards us from the park."

"Roger, I'll be right there." Matt was approaching the gangway down to the dock and could see Liz standing with Grace and Juliet by the row of vehicles Pete had recently collected parked along the street directly behind where the Irish Rover was docked. Matt looked beyond them and could see two females walking purposefully down the middle of the street.

At the top of the gangway, Matt turned to the guys who had followed him down to the main deck. "I'm going to walk out there and see what we have. Pete, stand by here and keep everyone else on board. Dave and Derek, head up to the sundeck and cover us from there. Get Dylan or Clare with a sniper rifle. I have no reason to believe these people aren't friendly, but we're not taking any chances." Without waiting for a reply, Matt turned and walked down the gangway. His stride was purposeful, but he did not want to appear to run.

Matt was standing next to Liz and Grace on the road in seconds. Juliet was hanging back between one of the vehicles. The two new arrivals were still approaching and about twenty meters to their front. As far as Matt could tell, no one had yet spoken.

The approaching woman appeared to be in her mid-thirties with ginger hair pulled back in a ponytail. She walked timidly, glasses framing her thin face and wearing a green Barbour jacket, jeans, and sneakers—or trainers, as they said in Ireland. Next to her walked a more confident, pre-teen version of herself, and Matt had no doubt this was a mother and daughter. Where the older woman appeared somewhat defeated and stressed, the girl had a bit of a swagger and cockiness that instantly endeared her to Matt. Knowing what he knew of the hardships these two had likely endured, it was interesting to see how each of these women had weathered the storm.

As Matt watched, he saw both women's eyes fixated on the holstered pistol on his belt. Both women stopped abruptly, and Matt raised his hand in greeting.

"Hello," Matt said, loudly enough to be heard but well below a shout.

"Hello," replied the woman, her face expressionless.

"We just arrived yesterday. You're the first people we've seen since we arrived. Is there anyone else here?"

Both women just continued to stare at him. The mother was about to speak, but the daughter beat her to it. "Where are you from? Are people alive where you came from?" Matt guessed she was about the same age as his son, Christopher.

"We're from the United States. We just crossed the Atlantic. Almost everyone is dead back in the States. The Black Pox took more than 98% of the population. I assume it's the same here. Is that correct?"

"Yes," said the mother. "Everyone's gone. There's some people in Cork, but not many. The pox took everyone. How are you still alive?"

"We're all vaccinated," said Matt.

Both women stared at him, the young teen subconsciously shaking her head slowly in disbelief.

"It's true. We were all vaccinated in the US and brought some with us. We heard that almost none of the vaccine found its way to Europe, but we brought some doses. I'm Matt, by the way. To my left here is Liz, and to my right is Grace."

"Nice to meet you both," said Grace.

After a pause, the mother replied, "My name's Rosie, and this is my daughter, Orla. None of the vaccines got to Ireland, as far as I know. There are seven of us now living here in Kinsale."

"Nice to meet you, Rosie, Orla," Matt said, nodding to both women. "Grace is the closest thing our group has to a doctor, so if it's okay with you, I'd like to ask her to go back to the boat and get some vaccine doses. We can vaccinate both of you right now and then the rest of your group as soon as you bring them here. Is that okay?"

"That would be fine, Matt. Thank you."

Without being asked, Grace turned and trotted back to the gangway. Although only in her second year of medical school at the University of Florida, Grace had assumed the role of the family physician since the pandemic began. Matt looked up to the sundeck and saw Dave and Derek watching intently, no weapons visible. Matt gave them a quick thumbs up.

"Are there more boats coming?" Orla asked.

"Not that I'm aware of," answered Matt. "It's just us."

"Why are you here?" Rosie said, a stoic look on her face but the slouch of her posture indicating her despair.

"Well, Rosie, that's kind of a long story. The short answer

is that where we were was no longer safe, and we felt Ireland would be a better place to start over. My sister-in-law's family is from this area, so I was somewhat familiar with it."

"Okay, and if I may ask, why do you have the vaccine? Is it readily available in the US? The last we heard, the entire world was being hit by the Black Pox, but we lost power and any news over six weeks ago."

"Another long story, Rosie. I'm unsure how familiar you are with US geography, but my family fled to Vermont after the nuclear attacks. A vaccine shipment was delivered to our local hospital, and we helped rescue the Army officer responsible for delivering it after criminals attacked him. We ended up with quite a few doses of the vaccine and are happy to vaccinate anyone still alive here in Cork."

Rosie's face visibly relaxed as she began to believe Matt's story, the stress of her ordeal seeming to wash away, likely for the first time in months. "I can't believe this is happening," she said. "Please tell me you're not joking."

"We're not joking, Rosie. I can only imagine how incredibly difficult things have been for you and your family. Please accept our help." As Matt spoke, he heard Grace jog up next to him. She already had two syringes and a vial of vaccine in her hand.

"Is that it? The vaccine?" Orla asked.

"Yes," said Grace. "This is it. If both of you wouldn't mind taking off your jacket and rolling up your sleeves, I can give it to you now."

"Uh, Matt, I don't want to sound ungrateful, but how can we trust you? I mean, at this point, we really have nothing else to lose, but getting an injection from complete strangers is something I'm not sure we should rush into," said Rosie.

"I understand, Rosie. I do. Please, wait one minute." Matt

reached down and toggled the microphone on his radio. "Clare, this is Matt."

"Go ahead, Matt."

"Would you mind coming out here? And bring Christopher and Laurie with you."

"Are you sure it's safe, Matt?"

"Dave, are we good?"

"Yeah, you're good. Nothing is moving at all. If someone had wanted to take a shot at you, they already would have," said Dave over the radio.

"Okay, Matt," replied Clare. "We'll be down in a minute."

In less than twenty seconds, Clare exited the gangway, followed closely by her two children, eleven-year-old Christopher and seven-year-old Laurie. As they walked up to the group, Matt turned to face Rosie. "Rosie and Orla, I'd like you to meet my wife, Clare, and my two children, Christopher and Laurie. We have all been vaccinated with the same batch of vaccine that Grace has in her hands. There are no side effects other than some pain at the injection site, and its effect on preventing smallpox is immediate."

Rosie seemed even more relieved, and Orla was smiling. They both took off their jackets and began rolling up their sleeves.

CHAPTER 7

November 12, 4:52 pm

The sun had recently set, casting deep shadows across the harbor as the temperature dropped considerably. Rosie sat in the main salon on the owner's deck, sipping iced tea despite the temperature. It was the first cold drink she had imbibed since mid-September.

After receiving her vaccination, Rosie had asked to return to their home up the hill from the harbor and retrieve her other children. While Orla was the oldest at eleven years, Rosie also had twin seven-year-old boys, Daniel and Nathan, as well as a precocious 5-year-old girl named Ella. As a result of the pandemic, Rosie had also taken in her best friend's children soon after the woman died of smallpox. Michael and Aoife were twelve and ten, respectively, and appeared to Matt as shy and polite, albeit still overwhelmed by the loss of their parents.

After providing the newcomers with a hearty, early supper, the children were currently all down in the living room of the main deck playing games with the children and young adults of Matt's extended family. From what Rosie had told them already, it was likely the first carefree playtime her children had enjoyed in months.

Stan, Marvi, Clare, Kim, and Molly joined Matt on the salon couches as they sought to learn as much as possible from Rosie. Matt did not want this to seem like an inquisition and hoped by having several of the adult women present, the conversation would flow more easily. Matt knew that having Pete, an attorney, and Dave, a criminal investigator, would have drastically changed the conversation's tone, so he politely asked them not to participate.

"I'm so sorry to hear about your husband," said Marvi. "Have you had any contact with anyone since he left?"

"No, we're pretty self-sufficient and have kept to ourselves," said Rosie. She had finished giving the group an overview of the last two months here in Kinsale. When the Black Pox hit, it hit hard. Ireland was completely unprepared, and before anyone knew what was happening, it seemed that the entire nation was infected. Hospitals were overrun, and the Gardai (police) were called out, as well as the military, but to no avail. By the end of September, almost everyone in Ireland had succumbed to the Black Pox.

Rosie and her husband, Richard, lived in a farmhouse about 1.5 kilometers on the back side of Kinsale, near the GAA fields where the kids played hurling and camogie. They owned over three acres of land and actually had a small farmstead, including pigs, chickens, and several goats. While the farmstead was mostly Rosie's hobby, Richard worked as an IT professional in Cork City. He was one of the first to spot the impending pandemic, and he immediately gathered significant supplies and self-quarantined his family well before the government implemented similar restrictions. Rosie had agreed to care for her best friend's two children, Michael and Aoife, while her friend went to retrieve her ailing mother from West Cork. Her friend never returned, so Michael and Aoife had become part of her family.

From what Rosie had told them, she and Richard had been extremely savvy in their preparations and had kept fully isolated from everyone. Once almost everyone had died, and as far as Rosie knew, everyone in the Kinsale area had either died or moved away, her family had methodically gathered all the supplies they would need to survive the winter. Her husband, Richard, was an excellent planner, problem-solver, and handyman. Together, they had wired a generator into their home, liberated a gasoline truck for fuel, added several animals to their farmstead, and scavenged a significant amount of supplies.

Everything seemed great until a bit more than two weeks ago, on October 25, when Richard left on a day trip to the outskirts of Dublin. He had a pickup truck with a trailer and had planned a trip to obtain a wood stove, solar panels, and a small wind turbine. There were two supply centers in particular that he was planning to go to near the Blanchardstown Mall area on the west side of Dublin. He had left before light on the morning of October 20th and expected to return later that day.

It had now been eighteen days with no sign of Richard. Rosie was sure that he was dead.

"We're so sorry, Rosie," said Clare. "Everyone has lost so much these last few months, but I can imagine how difficult this must be to have survived the pox only to lose your husband now. Is there anything we can do?"

"Well, what are your intentions in Kinsale? Are you just passing through?" Rosie asked.

"Our goal, Rosie, has been establishing our home here in Kinsale. We arrived yesterday, and as of now, we're planning to clear some of the homes over in Scilly and make that our base for the winter," said Matt. "We likely have enough vaccine for any survivors in County Cork, so eventually, we'd like to explore the area and hopefully find other survivors so that we might be able to build a small community."

"That sounds lovely, Matt. It truly does." A tear began to form in Rosie's left eye, sliding slowly down her cheek.

Several others immediately followed it. Clare, sitting next to Rosie, leaned over and wrapped her arms around the woman, realizing how utterly lonely she must have been these past few weeks. Rosie tucked her head into Clare's neck and began to sob. "I'm sorry," she said between sobs. "I didn't mean to turn into a blubbering eejit."

"Shhh," said Clare, hugging Rosie tightly. "It's okay. You're not alone anymore." Rosie continued crying, finally letting out the grief and worry she had bottled inside for the past few weeks. After a minute, Rosie gathered herself, thanking Molly for handing her a tissue.

"Rosie, we started with just Clare and I and our two children. In the last two months, our family has grown to number twenty-five. We have the means to protect ourselves, as well as to build a sustainable life. We're survivors, Rosie, and we all need to stick together. Whatever we can do to help you, ask. As far as we're concerned, even though we only met a few hours ago, I'd like to consider you part of our extended family if you want to be."

"Yes," said Stan, who until then had remained silent. "The world is going to be what we make it, Rosie, and there are good and bad people remaining. Good people need to stick together. We consider everyone on this boat part of one extended family —and we'd do anything to help each other. No matter what. If you need us, we'll be there for you."

Rosie made eye contact with each person at the table, who smiled back in turn. More tears started down Rosie's cheeks. Marvi, Molly, and Clare joined her, with tears streaking down their cheeks as well. Matt pretended to have something in his eye and quickly brushed it with his hand.

Clearing his throat as a bug seemed to have formed in it, Matt spoke softly. "I know it's a lot to take in right now, Rosie. A big group of Americans just showed up on a super yacht. But there's no need for you to change anything. Just know that you and your family are safe from smallpox forever, and if you need anything at all, we're going to be right here in Kinsale. We'd love for you to spend as much time with us as you'd like."

"Thank you, Matt. Thank you, everyone. You have no idea how much you've lightened the load pressing down on our shoulders. To even think about a future for my children has been something I've been afraid to even think of these last two months," Rosie said, a smile breaking through the tears like the sun breaking through the clouds after summer showers. "As I mentioned, we have a few pigs, goats, and chickens. With some help, we could gather up some additional stock, and I'd be happy to care for them. That would provide some fresh meat, eggs, and even dairy if we found some dairy cows. Other than that, I'm not sure how I can ever repay your kindness."

"We're not seeking repayment, Rosie. You're part of our group now, for as long as you want to be and with no pressure at all. Setting up some additional livestock at your place sounds like a great idea. Molly, maybe you can get with Rosie and figure out how we want to do that?"

"Sure, Matt," said Molly. "Sounds great. I wanted to look at establishing our own farm anyway, so this is perfect."

"Uh, Rosie," said Stan quietly. "I was hoping you could give us a bit more detail on our surroundings. I've kind of taken on the responsibility of gathering information about everything, and I know Matt is planning a trip to visit some of the neighboring towns and possibly up to Cork City. Is there anything you can tell us? Do you know of any people still alive in the area?"

"Yes, there are definitely people still alive. I haven't seen any personally, but I know that my husband, Richard, had several groups and families with whom he was in contact. There's a farmer and his family outside of Bandon—in Inishannon, as I recall. And there's another farmer over in Novohal, an older gentleman who was there with his wife and granddaughter, whom Richard traded with. And then there were at least two groups in Cork City. One group, over by Cobh, was one that Richard met with at least twice and seemed to like. He mentioned trying to get them to go with him to Dublin. The other group was on the city's north side, and Richard didn't trust them, so he only interacted with them once, I believe."

"You said he interacted and traded with these people. Was he worried about smallpox?"

"Yes, we're all deathly afraid of catching it. He always wore a mask and gloves, never got within ten meters of anyone, and always met outdoors. We mostly traded fresh eggs from our hens."

"What did these groups provide you?" Stan asked.

"With the farmers, we traded eggs for fresh corn and vegetables. With the one group near Cobh, we traded eggs for medicine and medical advice. They have a doctor."

"Do you remember how large these two groups were? You said your husband didn't like the group on the north side; was he afraid of them? Do you remember anything else he might have said about them?"

"No, Stan, I'm sorry. I can't really remember anything specific other than I'm positive the Cobh group had a doctor. Richard said that if anything ever happened to one of the kids, to bring them to Cobh, and that group would see us coming."

"Okay, that's good, Rosie."

"I believe the group by Cobh was maybe around ten to fifteen people, and the one north of town was a bit bigger."

"Did you and Richard ever discuss why you thought no one survived? We expected more survivors, to be honest."

"Yeah, we talked about it all the time. The thing that maybe you're not aware of is people flocking to Dublin and Belfast. Once everyone started getting sick, rumors were circulating like crazy. The official news from the government was to stay home and wait for a vaccine to be distributed. They encouraged everyone to keep their distance from each other and to limit any interactions outside of immediate families. However, after the first ten days or so, when things started to get bad, the rumor was that the vaccine would go to Dublin. People packed up their families and drove to Dublin. Almost none of them returned."

"When you say people, how many are we talking about, Rosie?" Stan asked.

"Mmmm, I'd say maybe fifty percent. I know our neighbors on both sides of us went to Dublin or Belfast. That was the other place. The first few days, everyone said Dublin. Then the rumors shifted to the UK having vaccines due to their special relationship with the Americans, and Belfast would have a million doses. Our neighbors on the north side of us went to Belfast. None of them returned."

"Okay. That's similar to what happened in parts of the United States. Did you ever think of leaving Kinsale?"

Rosie snorted. "All the time! Every day. But Richard and I knew we couldn't catch the pox if we didn't interact with anyone. We had plenty of food, a solid roof over our heads, and it didn't seem like there was a rush. As soon as we realized people weren't returning, we knew something bad was happening. There really wasn't any need for Richard to go two weeks ago, but he thought it would be safe. The worst that would happen is that he'd simply turn around. He wasn't even planning on going into the city, just a couple of major stores on the outskirts of Dublin."

"Did Richard have a gun, Rosie? How about the other groups?"

"No, we don't own a gun. Very few people we know own a gun; if they do, it's mostly a shotgun for hunting."

"We didn't notice any evidence of violence occurring in Kinsale. Did you hear about it elsewhere? In America, things became extremely violent across the country."

"Not really anything like that, Stan. Not that we've heard of, anyway. There was supposedly a massive fire in Dublin, but I think it was accidental."

"A fire?" Interjected Matt. "How bad?"

"Mmmm...I guess it happened maybe at the very end of September. It was after most people had already died, and the news had stopped broadcasting—even the radio. Richard heard about it from the group in Cobh. There was a massive fire that spread across almost all of greater Dublin. Even though many of the buildings are stone and brick, the buildings are so close together that the fire leaped from building to building and then roof to roof. The doctor told Richard that some group may have started it in several places to burn away the smallpox. Not sure it did any good, but from what we heard, downtown Dublin is pretty much a burned-out shell."

"Well, that's certainly interesting. We weren't planning to go to downtown Dublin, but like Richard, some stores there have items we may want. I guess it depends on how picked over Cork City is."

"There's still plenty of food, as far as I know," said Rosie. "We gathered almost a year's supply of rice, pasta, flour, and other staples without leaving Kinsale. We also grabbed enough canned goods to last us easily through the winter."

"Rosie, this might sound like a strange question," asked Matt. "My sister-in-law's family is from Carrigaline. Their last name is O'Riordan. You wouldn't by any chance know of them? Their family home is in the town center, almost across from Barry Collins' hotel."

"Not the O'Riordan Toyota folks, is it?"

"Actually, yes. That's her father, James."

"Well, I know who they are, but I don't know them personally. We bought a Rav4 from them a few years back. I don't have any news, though. Sorry."

"That's quite alright, Rosie," said Matt. "I feel like we've been grilling you here, and that wasn't our intention. Why don't we head downstairs and see how the kids are doing? You're welcome to spend the night, or we can escort you back to your place."

CHAPTER 8

November 13, 8:04 am

The Porsche Cayenne molded to the road's curves along the River Stick like a little black dress to a voluptuous woman. The R600 road leading north from Kinsale was a wide, two-lane road that followed every bend and turn of the River Stick as it meandered to the sea. Matt had always enjoyed driving on the left side of the road, and as he'd never been at the wheel of such a performance vehicle while driving the narrow roads of Ireland, Matt was tempted to push his speed higher. He could see the pickup truck getting smaller and smaller in his rearview mirror and realized Pete likely wasn't as comfortable steering from the right side of the vehicle and manually shifting with his left hand.

Matt reduced his speed, so the dashboard's electronic speedometer read just over 70 kilometers per hour, which Matt calculated as just over 40 mph. In the passenger seat, Dylan let out an audible sigh of relief. On the road behind them, Pete immediately closed the gap between their vehicles as they entered the small village of Belgooly. The R600 was the main road leading north from Kinsale into Cork City, but today's destination was the bustling town of Carrigaline, located about ten kilometers east of the R600 and halfway between Kinsale and Cork.

Matt knew from his previous trips that the Irish roads designated with the letter R were regional roads and were normally two-lane roads with painted lines and often a shoulder to pull over. N-roads were national roads—normally well-marked divided highways. L-roads, on the other hand, were local roads, and while open to two-way traffic, these roads were often not much wider than a single vehicle and seldom had any paint depicting a center line or shoulder. With the high hedges common along most roads in Ireland, navigating these narrow, twisty roads was always an adventure. With almost no risk of oncoming traffic, however, today's trip was much less nerve-racking than Matt's previous driving experiences in Ireland.

Spotting the painted wooden sign of the Huntsman Bar on the right side of the road in the center of Belgooly, Matt used his turn signal to let Pete know they would be turning right. The Cayenne's automatic transmission downshifted smoothly as Matt slowed to take the turn and accelerated rapidly onto the R611, which passed through the crossroads of Ballyfeard in the blink of an eye, followed by a straight shot into Carrigaline.

Matt was quite familiar with these roads as he had driven them dozens of times on numerous vacations to Ireland over the years. Matt's sister-in-law Tracy had grown up in the burgeoning town of Carrigaline, ten kilometers south of Cork, and had moved to the US for grad school at the University of Michigan, where she had met Matt's brother Donald. While Tracy and Donald had made their home just north of Boston, all of Tracy's family remained in Ireland, including her parents, her sister and brother, several aunts and uncles, and numerous cousins. Tracy's father, James, owned several businesses in the town, including one of the largest Toyota dealerships in this part of the county.

It was difficult to get used to the fact that there was no traffic on the roads, a constant reminder of society's extinction. That said, everything else looked exactly as Matt remembered from his last trip here the previous summer, except for maybe several new housing developments. On Matt's first trip to Ireland for his brother's wedding, Carrigaline had been a sleepy satellite town of fewer than three thousand people, and the O'Riordan family had owned the Toyota garage, a gas station, and a convenience store, as well as the town's small movie theater. In recent years, Carrigaline had exploded to more than fifteen thousand residents and had become one of the busiest satellite towns surrounding the city of Cork.

Matt eased off the gas and let the Cayenne coast down the hill as they entered the town from the southwest. R611 ended in a T-junction on the southern edge of town, with traffic turning left (north) onto the Cork Road. This was the central artery through the previously very congested town, and other than cars parked along the road, it was now completely empty. Pete closed the gap between their two-vehicle convoy, and Matt drove slowly through the center of town, fond memories flooding his brain as he drove. A delicious evening of Indian food at the Spice Restaurant on his right, drunken revelry downing pints of Murphy's with his brother Donald at Rosie's Bar, food shopping at the Barry Collins' SuperValu supermarket, and the memory of attending the wedding reception of Tracy's sister, Judy, at the Carrigaline Court Hotel.

Carrigaline's lone hotel, the Carrigaline Court Hotel, was situated on a roundabout at the very north end of the downtown strip along the Cork Road. Matt knew Tracy's family home was just a few doors past that on the left. The home, referred to as Benmore, had been built by Tracy's grandfather after the Second World War and sat on three acres surrounded by a classic Irish stone wall. As the town had grown, Benmore had become an oasis of green inside the center of Carrigaline, with oak and ash trees towering over a beautifully manicured lawn and garden.

This was where Matt's brother Donald had been on vacation with his wife and daughter when the cataclysm had begun.

Matt's pulse quickened as they neared the approach to Benmore's driveway. He had held out hope that his brother was still alive, but now that he was seconds away from finding out, his confidence waned, and a sense of pending grief overcame him. Dylan sat silently next to him and had not spoken the entire trip. While Matt was eager to learn the fate of his brother, Dylan, Derek, and Kelsey would learn the fate of their parents and sister, whom they had not seen or heard from since the cataclysm began.

Matt turned left into the gap in the ornate stone wall that signified the Benmore estate. He was not surprised to see the driveway in front of the house empty, as he knew the paved driveway wrapped around the left side to the rear of the home, where a stand-alone three-car garage was connected to the back of the house by a covered walkway.

Matt reached over and put his hand on Dylan's knee. "Whatever we learn here, at least we'll know."

Dylan looked straight ahead and just nodded. Matt could see Dylan's bottom lip quivering slightly and knew he was having difficulty controlling his emotions. As the SUV pulled around to the back of Benmore, Matt first noticed the two Toyotas parked in front of the garage. The second thing he noticed was that while all the blinds were up on the home's back windows, there did not appear to be anyone staring out at them. As soon as Matt stopped, Dylan jumped out of the passenger seat and ran toward Benmores's rear door.

"Mom! Dad! It's us! We're here!" As Dylan rushed to the back of the house, he was joined by Derek, who had similarly jumped out of Pete's pickup. Matt exited his car door and stood, looking 360 degrees around the grass yard. Matt registered the sound of Dylan and Derek opening the unlocked back door of the house and rushing inside, still yelling for their parents and grandparents.

His heart sank as he took in the large flower beds and the grass needing cutting. Next to the largest flower bed, just to the side of the garage, four wooden crosses held a silent vigil at the head of what appeared to be newly dug graves. From the few weeds beginning to take hold in the mounds of dirt, Matt estimated the graves were only a few weeks old. While he could still faintly hear Dylan's voice calling for his parents, Matt knew in his heart that there would be no answer.

The rear door banged open, and Derek rushed out. "The house's empty, Uncle Matt. No one's here."

Pete had walked over to the back door and called for Dylan to come out. Turning to Matt, Pete shouted across the parking lot, "House smells just a bit stuffy, Matt. Like no one's been here for a while." Matt knew this was Pete's way of politely stating that there was no smell of death or decay in Benmore, which might have been an encouraging sign without the existence of the four graves.

Derek rounded the back of the Porsche to where Matt stood and noticed the makeshift cemetery just as Matt had. Derek stopped abruptly in mid-stride, staring.

"I'm sorry, Derek," said Matt, stepping forward to embrace his nephew in a hug. Looking over Derek's shoulder, Matt saw Dylan watching them.

"No!" Dylan shouted. "Please, no!" He ran to where Matt and Derek stood, saw the graves, and kept running up to them. Matt released Derek from the hug, and the two of them rushed over to follow Dylan to the grave. Dylan knelt in front of the graves and peered carefully at each of the wooden crosses, which were simple pieces of 1"x3" pine lathing nailed together to form the cross. As Matt neared, he could see names written on the cross-piece of each marker.

The first words Matt read made his heart sink: Donald L.

Sheridan. *He's gone*, Matt thought. *My only brother is gone.*

Dylan and Derek were hugging each other, sobbing silently. At 20, Derek was two years older than Dylan, and he tried his best to console his younger brother while also being overcome with sorrow. Matt let the tears roll down his face, unashamed of his grief. He had known this was likely what he'd find, but some of him had still held out hope. His older brother had always been his hero, and if anyone could survive the cataclysm and pandemic, he knew that Donald could.

But he hadn't. Donald was gone.

Matt wiped the tears from his eyes and stepped forward to read the names stenciled on the other three graves.

James R. O'Riordan

Mary E. O'Riordan

Connor R. O'Riordan

What? Where were Tracy and Kirstie? Matt thought. James and Mary O'Riordan were Tracy's parents, and Connor was Tracy's younger brother who managed the Toyota dealership.

Matt felt Pete's presence behind him. "Hey, Pete, can you go check the house for me? This is Donald, as well as Tracy's parents and brother. See if there's any sign of Tracy or Kirstie in the house. Their luggage should be in one of the upstairs rooms."

"Sure, man," said Pete, placing his hand on Matt's shoulder. "I'm sorry about Don. He was a truly great guy."

"Thanks, Pete. I know you two always got along well," Matt replied, wiping the final tears from his cheeks.

"I'll go check the house. Be right back," said Pete.

Matt nodded and stepped forward to put his hands on the backs of both Derek and Dylan. "Boys, I'm very sorry about your Dad. He's been my hero since I was little and always will be. Let's be thankful that he, your grandparents, and your uncle received a proper burial." Matt paused, not sure exactly how to say this. "I don't know what to make of this yet, but there's no sign of your mom or sister. Until proven otherwise, we have to take that as a positive sign. Do you guys have any idea where they might have gone?"

As soon as Matt asked the question, the answer popped into his head—Judy's. Tracy's younger sister Judy lived in a cottage along the Owenabue River near the hamlet of Crosshaven. Judy was one of Matt and Clare's all-time favorite people—her Irish sense of humor, accent, and wit never ceased to keep them laughing hysterically on every visit. Matt and Clare often stayed at Judy's house when visiting Ireland, especially as Donald and Tracy normally occupied the guest rooms in Benmore. Clare and Judy had become close friends over the years, and Judy's youngest daughter, Millie, had spent the previous summer with Matt and Clare in Rhode Island.

The picturesque village of Crosshaven consisted of a handful of pubs, and its marinas catered to a serious sailing crowd, with dozens of sailboats docked and moored in the Owenabue along the town's shores. Behind the town, the terrain rose steeply several hundred feet to provide one of the most scenic overlooks of Cork Harbor, which lay on the other side of the hill from Crosshaven. A long-abandoned 16th-century military fort, Camden Fort Meagher, sat atop this hill above Crosshaven. Matt had always enjoyed the picturesque little village at the base of the hill. Judy's house was about a kilometer west of the village, on the side closest to Carrigaline, so only about five kilometers from where Matt stood in Benmore's back garden.

"Derek, Dylan, I think we need to go to your Aunt Judy's house. If your mom and sister are anywhere, that's the most likely place they'd be."

"You think they're alive?" Dylan asked, wiping tears from

his eyes.

"I don't know, Dylan. But we have to check," said Matt.

"They're dead, Dyl. I know it," said Derek, willing himself not to cry again. "You've seen this place. Just like Vermont. Just like Maine. Everyone's dead. Why would they be alive?"

"We have to check," said Dylan. "She might be gone, but she'd want us to look for her. And we can't stop until we know for sure."

"You're 100% right, Dylan," said Matt. "C'mon, guys. She only lives about five minutes away. When Pete gets done checking the house, we'll head there next. It's what your dad would want us to do." Both young men stood a bit taller, realizing for the first time that they now shouldered the responsibility for their family and their father's legacy.

At that moment, Pete walked out the back door, closing it gently but firmly behind him. He walked straight up to Matt. "No one's in the house, but I also found no sign of either Tracy's or Kirstie's luggage. Don had a suitcase in the guest room, and if I had to guess, I'd say that there was once another suitcase next to his that's no longer present. The second guest room looked like someone was staying there, but there's no suitcase or clothes. I found a pair of sandals that seemed to belong to a teenage girl."

"Okay," said Matt. "It'd make sense that maybe they relocated to Judy's. Did you see anything else?"

"Nothing to give any indication of where they might've gone."

"Okay. Let's go to Judy's. There'll be plenty of time to check through the house in more detail later on."

They each took their same seats in the SUV and pickup truck, and Matt led the way back around to the front of the house. It was still weird to realize that there was not a single moving vehicle on the street, but force of habit caused Matt to carefully look both ways before pulling out onto R611, the Cork Road. Heading back towards the center of Carrigaline, Matt passed the SuperValu supermarket and took a sharp left turn onto the R612 just after crossing the small bridge over the Owenabue River.

The R612 was also known as the Carrigaline Road, and Matt smiled as he thought how much common sense went into naming roads throughout Ireland. Instead of naming streets after people or trees as was common in the United States, in Ireland, the road was normally named after whatever town lay at the end of the road. While in the US, when asking directions, someone might give instructions to take Main Street, turn left on Maple Ave, and then follow it to Roosevelt Boulevard. In Ireland, when asking how to get to Killarney, one would be more apt to be told to take the next left onto the Killarney Road and follow it until it ends.

Matt's thoughts were clouded with grief over his brother's death, and he paid no attention to the picturesque scenery along the river. The tide was halfway out, and if Matt had cared to look, he would have noticed the muddy banks appearing beneath the tall seagrass that grew along the estuary. Instead, Matt's thoughts wandered to family gatherings at Christmas, watching his older brother's football games and wanting to be just like him, and Donald standing next to him at the altar as Matt married Clare. His window was down, but instead of noticing the sharp smell of the outgoing tide, Matt recalled the scents of Thanksgivings in Vermont where his brother carved a delicious turkey roasted by Tracy, surrounded by family. Matt's foot subconsciously pressed heavily on the pedal as he realized he'd never see his brother again. *I can't even tell Mom and Dad that he's gone,* Matt thought. *For all I know, my parents have been dead for weeks.*

Matt realized he was doing well over 100 kilometers per

hour in the high-performance SUV and that they were rapidly approaching Judy's home. The Drake's Pool scenic area flew by the left-side window, the passenger side in Irish vehicles, and Matt knew that Judy's house was just ahead on the right after the next sweeping left turn. Pete had fallen behind him on the R612 but caught up quickly as Matt slowed for the turn-off to Judy's house.

Matt braked sharply, almost missing the hidden turn into Judy's drive. The narrow entrance was marked by a small stone wall on one corner, and Matt juked to the right and then quickly back to the left as the gravel driveway rose sharply up a short hill. The treelined driveway paralleled the main road for about forty yards and then opened onto a bluff overlooking a bend in the river upon which three white stucco homes sat. Each home was surrounded by about a half-acre of land and offered commanding views across the river to the farmlands that sloped gently upwards on the far side. Judy's house was the first of the three, and Matt pulled into the gravel parking area behind her house next to a tiny Toyota hatchback with the O'Riordans sticker in the back window.

Matt's pulse quickened as the Porsche slowed to a crawl, and he could hear the crunch of the tires on the gravel. He looked over at Dylan, who had remained silent the entire trip, and realized Dylan was in no hurry to learn the fate of his mother. The enthusiasm Derek and Dylan had shown when running into the Benmore house had disappeared, replaced with a sinking realization that their mother and sister had likely suffered similar fates as their father.

"Wait here for a sec," Matt said. "I'll check the house."

"Okay, Uncle Matt," replied Dylan sullenly.

Matt got out of the Porsche at the same time Pete and Derek also exited their vehicle. Without a word being spoken, Matt and Pete walked slowly toward the back door of Judy's house while Derek stood silently next to his open car door. Matt noticed Derek scanning the yard for freshly marked graves, but the grass appeared undisturbed. Pete also noticed the lack of graves and gave Matt a hopeful smile.

Matt expected the rear door to be locked, but the knob turned smoothly in his hands. As the door swung inward, he braced himself for the putrid smell of death. Instead, all Matt could smell was the salty air of the estuary. He breathed a slight sigh of relief, his hopes rising that he was not about to find the decomposing bodies of his sister-in-law and niece.

"Hello!" Matt shouted. "Judy? Tracy?"

Silence.

"Anyone home?" He shouted again, to no reply.

Matt and Pete walked through a small mudroom and into a large kitchen. The kitchen was clean and tidy, with no dishes in the sink.

"I'll go check upstairs," said Pete, knowing that it would be much easier for him to be the one to find any bodies should they be present.

"Thanks," said Matt, recognizing the somber task Pete had volunteered to do for his friend. Unable to stand still and wait, Matt decided to walk through the rooms on the first floor. He wandered into the living room, dining room, and small den. Nothing appeared out of the ordinary, almost as if Judy had just stepped out for the afternoon. However, on closer examination, Matt noticed the lightest coating of dust on the wood table. Knowing Judy to be a fastidious cleaner, Matt surmised that she had likely been gone several weeks, if not longer.

As Matt continued to peruse the first floor, he heard Pete yell down from the top of the stairs. "Matt, there's no one up here, but you need to come up and look at a couple of things."

Matt let out an audible sigh of relief. He knew the odds were significantly against Tracy and Kirstie being alive, but until he had definitive proof, he continued to hold out a sliver of hope. He quickly crossed through the living room and took the stairs two at a time, meeting Pete on the upstairs landing.

"What'd you find?" Matt asked.

"A couple things. First, check the guest room," Pete said. Matt knew exactly the room Pete referred to, having stayed there on several occasions, and walked immediately across the hall into the large bedroom that looked out over the backyard. The bedroom was in disarray, with the green, flowered duvet haphazardly tossed across the queen-sized bed and several items of women's clothing strewn across it. At the foot of the bed sat two large suitcases, both open and about half full. Several pairs of women's heels and sandals lay discarded on the floor, as well as what looked to be a flowery dress.

Looking closely at the suitcases, Matt walked over and reached down to yank on the baggage tag hanging from the handle. Matt kneeled to get a closer look, unable to read the small letters while standing. "It's Tracy's bag," Matt said, reaching to examine the other piece of luggage. "And this one is Kirstie's. They must have relocated here from the Benmore house. But where are they now?"

"There's one more thing I wanted you to see. Follow me," said Pete.

Matt stood and followed Pete down the hall to the master bedroom. While the king-sized bed in this room was properly made, the room itself was in a bit of a shambles. The door to a large walk-in closet stood open, and numerous clothing items lay strewn across the floor. Matt tried to visualize the scene and concluded that this appeared to result from someone packing haphazardly.

"Have you checked Millie's room at the end of the hall? Is it in similar disarray?" Matt asked.

"It is. Not quite this bad, but looks like someone may have packed in a hurry," Pete said. "But Matt, that's not what I wanted you to see. Look at the nightstand."

Matt turned and stepped over to the nightstand next to the bed. It was a standard wooden nightstand, a bit too modern for Matt's conservative taste. On it was a lamp and a single sheet of A4 printer paper. One word was written in what appeared to be a female hand: Haulbowline.

"Whadda you think, Matt? Is that some kind of code? Like *haul* and *bowline*? Maybe referring to the nautical knot used by sailors? Towing something? Whadda ya think?"

"It's not two words, Pete," said Matt.

"It's not. Then what is it?"

"It's a place. An island, actually. In Cork harbor."

"An island? Interesting. Maybe it's their equivalent of Vinalhaven?" Pete answered, referring to the island off the coast of Maine, which their extended family had briefly called home before fleeing to Ireland.

CHAPTER 9

November 13, 4:35 pm

Liz had a laptop plugged into the large flatscreen television in the living room on the owner's deck of the Irish Rover as Stan stood before the others sitting in the couches and chairs before him. In addition to Pete, Dylan, and Derek, who had accompanied him on the trip to Carrigaline, Matt had also asked Dave, Kim, and Grace to listen in on Stan's briefing.

After confirming that Judy's house held no further clues, Matt decided to head back to Kinsale. Derek and Dylan initially opposed this, wanting to head into Cork and check out Haulbowline Island immediately. While Matt shared their intensity for tracking down Tracy and Kirstie, he also knew, as the leader of the extended family, that the mission to Cork required additional planning and preparation to ensure everyone's safety.

Consequently, after leaving Judy's house in Crosshaven, Matt led their two-vehicle convoy directly back to Kinsale, where he informed Stan of what they had learned and asked him to query QuAI with some specification information requests. Matt then had a heartwrenching conversation with Kelsey, informing her that her father had died. Kelsey was Donald's oldest child, and her motherly spirit had blossomed the last couple of months as she'd focused much of her attention on caring and teaching Matt's children. Holding her, Matt realized just how young most of those in the family were, and vowed, if at all possible, to ensure they could experience their teens and twenties with the youthful exuberance that he had. Despite wanting nothing more than to head into Cork, Matt spent the next two hours sitting with Clare and Donald's three children, sharing memories of the man they all loved dearly. It was a cathartic afternoon of shared grief, and now Matt was ready to move on to the next mission.

"Okay, everyone. I appreciate the condolences on losing my brother and Derek and Dylan's father. As we all know, losing family and friends has unfortunately become part of our daily lives. Our family of twenty-five is most important right now, and every action we take must be based on ensuring the safety and well-being of our family. Do I want to find Tracy and Kirstie? Yes, of course. But not at the expense of the safety of our family.

"As everyone knows, we found a piece of paper at Judy's with *Haulbowline* written on it. I believe that Judy or Tracy intentionally left this to let anyone who came to the house know that this is where they went. I could be 100% incorrect, but I don't believe I am.

"Ireland has a very small military—what they refer to as the Defence Forces. There is an army, an air force, and even a small navy. These naval forces are based on a small island in Cork Harbor. An island called Haulbowline." Matt looked at those assembled on the couches around him and saw everyone nodding their head in instant understanding. *What better place to serve as a safe haven than an island run by the Irish Navy? The same logic that made Vinalhaven an ideal destination for their family may also apply equally to those surviving in Ireland.*

"I see many of you nodding, seeing the logic behind my assessment of this clue. Most of you don't know, however, that Tracy's sister Judy has two children—a seventeen-year-old daughter named Millie and a twenty-three-year-old son named Rory. Rory is a newly commissioned ensign in the Irish Navy, stationed at Haulbowline." As Matt looked around the group, he could see the lightbulb had fully switched on. "Given this, I've asked Stan and Liz to query QuAI and get us as much information as possible about the current situation on Haulbowline and Cork City. Stan, the floor's all yours."

Stan nodded to Liz, who clicked a button on the laptop, which brought up an enlarged map of the area surrounding Cork City onto the large-screen television. Stan stood, clearing his throat to gain everyone's attention.

"I think we're all familiar with maps of the southern Irish coastline, but I wanted to spend a minute outlining Cork Harbor. As you can see, Cork's harbor is quite large, almost four miles east-west by two miles north-south. The northern edge is the large island of Cobh, spelled with a "bh" but pronounced "cove." This mostly residential island has a decent-sized commercial district along these quays, just north of Haulbowline Island. On the harbor's west side, Ringaskiddy forms the main port—and is highly industrialized, with numerous factories and pharmaceutical plants. Cork Harbor is the second largest natural harbor in the world, second only to Sydney, Australia. You'll also note that downtown Cork City is a couple of miles north of the harbor, requiring ships to transit more than a mile up the River Lee before entering Lough Mahon, which serves as the actual port of Cork.

"And here, right in the northwest corner of the main Cork Harbor, is the small island of Haulbowline." Stan used a small laser pointer to circle the island on the television monitor. He nodded to Liz, who clicked her mouse, which caused the screen to transition to an enlarged image of the island. "Haulbowline is about six hundred meters across by three hundred meters north-south and is split in the middle by this large concave harbor that almost splits the island in half. The island's west side is the naval base, while the east is a municipal park. While the harbor mouth opens to the north, towards Cobh, the island is connected to the mainland by a causeway that runs from the southern side of the small island to the port of Ringaskiddy.

"Liz and I have queried QuAI and studied all available satellite imagery. I can tell you with certainty that people currently live on Haulbowline. Based on the radio signals over the past few weeks, it's clear that this island has more RF signals than anywhere in Cork."

"How about marine traffic?" Matt asked. "Have you been able to detect ships moving in and out?"

"No ships that we've been able to detect. However, based on the type of marine radio frequency, it does appear that the same small boat has been transmitting frequently around the northwest part of the harbor, up to the quays of Cobh, and even up into the downtown area along the River Lee in Cork City."

"How do you know it's the same boat?" Pete asked.

"Good question. Actually, we are making an assumption. We know that it is the same RF signal that is being transmitted. So technically, it could be multiple boats using the same radio model to transmit. But I estimate it's most likely one single boat."

"Okay, fair enough," replied Pete, satisfied with the answer.

"Any estimates on the number of people?" Grace asked.

"No. Not with any level of certainty. I can tell you that QuAI has picked up dozens of RF transmissions each day from the island from what appear to be handheld radios similar to the ones we use daily. QuAI estimates eight radios are transmitting regularly, so I guess from my perspective, we could estimate there are at least eight people on the island. However, for all we know, a hundred are sharing eight radios."

"Okay, how about any visuals from the imagery? Anything

of significance?"

"Yes, there's a couple of things. First, there's a roadblock on the causeway. It appears to consist of several vehicles in a chicane to block traffic flow and create a funnel where only one vehicle can pass. This is consistent with someone attempting to fortify the island. Second, two large offshore patrol vessels of the Irish Navy are docked in Haulbowline's marina. These are consistent with the Samuel Beckett-class ships the Irish Navy uses—each about 300 feet long. One of those ships moved two weeks ago."

"Where'd it move?" Matt asked. "Out on patrol?"

"No. It moved from one dock to the other side, maybe 100 meters. Original images from September show both ships docked along the east side of the naval base, but two weeks ago, one of the ships moved to dock along the west side. We have no idea the significance of this activity other than it proves that people are alive at this location."

Matt sat back and looked at the others sitting around him. He saw the look of hope on Dylan and Derek's faces while the others appeared excited about the news. While Matt yearned for his sister-in-law and niece to be safe in the fold of a group of survivors on Haulbowline, he also knew that any contact with a large, organized group could spell disaster for his family. While Matt had no specific evidence of threats in Ireland, his experience over the last two months forced him to be ultra-cautious.

While Matt continued to think, Dave asked Stan a question. "Hey, Stan, what's that other small island next to Haulbowline? Does the military own that as well?"

Stan used his laser to point to a small, round island southeast of Haulbowline, towards the center of Cork's natural harbor. "That's Spike Island," replied Stan. "It's a former military fort and prison dating back to the late 1700s. It's now a tourist destination, and they give..."

"We've been there," interjected Derek. "My grandfather took us all to Spike Island a few years back. It was pretty cool. It's these enormous stone walls surrounding this huge parade ground. It used to be a fort in the 1800s but was used as a prison until fairly recently."

"Yeah, I remember," added Dylan.

"You're exactly right, boys," said Stan, attempting to regain control of his briefing. "Spike Island is about 100 acres compared to Haulbowline's 80 acres. However, we've seen no RF signals from Spike over the last month and have no reason to believe it's currently occupied."

Having heard enough, Matt stood up and motioned for Stan to have a seat. "Thanks, Stan. Good info, as always. Look, everyone, it's critical that we pursue all leads to see if we can find Tracy and Kirstie—and Haulbowline is our obvious next stop. While we've seen nothing yet to indicate hostile threats in Ireland, we must be cautious. We'll take the A-team—the same eight that went to Rockland. Dave, Kim, Grace, and I will go in one vehicle, followed by Pete, Derek, Dylan, and LT as our overwatch in the second vehicle. Stan, you and Liz will man the radios here on the Rover. We'll arrive right at first light, hoping to catch everyone half asleep. Questions?"

"What about taking the Hinckley?" Pete asked. "The four of us could head out to sea and around the coast to Cork Harbor. They'd never expect that."

"Good idea, Pete," said Matt. "But splitting the team adds a lot of uncertainty and doesn't give us as much flexibility. Depending on the sea conditions, it's a pretty long distance by water, probably at least an hour, if not longer. The threat level isn't high, and I think having two vehicles gives us a lot of options. Plus, if we show up with a boat, they'll know we have that capability—and I'm not sure I want to give that away so easily."

"Yeah, I hadn't thought that through," conceded Pete.

"We'll go fully kitted out as we have been, but I want everyone also to remember that we came to Ireland hoping it would be a peaceful place. So far, it has been. We don't want to be seen as the aggressors, but we want to ensure we protect ourselves. I'm hoping we'll meet some friendly faces tomorrow. Let's get some dinner and a good night's rest."

Everyone stood up and wandered out of the salon, leaving Matt, Stan, and Liz. "What's up, Stan? I could tell you wanted to speak to me about something else."

"Yeah," said Stan, sitting back in the overstuffed leather chair beside Matt. "In addition to Haulbowline, Liz, Juliet, and I have been doing our best to have QuAI do as much analysis as possible on Ireland. Some of the info QuAI has provided is pretty interesting."

"Okay," said Matt. "Such as?"

"Well, as we hoped, everything Rosie has told us seems to check out. Other than Haulbowline, there also appears to be a group of people on the north side of Cork out towards Blarney. QuAI estimates it's maybe 50-100 people from the RF signals, all handheld radios."

"Bigger than Haulbowline?"

"Yes, it seems that way. I believe over 30 different radio signatures are spread out across the north of the city. QuAI's analysis is that this group may be centered on a hotel just off the N20 in a business park."

"Okay, good to know. I don't think it impacts our immediate plans. What about the rest of county Cork? Or Killarney? Dublin? Galway?"

"As you know, QuAI has an incredible amount of info, but it's limited to what Liz, Juliet, and I can query and read. We've spent our entire effort in our local area for the past two days. I looked at QuAI's info on Dublin after what Rosie said about her husband not returning. While there have been sporadic RF signals throughout the city, nothing indicates that any major group is operating there. Almost the opposite. The satellite imagery shows the entire downtown destroyed by fire. It almost looks intentional, but it's hard to know for sure. Simply put, though, O'Connell Street, Temple Bar, and the Docklands are basically gone. The suburbs are intact, but QuAI is not indicating any major activity."

"And the west?"

"As you'd expect. Killarney has some activity, and Galway perhaps has the most activity in the country. And that's mostly from RF signals and some AI analysis of satellite imagery. Once things settle more, we can start looking at these areas in more detail."

"Fair enough," said Matt. "How 'bout Belfast?"

Stan and Liz both sat up a bit straighter at Matt's question. "That's a great question, Matt. We hadn't even put Belfast within the parameters of what we asked QuAI to look at. Frankly, it hadn't even occurred to me."

"Yeah. Many people don't realize Belfast's only a hundred miles north of Dublin—maybe 250 miles from Cork. With no speed limits and clear roads, it's probably only a three-hour drive from here."

"We'll add that to the queries."

"Okay, good. Anything more we need to know for tomorrow? What's your gut telling you, Stan?"

"You know me, Matt. I'm a glass-half-full kinda guy. I think tomorrow is going to go well. I don't know if your sister-in-law will be there, but I think we'll meet a well-organized group of Irish survivors tomorrow. They have no reason not to be friendly."

"Let's hope so, Stan. Let's hope so."

CHAPTER 10

November 14, 8:28 am

The early morning sun reflected on the windshields of the three vehicles deliberately parked on the two-lane causeway to form a chicane. With railings and no shoulder, the narrow causeway leading from Ringaskiddy to Haulbowline provided a natural chokepoint to control all land access to the island. The parked cars forming the chicane ensured that any vehicle approaching would need to slow to less than five miles per hour to navigate the obstacle.

Good tactics and planning, Matt thought as he peered through binoculars while lying prone in the tall grass of Paddy's Point, the strip of the mainland just before the start of the causeway. Behind Matt, what Matt considered his "A-team" sat in their two vehicles hidden by the buildings of the National Maritime College of Ireland. While Matt had moved forward to a position closer to the harbor's edge, Dave had entered one of the four-story buildings to scout from on high.

Matt had been lying hidden in the grass for about twenty minutes while reconnoitering the Haulbowline checkpoint and had learned three important facts. First, November mornings in Ireland were cold as hell. Despite wearing a heavy fleece, hat, and gloves, Matt's lower body had become soaked in the dew of the tall grass, and he had to fight the shivering to keep the binoculars steady.

Second, and more importantly, the two individuals manning the checkpoint appeared unarmed and unconcerned. The sentries were a young man and woman in their early twenties, and Matt could see them sitting on the hood of a small SUV, drinking what appeared to be coffee or tea from a thermos. The SUV was parked about ten meters on the far side of the chicane, and neither was carrying a sidearm or a rifle. From his current vantage point, Matt could not tell if any weapons were in the vehicle. The two sentries talked idly and seemed wholly unconcerned with scanning the approaches to the island.

Lastly, neither the man nor the woman wore a military uniform—both being fully bundled up in heavy winter coats, hats, gloves, and civilian hiking boots. The lack of military uniforms wasn't definitive in and of itself, but combined with the lack of weapons, Matt believed Haulbowline might not be under military control.

Having seen enough, Matt slithered backward from the tall grass and returned to the vehicles to brief his team. As he approached, he saw that Dave had rejoined the group.

"How was the view from upstairs?" Matt asked Dave.

"Good, man. Seems like they have just a simple checkpoint. The chicane is a smart idea, but it seems mostly oriented to get people to slow down. It's more of a checkpoint than a roadblock."

"Yeah, that's exactly the conclusion I came to," replied Matt. "For everyone else's benefit, there were two sentries—a man and woman in their early twenties—and they both appeared unarmed and not overly alert. No crew-served weapons on the vehicles and no personal weapons on the sentries. No military uniforms."

"And a single, handheld radio," added Dave. "Just sitting on the dashboard. Neither sentry used the radio the entire time I was watching."

"Good catch," said Matt. "I couldn't see the dashboard from my vantage point."

"Could this be a ruse?" LT asked. "Do you think they have guns hidden, or maybe these sentries are bait to lure us in?"

"Yeah," said Derek. "Maybe they want to get us out on that causeway and trap us?"

Matt looked at both of them, organizing his thoughts before answering. "You both bring up a good point, which I've been thinking about since we arrived in Kinsale. It's something Clare has noticed and talks to me about quite a bit." Matt looked at his "family" members assembled around him. "While we can never be too cautious, I think it's also important for us to recognize that our views on how the world currently works are based on our personal experiences over the last two months. For us, the world is a very dangerous place. One where we have been forced to defend ourselves against immoral aggressors on a regular basis to simply survive." Matt watched as almost everyone's heads subconsciously nodded in agreement. "While this is our reality, we must also recognize that it may not be true here in Ireland. Ireland doesn't have a culture of guns. The police don't carry firearms. The Irish are, for the most part, fairly non-confrontational and believe firmly in the rule of law.

"While our group might see a possible enemy behind every tree, it's possible, in fact, it seems wholly probable, that the survivors here in Ireland are not afraid of being attacked, robbed, raped, and pillaged. If you talk to Rosie, you'll see they only fear the Black Pox. They don't have any hopes for a vaccine, and their entire world has collapsed solely because of this disease. They don't fear their fellow man; they fear the pox."

Matt could tell that his words had hit home. As intended, he wanted his family to soften, begin to see the good in people, and not always see everything as a threat. He and Clare spent hours whispering about this in bed late into the evenings. While Matt's entire focus had been keeping his family alive, Clare focused on keeping them a family. She wanted her kids to play without care, her nephews to be teenagers and explore, and her friends to laugh, dance, and enjoy life. In short, Clare wanted her family to look forward to the future, not to be afraid of it.

"You make a good point, Uncle Matt," said Derek, to Matt's delight. "But what if you're wrong? What if it is a trap like LT said?" Matt looked at his nephew, realizing how deeply the last eight weeks had affected everyone, especially Derek. *You can't throw these kids into life-or-death situations against rapists and murderers and not expect them to be forever changed*, Matt thought.

"Well, Derek, that's why we'll always play it safe. Always," Matt responded. "But at the same time, we need to manage each situation appropriately and not unnecessarily escalate things if it's not warranted."

"So, basically," interjected Dave. "Your uncle's saying that we're not gonna start off guns a' blazing. We left the old 'shoot first—ask questions later' approach back in the States. Here in Ireland, we'll take the more civilized approach of asking questions *before* shooting. Did I get that right, *Uncle Matt*?"

"Uh, yeah, Dave. As usual, well said," replied Matt, shaking his head.

"So what's that mean for this morning, Matt?" Grace asked, attempting to keep things on track.

"What it means, Grace, is we're going to combine Patrick Swayze's *Roadhouse* rules with a little Teddy Roosevelt diplomacy. Be nice til it's time not to be nice, and speak softly and carry a big stick." Matt paused to make sure everyone was paying attention. "Grace, Kim, and I will take the lead vehicle and approach the roadblock. We'll carry sidearms but leave the long guns in the vehicle. This gives us the least aggressive approach. Dave, you and Derek head to where you were on the top floor or roof and get into an overwatch position with the M240B and the grenade launcher to cover us. I estimate it to be under 400 meters to the checkpoint, so you should have excellent coverage. Lastly, Pete—you, Dylan, and LT stay ready in the second SUV as a quick reaction force should we call. If this thing turns nasty, there's a good close overwatch position on the right side of the road, which will allow you and Dave to coordinate effective enfilade fires along the causeway. Hopefully, everything goes to plan, and I'll radio everyone to come forward. But as my old commander used to say, 'hope is not a course of action." Everybody good?" Matt saw nothing but bobbing heads in the affirmative.

"I love it when a plan comes together," said Dave, clapping his hands. "Let's do this."

CHAPTER 11

November 14, 8:47 am

As soon as Dave radioed down that he and Derek were in a good overwatch position on the building's roof, Matt drove slowly out of the Maritime College of Ireland's parking lot, waving to Pete, who was sitting in his idling SUV. Kim sat beside Matt in the passenger seat while Grace was buckled into the rear seat behind Matt. Kim had her M4 held low along her right leg, well below the level of the window.

Matt rolled south through the Maritime College's parking lot, then turned east onto the L2545 road. In less than a hundred yards, the L2545 turned sharply to the north and was a straight shot directly onto the causeway in less than five hundred meters. The blue-gray waters of Cork Harbor looked peaceful, with the green trees of Spike Island about a kilometer in the distance. Matt kept his speed at just twenty kilometers per hour, knowing that within seconds, the two sentries should be able to see him approaching.

"They see you," Dave's voice said over the handheld radio sitting in the cupholder. Matt could also hear Dave through the earpiece he had connected to the radio on his vest. "They're both standing in front of their vehicle. Still no weapons visible."

Matt continued to drive north onto the causeway, planning

to bring the Porsche Cayenne to a stop about ten meters short of the checkpoint. "Okay, Grace. You and I will get out slowly, keeping our hands empty and visible. Non-threatening. Kim, stay in the vehicle and be ready with the rifle. You can also keep Dave and Pete updated on the radio."

"Got it," said Kim. "Be careful."

"Matt," Dave's said through the radio. "The female has a hand-held radio and has spoken into it twice. My guess is the cavalry should be arriving shortly."

"Roger," said Matt, toggling the switch on his radio and speaking into his throat mic. "No firing unless we're fired upon. No exceptions." Matt brought the Cayenne to a stop. The two sentries stood before him, looking more inquisitive than scared. The one thing they didn't appear was threatening. Neither was armed, and neither looked in any way like they had military training. The two just stood there, staring at Matt and Kim through the windshield of the Cayenne.

Taking a deep breath, Matt slowly opened his door and stepped out. He could sense that Grace had done the same and was standing just behind him and to the left.

"How ye?" Shouted the young man in front of him. "How can we help ye? Please don't come any closer." Up close, Matt confirmed that the young man was no older than his early twenties. Exceptionally thin, with bright red cheeks that Matt wasn't sure were his natural complexion or a result of the biting wind coming off the harbor's water, the young man looked like a lost college student. His companion looked even younger and fit the classic description of an Irish ginger with locks of curly red hair poking out of her wool cap and emerald green eyes that sparkled from ten meters away.

"Hello!" Matt said back loudly, waving his hand in greeting. "We're looking for someone and hope that maybe you could help us."

"Are ye's American, then?" Replied the man, seeming to take a bit more notice of the newcomers.

Deciding not to answer the man's question, Matt continued with one of his own. "Ensign Rory Hogan? Or perhaps his mother, Judy O'Riordan? Would you happen to know them? We're relatives and hope they might have sought refuge here, possibly with a few others."

Clearly, these two weren't high-stakes poker players, and it was immediately evident on their faces that the Hogan and O'Riordan names meant something to them. The girl raised the radio to her lips and spoke too softly for Matt to hear. It was also not lost on Matt that the man and woman were now fully noticing his combat vest and staring at the pistol strapped to Matt's right hip.

"Matt, be alert," Dave said over the radio. "Two OD green SUVs approaching from the north at a very high rate of speed. Less than thirty seconds from you."

Behind him, Matt heard the passenger car door. Turning quickly, Matt saw Kim step out of the vehicle with the M4 in the safe hang position, muzzle pointed down but her firing hand on the pistol grip. The man and the young woman jerked as if plugged into a light socket, taking two steps backward.

"We mean you no harm!" Matt shouted, raising both hands with palms facing forward, hoping to de-escalate the situation. "Judy O'Riordan is my sister-in-law, and Rory is my nephew by marriage. Please. We've come a long way and want only to talk." Judy was divorced and had retaken her maiden name of O'Riordan, while Rory and Millie shared the last name of Hogan.

Before the young man or woman could reply, two SUVs sped up to the north side of the chicane and quickly maneuvered through them, stopping just behind the two sentries standing in the middle of the causeway. Both vehicles' driver and passenger doors flew open, followed quickly by four individuals. Matt's first glance showed the occupants of the first vehicle to be two young men dressed in gray military camouflage uniforms. The second vehicle consisted of a man and a woman around Matt's age, both in civilian attire. None of the four appeared to have any weapon.

Both sentries turned towards the older civilian man and took several steps backward. It was clear this man was in charge, surprising Matt, who initially assumed the older of the two military men was the leader. With no obvious threats visible, Matt focused on the civilian leader when he heard a shout from the younger of the two military men.

"Matt Sheridan? Is that you, Matty?"

Looking over, Matt noticed that the younger man was none other than Rory Hogan—Judy's oldest son, whom Matt had spent considerable time with while visiting over the years. With an overwhelming sense of relief, Matt rushed forward towards Rory, who was running forward to embrace Matt.

"Stop!" A tremendous shout came from the civilian male, causing Matt and Rory to stop dead in their tracks without even thinking. "Move back now, Rory. You've no idea if these people are infected."

Coming to his senses, Rory understood his almost fatal mistake and quickly took several paces backward.

"It's okay," said Matt calmly, raising his hands. "All of us are vaccinated."

"Are ye langers or just mad?" Asked the man, his West Cork accent evident. "I'm not sure how ye survived this far, but I can assure you there's no vaccine hereabouts."

"Doc, this is Tracy's brother-in-law, Matt Sheridan," Rory quickly explained to the man. "I have no idea how he got here, but he's family."

"That's all well an' good," said the man. "But you know the rules. We need to quarantine these people before we let them close. No exceptions."

"Uh, Doc, is it?" Matt said. "I apologize for the abrupt approach, but maybe we could start things over. First, I'd like to know about my sister-in-law, Tracy, and her daughter, Kirstie. Are they alive?"

"Yeah, Matt," answered Rory. "They's both healthy and back at the base. I'm so sorry, though, Matt. Donald passed away of the Pox. Along with my Grandad and Grannie, and Uncle Connor."

"I know, Rory. We saw their graves at the Benmore house. I'm so sorry for your loss as well." The relief Matt felt hearing that Tracy and Kirstie were alive was one of the best feelings he'd had since the Cataclysm began.

"Yeah," said Rory. "Seems like almost everyone is gone now. But we've been lucky here on Haulbowline."

"Matt?" Interjected the man referred to as Doc. "My name is Kevin Cross, and this is my wife Beth. I'm a medical doctor and have become somewhat of the de facto leader of our band of survivors."

"And I'm Lieutenant Seamus Duffy," said the other military male, who had remained completely silent until just then. "I'm the senior surviving military officer here on Haulbowline and was Rory's supervisor before the world ended. I've heard quite a bit about you. A pleasure to meet you."

"It's a pleasure to meet all of you," said Matt. "Next to me here is Grace Heck, and Kim Carney is on the other side of the vehicle. I'm confident we will all have plenty of time to get to know one another. First, though, the most important thing is to vaccinate all of you." Matt paused as he saw the look of disbelief on Kevin's face. "Kevin—Doc—please listen to me for a second. You're a medical doctor, so you'll fully understand this. We recently arrived in Ireland after traveling here by boat from the state of Maine in the United States. It's a long story, but at the end of September, we were able to access a considerable number of doses of the updated Black Pox vaccine. These came directly from the US government. The case Grace is carrying here contains several vials of this vaccine, and we'd like you to administer it to all of your people as soon as possible."

"Matt, please forgive me for being a bit skeptical, but this is all quite a lot to take in," said Kevin.

On her own, Grace took several steps forward and unslung the small bag she was carrying slung over her shoulder. Reaching into the bag, she pulled out a pack of antiseptic wipes and began wiping down one of the vials. She then bent down and set the vial on the pavement in the middle of the road. "Kevin, as Matt said, I'm Grace. I'm also a second-year medical student at the University of Florida and the closest thing our group has to a medical professional. I've been the one administering this vaccine and was present when we received it from the government. The military officer safeguarding this shipment is also a part of our group. Please. Have a look at this vial so we can move things along."

Grace took several steps back to stand next to Matt, and they both watched as Kevin stepped forward to examine the vial. Matt reached down and toggled his mic. "Derek, Dylan, I'm standing here with Rory. Your mom and sister are on Haulbowline and safe." Matt would have preferred to tell them in person but didn't feel right keeping this information from the boys for even a second longer than necessary.

"Thanks, Uncle Matt," replied Derek. Matt could tell from the frog in Derek's voice that he was sobbing. He knew how heart-wrenching yesterday was for the boys and was glad to be able to give them some good news for once. That task complete, Matt shifted his attention back to Kevin.

"Kevin, we're happy to answer any questions you have, but I think the first order of business is getting you all vaccinated. As long as you're not infected, the vaccine provides instant immunity."

"Yeah, Matt, I just need to think through this for a minute. Getting the vaccine has never been an option for us. I still am having a hard time believing you just showed up with vials of vaccine."

"Hey, Doc," said Rory. "I'm happy to go first. You don't know Matt, but you'd trust him completely if you did. In fact, I insist on going first."

Without waiting for any further permission, Rory stepped forward and walked directly up to Grace. Grace looked over at Matt, who nodded once in the affirmative. She reached into her pack, withdrew a syringe, and proceeded to load it with the correct dosage while Rory stripped off the top of his camouflage uniform to bare his upper arm.

"Doc?" Lieutenant Duffy asked. "Can you give me any valid reason not to get this vaccine now other than fearing the unknown?"

Kevin looked over at the lieutenant, unable to provide a good answer. This hesitation was all Seamus Duffy needed, and he quickly strode forward and began removing his top. As he did so, Grace completed injecting Rory, who promptly walked over to Matt and wrapped him in a huge hug.

"Jesus, Matty. It's so damn good to see you. You've no idea how happy Tracy, Kirstie, and my mum will be." Matt squeezed him back tightly, realizing the family group he was responsible for had just grown in size.

Releasing Rory, Matt looked up to see that Kevin had made up his mind. The doctor and his wife were now walking up to Grace and motioning for the two sentries to follow them. Looking over to Matt, the doctor said, "Matt, I'm sure ye've conquered many obstacles to get here and keep your family alive. I hope to God Almighty that you're right about this vaccine. If you're wrong, you've doomed us all."

"Kevin, I don't take your trust in me lightly. There are so few survivors left. We must take care of each other."

The next few minutes were spent administering the vaccine, followed by handshakes and hugs. It was the first time the Irish survivors had been in close contact with anyone outside their group, and the positive vibes were contagious. Matt quickly learned that the Haulbowline group consisted of twenty-six survivors, eight of whom were members of the Irish Naval Service.

Matt called forward Pete and Dave's teams, and they all planned to tour the Haulbowline facilities while reuniting Derek and Dylan with their mother and sister.

CHAPTER 12

November 14, 10:16 am

Under a gloomy November sun, Matt watched with a hopeful smile the mother and child reunion on this strange and mournful day. Seeing his sister-in-law Tracy tightly hugging her two sons made Donald's loss even more pronounced. While both Tracy and Kirstie appeared in good health, the absence of their father made the reunion bittersweet.

The last hour had been a blur of introductions, vaccine administrations, and a quick tour of the facilities at Haulbowline. Tracy's sister Judy O'Riordan hadn't changed one bit since Matt had last seen her—the combination of her Irish slang and wit had everyone laughing within seconds. At seventeen, Judy's youngest daughter Millie had grown into a lovely teenager. Matt could see the strain etched on all their faces from the lack of updates from the middle daughter, Katie, who had been away at university in the Netherlands when the pandemic began. The last they heard, Katie's boyfriend had become ill, and Katie had vowed to stay by his side.

The eight sailors, Dr. Cross and his wife Beth, and the O'Riordan/Sheridan ladies were accompanied by twelve others to make up their complement of twenty-six. Matt and his group were introduced to all of them while Grace administered their vaccines. Matt found it impossible to remember everyone's name but was confident there would be plenty of time to learn everyone's story.

The twenty-six survivors on Haulbowline had spent the last six weeks improving their living situation, and the small island offered both security and convenience. The group had rigged several trailer-mounted generators to provide electricity throughout their selected accommodation buildings, which they had turned into their new home. After a quick tour, Matt's group was invited to tea and biscuits in a cozy, well-appointed dining hall, which Matt assumed must have been the senior officer's mess.

The large, round room felt like a combination of an upscale quayside restaurant and a modern military mess hall, with expensive wood furnishings and walls adorned by various plaques, guidons, and pictures of former Naval commanders. The vaulted ceiling was covered in planks of blond wood, while the floor-to-ceiling windows provided an amazing view across the harbor. An enormous wooden table that could easily seat twenty was positioned at the end of the room, with just shy of a dozen other square or rectangular tables with seating for four or six, respectively.

Matt's gang were offered seats around the large table while Judy, Tracy, and a couple of the others brought out mugs, pots of tea, and trays of biscuits. The seats quickly filled up with most of the senior members of the survivor's groups while the junior seamen and children occupied several of the smaller tables. Matt knew that Dr. Cross and his group were eager for information, but so was Matt.

"So, Kevin, you've set yourselves up quite well here. How'd you end up here? Are you affiliated with the Navy?"

"Not directly, Matt. At least not anymore," answered Kevin, taking a sip from his mug. "I was a Medical Officer in the Defence Forces for eight years but left active service about five years ago. Until the government released all Defence

Force personnel from their obligations, I held the rank of Commandant, which I believe you call a Major. I was actually stationed here at Haulbowline, and that's how I met my wife, Beth."

"Beth was in the military as well?" Grace asked, looking at both Kevin and Beth, who was sitting next to him.

"No," answered Beth. "But my father was the Commodore and the flag officer who commanded this installation. Kevin and I met at a military ball. I'm a surgical nurse, so we also work together."

"Ahh, that makes sense," said Matt. "So, how'd you end up here after the pandemic?"

"Pure luck, honestly," said Kevin. "The first signs of the pandemic began while we were on a two-week sailing vacation to west Cork, something we'd always wanted to do. For two glorious weeks, we were either on our sailboat or in an isolated cabin at the very tip of West Cork near Crookhaven. As such, we had almost no contact with anyone at all. Upon returning to our slip in the Cork Harbor Marina, over in Monkstown, we immediately knew something was wrong. Our first stop was to see Beth's mum and dad, the Commodore." Kevin paused, a look of grief crossing his face as he remembered the details. "They were all gone. The base was almost completely deserted, and those remaining were dead, including both of Beth's parents."

"Is that how you linked up with Rory?" Matt asked, alternating his look between Kevin and Judy's son. "Were you stationed here throughout the pandemic?"

"No, Matty. I was actually with a small group out at Elfordstown, guarding the satellite station there. I believe we got back here to Haulbowline the day after the Doc and Beth returned."

"Elfordstown?" Matt asked, never having heard of that

town.

"It's just north of Midleton," answered Seamus, the Lieutenant and Rory's superior officer. "A small town approximately thirty kilometers northeast of here. Elfordstown Earthstation is part of the National Space Centre. I was assigned, along with Rory, as an officer on the *LÉ Samuel Beckett*, one of the three newer offshore patrol vessels stationed here at Haulbowline. Just as the pandemic began, I was tasked with taking a team of twelve to guard the Elfordstown facility. This team consisted of Rory, two non-commissioned officers, and eight seamen. We were there for two weeks when we lost contact with our headquarters. Our last radio transmission told us to go home to our families. We immediately returned to Haulbowline, where everyone was gone except Doc and a few others."

"Wow," said Matt. "Were you following what was happening while at Elfordstown?"

"No. The Space Centre consists of very sensitive satellite dishes, and cell phone reception was non-existent at the facility. We had some information from the internet at the beginning, but we lost that during the first week when the facility shut down and its personnel went home."

"That's crazy," said LT, speaking for the first time. "You guys were lucky to be assigned to a remote location."

"Yeah," said Seamus, the other LT, morosely. "Although I have difficulty believing there's any luck left in the world. In addition to everyone being dead, three of my men left Haulbowline and never returned. I can only assume they perished as well."

Trying to avoid a pity party, Matt quickly changed the subject by asking about others at the table. Shifting his gaze to the older gentleman across the table from him, Matt asked, "And Tom, was it? Are you retired Navy? What brought you here?"

"Heavens, no. I'm a retired professor from UCC. That's University College Cork. I was at home with my daughter, Sarah, and our two boarders over in Monkstown," Tom replied, motioning towards the handsome woman in her late forties sitting next to him. Tom was a small, wiry man with gray hair and a ruddy complexion. Appearing to be in his early 70s, Tom had the physique of a marathon runner.

"Borders?" asked LT. "As in border collies?"

Tom laughed. "Heavens, no, young man. Boarders, as in those two lovely ladies at that table over there who are undergraduates at UCC. They rented the small apartment above my garage." Tom pointed his hands at two women sitting with several other young women and a few of Rory's sailors at a table across the room. One of the women Tom pointed at was one of the sentries manning the checkpoint earlier that morning.

Everyone smiled at the mixup in language. Matt knew from his experience in Ireland that while Americans and Irish both speak English, it is often quite difficult to understand each other given the accents and the use of different words.

Tom continued his story. "My wife died several years ago, and it was just Sarah and I weathering out the storm. We had plenty of supplies and were content to stay home when John came by—ah, I guess I should say Petty Officer Cassidy came by. John and Niamh lived next door to us with their two children. We had left some supplies outside for Niamh at the beginning of the pandemic, and when John came back from Elfordstown—you see, he was part of Seamus's guard detail there—well, John came by to get his family next door and offered to have us follow them to Haulbowline."

"But weren't you worried about the pox?" Grace asked.

At this, Kevin raised his hand to answer. "Grace, we were

very worried. But at the same time, I knew we needed to gather survivors to build a community. We set up very specific protocols when Seamus released his men to check on their families. They could take as long as they wanted to gather their families, but everyone would be required to quarantine for a minimum of ten days upon returning to Haulbowline. Beth and I found a small group of five survivors here on Haulbowline, mostly dependents or girlfriends. Tom and Sarah, Petty Officer Cassidy's family, and Rory's four family members became part of our community. Those first ten days were difficult, with everyone forced to stay quarantined on different parts of the naval base. But by mid-October, we were all together and, for the last month, have accomplished a lot in making this our home."

"Remarkable, actually," agreed Matt.

"Well, we've been quite fortunate. Tom and Sarah are both professors of engineering. Tom is an electrical engineer, while Sarah holds a doctorate in mechanical engineering. With the tools and equipment on the base, they've been instrumental in restoring our electricity, keeping our water fresh, and our accommodations heated as winter approaches."

"Mmm," agreed Matt. "And what about Cork? Have you had any interaction with other survivors around the city?"

"Some, but not many," said Kevin. "With no known vaccine until this morning, our focus has been maintaining our separation from anyone and anything that could infect us. We gathered enough supplies for the winter and planned to hunker down on Haulbowline and see what the Spring would be like."

"Fair enough," said Matt. "Survival is always paramount. So, I assume you've seen no threats?"

"No, mate. This isn't America. Everyone who's survived is doing just like we are. We've met a few people around the area, mostly single families or sometimes a small group of families who've remained isolated from the virus. All are doing reasonably well given the plentiful availability of supplies." Kevin took a sip from his mug of tea. "I must say again, Matt, we are eternally grateful for you providing the vaccine to us. If I might ask ye, you mentioned you came ashore down in Kinsale, but what are your intentions moving forward? And how much vaccine do you have?"

"Honestly, Kevin, we haven't thought too far into the future. We plan to make Kinsale our home through the winter, and we've been taking steps to do so. Our biggest long-term concern is sustainable energy. We're in the process of hooking up generators, but at some point, the supply of diesel and petrol is going to become ineffective. As for vaccine, we have several thousand doses." Matt had no reason not to trust Kevin, but he felt it unnecessary to inform him that they still had just over 9,700 doses remaining.

"It's been a long, emotional morning for everyone. Here's what I'd like to do," Matt continued, looking to Tracy sitting to his right and squeezing her hand. "First, I'd like to get Tracy and Kirstie to Kinsale to be reunited with Kelsey and the rest of the family. Second, I'd like to leave you with our satellite phone so that we have some reliable communication. Lastly, I'd like to come back tomorrow and discuss with you a plan for identifying survivors and getting them vaccinated. The quicker we can do that, the easier it'll be to start building a strong community. America's devolved into chaos and violence, but if we do this right, Ireland can be a safe place for us all to start fresh and raise our families."

"Excellent plan," said Kevin, accompanied by affirmative nods from everyone around the table.

"Grace will leave you one full vial and the remainder of what we used this morning, along with syringes. That's about seventy-five doses. Feel free to use as you see fit."

CHAPTER 13

November 14, 9:51 pm

The slight rocking of the Irish Rover only added to the feeling of comfort as Matt nestled into the soft duvet, propped up on several pillows with Clare's head resting on his chest. They had purposely left the thick drapes open this evening so that they could see the moonlight reflecting on the River Bandon as they looked south across Kinsale Harbor. Today had been a good day. Especially after yesterday.

"I'm so happy for those kids, Matt," said Clare. "I still can't believe you actually found Tracy and Kirstie. And that they're healthy." Their children, Chris and Laurie, had elected to take sleeping bags down to the floor in the main salon so that they could have a slumber party to celebrate Kirstie's return.

"Yeah. It was a special day. Things seem to be working in our favor a bit. Finally."

"The look on Tracy's face sitting at the table tonight at dinner, surrounded by all four of her children." Clare paused, not wanting to cry again. "I can't even imagine what the last two months must have been like for her." Clare abruptly sat up, tossing off the covers and wrapping her arms around her knees as she tucked them into her chest. "Promise me, Matthew Sheridan. Promise me that I'll never be separated from our children. I don't think I could handle it."

Matt reached up and brought his wife into an embrace. "I promise you, honey. Everything we do, every day, is for this family. And I can only do the things I do knowing that you're with Chris and Laurie. That's what makes us strong."

"What's next, Matt? I mean, other than just surviving. What's the plan? Is Ireland all that you hoped it would be?"

"Yes," replied Matt instinctively, then was silent for a moment. "And no."

"What do you mean, no? I thought everything seemed to be better than you hoped."

"Yes, overall, I can't complain about a single thing. Kinsale is as expected. There don't appear to be any real threats. Finding Tracy and Kirstie alive and healthy has honestly been a bonus, as realistically, there was a 99% chance they were dead along with everyone else. I mourn Donald, but given all that's happened, we're just so damn lucky to have everyone that we do."

"So why did you say '*and no*'?" Clare asked.

"Well, it's been something Stan, Pete and I have been discussing—long-term sustainable energy. We got somewhat spoiled at Vinalhaven with the wind turbines and having 24/7 electricity. Ireland has quite a few small wind farms, but none are near us here in Cork City. They're all west and north—parts of the country we aren't familiar with."

"And gas and diesel will eventually be useless, right?"

"Yes. I mean, with some care and planning, we should be able to get at least a year out of the fuel we have, maybe even two years. But I'm thinking much farther down the road."

"So if not Ireland, then where?"

"No, no, Clare. I'm not saying Ireland isn't our final destination. You asked if it was all that I hoped it would be, and I'm pointing out what I think is our biggest long-term challenge. Remaining near the sea is critical for us in terms of logistics, security, and food. But if we want to attempt to live with all the conveniences we're used to, we need to put considerable effort into ensuring we have a sustainable energy source. Solar in Ireland is a non-starter. It's sunny about ten days a year, and even on those days, it probably rains. The wind is our only manageable solution."

"So maybe we need to find these wind farms and see if any of their technicians survived?"

"You sound exactly like Pete!" Matt said, smiling. "And honestly, two people in Haulbowline might be instrumental in this. You'll meet them soon, but there was an older gentleman named Tom Ryan, along with his daughter Sarah. He's got to be in his seventies, as she's probably in her late forties. They're both engineering professors at UCC. His specialty is electrical engineering, and hers is mechanical. We'll find out soon, but hopefully, between them, they know something about wind turbines."

"Well, that's good."

"Yep. And I really liked the guy in charge there—Kevin. He's a former military doctor—a surgeon. He's very sharp. A good leader. Cares for his people and seems to be quite cautious—which I like. His wife, Beth, is a nurse. You'll like her. And Rory's boss seems top-notch. Seamus is a lieutenant, equivalent to our O-3 captain, who seems to know what he's doing. They have two working warships, and I'm hopeful he, Rory, and the half dozen sailors they have can run those ships if we ever needed them."

"I can't wait to meet them. Maybe we should invite them all down here for a social event. Whadda ya think?"

"Yeah, I'd like that," said Matt. "Let's give that some thought tomorrow. I'm not sure about the logistics of that —transporting everyone and cooking all the food. We might need to start with smaller groups."

"I'll talk to Marvi and Molly tomorrow. Oh, and Tracy, of course. Between the four of us, we'll plan something. Tracy can tell us all we need to know about Haulbowline."

"Okay. The next week is going to be busy. We now have almost sixty people between Kinsale and Haulbowline, and I want to divide some tasks so that we can accomplish some of the things we've discussed. I'd love to get in touch with as many people as possible throughout greater Cork, but short of going door to door, I don't see an easy way to get them to come out of their houses. Everyone is still so afraid of contact that they've hunkered down, and I guess that most survivors are not on the main thoroughfares."

"You need the ice cream man," said Clare, deadpan.

"What? What are you talking about?" Matt shot back, thinking she was being flippant while he was talking about a real obstacle.

"Hey, easy there, cowboy. I was just offering a helpful solution."

"What could ice cream possibly have to do with distributing the vaccine?" Matt said in the condescending tone Clare absolutely hated.

"I didn't say ice cream, Matt. I said the ice cream *man*. Don't you remember the ice cream man when we were little? No matter what time of day, whether we were playing indoors or outdoors, you could hear that music playing a mile away, and everyone instantly ran to get money from their parents. My favorite was always the chocolate eclair!"

Matt laughed, fully understanding Clare's idea and realizing it solved their problem of contacting survivors. "You're a goddamn genius, Gump!" He shouted, sitting up to kiss his wife on the lips. "Seriously, that's a great idea. Mine was a bombpop, by the way."

CHAPTER 14

November 15, 5:39 am

Wiping sleep from his eyes, Matt was surprised to see his sister-in-law sitting at the yacht's dining room table, cradling a mug of coffee. He had figured on being the first one awake on the yacht, wanting to get an early start on putting the finishing details on the day's plan.

"Hey, Tracy. How'd you sleep?" Matt asked, walking into the room. He was wearing faded jeans and an old desert-tan t-shirt depicting his old Special Forces team's logo—a caricature of a Mongoose eating a snake. Matt noted that Tracy was still wearing the same outfit he had seen her head off to bed in—a pair of sweatpants and a Michigan Go Blue sweatshirt. Tracy was four years older than Matt, the same age as his brother Donald. With long, natural blonde hair and brown eyes, she had the lithe build of a runner, although, to Matt's knowledge, she'd never run a single mile and was naturally thin. Often jokingly referred to as the family's Martha Stewart, she was one of those rare people who always made anyone feel completely welcome and at home, no matter who they were. Her home was always the hangout for all her kids' friends, and in all the years Matt had known her, he couldn't think of a single time she had ever spoken badly about someone.

Looking up, she smiled warmly. "I don't seem to sleep much

nowadays, Matt. But as far as sleep goes, the bed on this yacht sure beats anything I've slept in recently. You have yourself quite a setup here."

"Yeah, well, we've had a lot of ups and downs the last few months. As we all have," he said, both of them immediately thinking of Donald's body lying in the fresh grave in Carrigaline.

"Let me get you some coffee, Matt. I just made a pot," said Tracy, standing up.

"Sit. Please. I can get it," Matt said, motioning for Tracy to stay in her seat.

Instead of sitting, Tracy stepped over to her brother-in-law and wrapped her arms around him, burying her head in his chest. "I know I thanked you yesterday, Matt, but seriously, you have no idea how grateful I am for what you've done for Kelsey, Derek, and Dylan. The only thing that kept Don and I going these last couple of months was knowing that our children would be safe with you. We had no idea how you were faring, but we knew if anyone could make it through this, it would be you and Clare. Thank you, Matt. Thank you, thank you, thank you." Tracy sniffled as tears dripped down her cheeks and onto Matt's t-shirt.

"Shhh," said Matt. "We're family. If anything, the three of them cared for us as much as we did them. You have no idea how proud I am of each of them. They've been instrumental in keeping all of us alive."

"They certainly had some interesting stories to tell last night," Tracy said, composing herself and wiping away the tears. "I feel like I should be a bit more upset learning you taught my baby boy to set up a claymore mine and my oldest son to use a machine gun." She tried to smile through her drying tears.

"Well," said Matt a bit sheepishly. "I have to admit, they're quick learners. And don't forget, I did teach them how to play Texas Hold'em as well on the voyage over here. Let me get you a refill." Matt quickly grabbed Tracy's mug and went into the kitchen for more coffee. Returning in just a few seconds, he set Tracy's mug in front of her as he took a chair across the table. "How bad was it, Tracy? You've heard our stories from Woodstock and Vinalhaven, but how was it here? How were Don's last few days? And your parents?"

Tracy took a sip, using the hot liquid to wash the edges off these raw memories. "Honestly, Matt, looking back, it just seems so frivolous. So arbitrary. The nuclear attacks on the US caused quite a disruption here and everywhere. And the President's retaliation against the Muslim world brought everything to a standstill.

"When the first reports of the Black Pox started filtering around, we thought we'd be fine. Donald has a bit of that Sheridan prepper gene in him, and with my father, we stocked up on everything we could possibly need. We also stocked Judy's house down in Crosshaven and figured between the two places, we'd be fine, and each of us would have a backup location should something happen."

"So you, Donald, and Kirstie stayed with your parents at Benmore while Judy and Millie hunkered down in Crosshaven?"

"That's right. And my younger brother, Connor—he was staying with Judy. And for the first two weeks, everything was fine. Until the morning of October 3rd."

"What happened?" Matt asked.

"It was just something so stupid. My brother Connor went to check on our cousin Ronan. He lives just outside of Crosshaven up towards Myrtleville. We'd been able to travel back and forth no problem between Crosshaven and Benmore, but we had strict protocols that we never got out of the car and never came into contact with anyone else."

"Okay," said Matt, already seeing where this was going.

"So that day, Kirstie and I were working in the garden at Benmore when Connor came over. He went into the house, and we thought nothing of it. A few minutes later, Don came out, white as a ghost. He had Kirstie and I stand up and said he was now quarantined. Connor had broken the rules and went into Ronan's house, where he found Ronan dead of pox. He panicked and rushed home to tell my parents. He didn't even think about the fact that he might be contagious."

"So Donald saw the issue immediately and placed himself, his parents, and Connor in quarantine?"

"Yes," said Tracy, tears beginning to well up in her eyes again. "He said it was just a precaution and we shouldn't worry. Just for Kirstie and I to take the other car and stay with Judy and Millie. He said everything would be fine in ten days, their quarantine would be over, and we could resume living as a family."

"But it wasn't fine," said Matt quietly.

"No. It wasn't." Tracy sniffled away the tears, sipping her coffee and composing herself. "There was no drama, and honestly, nothing for us to do. Kirstie and I visited daily while keeping our distance, and on the fourth day, Donald came outside. Instead of staying ten meters away, he yelled for us to stay in the car. I could tell right away he was sick. His eyes were red, he was sweaty with fever, and his nose was running. He said my parents and Connor were sick and unable to get out of bed. There was nothing anyone could do. I had Kirstie say goodbye to her father and took her back to Judy's. I then returned, and Don and I talked for several hours in the back garden, keeping ten meters between us. If not for Kirstie and the hope of reuniting with Kelsey, Derek, and Dylan, I would have gladly gone into the house with Donald."

"I know you would have, Tracy. I know," Matt said.

"That was it, Matt. I just said my goodbyes, unable to hug or kiss him. He watched me drive away, and I knew I'd never see him again."

"Did you bury him? Weren't you worried about the pox in the house?"

"Rory did that," she said. "We didn't go back to the house for almost two weeks. A few days after moving to Judy's, Seamus and Rory invited us all to Haulbowline, where we've been over the last month. About two weeks ago, Rory and some sailors wore these HAZMAT suits to Benmore. They had already dug four graves and buried my parents, brother, and Donald in the back garden. We waited a few days, then Rory took Judy, myself, and the kids, and we had a short graveside service for them all. It was nice. Peaceful."

"I'm so sorry, Tracy. I can't imagine how difficult that's been for you."

"I'm sorry, too, Matt. I know how much your brother meant to you. And I know how proud he was of you and how he slept at night knowing you were caring for our children."

"We're all together now, Tracy. And nothing is going to split us apart. Nothing. This family is all we have."

"You've done such amazing things, Matt. This big family you've put together, everyone seems to just fit."

"Yeah, it is amazing. There's twenty-five of us, twenty-seven with you and Kirstie, and an even thirty if Judy, Rory, and Millie want to join us. Together, we're strong. As strong as anything on the planet."

"You believe that, don't you?"

"I do, Tracy. I absolutely do."

CHAPTER 15

November 15, 1:12 pm

Matt just loved when a plan came together. He leaned back on the hood of the Porsche Cayenne, enjoying the warm sun on his face as it tentatively tried to poke through the November clouds. Today seemed slightly warmer than the last couple of days, but Matt wasn't sure how much of that warmth was simply the feeling of finally feeling like they were making progress.

They were stopped in the center lane of the N40, otherwise known as the South Ring Road, on the south side of the city of Cork. With three lanes running east and west, this was the central artery moving traffic on the southern edge of what was once Ireland's second-largest city. Today, the highway was completely deserted. Their convoy had stopped two dozen meters short of what appeared to be a major police checkpoint consisting of more than a half-dozen Gardai police vehicles. These would be perfect for Matt's plan.

After yesterday's emotional reunion, Matt had invited Kevin and his core team in Haulbowline to join his family for breakfast aboard the Irish Rover this morning. Kevin and his gang had arrived in two vehicles just after 8:00 a.m., and the last few hours had consisted of Matt outlining his plan to move things forward. To build a community. To start fresh.

The plan was not new, nor was it really Matt's. The "adult

council," as Matt had taken to calling it, had spent countless hours on the voyage over, as well as since their arrival in Kinsale, discussing priorities, options, and objectives for how best to ensure their extended family's survival and success on the emerald isle. With Juliet serving as the designated scribe, each discussion provided greater and greater detail, which Juliet had captured in a series of PowerPoint slides. After his pre-dawn coffee with Tracy, Matt sat down with Juliet and added individual names and some additional specificity to these slides.

With Kevin and his team of Seamus, Rory, Tom, and Sarah, now a part of Matt's newly expanded adult council, gathered in the main salon, Matt laid out his plan for the combined group's next several weeks of activity. He proposed dividing their efforts into six main functional areas and assigning individuals to a specific area, at least for the short term. The six areas Matt proposed were Community/Health, Security, Survivability/Sustainability, Comfort/Food/Family, Intelligence, and Special Projects.

Expanding their community and ensuring everyone's health would fall to Kevin, Beth, and Grace. Their initial focus would be conducting community outreach, getting the vaccine to as many survivors as they could identify throughout County Cork, and gathering the necessary medical supplies and equipment their community might need.

Matt assigned Security to Dave, along with Seamus, Rory, and LT. Others would help, as security was everyone's responsibility, but the main tasks of responding to threats and ensuring they were protected would fall to these four.

Survivability and Sustainability were possibly the most important functions, allowing them to rebuild as a community. Matt proposed Pete and Kim from the Kinsale group should work alongside engineering professors Tom and Sarah to tackle some of these problems. Again, they would have help from whoever was needed, but the four of them would be the brains behind establishing sustainable energy and gathering all equipment and technology required for them all to keep their society functioning at a 21st-century level.

Matt referred to the next group as the "Seven Moms" and stressed that this was the single most important functional area—which is why the six mothers in their group were in charge. Clare, Molly, Marvi, Michelle, Rosie, Tracy and Judy. Each of these ladies brought something unique to the extended family. These ladies would ultimately be the ones to decide how they all lived, what they ate, and tasking the other groups with the priorities needed for their children and families to succeed in this post-cataclysmic world.

The remaining two functional areas, Intelligence and Special Projects, Matt labeled as belonging to Stan and himself, respectively. Matt also tentatively assigned Liz and Juliet to the Intelligence section under Stan while reserving Derek and Dylan to assist Matt with special projects. Matt and Stan had agreed to refrain from mentioning QuAI until the relationship with the Haulbowline survivors was more firmly established.

Matt had no intention of micro-managing any of the functional areas, and his goal in establishing them was to give the amazing people in his family the responsibility to focus their efforts and energy. With more than 98% of the world's population dead and the island nation of Ireland virtually abandoned, the survivors had more tasks than they could ever hope to accomplish. By dividing their intellect and expertise, Matt's goal was to resurrect their pre-pandemic way of life as much as humanly possible.

Standing in front of the Porsche Cayenne on the N40, leaning back on the hood to enjoy the heat of the engine permeating through the vehicle's metal surface, Matt was now witnessing his plan for dividing labor being put into action. To his front, Dave supervised LT and Matt's two nephews in jumpstarting four Gardai vehicles and filling their tanks with fresh petrol. The predominantly white four-door wagons were marked in the blue and highlighter-yellow markings of Ireland's police force, formally known as the Garda Siochana. Behind Matt, two olive-drab Toyota Landcruisers of the Irish Naval Forces pulled up and discharged Kevin, Beth, and Grace, along with four Irish seamen and four of Kim's MIT students. Pete, Tom, and Sarah had taken one of the Kinsale SUVs and gone to Curry's—a large electronics store just off the motorway one exit to their east. Matt expected them to return shortly, and the next part of the plan would commence.

"Hey, Matt," Kevin greeted him, walking up from where he had parked the Navy Landcruiser. "Any issues with the Gardai vehicles?"

"None at all," replied Matt. "These guys have pretty much gotten it down to a science. We have a couple of those portable battery jumpstarters, as well as full cans of petrol. It looks like the Gardai just abandoned this checkpoint when things got rough. There were no bodies in any of the vehicles."

"Yes," said Kevin. "We've only explored a few areas to get required supplies, but it seems that most people died in their homes. Was it not like this in the States?"

"It depends. We had a lot of violence in the country leading up to the pandemic and even after the pandemic hit hard. Many people were killed on the roads, in stores, and around hospitals. But like here, most people died in their homes."

"The vaccine makes all the difference. We would never have approached this checkpoint or gone into any building that might have been contaminated. Our fear of smallpox was too great, so we've lived pretty austerely for the last six weeks. I suspect the remaining survivors are scattered around the countryside, mostly keeping to themselves and deathly afraid of any contact with outsiders."

"That's where Clare's ice cream truck idea comes into play. I'm hoping the Gardai vehicles, with their sirens and public address systems, will alert people to the fact we have the vaccine."

"Ah yes, we call them ice cream vans here," said Kevin. "And I agree. Your idea's a good one."

Earlier that morning, Juliet and Amey went to a stationary supply store in Kinsale and found a few reams of brightly colored paper. They had quickly made a simple flyer and printed several hundred copies on one of the laser printers on the yacht. Now, the plan was for teams of two, one Irish Navy and one of the MIT students, to drive designated routes around the towns south of Cork. Sirens blaring, they were to post the flyers on conspicuous areas in villages that seemed likely survivors would go to for supplies.

"Thanks for supporting this initiative," said Matt. "The routes you and Seamus put together are just what we need."

"It's a good idea, Matt," said Kevin. "This week's focus will be the villages between Kinsale and Cork, east to Ringaskiddy, and west to Inishannon. That's a 20-kilometer diameter circle. Each team will handwrite specific times for each location and retrace their route daily for the next week. Hopefully, this will cast a net wide enough to catch most of the survivors in this area."

"And every flyer says that we will have vaccines available every day at noon at the car park in downtown Carrigaline, where the Owenabue River crosses the Cork Road."

"Spot on, Matt. This will work."

Just then, Pete's SUV came rocketing up the motorway from the east and stopped behind their gaggle of vehicles. As Pete, Tom, and Sarah exited the vehicle, Matt noticed they each carried several large plastic shopping bags.

"Any luck, Pete?" Matt asked.

"Oh yeah," answered Pete. "Sarah knew exactly where to go. Curry's had everything we wanted. These bags are just what we found on the shelves. Tom thought to check out the warehouse area, where he found boxes containing more than two hundred radios."

Matt and Kevin watched as the three newcomers emptied their loot onto the Cayenne's hood. Each of their bags had several sets of handheld VHF radios and large packs of AA batteries.

"Okay, everyone," Pete said in a loud voice to get the attention of the MIT students and Irish sailors. "Come grab a box, pull out the radios, and fill them with batteries. Let's put everyone on Channel 1 for now and do a radio check."

In minutes, more than a dozen radios had been confirmed to work. With the Gardai vehicles started and filled with petrol, Kevin and Grace briefed the four two-person teams while handing out their routes and a stack of colorful flyers. Dave had insisted that each group was armed, and Matt was pleased to see each team member wearing a holstered sidearm. The Irish sailors each also had a futuristic-looking rifle, a Steyr Aug, slung over their shoulder. While no one expected any trouble, the Americans knew that bad things could happen without warning.

After they all watched the four Gardai vehicles depart, Beth, Grace, Tom, and Sara took one of the OD green Landcruisers and returned to Haulbowline. They had plans to get things ready for manning a vaccine station in Carrigaline at noon the next day.

Matt gathered the remaining personnel around the front of his Porsche. Dave, LT, Derek, and Dylan stood to Matt's left. Pete, Kevin, Seamus, and Rory stood across the hood from him while Kim positioned herself directly at Matt's right side.

"Okay, folks," said Matt, looking around and making eye contact with everyone. "This next task I'll put firmly under the heading of 'special projects.' Kevin, you're probably wondering why Dave and I asked you so many questions about your time in the Army this morning. The bottom line is this: our experiences in the post-cataclysmic US were filled with extreme violence. While things here appear peaceful, our experience proves that it is now a cut-throat world where the rule of law no longer encumbers evil people."

Matt looked directly at Kevin and Seamus. "You've already noticed and commented that all of the adults in our group carry at least a sidearm at all times. You'll note that Dave, LT, and I are seldom without our full kit and an assault rifle."

"Yeah," said Seamus. "We've noticed. A bit cowboyish, isn't it? No one here carries a gun."

"You're right," agreed Matt. "And that's exactly our special project today. Our group came here with the ability to defend itself against a very organized enemy. I have no intention of ever allowing an enemy to arm itself and organize against us."

A light bulb seemed to go off in Kevin's mind, and Matt could see it in Kevin's eyes. "Collins Barracks," said Kevin, thinking out loud.

"You got it," confirmed Matt. "The Irish Defence Forces are scattered all over the country, but their main firepower is concentrated in only a few facilities. The main facility in Munster is Collins Barrack, just up the road in Cork City."

"You're going to seize all of the guns and ammunition?" Rory asked, a bit incredulous. "They have artillery, Matt. Probably thousands of individual weapons. We can't possibly take everything."

"Oh, I don't want to take it," said Matt. "I just want the keys so no one else can take it. Kevin, can you help us out?"

"Yes," Kevin replied. "I think I know just the place."

CHAPTER 16

November 15, 2:45 pm

The Porsche Cayenne automatically downshifted to its lowest gear as Matt steered their three-vehicle convoy onto the steep incline of St. Patrick's Hill. The drive through the city of Cork had been one of the most impactful experiences since the cataclysm, and Matt was still trying to wrap his head around it.

Cork City was empty. Motionless. Abandoned.

The city of Cork straddled the River Lee—several wide bridges crossed the river, linking the brick sidewalks of the central market area on the south with the businesses on the steep hill overlooking the entire site, both named after Patrick, the saint who banished snakes from the emerald isle. Large, historic, and vibrantly colored stone and brick buildings lined the quayside on both sides of the river. Once lauded as the European Capital of Culture, the last time Matt had been here, the city had seemed so vibrant and alive. People window-shopping along the wide sidewalks of St. Patrick's Street in front of the Brown & Thomas department store or the famed English Market. Buskers, homeless people, students in their matching school uniforms and backpacks, and tourists speaking a myriad of Slavic and Asian languages.

No more. Like its inhabitants, Cork City was dead.

Except for the animals. Dogs wandered freely through the

streets, some solo and others in small packs. Glancing down some of the side streets often revealed groups of cats. Matt had no idea if these were former pets or feral cats, but they seemed content to sit in the sun along stone walls, dumpsters, and doorways. And the rats. No longer hiding in the shadows and darkness, large rats seemed to be almost everywhere.

Kevin was riding shotgun in the Porsche SUV, with Kim behind him in the backseat. Dave drove the vehicle behind Matt, with Rory in the final vehicle of the trio. Kevin's running commentary as they drove through the city streets was more for Kim's benefit, as Matt was already extremely familiar with the city, and Matt found his mind wandering a bit.

As he drove, he realized this was the first major city he had visited since waking up to nuclear terrorism in the United States. For some reason, he expected to see death—and its absence bothered him. There were no bodies in the streets, no signs of violence or destruction, no evidence other than the lack of humans to prove that the world as everyone knew it had ended.

Driving slowly through the abandoned city streets, Matt rolled his window down. While he couldn't see death, he could smell it. Nothing overpowering like the makeshift morgue at the Woodstock Inn back in Vermont, but more the faint, sweet odor of decay wafting on the gentle November breeze floating through the city first built as a trading port in the 10th century along the River Lee. Matt couldn't help but wonder at all the challenges and hardships the people of Cork had overcome over the last one thousand years. The city survived the Norman conquest, the Black Plague, the English occupation, the Great Famine, and the Irish Civil War, to name just a few.

Yet it had failed to survive the Black Pox pandemic.

As Matt steered up the steep incline of Patrick's Hill, he had no idea why the death of Cork City seemed to bring such emotion. As he passed the gated entrance to St. Angela's

College on the left, the high school attended by Tracy's mom, Matt wondered if his daughter would ever have the opportunity to attend school with other children. As they crested the top of Patrick's Hill and Kevin motioned for Matt to turn right onto the Youghal Road, Matt saw a sign for the Christian Brothers sports fields. He knew Tracy's father, brother, and even Rory had all attended Christian Brothers, likely all spending considerable time on these very pitches. *Would Christopher ever get a chance to play football, soccer, or rugby and know the pure joy of giving his all with his teammates on the field of play?*

"This is the start of the barracks, Matt. Here on the left," Kevin said, snapping Matt out of his reverie. Their road narrowed to one lane with a double-yellow lane painted along the left side and annoying speed bumps set every hundred yards. Matt knew the Irish referred to these speed bumps as "ramps," but that seemed to make them even more annoying. *Ramps to what?*

Stone walls enclosed both sides of the road. The wall on the right side of the road appeared much older than the one on the left. Matt knew over the right wall was a playing field, while the left wall protected the headquarters of the Irish Army's 1st Brigade. In addition to eight feet of solid stone, this wall was topped with three-foot-tall metal spikes spaced inches apart, making it impossible to see or climb over.

"Just ahead," said Kevin. "You'll see the entrance."

Matt slowed the SUV as they approached the entrance, with a large, modern guard booth centered between the entry and exit lanes. Matt's first inclination was to pull into the right-side lane before seeing two signs with red circles signaling him to stop.

"Wrong side, Yank," said Kevin, laughing. Smacking himself in the forehead upon realizing his mistake, Matt immediately turned the wheel sharply to the left and towards the proper entrance lane.

"Hey, maybe it's time we get you guys driving on the proper side of the road now—the right side!" chided Kim.

"Sure, Kim. No problem. And whilst we're at it, maybe we could implement the imperial measurement system instead of the metric?"

The three chuckled as Matt pulled slowly into the entrance to Collins Barracks, followed closely by the other two vehicles in their convoy.

"Continue straight, and then take a right in about a hundred meters. We'll check the main parade grounds first, then swing back to brigade headquarters," directed Kevin. Matt drove slowly along a narrow lane—a large, modern green structure appeared on their left, while a long, low-slung brick building followed the road on the right-hand side. "That's the new gymnasium there on the left," said Kevin.

"And to the right?" Matt asked. "Looks like a headquarters building, with the old armored cars on concrete stands."

"Yes, that's exactly right," replied Kevin. "This is the headquarters of the first brigade. We'll park in back as that's the best entrance. Up on the left, there, past the gym, are the main barracks and dining facility. Turn right. Here!"

Matt turned ninety degrees to the right, passing a narrow lane leading back towards the entrance and the brigade headquarters. A long row of single-story brick buildings framed the left side of the narrow road, and suddenly, Matt found himself driving onto the north end of a large, open, paved square. Kevin pointed, and Matt steered their convoy into the center of the large parade ground. While the US Army favored grass parade grounds, Matt knew that military barracks in the UK and Ireland were often centered around a paved or bricked square, with the various battalion and company-level orderly rooms arranged along each leg of the square. The parade ground at Collins Barracks measured approximately 150 meters on each side, and other than a dozen military trucks parked along the northern edge, was completely devoid of people or equipment. The letter "H" was painted within a white circle at the center of the parade ground, indicating the square doubled as a helicopter landing zone.

"An entire infantry brigade is stationed here?" Matt asked. "Place doesn't seem that big."

"Actually, this is currently the headquarters and some of the support units, including an artillery regiment, cavalry squadron, engineer, and military police companies. The infantry battalions of the brigade are in Galway, Limerick, and Kilkenny."

"Okay, that makes sense. Is this what you expected? It's empty."

"Yes. Remember, when it became clear the pandemic would be the end of us all, the Taoiseach absolved all government employees of their oaths and obligations, including the military and police. He wanted everyone to be able to spend their remaining days with their families and hoped more people might be able to survive in isolation."

"Tee-shack?" Kim asked. "What's a tee-shack?"

Kevin chuckled. "Taoiseach is what we call our prime minister. Ireland's head of government." Kevin pointed to a gap in the buildings along the square's southwest corner. "Head through that gap, Matt. That will take us right up to the small parking area at the entrance to the 1 Brigade headquarters."

Matt drove slowly across the edge of the open square, turned right onto another narrow lane, and then guided the Porsche into one of a dozen parking slots behind a modern brick building. A sign on the front of the building clearly showed this to be the headquarters of the Irish Defence Forces

1 Brigade. All parking spots except one were empty in the row along the building.

"Place looks empty," said Matt.

"Well, this office is always manned, twenty-four hours a day, seven days a week," answered Kevin. "As a doctor, I was exempt from the duty rotation, but I know all of the junior officers in the regular units rotated through manning the front desk. There's a small room off the reception where they keep a cabinet with all the keys on the installation. For the medical clinic, whoever closed up at night would have to bring the door keys here for safekeeping. I would assume all unit armorers were required to do the same."

"That's exactly how they do it in the US military as well. Let's go inside."

The three exited the Porsche and gathered on the sidewalk with the occupants of the other two vehicles. Dave, an M4 assault rifle hanging across his chest from a single-point sling, immediately took the initiative.

"Matt, maybe LT and I should have a quick look first. Make sure everything is safe." LT stood beside Dave, holding a Halligan breaching tool.

"Go for it," said Matt. Everyone stood and watched as Dave and LT cautiously approached the glass front doors about twenty meters from the parking area. With the power out, seeing what was inside the glass doors was impossible. Dave walked up to the door and tentatively pulled on the handle. The door swung open easily. Both Dave and LT immediately turned away, covering their mouths. As Dave pulled a bandana over his face, it was clear to everyone that there were dead bodies inside. They watched as Dave turned on his flashlight, and he and LT entered the building, letting the glass doors swing closed behind them.

The front door opened less than three minutes later, and

Dave walked down the sidewalk to the assembled group. "The building's clear. One deceased individual curled up on the floor behind the main desk. I think it's the Regimental Sergeant Major from the insignia on his uniform."

"Props, man," said Matt. "Guy held the fort and was the last man standing."

"That's not a surprise," said Kevin. "Was it a gray-haired guy with a handlebar mustache?"

"Ahh, doc. Sorry, but he's been decomposing for two months. Pretty hard to tell what he looked like. He had a name tape on his uniform. O'Callahan. And from the rank, he was an RSM."

"That's him," replied Kevin. "A true soldier's soldier."

"He probably sent everyone else home," said Matt. "Either back to the barracks or home to their family." Shifting to Dave. "Did you find the cabinet with the keys?"

"Yeah," said Dave. "I popped it with the Halligan, and LT is now putting everything in a small box. All the keys were labeled, as well as some instructions in a binder. He should be out in a second. The rest of the building is empty."

"What more do you want to see?" Kevin asked.

CHAPTER 17

November 18, 8:24 am

Matt overheard the ladies gathered at the Raffeen House's large dining room table say that Thanksgiving was now ten days away. Looking at his watch, he noted that it was November 18th—three days since they had gone to Collins Barracks and a week since their arrival in Kinsale. Sipping hot coffee from his mug, Matt couldn't help but feel a touch of pride in all they had accomplished so far.

Matt sat in one of the overstuffed wingback chairs in the front drawing room, enjoying the view across the lawn to Kinsale Harbor. Directly in front of the house on the far side of the harbor floated the Irish Rover at the same dock it had been since their arrival. Taking another sip, Matt knew he still had about twenty minutes before leaving the Raffeen House and going to the Irish Rover for his scheduled meeting with Stan and Pete.

The last evening had been their second night sleeping at the Raffeen House. As much as Matt enjoyed the luxuriousness of the megayacht, he had to admit there was something special about sleeping in what he felt was his own home. As one of the family's highest priorities, everyone had worked together to make this neighborhood in Scilly livable for everyone.

Upon returning from Collins Barracks three days ago, Pete

had engaged Tom and Sarah's assistance in setting up three trailer-mounted generators in series just up the hill from the Raffeen House and directly in front of the Spaniard Inn and the Man Friday restaurant. Using heavy-duty cables liberated from an electrical supply warehouse in Cork, they efficiently ran electricity to each of the half-dozen homes selected as their new residences. As a bonus, Pete had wired up the Spaniard Inn as well, planning to set this up as the communal dining and social spot for the extended family. Tom had solved the issue of constantly fueling the generators by configuring a special hose to allow Pete to park one of the several fuel tankers he had acquired and have the generator drain the tank on the trailer. With each tank providing more than 20,000 liters of fuel, it was now simply a question of swapping out the tank trailers weekly.

Matt, Clare, and their two children occupied three of the five bedrooms in the Raffeen House, and Clare had invited Kim to make this her home as well. Since Kim's brutal assault and rape at the hands of The Base's barbarians at the Samoset Resort, she had rarely left Matt's side. Matt had almost forgotten this during their cross-Atlantic trip as everyone was crammed into the Irish Rover, but since their arrival, he had to get used to it again. He was concerned that Clare might become jealous, but since the first day Kim and her group had joined them on Vinalhaven, there had never been an ounce of jealousy or resentment. If anything, the opposite had occurred. Clare and Kim had become best friends. *Maybe I should be the one jealous of their relationship?* Matt thought to himself as he heard them laughing at the dining room table.

Looking through the drawing room doorway into the dining room, Matt could see his wife sitting with what everyone now referred to as "the Mom's Group." Molly, Marvi, Michelle, and Tracy were the mothers at the table, with Kim being the only group member without children. From what Matt could overhear, they were planning the finer details of the first Thanksgiving feast to be held in post-cataclysmic Ireland. While Matt had enough on his plate not to be concerned with the details of the holiday, he took pride in all they had accomplished since arriving in Ireland.

With the addition of electricity, the extended family now fully occupied a half-dozen homes on the Scilly peninsula. Dave and Michelle occupied the small house on the water directly to the right of the Raffeen House as one faced the water. Tracy, her sister Judy, and their children Kirstie and Millie had taken over the four-bedroom cottage immediately behind Raffeen House. To the right of Dave and Michelle's, stood the Pallace Wharf House. This large, 18th-century home had ten bedrooms and a unique, U-shaped front yard that allowed boats to be protectively docked. With the Scilly peninsula being a finger jutting into the very northern part of Kinsale Harbor, Raffeen House occupied the southern quadrant of the peninsula's very tip. The Pallace Wharf House occupied the north quadrant, and the homes occupied by Dave and Michelle and Tracy and Judy were sandwiched between the two larger homes. Behind these homes and heading uphill, about where the first knuckle would be on a finger, were a half-dozen other homes, the larger Spaniard Inn pub, and the Man Friday restaurant.

Matt smiled while thinking of how his extended family had decided on their new residences. Molly volunteered to manage the Pallace Wharf House, and her free bedrooms quickly filled with Kim's MIT students, Kelsey, Derek, and Gianna. Making the biggest splash, two couples formally emerged during the housing assignments. Grace and Dylan declared their intention to live together and were quickly followed by LT and Amey. The two couples had already selected a quaint bungalow behind the Pallace Wharf House. Neither Tracy nor Molly were thrilled with this decision, but given how quickly everyone had been forced to grow up these last two months, they quickly gave their full blessing and support.

Stan and Marvi had agreed to remain living aboard the Irish Rover. Matt had encouraged them to move into the owner's suite, but they were content to remain in the Captain's cabin where they'd been since leaving Vinalhaven. Along with the White's daughter, Juliet, Pete, and Liz planned to remain living aboard the yacht. Matt fully supported this, as the yacht remained the family's greatest asset for security and survivability. Should something happen in Ireland, the Irish Rover could offer a place for the extended family to live while relocating to a safer location almost anywhere in the world. It also made sense that these two families, both with considerable naval experience, remain as close as possible to the Irish Rover to assist in maintaining it should it be needed in the future.

Matt continued to be satisfied that Ireland remained free of any substantial threats to his family's future. There was nothing so far to indicate a violent band of survivors like the Nomads in Woodstock or an organized group bent on accumulating power through intimidation, slavery, and conscription like The Base. Like their historical stereotype, the surviving Irish seemed content to live peacefully and get along with their neighbors.

Grace and Kevin had made significant strides with their mobile vaccination teams. In just the last three days, the posters they'd disseminated had resulted in eighty-three individuals vaccinated. Amey had become the designated record keeper, and she was working with Stan to build a database with QuAI that would allow them to keep track of all the survivors they vaccinated. The hope was that this information would allow them to build communications platforms that would then lead to rebuilding local communities. So far, the eighty-three survivors comprised eleven groups ranging from thirty to two individuals and included the large group Rosie had mentioned living on the north side of Cork City.

Based on interviews with the new survivors, the sirens and flyers had worked very well, and Kevin and Grace planned to increase the radius of their four mobile vaccination teams. Continuing to focus on County Cork, the next ten days would push farther west and north to Bandon and Mallow. Kevin's goal was to hopefully get to both Killarney and Limerick by the beginning of December.

QuAI predicted another two hundred survivors by the end of the month, potentially reaching as many as four thousand throughout the republic by the end of the year. Matt knew the more survivors they vaccinated, the less secure his extended family became. He and Dave discussed this daily—often several times a day. They both believed that while the Irish might be peaceful, fun-loving people, the fear of contagion had kept violence away from the island nation. The Black Pox had killed about 99% of the population, and those who survived remained deathly afraid of coming into contact with anything that could give them smallpox. Consequently, the survivors they'd come across were barely managing to survive as they were still fearful to forage into new areas that might contain infected corpses. Now that they were vaccinated, Matt and Dave believed that people were much more likely to come into contact and possibly conflict as resources became scarce. Some survivors would work hard to build a better life, while others would take what others had worked hard for. It was human nature, pure and simple, and the driving force behind Matt's desire to control as much heavy weaponry in the country as possible.

The other thing Matt and Dave feared was something they hadn't previously considered but was brought to their attention by QuAI's latest report. At some point, likely by Spring, according to QuAI, they were going to reach the magic number of 9,700 survivors. This was the limit of their vaccine supply.

Matt had intentionally continued to be vague with Kevin and Beth regarding the true number of doses they had available, and Matt had sworn Grace to secrecy. It wasn't that he didn't trust Kevin or the other Irish survivors; it was simply a temptation that he didn't want to burden them with. Like gold, the scarcer the vaccine became, the more it was worth. At this point, they still had a difficult time picturing 10,000 survivors. But as the number of survivors increased and the amount of vaccine decreased, it would become more evident that they would quickly run out.

Matt had a recurring nightmare of a line of 1,000 survivors and realizing they only had nine hundred doses left. Who was going to play God?

While both Matt and Dave knew that, at some point, this issue was going to reach critical mass, their main focus in the interim was gaining control of the weapons that could most threaten their family. The day after retrieving the keys from Collins Barracks, Dave had taken LT, Derek, and Dylan to inventory the various unit arms rooms. The good news was that Dave had found the armories almost exactly as he'd expected. The Irish and US armies seemed to have similar protocols for storing armaments and munitions. Dave's team had done a quick inventory of over a dozen arms rooms of various sizes and found a munitions bunker where the 1st Brigade stored its ammunition, explosives, large-caliber munitions, and artillery shells. At Matt's instruction, Dave had left all the weapons and munitions in place—for now.

One of the items on the agenda for Matt's upcoming meeting with Stan and his intel team was the planned trip north to Dublin. Dave desperately wanted to put eyes on the Irish Army's base at Curragh Camp in Kildare, and Pete and Tom had a list of some major items they could only find in the major supply centers on the outskirts of Dublin. They planned to send a convoy north towards Dublin in three days, and Matt wanted to ensure they knew all potential threats. Rosie's story that her husband had failed to return from Dublin had never sat well with Matt, and he wondered if something might be going on up there. As always, he was fearful of anything that had the potential to bring harm to his family. And what he feared most were the threats he didn't know.

CHAPTER 18

November 18, 9:03 am

Matt dropped his backpack, his body armor, and his assault rifle on the chair in the yacht's office just off the owner's suite that he and Clare had called home for the last month. Stan was planning to continue to use the captain's office, where the QuAI computers had been set up, so Matt thought he would likely continue to use the Irish Rover's plush owner's office as his own.

After removing his equipment, he walked to the formal salon just behind the office, where Stan, Pete, and Liz sat drinking coffee on the two opposing couches. Matt poured a cup for himself and took a seat at the far end of the sofa Pete occupied.

"Another beautiful day in the Emerald Isle," said Matt in greeting. "How's everyone this morning?"

"Excellent," replied Pete, while Stan and Liz nodded affirmatively.

"Is Juliet going to join us as well?" Matt asked.

"Not this morning," said Stan. "She left an hour ago with Amey and Grace to go to Haulbowline. She's helping Amey with the database and making sure we capture the information we need from newly vaccinated survivors for QuAI to be the most helpful to us." Stan motioned for Liz to turn on the television, and with a few clicks of a remote control, the large-screen television at the end of the sofas came to life. Typing quickly on the tablet she held on her lap, a PowerPoint slide with a meeting agenda slid onto the widescreen television.

"Got it," said Matt, after quickly reading the several bullet points. "Pete, you're the one who asked to be included in the meeting, so why don't we start with your agenda item? Is it okay if we skip to that, Stan? I know Pete has a lot on his plate."

"Sure, that will work fine. And before you ask, Matt, no, there's not a deck of slides piled up behind the agenda. Liz and Juliet have a tendency to favor PowerPoint, but I know that you absolutely hate it. All we have are a couple of QuAI-produced maps that I think will be helpful for our discussions. Pete, why don't you start us off."

"Thanks, Stan. The last few days, the Sustainability team has really focused on improving our living conditions here in Kinsale. With the help of Tom and Sarah, who've been instrumental, we've been able to wire several 400 kVA trailer-mounted generators into a local grid consisting of eight houses plus a pub and restaurant. I've been told this is more than enough power. We've also configured some diesel trailers so that we can easily replenish the generators' fuel supply. But of course, at some point, the diesel will expire."

"Does Tom or Sarah have any thoughts on that?" Stan asked. "The shelf-life of diesel?"

"Well, Tom's confident that if properly stabilized, we'll get at least twelve months out of it. It's not really a question of diesel working or not working, it's more that it begins to degrade. He says we'll start to see degradation in about a year, and after that, it's a bit of a crap shoot. Best case, diesel will work for about two years, maybe a bit longer if we mess with the stabilization. But at some point, it's going to start causing mechanical issues with our generators, and Tom thinks that will start happening in about a year."

"Okay, fair enough," said Matt. "Great work, by the way. I have to admit, it's been nice to wake up in a house. And to spread out a bit."

"Yeah, the feedback has been overwhelmingly positive," said Pete. "So what I wanted to bring up are two things. First, the next priority for my team is communications. I've talked at length with both Tom and Sara, and also with Stan and Liz, and here's the plan. Liz?"

Liz touched her tablet, and the television screen flipped to a map showing Cork City at the top and Kinsale at the bottom. Matt noted the town of Carrigaline just east of center, with Haulbowline at about the one o'clock.

"This is an elevation map of the local area," continued Pete. "Note the highlighted areas in red. These are the points of highest elevation. This is hardly a mountainous area, and in fact, could barely be considered hilly, but there is definitely some terrain undulation. You can see the elevation is considerably higher to the west and north of Cork City, but in our area, there is a finger of higher ground running just along the south edge of the N40 motorway. The highest point in our area, at just under 600 feet, is just on the east side of the Cork Airport, about halfway between Kinsale and Cork City. With me so far?"

"Yep," said Matt.

"So, talking with Tom and Sarah, we think that this is the perfect area for us to set up a radio repeater. Tom and I were out there yesterday, and there's already a tower there. It already has the equipment in place, all we would need to do is run power to it and then configure some software."

"And what will that get us?" Matt asked. "Cell phones?"

"No. I don't think we'll ever have a cell phone network

again, at least not for a long while. That would entail an entire system, and frankly, we don't have the technical knowledge. What this would do is allow us to use our handheld VHF radios for about a twenty-kilometer radius centered on the Cork Airport."

"So basically, we could talk on the radio from here all the way to the north of Cork City, west to Bandon, and all the way over to the eastern shore of Cork Harbor?"

"Exactly, Matt. Your walkie-talkie in Raffeen House could talk to Kevin at Haulbowline or even Dave at Collins Barracks on the north side of Cork City."

"Fantastic!" said Stan.

"I agree," said Matt. "That's a game changer. Especially with a ready supply of walkie-talkies and rechargeable batteries."

"Exactly," said Pete.

"So what's the catch, Pete?" Matt asked. "Why aren't we doing this."

"Well, the catch is that there's some specialty equipment Tom needs, and the only place he knows that has it is on the outskirts of Dublin."

"It's not available in Cork?"

"No. We've pretty much exhausted what they have in Cork. These are some specialty connections for the generator, as well as some hardware and software specific to the radio antennae and the repeater."

"Okay. And Tom knows where to go in Dublin?"

"Yes. He's very familiar with the place. So is Sarah. They said it's normally about a 3.5-hour drive, but with no traffic or speed limits, it's probably more like 2.5 hours."

"Okay," said Matt. "Dave's been itching to put together a trip up that way as well. We've talked about doing it in a couple of days, why don't we add your stop into the mix? Please get with Dave and let him know the specifics. He's the security guy, so he can plan the convoy route and all the details."

"Thanks, Matt. This will be a game-changer for our communications."

"And while you're thinking about it, Pete, think through anything else you might need. We might as well get everything we can think of. Hey, what about satellite phones? We could use more than the three we have."

"Actually, Matt," interrupted Liz. "Satellite phones are probably not going to happen."

"Why not?" Matt asked. "There have to be stores in Dublin that sell satellite phones."

"Oh, definitely, Matt. But the phone isn't the issue. The issue is the account. Our phones work on the existing satellite network because they're already programmed with access to an account. We can try it, but I don't think a new satphone, even if they have a pay-as-you-go card or something like that, will be able to register itself on the network. Most of those protocols take some form of human approval in the process or require computer approval from a terrestrial computer system like Visa or Mastercard that no longer works."

"Damn," said Matt. "Makes sense. I never thought of it like that."

"Yeah," agreed Pete. "Me neither."

"That's why you pay me the big bucks, Dad," laughed Liz.

"Okay," added Stan. "So it looks like hand-held radios it is. And that brings us to the next slide, please, Liz." Liz tapped her tablet, and the screen changed once again. It had the same map, but instead of elevation, there were hundreds, if not thousands, of yellow and blue dots. "We had QuAI generate this map using the Hawkeye 360 satellite system. These are the RF signals we've generated over the last week. The green dots are from our group, and the yellow dots are from the Irish. Do you see how some yellow dots appear to draw circles and lines on the map? I asked the MIT students working on the mobile vaccine teams to key their radios frequently while driving, as I wanted to test this out. In essence, by keying their microphones and using QuAI, we've generated a rudimentary GPS tracking system."

"Amazing," said Matt. "Can QuAI distinguish different radios?"

"Mmmm, yes and no," answered Stan. "Technically, no. The RF signals don't have a unique signature, but there are some distinguishable differences. But with some forethought and the right prompts, we can tell QuAI what to look for, and with machine learning, she can attach a person or a group to a set of patterns. It might not be 100% accurate, but she should generally be able to distinguish at least groups. That's why I recommend our family use specific brands and types of radios, and we then give out other radios to different survivor groups. This will let us track things as needed."

"A bit Big Brother-ish, don't you think?" commented Pete.

"Exactly!" Stan said. "We are Big Brother, so anything that gives us an advantage or provides even an ounce more security benefit for our family is something we need to do."

"Agreed," said Matt, while Pete nodded his head in agreement as well. "It could also be a 911, right? We could set up a pattern of keying the mic to alert QuAI as a distress signal, right?"

"Yes," said Stan. "That's a great idea. Liz and I can put that together and get it out to everyone."

"Okay. Pete, please ask Tom for a list of stores in Dublin that would carry a large inventory of hand-held radios. We'll want to stock up."

"Will do. I'm gonna head out if you guys don't need me anymore. I'm meeting with Tom to go over to Rosie's farm and set her up with electricity. She and Molly are also trying to set up a winter grow house, so we might have some fresh vegetables at some point."

"Sounds good. Don't let us keep you," said Matt.

The three watched Pete grab his things and head down the central staircase. They were all still getting used to the fact that the yacht was empty, as for the past month, there had normally been at least twenty people on board at any given time.

"So, Stan, Grace told me we're up to eighty-three survivors vaccinated already? I know Amey and Juliet are collecting info on everyone for QuAI, but do we have any preliminary thoughts?"

"The data pool is still too small to make any sweeping generalizations, but there are two relevant items. First, the survivors so far comprised eleven different groups. Of these eleven, only three had a firearm - and these firearms consisted mostly of single- or double-barrel shotguns and two .22 rifles. Not a single handgun among the survivor population - not including Haulbowline, of course."

"And is that good or bad for us?" Matt asked.

"Well, it's a double-edged sword," replied Stan. "On the one hand, unarmed survivors pose very little threat to our family. They have no capacity to mount any reasonable attack against us, which in turn allows us to reduce our security posture and still know that we're safe.

"And on the second hand?"

"The survivors are incapable of defending themselves against an external threat. They offer us no buffer against an attacking force, nor are they realistically capable of being organized into a defensive force, even if we were to provide the weapons."

"Okay. I think, given what we know now, my preference is that the survivors pose no threat. It will make identifying any significant threats easier, I would think."

"Yes," said Stan. "I'd agree with that."

"And what about the number estimates? Does QuAI still think we're on track to find 4,000 survivors in the next six weeks?"

Stan turned to Liz, clearly wanting her to answer this question. "Yeah, Matt. She's predicting 4,000—at a minimum. To date, the survivors have all stayed close to their homes. Now that they're immune, it's only natural that they go search out relatives and friends. This traveling will exponentially increase the numbers of survivors who become aware that a vaccine is available—and those people will be drawn to us like magnets."

"Yeah, makes sense," said Matt. "What do you think of Dave's proposal that we move the vaccination center out of Carrigaline and up to the N40 motorway on the west side of Cork? He wants us to keep it as far away from us as possible, and he wants a security checkpoint to check the vaccination team's backtrail to ensure they aren't being followed home. Is that overkill?"

"Considering the population is almost entirely unarmed, it's likely overkill. But I completely agree with Dave on this, Matt. We can never be too careful. Not ever."

"Yeah, I hear you." Matt made a mental note to speak with Dave that evening and put in place his counter-surveillance checkpoints. No one needed to know their setup in Kinsale. "Speaking of that, Liz, have you talked to Dave about the surveillance network he wants to implement around Kinsale? Kind of like what we did in Vinalhaven?"

"Yeah, Matt. We've spent a lot of time on that. Pete didn't mention it, but Dave and I gave Pete the specs for the generators we'd need to have 24/7 power for an extended Wi-Fi network that would give us about a two-kilometer radius around the harbor. There are six roads that anyone approaching Kinsale would have to travel on, and we could put cameras on all six routes. We could also have pan-tilt-zoom cameras all around the harbor and the neighborhood in Scilly."

"And we'd monitor them 24/7 from the Irish Rover?" Matt asked.

"Well, I propose we have QuAI monitor them 24/7. As we saw in Vinalhaven, her machine learning capability is more than capable of identifying approved vehicles and personnel and alerting us when necessary."

"Okay. Fair enough. I like it. When do you think we can have this up and running?"

"Within three days after the trip to Dublin. We left many cameras in Vinalhaven, so we'd need a fresh supply. Tom says we can get most of it in Cork, but he knows several warehouses in Dublin that will have the best equipment and as much as we need. With the cameras and the portable generators, we'll easily be able to set up an extended Wi-Fi network and a web of surveillance cameras."

Matt nodded, pleased that they could replicate their communications and security network from Vinalhaven.

Stan spoke up, changing the subject. "Matt, you said you wanted a more global threat assessment and an update on what was happening back in the US, especially regarding any continued efforts by the government to find us."

"Yes, definitely," said Matt. "I feel like we've been solely focused on setting up here in Ireland. I don't want to lose visibility over what's happening back home or worldwide. Whadda ya got?"

"Okay, well, first let's talk about the 2nd US Civil War, which is about to start its 20th day. As you'll recall, and we've discussed several times, President Moravian—and I use the term "President" lightly as I think the man's a complete menace—launched a two-pronged attack against The Base utilizing both land and naval forces. Along the James River in Virginia, the 82nd Airborne, supported by naval littoral combat ships, captured Richmond within the first week. Likewise, the northern prong, consisting of an aircraft carrier and a degraded 2nd Marine Division, struck up the Delaware to seize Philadelphia. They too were initially successful in accomplishing their immediate objectives, although not without taking significant casualties."

"What a fucking mess," said Matt. "Less than 2% of our country survived, and these assholes insist on launching a civil war."

"Yeah," agreed Stan. "And it looks far from over. Failing to learn anything from our involvement in Iraq or Afghanistan, the government forces have focused on a conventional attack while failing to notice that The Base had switched to unconventional warfare. While the initial battles were being waged in Richmond and Philadelphia, it appears The Base did two things. First, their leadership abandoned Philly and then immediately initiated significant guerrilla operations against the government forces."

"Where'd The Base headquarters go?"

"York, Pennsylvania."

"Seriously?" Matt asked. "What the hell is in York, PA? Isn't that in southern Pennsylvania? I feel like I've driven through there on the way to Gettysburg."

"Exactly. It's about two hours west of Philly. As to why? Someone in The Base is clearly a US history buff. While Philadelphia was the first capital of our country, York held that distinction for nine months in 1777 during the Revolutionary War. If it was good enough for the Founding Fathers when the British invaded, The Base feels like it will be good enough for them. They're attempting to convince their followers that the government forces are actually the invading force."

"Interesting."

"Yes, and as you mentioned, it is quite near Gettysburg. The Battle of Gettysburg did not occur as a fluke. It's the confluence of several mountain chains, and funnels ground travel from the south and the east into one area. Honestly, it's not a terrible place for The Base to go. It gives them many options to run a guerrilla campaign."

"And you said they've already conducted guerrilla attacks?"

"Yeah. So far, they've succeeded in sinking three ships—two in the James River and one in the Delaware River just outside of Philadelphia."

"How? Please tell me they don't have anti-ship missiles?"

"Not exactly. But they have both Javelin anti-tank missiles, tanks, and scuba divers. They've successfully employed a combination of all three to devastating effect. So much so that Admiral Cryover, the guy in charge of Norfolk, has temporarily pulled back the ships to parts of the river outside range of the shoreline. This has left the ground forces, especially the 82nd in Richmond, without fire support. Picture Fallujah and Helmand province without artillery or helicopter gunships. They're starting to get chewed up, one small bite at a time."

"Jesus. What a shit show." For as little as Matt was surprised, he found himself sad for the soldiers on the ground.

"The good news for us," Stan continued. "Is that the government seems to have put finding us on the back burner. The ship dispatched to apprehend us in Vinalhaven was ordered to support the attack on Philadelphia. So far, QuAI has found nothing to indicate that anyone suspects we've fled to Ireland."

"Speaking of QuAI, is Cheyenne Mountain still attempting to kick her out of the government systems and databases?"

"No," Stan chuckled. "QuAI has reconfigured many systems to show she no longer has access. Additionally, she's embarked upon removing the government's access from their own remote systems in a very systematic way."

"Wouldn't that tell them that QuAI is still active?" Matt asked.

"Normally, maybe yes. But not the way QuAI is doing it. She's making it look like these remote systems, networks, and satellites are dying off due to battery failures or glitches in their system that can no longer be fixed as all the technicians are dead. Cheyenne Mountain believes these satellites are simply going offline—when in reality QuAI now has complete control over them."

"Jesus, Stan. This is some pretty scary AI shit. Like Skynet in the Terminator movies. Are we sure we have control of this thing?"

"Sort of, but it's now entirely irrelevant, Matt."

"Sort of? Irrelevant? Please tell me you're joking, Stan."

"Look, Matt, I'd be lying if I told you I controlled every aspect of QuAI. The entire point of machine learning and artificial intelligence is that computers can learn faster and absorb more than humans. I can direct QuAI's efforts and have access to every piece of data she has, but what she does most of the twenty-four hours of the day is up to her. Based on our queries and our prompts for priority information requirements, she gathers info and does what she thinks is correct."

"And what if at some point her definition of 'correct' differs from yours."

"That's not a concern."

"And why not, Stan?" Matt asked, a bit incredulously.

"Matt, more than 98% of the world's population is dead. About 100% of the world's electricity has ceased operating, with only batteries remaining along with the generators the remaining humans are operating. Exactly how much power do you think computers will have over a world that is already dead?"

Matt thought about this for a second and then smiled. "Pretty good point you make there, Stan."

"Trust me, Matt. I have control over QuAI."

"And no one can take that control away from you? Ever?"

"No, never. Only Marvi and Juliet have access to the main systems in Charlottesville." Stan paused, seeming to collect his thoughts. "I wasn't going to say anything, Matt. Not because I don't trust you, but because I didn't think it was necessary. Since our arrival here, I've added access for you, Clare, Liz, and Pete. I've also added Christopher and Laurie, who are our next generation. If anything ever happens to me, the eight of you can access QuAI."

"How?"

"Just get on the QuAI computer—she'll direct you how."

"Okay."

"But Matt," added Stan. "Please don't tell anyone but Clare. I'll tell Pete myself. Liz, I don't want you ever to discuss this—with anyone."

"Okay, Stan," said Liz. "I won't."

"I'm serious, Liz. Right now, we think the vaccine is the most valuable thing in the world—it's not. It's not even a fraction of the value of QuAI. And should anyone learn that the full system is still operational underneath Charlottesville, I fear they'll stop at nothing to gain access."

"Stan, I get your point," said Matt. "But do you think an AI computer is more valuable than the vaccine? You said yourself that the various systems worldwide have already died or are dying without electricity and human technicians."

"Yes, Matt, I did say that. What I didn't say was that QuAI is the only thing that can bring those systems back to life."

"Mmmm," thought Matt. "Okay, good point."

"And you keep mentioning the vaccine running out..."

"Yeah, I do."

"Matt, QuAI has the formula for making more vaccine."

CHAPTER 19

November 20, 10:50 am

"Okay, Pete. We're breaking off here at Exit 12. We'll catch up to you guys in Blanchardstown," said Matt into the mic of the handheld VHF radio tucked into a pouch on his tactical vest.

"Roger, Matt. See you in a couple of hours."

"Be careful, Pete. You're less than thirty minutes out, but as we discussed, Dublin is a complete unknown."

"Roger, no worries, mate—as Kevin here would say."

Matt smiled as he steered the Porsche SUV into the left-hand lane and slowed for the upcoming exit. Pete's convoy of the SUV he and Kevin occupied, followed by a cargo van and small panel truck, whizzed past him in the right lane. While driving on the left in Ireland had never been an issue for Matt, he always found the highways, or motorways as they were referred to in Ireland, to be the most difficult to internalize. It didn't feel natural to pass vehicles on the right or exit a highway to the left. *Oh well, I better get used to it if Ireland's going to be our home.*

Matt looked in the rearview mirror and saw Dave's SUV closely behind him, followed by another cargo van driven by Rory. This trip to Dublin involved four of Matt's "teams," including his own special projects element. The sustainability team with Pete and Tom was the main effort and had the goal of gathering all the supplies and equipment needed to establish the communications network around their area of Cork. Kevin agreed to drive for Pete, not just because he was familiar with Dublin and its surrounding areas, but because he wanted to leave some flyers and try to identify survivors in the greater Dublin area. So both Kevin and Beth of the health group had come along on the trip and would supervise that aspect of the adventure. Their three vehicles were now continuing up the M7 motorway with their first stop at several of the large box stores in the Blanchardstown shopping area.

Dave, leading his security team, was following Matt's Cayenne as they took the Kildare exit off the motorway and headed south on the Curragh Chase. In the past, the majority of motorists taking this exit would turn north toward the famed Curragh Racecourse, one of the most famous horseracing venues in the world. The road to the south of the exit looked just like it did going north—completely flat ground covered by the greenest of grass broken only by the darker green of a tree line a mile off in the distance. Instead of horse tracks, all Matt saw were sheep. Dozens of them, most with a slash of red spray painted on their dirty wool coats. Matt slowed his speed as several of the sheep wandered across the narrow two-lane road, and with his window down, he could hear their faint bleating as he passed.

Just past the sheep, two bright red signs, one in English and one in Irish, proclaimed that Matt's convoy was approaching a military installation. Matt had never been here but knew from QuAI and Kevin that this was Curragh Camp—home to Ireland's Defense Forces Training Centre. Dave had queried QuAI regarding the location of all the major military weapons systems in Ireland, learning that Curragh Camp also contained the Irish Army's only mechanized infantry company and armored cavalry squadron. Second only to Collins Barracks in Cork, Curragh Camp was Dave's highest priority, and his goal on this trip was to gain control of the armories for both of the military units, thereby preventing the threat of anyone gaining access to armored vehicles with crew-served weapons that would be extremely difficult for their family to defend against.

Matt, with Kim sitting in the front seat next to him, had a different goal for visiting Curragh Camp, and he had mentioned it only to Stan, Kim, Dave, and Pete. It wasn't that his project was a secret; it was just that Matt wasn't sure he would be successful. The items he was after were not essential to his family's safety or success, but they would definitely enhance their security capabilities.

"We're turning left at the next intersection," Dave said over the radio.

"Okay. Kim and I will turn right and loop around to the west half of the base, as planned," Matt spoke into the radio mic clipped to his vest just under his chin.

"Roger. Once we take care of the Infantry Wing, we're going to head to the Cav Squadron and then the Mech company. Shouldn't take us more than an hour."

"Okay. I'll keep you updated when we get to the ARW," replied Matt, signing off. Matt had reviewed plenty of satellite imagery of Curragh Camp earlier this morning, and Kim held a satellite printout with various buildings labeled in red pen.

The installation was shaped like an elongated jelly bean, with the long access running generally east to west. The entrance road they were on entered from the north and bisected the camp with about 1/4 of the base to the east and 3/4 of it to the west. Dave had turned left, heading east into the most built-up area of the base. This eastern quarter contained most of the training schools on the base, including the United Nations Training School, the Infantry Wing, and the Military College.

Rory, now an ensign in the Irish Navy, had attended Stage 1 of the Cadet School here at Curragh Camp before completing his training at the National Maritime College in Ringaskiddy, just outside the causeway to Haulbowline. Rory had proven a font of information regarding Curragh Camp that was now driving their current plan.

Dave, Rory, Derek, and LT were planning to stop first at the Infantry Wing to take control of the keys to that arms room before moving to the armories of the 1st Mechanized Infantry Company and the 1st Armoured Cavalry Squadron.

Matt and Kim had turned their vehicle to the west, with a target of a small compound located in the southwest corner of the installation. As Matt drove through the empty installation, he was reminded of the older military installations he had trained at, such as Fort Devens, Fort A.P. Hill, and even parts of Fort Bragg.

The US Army referred to the older buildings on these installations as "World War II-style barracks," and Matt had spent considerable time in these white-clapboard, two-story, open-bay barracks with communal bathrooms and no air conditioning. While the buildings on Curragh Camp were all made of red brick instead of white-painted wood, the way each building was set in line with the others in rows harkened back to the same era of architecture and planning as the older American barracks.

The morning was cold, and as usual for this time of year in Ireland, it felt as if it could rain at any moment. Matt wasn't sure if it was the gray sky or the overgrown grass that gave the place a sense of utter abandonment.

"This place would make the perfect set for a horror movie," Kim said, riding next to him. "I keep waiting for a black cat to dart across the road in front of us."

Matt looked at her, attempting a smile. "I agree. I'd laugh, but the hair on my neck just tingled, and it's not 'cuz I think Michael Meyers is in one of these buildings. I get the distinct feeling we're being watched. Keep your head on a swivel. Especially second-story windows and roofs."

Kim knew from the look on Matt's face that this was not to be taken lightly. She increased her vigilance, watching her side of the road. She saw what appeared to be a military museum, with a dozen or more military vehicles, tanks, and artillery pieces set on concrete pads outside a one-story green building. Across the street was a small kiosk of a building with a sign on top saying "Asian Cuisine."

Matt turned the car to the right and knew their destination was just one kilometer ahead. To the left appeared a modern recreation center with an indoor pool and playing fields behind it, while on the right were open fields in need of mowing. Next came massive white buildings on both sides of the road, and Matt knew instinctively that these were motor pools for the mechanized infantry and armored cavalry squadron. Just ahead was his target.

The ten-foot high green fence topped with barbed spikes let Matt know he was in the right place. He could barely see the tops of several buildings inside the compound. It instantly reminded him of the 75th Ranger Regiment and 3rd Ranger Battalion compounds at Fort Benning—where he had spent significant time. There were no signs, no fanfare, just some ordinary buildings surrounded by a simple fence to protect it from prying eyes. This was the home of the Army Ranger Wing of the Irish Defence Forces.

Matt felt bad that until that morning, he didn't know that much about the Army Ranger Wing, or ARW, as they were often called. While the ARW traced its lineage back to a small group of Irish officers and NCOs attending the US Army Ranger School in the 1960s and 1970s, the unit had progressed considerably, and Matt felt they were closer to the equivalent of the US Army's 1st Special Forces Operational Detachment-Delta, often called Delta Force or the Unit, than they were to the 75th Ranger Regiment. Estimated to have approximately 125-150 members, the ARW was Ireland's Tier 1 force focused on counter-terrorism, hostage rescue, and anti-hijack missions. As Ireland's only special operating force, they also incorporated several additional Special Forces and Ranger missions into their repertoire, such as counter-insurgency, raids, ambushes, and capturing key objectives. In short, they were the elite of the elite of the Irish Defence Forces.

Matt held very little hope that any of the Irish Rangers had survived the pandemic. He knew these men would likely have been used to protect key members of government and critical installations as things began to deteriorate, not to mention the possibility that some were likely deployed overseas. He couldn't imagine a scenario where they would have been able to sequester themselves from the virus. Still, just in case, he drove extremely slowly through the open gate of the entrance to the ARW compound.

A large car park spread out before him with space for at least fifty vehicles. The road continued to the right with two larger multi-story brick buildings, similar to others on the post, within the 10-foot high perimeter fence. Directly in front of Matt as he pulled in appeared to be a smaller compound containing a single wide two-story white building. On the fence in front of the main entrance to this inner compound was painted a large black patch with an upright red sword surrounded by a golden wreath and another symbol. Above the patch was a tab similar to the US Army's Ranger, Special Forces, or Airborne tabs, except this one said Fianóglach. Matt knew this was the shoulder patch and tab of the Army Ranger Wing.

Matt pulled the Porsche Cayenne into a spot just to the left of the entrance and immediately in front of a memorial to the unit's fallen soldiers. He and Kim exited the vehicle and walked to the gated pedestrian entrance to the inner compound, protected by a small, abandoned guard house. The main building was bland, looking like an old two-story brick building on any military installation. Nothing about the place, besides the perimeter fence and unit patch, signified that this was the home of the most elite unit in the Irish Defence Forces.

Matt realized he had left the Halligan tool in the vehicle, but before heading back to get it, he decided first to see if the front door was unlocked. It was. Opening the door and holding it for Kim to enter and clear the room, they both took an initial step back due to the stench. The decaying smell of death permeated the entire entrance area, and both Matt and Kim quickly pulled up the bandanas they wore around their neck for just such a purpose.

The entrance room had minimal natural lighting, and they both immediately turned on the flashlights attached to the barrel of their M4s. Kim went in and quickly turned to the left while Matt followed her and cleared the right half of the room.

"Clear," Kim said. They both took in what appeared to be a standard entrance area—what in the US Army, they might call a CQ desk fronted by several lobby chairs for waiting. A huge wooden carving of the ARW unit patch took up almost the entire rear wall, while the other walls were adorned with various framed pictures of the unit members in action or in formal dress uniforms.

What made this room different from most lobbies was the dead man sitting at the entrance desk. He was in military uniform, his head lying on the desk as if he had leaned down to take a quick nap. Matt walked closer and peaked at his fatigues, noting the rank of lieutenant colonel. Matt wasn't sure exactly what rank the commanding officer of the ARW would be, but guessed that, in all likelihood, this was him.

The desk blotter in front of the man was empty except for a single piece of paper and a pen. On the paper was written:

Glaine ár gcroí, Neart ár ngéag, Agus beart de réir ár mbriathar

May God have mercy on our souls

"That's the unit motto," said Kim. "I saw it in some of the material QuAI gave us. Just a sec, I think it's in this packet with the map." Kim took out a folded-in-half stack of paper, opened it, and began quickly leafing through the half-dozen pages. "Yep. Here it is. Their motto translates from Irish to English: The purity of our hearts, the strength of our limbs, and our commitment to our promise."

Matt and Kim both paused momentarily, wondering what this man's last few hours must have been like. Matt imagined this was the ARW unit commander, having just sent his troops home to their families and knowing he would never see his own family again. *He must have been a hell of an officer.* Matt thought to himself. *I only wish I had half the fortitude this guy had.*

"It's like the Sergeant Major at Collins Barracks. The last man holding the fort. The Captain going down with his ship," said Kim, her voice low in a show of respect.

"Yeah," agreed Matt. Without realizing he was even doing it, Matt briefly came to the position of attention and rendered a quick hand salute to the fallen officer. "Rangers lead the way," he whispered, the motto of the US Army's 75th Ranger Regiment.

Kim just stared at Matt, letting him have this moment and knowing this man's death meant something different to Matt than to most. After a few seconds, Matt broke from his reverie.

"Okay," he said. "It looks like offices to the right and then a long hallway to the left. I'm guessing these are the admin or command offices here to the right, and what we want is somewhere down the left hallway. Let me quickly clear these offices, and then we'll move out to see what else is here."

Matt darted into the offices, confirming they were indeed the command group's offices, now empty. He and Kim proceed methodically down the long hallway in the other direction, which had a half dozen open doorways. They paused at each door, sweeping their flashlights to confirm that these were the administrative offices. While they meant nothing to Kim, Matt knew from the numbers on the door plaques that these offices included personnel, logistics, and operations staff.

The hallway turned to the right, ninety degrees to the main building, and through a window, Matt could see that this building was actually a rectangle with a large, open courtyard in the center. The courtyard was paved and reminded Matt of a prison yard, with painted lines for soccer and basketball. He could also see individual entrances to various building sections immediately to the rear of the hallway they had just cleared.

"Bingo!" Matt said. "Those doors are what we're looking for."

"That's the armory?"

"I'm sure of it," said Matt. "One of those will be the armory; the others are likely team rooms for the individual sub-units. They'll each have their areas to plan, store their gear, and prepare for missions."

"Okay," said Kim, pushing open the door that led to the inner courtyard.

"Wait," said Matt. "We need to find the keys first. They have to be in one of the rooms we just cleared."

After ten minutes of searching the various offices, Kim finally found a wall-mounted key box. Not wanting to go back for the Halligan, Matt tried using his sheath knife to pry open the lock. Succeeding only in slightly denting the box's door and not wanting to damage his knife, Matt realized the Halligan would be necessary.

"Gimme two minutes, Kim. I need to run out to the Porsche to get the Halligan. See if you can find a diagram of this place that labels each room. That'll help us when we get the keys."

"Okay, Matt. I'll be here."

Matt quickly walked through the lobby and out the front door. He immediately pulled down his bandana, relishing the taste of fresh air. His mind was still thinking about the lonely bravery of the ARW commander as he walked down the path and out the front gate to where their SUV was parked.

Wham! Something slammed into Matt's chest with enough force to cause him to backpedal and lose his balance. He hadn't heard a gunshot, but it felt like someone had slammed a railroad spike into his chest. *They say you never hear the shot that kills you.* Matt shook his head quickly, having not heard a gunshot and realizing he must be in shock. He had this vivid image of a stick poking out of his chest. Off balance, he stumbled backward, snagged his boot on the overgrown grass, and fell backward onto the ground. Later, he would realize this simple reaction would save his life.

What appeared to be an arrow flew directly by Matt's left ear, so close he could feel the feathers whoosh by his head. Looking down, he realized he had indeed been shot, but not by a bullet. Thirty inches of aluminum arrow protruded straight out from his vest, wedged into his equipment, and from the pain, Matt felt sure it was embedded in his chest. Sitting on the ground, the arrow sticking straight out, Matt quickly grasped his M4 and raised it to search for enemy targets.

Matt reached down to toggle his mic. "Kim! Kim! I'm out front. I'm hit. Enemy is somewhere in the car park."

Having fallen back through the pedestrian gate, Matt could only see a sliver of the parking lot through the small opening.

He realized how lucky he was—if the shooter had waited for him to take two more steps, he would have fallen in front of the perimeter fencing and would be fair game with no cover. As it was, with him sitting on the grass inside the perimeter fence, he was concealed from anyone in the parking lot targeting him. However, as Matt had learned long ago in the Army, there is a distinct difference between concealment and cover.

Matt jolted to his right as another arrow came screaming through the thin green tarp covering the chain link of the perimeter fencing. Training his weapon on the open doorway, Matt heard someone running in the parking lot and just caught a quick glimpse of a short body dashing behind a car in the parking lot. Not sure how badly he was wounded or if he could stand, Matt searched around frantically for something to hide behind. Ankle-high grass was all he could see. *Where the fuck was Kim!*

Looking down at the arrow, Matt thought of pulling it out. He knew that would not be the smartest thing to do, but he could not move and seek cover with a couple of feet of arrow shaft sticking out of his body. Not getting shot again was his highest priority at the moment. He reached his left hand under his vest and his shirt, attempting to feel where the arrow had pierced his chest. The pain had become a sharp ache. As his hand slid under his vest, Matt could immediately tell that the arrow had not fully penetrated through the woven kevlar material designed primarily to stop bullets. *Thank god!*

The pain was significant, but knowing he wasn't seriously wounded, Matt yanked on the arrow's shaft. Pulling at it, Matt knew instantly why Kim had not come to his rescue. The arrow had pierced right through the plastic center of his small handheld radio, rendering it inoperable. It was lodged so deep in the kevlar fibers that Matt couldn't pull it free.

A fourth arrow came flying through the fence. Matt knew the archer was firing blindly and couldn't imagine the guy had an endless supply of arrows.

"Kim!" Matt yelled. In seconds, Kim came running to the entrance door. Seeing Matt lying on the ground with an arrow stuck in his chest, she immediately came bounding down the stairs. Matt started to get to his feet, and Kim helped him stand.

"What the fuck?" Kim shouted. "Are you okay?" Realizing they must be under attack, Kim reached for her M4 and began scanning the inner courtyard for targets.

"I'm okay, Kim. I'm okay. Somebody shot me with a fucking bow and arrow. Help me get back inside. I need to catch my breath." The pain in Matt's chest was approaching unbearable, and he was having difficulty breathing.

Once inside the safety of the building's entrance, Matt reached out and grabbed the mic from Kim's radio. "Dave, this is Matt. Urgent."

"Yeah, Matt, what's up?" Came Dave's instant reply.

"We're pinned down in the ARW compound by someone with a bow and arrow. Can you approach them from behind? I want to take them alive if at all possible."

"Roger," replied Dave. "We're just down the street at the Mech Company's area. We'll approach on foot. Give us five minutes."

Kim used the time they were waiting to check Matt's injury. Realizing the arrow was not embedded in his skin, she used both hands to pull it free from his vest. The arrow had gone straight through the radio and penetrated Matt's vest to the point where it was impossible for her to pull it free of the kevlar fibers. Unbuckling the vest for him, Kim gingerly pulled the entire assault vest over Matt's head.

"Jesus, that feels so much better," Matt said, lying back against the wall.

"Let me see." Kim pulled up the fleece and t-shirt Matt was wearing. An angry purple welt was already visible on Matt's chest, just to the right and below his breastbone. She probed around it gingerly as Matt winced and pulled away.

"Sorry, I just need to see if you've broken a rib. There's no external bleeding, but you need to get to Kevin ASAP to make sure there's nothing wrong internally. Jesus, Matt. What the fuck are you doing getting shot by an arrow?" Kim had flipped from triage mode to now being concerned that Matt had almost been killed.

"I don't know, Kim," Matt said, smiling slightly. "It's not like I went out there asking to be shot."

"Who do you think it is? One of these Ranger guys?"

"No, definitely not. Honestly, I think it might've been a kid."

Matt reached over to grab Kim's radio handset again. "Dave, are you in position? There's a chance this guy could be a kid. Try to take them alive if possible."

Before receiving a reply, Matt heard a single gunshot followed by lots of yelling.

"Get down! Drop it! Stop!! We're not going to hurt you!" The yelling came from several voices, and Matt recognized Dave and Derek's voice immediately. Through the open door, Matt heard heavy footsteps running across the parking lot's pavement before someone yelled, "I got him!"

Thirty seconds later, Dave's voice came over the radio. "We got them, Matt. Where exactly are you?"

Kim toggled her handset. "Just inside the pedestrian gate, to the right of our SUV."

"Gotcha," replied Dave.

Matt stood up to meet Dave outside. Kim carried his assault vest and gear while Matt slung his M4 over his shoulder, refusing to go unarmed even momentarily.

"What happened to you?" Dave asked, walking through the pedestrian gate.

"I'm okay," replied Matt. "Who was it? Did you catch them?"

"You wouldn't believe me if I told you," said Dave, motioning for Matt to follow him back into the parking lot.

As Matt and Kim walked out the gate, they first noticed Dylan sitting on the curb in front of the ARW memorial statue, a child on each side of him. From behind, the two children could have easily been Christopher and Laurie, Matt's kids. To Dylan's right, a young boy of eleven or twelve with light brown hair in desperate need of a trim sat with his arms across his chest, a defiant look on his dirty face. On Dylan's right was an adorable young girl with unkempt, curly red hair, bright blue eyes, and the same grimy face as her brother. Unlike her brooding and silent brother, the girl had a mischievous smile and seemed to be chattering a mile a minute in a conversation with Dylan. A few feet on the far side of Dylan stood Derek and LT, M4s hanging from single-point slings, along with Rory, who carried only a holstered sidearm. Matt could see a compound bow and a quiver with several arrows in Derek's hands.

Ignoring the pain in his chest, Matt went straight over to the children sitting on the curb and knelt before them. "I'm the one you shot. You don't have to worry, I'm okay. My name is Matt."

The young girl stopped talking, and the boy looked straight ahead defiantly, refusing to make eye contact with Matt.

"Why'd you shoot me?" Matt asked the boy.

The boy continued to look straight ahead.

"What's your name, young man?" Matt continued his questioning. "Were you trying to protect your sister?" No answer. "You're a pretty good shot with that bow. Who taught you to shoot like that, your father?"

The boy's bottom lip started to quiver, and Matt watched a single tear fall from the young boy's left eye, carving a downward path through the dirt caked on his cheek. Matt looked at Dylan and raised his eyebrows.

"Matt, this young lady here is Caroline Mooney. She's seven years old and lives with her brother, Mick, who's eleven."

"Well, hello, Caroline. Such a pretty name," Matt said, extending his right hand in greeting. "My name is Matt, and it's a pleasure to meet you." Caroline giggled and shook Matt's hand shyly.

Matt reached out to extend his hand to young Mick. "Nice to meet you, as well, Mick. No hard feelings, right?" The boy stared straight ahead, tears still slowly running down his face.

Dylan looked over and playfully nudged the young boy next to him. "Hey, Mick. Matt's my uncle and the toughest guy I know. The fact you shot him with an arrow—I think that now makes *you* the toughest guy I know." The boy looked at Dylan and smiled ever so slightly. "C'mon, Mick. We're here to help you and your sister. But you have to talk to us if we're gonna be friends."

Mick looked at Dylan and then back to Matt, still kneeling in front of him with his right hand extended in greeting. Seeming to make a decision, Mick slowly extended his hand and shook with Matt. "Uh, hi, Matt. I'm awful sorry for shooting you with my bow. We thought you was stealing and going to hurt us."

"I understand completely, Mick," said Matt. "I have a son your age, and I'd be extremely proud of him for trying to protect his sister."

Dave appeared at Matt's side, holding the boy's compound bow and quiver of arrows he'd just taken from Derek. "Mick?

I'm Dave. I apologize for having to tackle you. Are you hurt at all?"

"No, I'm okay," answered Mick.

"Good. Here, buddy. Since we're all friends, I want you to have your bow back." Matt looked at Dave quizzically as Mick took the bow and quiver from Dave's outstretched hand. Matt had the utmost respect for Dave's judgment, so remained silent. "Where do you live, Mick? Is it just you and your sister, or are more people living with you?"

"It's just my sis and me," Mick replied. "Me dad is overseas, and me mum died fifty-five days ago. Not sure when me dad will be comin' back, but me mum said to take care of Caroline until he does."

Matt looked at this young man, realizing that Christopher and Laurie could easily be in this exact situation, alone in a world gone mad. "Was your Dad a Ranger?"

"My dad IS a Ranger," replied Mick.

Matt immediately realized his error and felt terrible, not wanting to take away this small glimmer of hope while knowing there was no chance his father was coming home. "Well, before all this, Mick, I was a Ranger in the American Army. And so was Dave, here. I'm looking forward to meeting your father someday. I bet we have a lot in common."

The boy brightened immediately. "Is that why you have guns? My dad carries a rifle just like yours on operations."

"Yeah, Mick. That's right. We carry rifles to protect ourselves and our families. How much do you know about what's happening in the world, Mick? And around Ireland?"

"I know just about everybody's dead if that's what you mean. Smallpox. Black Pox. It's killed everyone, including me mum."

"Where do you live, Mick?" Dave asked.

"We live over on Orchard Park, the estate just outside the south gate. Our mum died in her bed from the Black Pox. She told us to stay away as soon as she knew she might be sick. So we moved into Paddy McGee's house next door as they left town and gave Mum the keys. We've plenty of food from the Centra. We wanted to bury her, but she said to go to Paddy's and not get near another person, living or dead, no matter what. She also said not to let any bad people hurt my sister. I'm sorry, Mr. Matt, but I thought you were a bad person."

"That's okay, Mick," Matt said, patting the boy on his knee. "You were protecting your sister. That makes you a hero, like your dad."

Kim flipped through the pages she'd printed from QuAI. "I see it," she said. "They live just south of here, maybe five hundred meters as the crow flies." Kim held out her paper so Matt and Dave could see where the children lived.

"Okay, Mick, Caroline, I'll tell you what," Matt said, clapping his hands and rubbing them together. "Dylan here is going to have you sit in the backseat of one of these SUVs, and he's going to get you something to eat. Sound good?" Both children nodded. "Dave, Kim and I have a few things we need to do; then we'll go by your house and discuss the future. Okay?"

"Okay," said Caroline, with Mick just nodding.

CHAPTER 20

November 20, 12:37 pm

Matt reclined back in the front passenger seat of the Porsche Cayenne as they sped north on the M50 motorway, following Rory in the cargo van along the eight-lane beltway encircling greater Dublin. He was pretty sure he had cracked, if not broken, a rib, as the pain and swelling in his chest was considerable. *Better than being shot by a gun*, he thought, closing his eyes and trying not to breathe deeply.

Derek was riding in the rear passenger seat and somehow felt the need to read every highway sign out loud and make some comment. “Exit 1. N4 to Galway or south to Palmerstown on R148. Says there’s a toll ahead. I’m guessing no toll booth attendants.”

Derek had pretty much read every highway sign since they’d left Kildare, traveling north on the N7 until merging onto the M50 to travel clockwise around the Dublin suburbs. From experience, Matt knew they were getting off on Exit 2 towards Blanchardstown. His mind wandered to Derek’s comment on tolls, and Matt knew there was no toll booth. It was an automated toll, and Matt was always irritated that you had to download an app and pay a few euros online within 24 hours to prevent being fined. Needless to say, over the years, he’d paid plenty of fines.

"Rory will know the way, Kim, but we should be exiting at the next exit. Follow signs to Blanchardstown Shopping Center," Matt said softly, trying to remain still and keep the sharp, stabbing pain at bay.

After leaving young Mick and Caroline to have a delicious and exciting lunch of MREs with Dylan, everyone else had gone back into the ARW compound. With the diagram Kim had found along with the Halligan tool, Dave easily opened the key box, and they found the areas they were looking for. It took them about forty-five minutes to shuttle everything to the cargo van, but they now had all of the items Matt had been looking for. These included three dozen encrypted handheld radios and the same number of the latest night vision devices, both thermal and infrared. While the inexpensive VHF radios found at the local electronics store had proven extremely functional, Matt was concerned that it would prove more and more difficult to maintain secure communications within the family as their community grew. Likewise, while they had a dozen or so night vision devices liberated from the Nomads in Woodstock, Matt knew that the ability to see at night was the ultimate differentiator on the battlefield, and he wanted to ensure his family maintained more than enough capability to operate at night.

The other items loaded in the van were some specialized weaponry and medical kits. The Irish Army used the Steyr Aug A1 as their standard individual rifle. This bullpup assault rifle, made mostly of molded composite plastic, had always looked to Matt like a kid's toy gun, even though he knew it to be a reliable weapon fielded by several of the world's militaries. The ARW, however, used the HK416 assault rifle as their main rifle, and Matt had taken two racks of ten rifles each, along with suppressors. Chambered in 5.56mm and made by Heckler & Koch, the HK416 was considered one of the world's best assault rifles and was used by many of the world's elite Tier 1 special operations forces. Matt had also grabbed several suppressed HK417, similar to the HK416 but chambered in 7.62 and capable of being used as a sniper rifle, as well as two Accuracy International .50 caliber long-range sniper rifles. While the Remington 700s that Matt currently had could hit targets out to more than 800 meters, these .50 cal sniper rifles could drop targets almost a mile away—with the right person pulling the trigger. In addition to a significant supply of ammunition for all of the above, Matt grabbed a half-dozen field trauma kits with everything needed to respond to just about any battlefield injury.

Dave had been very energized by Mick and Caroline. While he and Michelle rarely, if ever, spoke about it, Matt knew they desperately missed their two children—both of whom were serving in the US military. Their daughter, Daphne, was stationed with the US Air Force in Japan, while their son, Max, was an infantryman in the 101st Airborne Division. Given all the available information, Matt knew that Dave and Michelle assumed their children had not survived. Matt saw the twinkle in Dave's eye as he chatted with Mick and Caroline, and Dave had specifically asked for them both to ride with him in his SUV—which is why Derek now rode with Matt. Dylan and Dave had established the best bond with the two children, and Matt sincerely hoped the ride to Dublin was going well for everyone.

Matt opened his eyes as he felt Kim steering the SUV off the exit ramp to the left. He adjusted his seat, wincing with the sharp pain the movement brought to his ribs, and watched as they sped north on the N3 and took the first exit. Matt listened as Rory and Kevin spoke over the radio, with Kevin providing specifics as to where to link up.

Kim handled the Porsche exceptionally through several small roundabouts, although failing to register the "Hump" sign as indicating a serious speed bump. The Porsche popped over the bump at about 20 mph, and while Derek quite enjoyed the sensation, it felt to Matt like someone had just shoved a knife into his chest.

"Easy there, Mario. Let's try to take it easy. I'm an old man," Matt said, trying to keep it light.

"Sorry, Matt," replied Kim. He knew she would never do anything to cause him pain intentionally.

The Blanchardstown Mall, possibly the largest in greater Dublin, was off to their left. Matt had never seen the parking lots completely deserted. To his right were several box stores, and up ahead was the ten-story Crowne Plaza Hotel. Kim drove left at the roundabout in front of the hotel, keeping the mall to their left as they proceeded along the backside of the shopping center. Matt saw the green and white sign of a Starbucks, as well as the logo for the Captain America restaurant. Matt had eaten there several times, always completely embarrassed as an American coming to Ireland to eat in a Captain America chain restaurant. However, the first bite of the buffalo chicken wings always erased that embarrassment. Matt vehemently held that Ireland was home to the best chicken wings in the world, hands down, and the current front-runner for the very best wings in Ireland, in Matt's humble opinion, was the crispy buffalo wings at Captain America.

Matt was never sure whether it was the taste of their buffalo sauce, the crispiness of the fry, or the freshness of the chicken, but the result was always a winner. *I wonder if they have the recipe posted in their kitchen? Maybe we should stop to see if we can find it?* Matt thought. *And maybe I've eaten my last buffalo chicken wing? What kind of world will my kids live in if they can't eat chicken wings and watch the Patriots on Monday Night Football?*

Matt saw Pete's convoy of vehicles parked in the lot to their right, and Kim followed Rory into the parking lot. They were parked in front of a large electrical store, and Matt could see Pete and Tom loading things into the back, along with several of Rory's sailors who had volunteered to help. By the time

Matt gingerly dragged himself out of the SUV, Rory and Dave were already standing with Pete, Kevin, Tom, and Sarah—undoubtedly discussing their adventures at Curragh Camp and their two new additions.

Kevin reached into the front of one of their vehicles, pulling out a small backpack. Slinging it over his shoulder, he walked with Dave to the SUV where Dylan and the two children sat. Not feeling like he would add anything to the situation, Matt watched as Kevin knelt down and quietly spoke with the children in the backseat for a minute. Kevin then reached into his bag, withdrawing two syringes and a vial of vaccine. Mick and Caroline stoically rolled up their sleeves and allowed themselves to be vaccinated.

Dave and Kevin then walked over to where Matt stood leaning against the Porsche, Kim at his side.

"Dave tells me you've been playing your Yank game of cowboys and Indians with our new friends," Kevin stated, smiling a bit.

"Yeah, Doc. I'd laugh with you, but it hurts like hell. I think I got pretty lucky," replied Matt as Kim reached over to pull up his shirt and expose the wound.

"I'll say," said Kevin, tenderly probing the edges of the discoloration. "Having trouble breathing?"

"Not really," replied Matt. "I mean, not when I stay perfectly still. My lungs are okay, though, if that's what you're asking."

"Yeah, that's my concern. A bruised or cracked rib is just pain, but if it's fully broken, we must worry about the sharp edge puncturing your lung or something else."

"Can you just tape me up? I broke a couple of ribs playing football back in the day, and the Doc just taped me up and told me to take it easy."

"Well, we don't do that anymore, Matt, but that shows your

age. I will insist that you take it easy and will put Kim in charge of ensuring that happens. As for the tape, that will only restrict your ability to breathe, and despite the pain, I want you to try to breathe as deeply as you can. Other than puncturing a lung, pneumonia is the biggest concern with a broken rib. If you continually take short breaths, you're at risk of a collapsed lung or pneumonia. Expanding your lungs fully will prevent that."

"Uh, yeah. Okay, Doc. I'll go sit in the car and breathe."

"Good idea, Matt. Pete can brief you just as easily while you're sitting down."

Kim opened the door, and Matt retook his seat in the front left passenger seat as Pete walked around the vehicle. "How's everything going?" Matt asked, not liking the fact that he couldn't stand up and talk like everyone else.

"All good, Matt. How're you? Did that kid really shoot you with a fuckin' arrow?" Pete was serious but also trying not to laugh.

"Yeah, Pete. Right in the chest. Would have killed me, I think, if I wasn't wearing a vest. His second shot just narrowly missed my face, the little fucker." Matt paused, trying to breathe slowly. "He's a good kid. Just trying to take care of his sister. His dad was an Irish Ranger.

"Damn," said Pete. "What a fucked up world, man. Every time I get focused on building something for our extended family's future, something snaps me back to reality. We really fucked over our kids, didn't we? I mean, we're protecting them, but for what? To eke out an existence and always wait for the next threat? The next enemy? The next catastrophe?"

"Hey, buddy. Remember, we're just playing the hand we're dealt. And honestly, look at us. We're doing a pretty goddamn good job. Our kids wake up in a warm bed each morning, excited about what the new day will bring. They're not living in fear. They're not huddled alone in an empty house taking potshots with a bow and arrow at passersby, like Mick and Caroline here. We're building a community. A society, Pete. Think about the days back at UVM, sitting on the porch at 440 Pearl Street, drinking beer at FADC on a Friday afternoon. Did you ever think you'd have this much responsibility or make this much difference in people's lives? We're literally saving the human race, Pete."

"Yeah, Matt. Sometimes I wonder what's the point. I mean, I see you sitting here after almost getting killed by a fucking arrow by those kids, man. So what is the point, exactly?"

"You just said it yourself, Pete," said Matt, nodding towards where Mick and Caroline sat in the vehicle with Dylan. "They're the point. Right there. Mick and Caroline. Dylan and Derek. Liz, Juliet, Christopher and Laurie. We're doing this for them and hopefully the thousands like them."

"Yeah, yeah. I hear ya, man. I do," said Pete. "Thanks for the pep talk, coach."

"No problem. What're friends for? So, did you guys find everything you needed?"

"We did. And then some. Kevin posted some flyers around the mall for a vaccine—he wants to come back next week and see if anyone shows. And Tom and Sarah are literally geniuses. I think we have every electronic and mechanical item we'll need for our communications and surveillance network. As a bonus, we found a warehouse for wind turbines with parts, accessories, and more. We left it in place, but Sarah gathered some of their books and laptops in hopes that they can figure out the best way to build a sustainable energy supply."

"Awesome. How much more do you guys have to load up?" Matt asked.

"I think we're done. We can probably get going here in just a few minutes."

"Excellent. Would you mind asking Dave to come over? Once you're ready, let Dave know, and we can head back to Cork."

"Sounds good. Rest easy, Matt. We need you healthy." Pete walked away, and after a few words with Dave, Matt watched Dave walk over to where Matt sat in the car.

"All good, man?" Dave asked as he approached the open passenger window.

"Yeah, Pete's just about ready to leave," Matt said. "I was thinking. Given all that's happened today, I think you should postpone the side trip to Kilkenny." The plan for the day had included all six vehicles traveling north to link up in Blanchardstown. However, on the return trip, Dave planned to take Rory, LT, Derek, and Dylan and detour to Kilkenny, while Matt and Kim would continue with Pete and Kevin's group to Cork. Kilkenny was home to Stephens Barracks, where the 1st Brigade's 3rd Infantry Battalion was. Dave planned to secure the armories at this location, similar to how they'd proceeded at Collins Barracks and Curragh Camp.

"Yeah, I was going to mention that to you. I agree. Let's get back to Cork and get Mick and Caroline settled. I can take a trip over to Kilkenny any day this week."

"Okay, sounds good. I think..."

The high-pitched sound of a car's revving engine caused Matt and Dave to instantly jerk their heads back towards the main road to their right. A metallic blue BMW 3-series accelerated rapidly along the road, heading east to west from the Crowne Plaza towards the movie theater, the driver redlining the engine to get the most acceleration possible.

"Stay put, Matt. I got this," Dave said, moving quickly away from the Cayenne towards where the others were grouped by the panel truck. Matt could hear Dave shouting instructions to everyone.

"LT, Derek, take up positions at the rear of the cargo van. Don't engage, but track that vehicle. Dylan, keep the kids down on the floorboards. Kim, Rory, and Pete—I want you to watch everything to our backs. This vehicle could be a ruse, getting our attention so someone can sneak up behind us."

Everyone moved to their assigned spots.

"Do not engage," Dave yelled. "Not unless we're fired upon first, or you see hostile intent."

Fuck it, Matt said to himself. *I'm not going to sit here like an invalid. I just have sore ribs.* Matt opened his passenger door, grabbed the M4 from where it was wedged on the floorboard, and took a position behind the Porsche's engine block.

Matt sighted through the ACOG scope on his M4, giving him four times magnification. He watched as the BMW bounced over one of the large speed bumps and then slowed to enter the roundabout in front of the McDonald's. The car sped fully around the roundabout and headed back towards the Crowne Plaza. In seconds, it would pass near where their convoy was parked, about 100 meters from the road.

Matt wished he had his assault vest on, as his binoculars would have come in handy right about then. Matt turned his head quickly and saw that Dave had pulled out his binoculars and was staring intently through them while watching the approaching vehicle.

"Two young adult males," Dave said loudly. "No visible weapons. Hold your fire."

Matt sighted through the ACOG, placing the driver in the center of his reticle. Instead of accelerating, the BMW slowed considerably and then turned sharply into the far side of their parking lot. Matt could now see the driver and passenger clearly—two young men who appeared in their early twenties.

"Hold your fire," Dave shouted again. Matt saw the BMW's

passenger waving a brightly colored piece of paper from his window.

"They have our flyer," Matt shouted, wincing in pain.

"Weapons safe!" Dave shouted. "They have our flyer! They have one of our flyers!"

The BMW approached slowly towards where Matt's vehicle was parked. Dave let his M4 drop on his sling and began to walk slowly towards the BMW, now stopped about thirty meters away.

"Cover me," Dave said quietly as he passed Matt. Matt refocused his reticle on the driver and kept his non-dominant eye open to watch Dave walk towards their vehicle, his hands raised in the universal symbol of calm. It did not appear that the two individuals in the BMW were intent on causing them harm, so Kevin jogged up to stand next to Dave.

"Hello there," Dave said. "Would you two mind stepping out of your vehicle?" Despite trying to sound non-menacing, Dave's voice carried the authoritative command of a police officer.

The two men opened their doors and stood up in their open doorways. The driver was tall, at least matching Matt's 6'3", if not taller. Sporting shaggy, light brown hair with bangs that almost covered his eyes, the young man had the lean muscles of an athlete and was wearing faded jeans and a red 1/4 zip fleece. His fleece was embroidered with a white "S" on its left breast, an outline of a tree appearing across the "S." Matt looked closely and recognized the logo of Stanford University.

The other man was quite a bit shorter, maybe 5'10", and had the muscular build of a rugby player. Or maybe Matt was projecting that, as the man wore a rugby shirt with the words Sport Ireland emblazoned across the front. This man appeared a bit older, probably in his late twenties, whereas the driver appeared college-aged.

"Thank you," said Dave. "What can we do for you, gentlemen?"

"We saw you posting these flyers. Is this true?" The driver asked Dave, in what Matt was sure was an American accent.

Matt didn't hear Dave's reply as Kim nudged him in the side, sending a bolt of pain through his chest that caused Matt to gasp audibly. "Sorry, Matt! But I think I see two people on the roof behind us, and I'm pretty sure I saw the barrel of a gun."

Matt turned as quickly as he could, raising his rifle and sighting through the ACOG. He saw the heads of two people, one man and one woman, in their late teens or early twenties. He did not see a weapon.

"Dave?" Matt yelled. "We have two people on the roof behind us. Cover those guys. This could be a trap." Matt placed his finger on the trigger, just waiting for one of these people to show a weapon. "Derek, LT, cover the rooftops behind us to the right. I've got the two on the left."

Dave began to move towards the two men from the BMW, who quickly retreated to their car. "Stop!" Dave yelled, bringing his M4 to bear.

"Wait! Wait!" Screamed the driver. "We mean you no harm! We're just trying to see if you're for real! Don't come closer! You'll infect us!"

Dave stopped short, Kevin standing next to him. He told the driver, "Tell your friends to come down from the roof. Anyone else you have out there, you better signal for them to show themselves. Now! My friend over there has an itchy trigger finger, and he's already been shot once today."

The driver stood back up and began waving both hands over his head, crossing them as he waved. "It's okay! You can come down!" He shouted. Turning to Dave, the young man continued. "I'm sorry. We weren't sure if you were legit or just looters. When I saw your guns, I decided to put in place some insurance. The only people are those two on the roof. They're armed, but please don't shoot them."

"Okay," said Dave. "No one is going to shoot if your friends stay calm. I want both of you to keep your hands where we can see them." Dave turned and jogged over to where Matt crouched behind the hood of the Cayenne. He handed his binos to Matt, then turned and returned to stand with Kevin about ten meters from the BMW.

Matt trained the binos on the far left corner of the big box stores surrounding the parking lot. He vaguely noticed the Homestore+More sign and focused on the two individuals rounding the corner. Clearly, these were the same two from the rooftop—a young man carrying what appeared to be a .22 rifle and a woman carrying a semi-automatic pistol in her hand. Both had their weapons pointed down, with their other hand held high.

"John! Sharon!" The BMW driver yelled. "Walk over to us. Everything is okay."

Everyone waited patiently as John and Sharon crossed the open parking lot to stand beside the BMW passenger.

"Okay," said Dave calmly. "John? Sharon? My name is Dave." The two nodded at him blankly, almost in shock. "I'd like the two of you to place your weapons inside the BMW. Yep, just toss them right in." Dave watched as they complied, and then he let his M4 fall onto his sling to dangle along his side. "See, no need for guns, right?"

Matt stood up and walked over to stand next to Dave, his rifle also hanging by his side. Without waiting to be told, Kevin started speaking. "My name is Dr. Kevin Cross. I'm also a Commandant in the Irish Defence Forces. These here are my friends. You've met Dave, and this other gentleman is Matt." Kevin paused for a second. "Our flyer is for real. We do have smallpox vaccine and would be happy to give you each an immunization. It's effective immediately. No more worrying about contracting the Black Pox."

"Are you serious, Doctor?" The woman named Sharon said in a heavy Irish accent, a look of disbelief on her face.

"Yeah, Doc. How do we know you're telling the truth?" Queried the BMW driver. Matt again noticed this man sounded American rather than Irish.

"What's your name?" Kevin asked the driver.

"Liam. Liam McCusker."

"Well, Liam, I'd be happy to show you my wallet with both my medical and military credentials. I'm also happy to show you the vaccine vial so you can read the label. Other than that, you'll have to trust us."

"Where'd you get the vaccine?" Liam asked. "I didn't think there was any in all of Europe."

"There wasn't. Until about a week ago. Half of us here are from Cork, but the other half are American. They just recently traveled here, and while I'm sure they'd be happy to share their story, the bottom line is that the vaccine is legitimate. My wife and I have taken it, and I've administered it to more than a hundred survivors in the Cork area. I'll happily give the four of you a vaccination right now."

"How much do you have? How, ah, how many doses?" Liam asked tentatively.

"Enough," said Matt sharply. "Why do you care?"

"Well, uh," the young man stuttered a bit. "It's just that, uh, there are more than just four of us. I'd like to make sure our entire group could be vaccinated."

Matt relaxed, realizing the young man was looking out for his group and not trying to see how much of the commodity they had. "How many are in your group?" Matt asked.

Liam looked to his friends to his left and right, searching for support on whether to divulge this information. Receiving no help from his friends, Liam made his own decision. "There's one hundred and six of us, including the four of us."

Matt, Dave, and Kevin looked at each other, shocked at how many were in Liam's group.

"We can vaccinate all of you, Liam," said Matt. "We'd be happy to. It's one of the reasons we came to Dublin, to connect with other survivors. My name is Matt Sheridan. Let's let Doc here vaccinate the four of you, and then we can figure out how to help the rest of your group. Is that an American accent I detect, Liam?"

CHAPTER 21

November 20, 2:41 pm

"Sorry, lads. This is the best we can do for the moment," said Shane, the passenger from the BMW, as he handed open brown bottles of Guinness to Matt and Pete. Matt accepted the beer, saying a quick "Cheers" before taking a deep slug. Despite not loving stout, the beer tasted great.

Matt watched as Shane took the seat to his left, both of them facing the open fire burning in the fire pit to their front. A neat, four-foot-high stack of split logs was stacked on the far side of the fire pit, with more than a dozen folding chairs positioned around it. At the moment, Pete, Matt, and Shane were the only occupants.

Beyond the stack of wood, about thirty meters away, Matt was staring at the facade of a modern, white building, a swirling "S" logo and the words "Sport Ireland Institute" emblazoned on its wall. In front of the building, spilling into the car park, Kevin, Kim, and the others were methodically administering vaccines to the more than one hundred survivors who had called this place home for the last two months.

After leaving the Blanchardstown Center, Matt's convoy followed Liam and his three cohorts south towards the M50. However, instead of getting on the N3 motorway, which would lead to the M50, Liam turned left at the now-defunct traffic light onto what Kim's map labeled Snugborough Road or the R843. After exactly one kilometer, Liam turned right at an extremely large building with a curved rooftop. Open gates marked the turnoff entrance, where Matt first saw the logo printed on the building to his front. Sport Ireland Campus, the sign read.

As they drove, it became evident that the first large building they had passed was the National Aquatic Center, complete with what appeared to be a large competition pool and an indoor water park. Liam continued past the indoor pool, juking through a roundabout and heading towards an even larger building. On both sides of the road, Matt could see cricket, hurling, and soccer playing fields. As they approached the large building to their front, it became clear this was two buildings joined in a T. One appeared to be an indoor arena, while the other was an indoor soccer or football field. This second building, easily forty feet high, had ten-foot-high glass windows encircling its base, and with the afternoon light shining in, Matt could see bright green artificial turf and what looked to be several large tents.

Liam's BMW followed the curve of the narrow road another few hundred meters before pulling into the car park of the building where they currently sat.

"So, Shane, you trained here before the pandemic?" Pete asked, taking another swig of beer and savoring the taste.

"Yeah, mate. I played football for the Irish Rovers for four years before hangin' up me boots and comin' to Sport Ireland as a trainer and coach. That's how I knew Liam, I was his strength and conditionin' coach right here in this building when everythin' went to shite."

Matt hoped that Pete knew enough to know that football in Ireland was not the same as in the United States.

"That's great," said Pete. "Matt and I both played a little football back in high school. But football's different in the US. What you call football, we call soccer."

Shane started laughing and almost snorted his beer. "Ah, yeah, we call it soccer here as well, mate. Football here is Irish football or Gaelic football. A bit more like Australian Football or even rugby than your NFL. It's not a game for pussies."

Matt couldn't help but laugh. He wasn't sure if Shane was putting down American football or if he was trying to explain Irish football a little better. Matt had often watched Irish football on television and a couple of times in person and did not doubt that those who played it were some of the toughest athletes on earth. Matt couldn't help but like Shane.

"So Liam was training here as well?" Matt asked Shane, rescuing Pete.

"Yeah, Matt. He's a swimmer, one of the best Ireland's ever had. He's a Yank like you lot, but his mum is from Cork so that also makes him Irish. Speak of the devil." Shane pointed with his beer bottle towards the building, and Matt turned to see Liam and Kim walking their way. Liam had another six-pack of Guinness in his hands, and they both walked up to take seats on the far side of Shane.

"Matt, Pete, we can't thank you enough for providing us with the vaccine," Liam said as he opened a beer and handed it to Kim before opening a second for himself.

"Think nothing of it," said Matt. "We're glad we could help."

"Matt," interjected Kim. "Liam was actually raised in Florida and just graduated from Stanford. He was a swimmer there—a really good one."

"Wow," said Matt. "Small world. Did you two know any of the same people?" Matt recalled that Kim had done her Ph.D. in marine biology at Stanford.

"Oh, no," said Kim. "I left Palo Alto probably in Liam's freshman year, but as a Ph.D. student, there was no overlap in social circles. Although I likely attended one or two of his swim meets, and we probably attended the same football games."

"So, Liam," Matt asked. "Shane told me you were training here when everything went to shit. How'd you end up with a hundred people on the Sport Ireland campus?"

Liam took another sip of beer, thinking how best to tell what was likely a very complicated story. "Well, honestly, it just happened. The Sport Ireland campus here has training centers for a lot Ireland's national teams—people training for the Olympics. I was here training for several months at the National Aquatic Center when the nukes went off. I first tried to get back to Florida, but most transatlantic flights were canceled, and those that flew were ridiculously expensive. I was staying in a small flat just off campus on the other side of the pool; we drove by it on the way in. I had three flatmates, all swimmers. They all went home. They invited me, but at the time, I thought I'd get a flight home myself, so I declined. Then people started getting sick, people in the apartments near me. I didn't want to be near anyone, and since they closed all airports, I decided the campus here might be the safest place. I came to the Institute, knowing they had a locker room, kitchen, and couches..."

"And there I was," interrupted Shane. "My mum and dad passed several years ago, and my only sister lives in Sligo with her husband. I lived in a flat right near to Liam and came to the same conclusion he did. So we were the first two."

"And the others?" Matt asked. "How'd you get to a hundred without getting infected?"

"Well, it kind of just happened. Mostly word of mouth. Almost everyone you see over there is either an athlete, a foreign student, or their siblings," said Liam, motioning towards the line of people waiting to receive their vaccination.

"People were getting sick and dying at that time, especially in Dublin. Everything was closed, the electricity was still on, and cell phones still worked. For about the first week or ten days. People Shane and I knew, mostly athletes but some foreign exchange students at Trinity or UCD, were frantically looking for a place to go. We invited them here."

"Okay, but how'd you know they weren't already contagious?"

"Oh, easy. Everyone slept outside. The weather was pretty good, and we liberated a bunch of tarps and tents from an outdoor sporting goods store in Blanchardstown. We also loaded up with canned goods. We made everyone keep at least twenty meters apart, and we kept them supplied with bottled water and canned goods. The government had put out that there was a 3-7 day incubation period, so we logged everyone's arrival, and on the eighth day they could move into the Institute."

"Smart," said Pete. Matt couldn't help but agree—very smart.

"So you're in charge?" Matt asked.

"Mmm, yeah, I guess. But it's not official or anything. It's just how it worked out. Shane and I put this together kind of by accident, but the first people that came were friends, and then after that, it was friends of friends or acquaintances of friends. It just came together, and we all got along. People can leave anytime they want, but if they leave, they must go through the seven-day quarantine to return. That's our only hard and fast rule."

"How do you keep supplies for 106 people?"

"We've set up a rotation of two foraging teams of four people. Sharon, John, Shane, and myself are currently on one of those foraging teams. We gather supplies, which are dropped off across the street in those old Quonset huts along the road.

Foraging teams do one week on, then one week of quarantine. You may've seen the tents on the indoor pitch when we drove in. That's where we're staying. Two tents are on one side of the pitch, twenty meters apart, and two tents are on the other end. The foraging teams stay as a group of four and never get closer than ten meters with another foraging team. And the quarantined foraging teams keep their distance and wait seven days before rejoining the main group here at the Institute."

"It's interesting that you decided to go off campus as the leader, knowing you'd have to quarantine," said Matt.

"Yeah, well, like I said, it's not really an official position. Shane and I talked about it, and for the first six weeks, we purposely kept ourselves off the foraging teams. We knew we were more valuable to the group staying here. But this week, I don't know, I just felt that it was time to see what the world had become outside our isolated campus. We had already gathered enough provisions to last us through the winter, and Shane and I had some ideas on things we might want for the future. Things to help us build our community for the long term." Liam took another sip from his beer. "I have a hard time believing in God after all that's happened, but I guess it must have been fate or something that brought us together. We really can't thank you enough. You guys've given us all a new lease on life. There's so much we can do now without constantly worrying about getting infected."

"You're very welcome, Liam. Like I said, we're so glad we could help and happy we linked up. We've put those flyers around Cork over the last week and so far have given about a hundred vaccines. We never imagined finding a group as large as yours in one place. You've done an incredible job keeping your group safe. Seriously."

"Thanks, Matt. From the brief story Kim told me of your adventures, it seems you've done quite an amazing job yourself."

"I have years of crisis management and combat experience, Liam. I never would've been able to do all this just out of college, like you have."

"So where do we go from here, Matt?" Liam asked. "Do we pledge our undying loyalty to you now?" Matt looked at Liam, hoping he was joking. Seeing the young man smile, Matt couldn't help but laugh despite the pain in his chest.

"Are you prepared to bend the knee, Sir Liam?" Matt asked, continuing the joke and causing everyone around the fire to laugh.

"But seriously, Matt. I hope there's a way for our groups to stay in contact and maybe work together. Kim said the estimate is almost 99% of the world has died. That means there can't be that many people left in Ireland. We need to all stick together and help each other if we can."

"Yeah, Liam. We definitely need to stay in touch and work together." Matt looked around, trying not to twist his torso too quickly. The handful of Motrin he'd swallowed back at Curragh Camp had dulled the pain significantly, but moving still sent spikes of sharp pain through his chest. "Kim, where's Dave?"

"He's over with Kevin helping to keep things organized," answered Kim. "I would think they're pretty close to being finished."

"I don't have my radio. Would you mind radioing him and asking him to bring one of the satphones from the cargo van?"

About five minutes later, Dave and LT walked over to the group sitting by the fire. Dave handed Matt a small zippered canvas bag. "Here you go, Matt. I just tested it and programmed in our two numbers and the number for the phone we gave Kevin at Haulbowline. I've noted the number in our phone as well." Matt knew inside the bag was an Iridium satellite complete with a charging cable and an externally mounted antenna to allow the phone to be used indoors. This was one of a dozen similar satellite phones they had found in the ARW compound, and unlike new phones at an electronics store, these phones were already registered and operational.

Matt took the bag and then passed it to Shane. Matt said to Shane and Liam, "Here's a satellite phone. Our three satphones are programmed into it already. This should allow us to keep in touch. We monitor our phones 24/7, and I'd suggest you do the same. So far, we've seen no real threats here in Ireland, but you never know."

The small group continued to chat around the fire, getting to know each other, while more and more newly vaccinated campus residents meandered over to the fire and began mingling in small groups with the folks from Cork. Matt couldn't help but notice that while almost all of Liam's people were in their late teens or early twenties, many clearly athletes and exceptionally fit, there were a handful of older adults and children between six and fourteen. If Liam and Shane could continue to manage this group with the discipline they'd shown that past six weeks, Matt did not doubt that these survivors would quickly establish a small community.

After about thirty minutes, Dave signaled everyone that it was time for them to go. Matt was clearly showing signs of significant discomfort, and Dave wanted to get back to Kinsale as soon after dark as possible. Kevin asked Liam to coordinate with any survivors his group identified, and he'd return when needed to provide vaccines.

As they departed, Matt quietly invited Liam to bring a small group down to Cork for the Thanksgiving celebration the moms had planned for the 28th of November. Liam said he was looking forward to it.

CHAPTER 22

November 20, 10:11 pm

Lying down hurt like a bitch.

So Matt followed the adage: if it hurts, stop doing it.

As a result, Matt was now sitting in one of the Irish Rover's overstuffed leather chairs, his feet propped up on an ottoman. Tucked under a heavy duvet, Matt read a book on the Spanish Armada's involvement in the Seige of Kinsale in 1601. Kelsey had taken the children to a bookstore in Kinsale and allowed them to choose a book to read. Christopher thought this book would be a good gift for his father, and Matt was enjoying learning about the history of the harbor where he now sat.

On the way back from Dublin, they had stopped first at Haulbowline to unload the panel truck and cargo van full of the supplies Pete's team had gathered. While there, Kevin took a moment to conduct a more thorough examination of Matt's injury. Despite not having an operational X-ray machine, Kevin was fairly certain that Matt's rib was not broken. Severely bruised and most likely cracked, but he didn't think it was broken. While not changing Matt's discomfort or level of pain, it was excellent news that meant he would likely return to normal in a week or two rather than the six weeks it would take to heal a fully broken rib.

Upon arriving back at Kinsale, Matt and Kim had gone

straight to the Raffeen House with Dave and the newest two members of their family: Mick and Caroline. Michelle was already at the Raffeen House cooking dinner with Clare, Tracy, and Judy while Kirstie and Millie entertained young Christopher and Laurie. Matt noticed that while he and Kim gave everyone a rundown on the day's events, Dave took Michelle into the den for a private conversation. Returning a few minutes later, Dave said he had something to ask the group.

"Michelle and I have talked briefly about it, and we'd like to offer to have Mick and Caroline stay with us next door. They're the matching ages of Chris and Laurie, and having them next door would allow them all to learn and play together. Matt, I know you mentioned having them bunk tonight with your kids, and while there's merit in that, I also think it might be important to give them their own space right from the beginning. We have two spare bedrooms in our cottage, and frankly, if we can make a difference in their lives, we'd like to give it our best effort."

Matt and Clare looked at Dave, realizing this could be the most heartfelt thing they'd ever heard him say. Michelle, who had just learned about Mick and Caroline a few minutes previously, had tears in her eyes.

"Of course, Dave," said Clare without hesitation. "That is definitely the best place for them, and I agree they should start living with you immediately. Thank you both for volunteering." Clare knew that Michelle often felt the odd person out, with Clare, Marvi, Tracy, and Judy all having children present and even Molly having her granddaughter. "After dinner, we should all head to your place and help set up those rooms for the kids. Tomorrow, we can go into Kinsale and find some clothes and kids' things at the stores."

They'd all eaten dinner, and Matt had decided to head off to bed early. As soon as he lay down, he realized sleeping on a regular mattress would be impossible for at least a few nights. No matter how many pillows he used to prop himself up, he found breathing quite difficult and painful. Clare and Kim both suggested he sleep on the Irish Rover.

Pete, who had accompanied them back to the Raffeen House after dropping LT, Derek, and Dylan at their homes in the neighborhood, had offered to bring Matt back with him to the Irish Rover. Matt didn't love being separated from his family, even if they were just across the harbor, but Dave assured him he'd take care of them, and the most important thing for Matt was to rest and recover.

On the Rover, Stan and Marvi had helped make sure Matt was comfortable and stocked with pillows, blankets, and a bottle of water and then had headed off to bed. Pete and Juliet had also gone down to their berths below decks while Liz had chatted with him for the last hour. She had taken to staying up quite late at night, committed to working with QuAI—writing new queries and reading the intelligence reports the AI computer spit out almost constantly. Her schedule consisted of catching a few hours of sleep from about 4-8 a.m. and then taking a longer nap in the afternoon from 2-6 p.m.

Although Matt enjoyed reading about Don Juan del Aguila's last Spanish Armada and the 100-day siege of Kinsale, the book, originally written in 1768, was a tad dull. He felt himself dozing off and welcomed the arrival of sleep.

"Matt! Wake up!" Matt heard the voice at the same time someone gently squeezed his shoulder. Swimming up from the depths of slumber to open his eyes, Matt saw Liz standing before him, framed in the light of the reading lamp Matt had left on when he fell asleep. Her voice wasn't frantic, but it carried a sense of urgency also reflected on her face.

"What's up, Liz? Everything okay?"

"Stan and my dad need you in the captain's office. It's

important."

Matt pulled his feet off the ottoman and attempted to stand up quickly. Shooting pain knifed through his chest, and he gasped audibly.

"Easy, Matt. Let me help you," Liz said, gently supporting Matt's shoulder and helping him stand.

"Thanks, Liz. Guess I forgot about the ribs." Shrugging it off, Matt followed Liz across the salon and down the narrow corridor to the captain's office just short of the bridge. Stan and Pete were already sitting in office swivel chairs. Stan pointed to an empty third chair and motioned for Matt to have a seat. Matt looked at his watch and noticed it was 4:47 am.

"What's up, guys?"

"Something interesting's happening back in the States. QuAI just intercepted satellite phone communications between the Navy staff in Norfolk and some folks at Cheyenne Mountain. The Navy's radio communication is encrypted, but when they use satphones, QuAI can often intercept."

"Okay. So what're they saying?" Matt asked.

"It seems as if The Base has just launched a very effective point counterattack in Richmond and Philadelphia. They've massed dozens of Javelins and attacked the Navy's carrier and two more littoral ships in the James River outside Richmond."

"Javelins? Hmmm, interesting. Were they effective?"

"Apparently, very effective." Matt knew the Javelin was a man-portable anti-tank missile that was fire-and-forget and extremely effective against armored vehicles and bunkers. He'd never heard of it being used against a ship, but with a range of 4,000 meters, he guessed it would be quite effective against anything within that range.

"What about the ship's CIWS?" Matt asked, pronouncing the acronym as Sea-WIZ. As former Navy officers, Matt knew

Stan and Pete would be very familiar with the acronym, which referred to the Phalanx close-in weapon system—a Vulcan autocannon capable of shooting 3,000 20mm rounds per minute to destroy any incoming missile.

"I don't know. I think maybe they overwhelmed it. It sounds like the two littoral ships are dead in the water, while the carrier took significant damage to its superstructure."

"Interesting," said Matt. "Not good for the Navy. I didn't think The Base would fight back so directly."

"The Base's attack isn't why I woke everyone up, Matt," said Liz. "It's what QuAI says the Navy admiral and the President are discussing."

"And what's that?" Matt asked.

"It seems they're about to nuke York, Pennsylvania," Stan said with an ominous tone.

"Are you fucking serious? They're going to nuke a US city?" Matt was incredulous.

"Well, they're certainly talking about it."

They all paused to collect their thoughts just as Juliet walked in carrying a tray loaded with mugs of hot coffee. Everyone but Liz took a mug and sat back in their chairs while Liz typed away at the QuAI terminal. Matt wondered what Stan must think, having personal history with both President Moravian and the admiral commanding Norfolk Naval Base. Matt knew he didn't think much of either of them.

"Holy shit!" Liz blurted, staring at her computer screen and furiously punching at her keyboard. Suddenly, the 27-inch computer monitor behind Stan sprang to life with a thermal satellite image of the eastern seaboard of the United States. "QuAI just detected a nuclear detonation centered on York, Pennsylvania."

"Jesus," said Pete. "These guys are fucking maniacs."

"Are you sure, Liz?" Stan asked calmly.

"Well, I'm sure that QuAI says she's detected a blast." Liz kept reading her screen as information scrolled across it. "She estimates it to be two 90-kiloton W76-1 warheads launched from a single missile by an Ohio-class submarine docked in the Elizabeth River inside Naval Station Norfolk. The warheads detonated above ground, thereby minimizing any fallout, and were spaced four kilometers apart and centered on York. Everything within three kilometers is gone, and everything within six kilometers is likely destroyed or burned."

"Jesus," Pete repeated.

Matt stayed silent, sipping his coffee and watching Stan stare out the window. There wasn't much to say. The man holding the title of President of the United States, who by all indications had no business being in that position, had just used nuclear weapons on his own country. With 99% of the population gone, Matt guessed the bombs likely killed a couple of thousand people at the very most, depending on how many people The Base had centralized at their new headquarters.

"Liz, honey," Stan said, just above a whisper. "Do me a favor, please. Query QuAI and ask her to display the satellite and RF signals at a radius of fifty kilometers around York, Pennsylvania, and for the thirty minutes before the nuclear detonation through to the current time. Let's see what QuAI can pull up. Please send it to the monitor behind me."

While Liz typed away at her terminal, Matt and Pete swiveled their chairs slightly to watch the monitor behind Stan. Stan sipped his coffee, focusing his gaze out the window and consumed with his thoughts.

In less than a minute, the image on the monitor changed from the thermal image of the nuclear explosion to a map of eastern Pennsylvania showing timelapse with multiple blue and red dots appearing and flickering off. A key in the bottom right showed that blue dots were RF signals and red dots were satellite calls.

"They didn't get them," said Stan. "They goddamn used nukes on Pennsylvania, and they didn't even fucking get them. They have a serious fucking leak."

Everyone in the room turned from the monitor to stare at Stan. Since Matt had known him, he could count on one hand the number of times he'd heard Stan use profanity. Stan never seemed to get rattled and was always quite proper in his speech.

"What do you mean, Dad?" Juliet asked. "You mean they didn't get The Base?"

"Yeah, Jules. Look." He pointed to the screen as the timelapse scrolled through from the beginning. "See the red dot there just north of town. It starts about twenty-five minutes before the nukes, and my guess is that it's probably not too long after The Base attacked the Navy ships. The call lasts for about five minutes and then ends. Then, five minutes later, just fifteen minutes before the nukes, another call in the same location. It lasts for ten seconds. Immediately after that, all hell breaks loose. Look at all those blue dots. Someone is sending out the alarm over the radio."

Matt sat back, immensely impressed by Stan's logic. Stan had nailed it.

"Is ten minutes enough?" Pete asked.

"Who cares?" Stan replied. "I mean, let's be real, I hope the nuke killed them all. We've seen firsthand what a bunch of goddamn savages The Base is. But in my mind, I think fifteen minutes is plenty of time for a lot of them to get outside the blast radius. Think about it. If they're only doing sixty kilometers per hour—and I assume they'd be pushing well over a hundred kilometers per hour to get away from an approaching nuke—even on city streets. They're moving at one kilometer per minute. They need six minutes to get out of the blast radius. So, I guess it depends on how fast they reacted. But the real issue is that someone in Cheyenne Mountain told them. As we thought—The Base has a mole inside the President's inner circle. No one else would have known that far in advance."

"I mean, that's good info. But do we really care?" Matt asked. "About the mole, I mean."

"Not really," said Stan. "I'm as patriotic as anyone, but Moravian has brought all this trouble upon himself. He and that jackass Admiral Cryover down in Norfolk."

"What about our situation, Stan?" Matt asked. "Any initial thoughts on what, if any, impact this morning's developments have on their search for you and me and the vaccine?"

"None at the moment. I think The Base is either neutralized, or more likely, a few of their leaders escaped, and they'll likely be replaced with even more savage barbarians. But I don't think we need to worry about The Base trying to find us. As for Moravian and his folks, only time will tell. I think coming after us in Maine was about gaining access to QuAI. We've done a lot to have QuAI appear to be completely offline. We'll know if they detect QuAI and should have plenty of warning if they pick up our scent and continue the hunt.

"Yeah, agreed," said Matt. "This latest nuclear stunt has me worried, though. If that maniac who calls himself a President is willing to use nukes so quickly against fellow Americans, would he consider using them to neutralize QuAI? He clearly sees QuAI as a threat."

"Good point, Matt. But I'm not sure he thinks of QuAI as a threat—I think he wants what minimal capabilities he thinks we've retained, and I think he wants my expertise in helping him build another supercomputer. What I've been carefully watching and have as QuAI's number one information priority is anyone attempting to access our underground data center in Charlottesville. If he sends the Army after QuAI, then I'll believe he may do something stupid to track us down."

"Well, let's hope this morning was Moravian's last stupid act. I don't mind so much if The Base and the US military keep focusing on each other. It's a complete waste of what precious life we have left on the planet, but now, I only want to be left alone."

CHAPTER 23

November 28, 1:52pm

Matt dropped back to pass with Clare rushing in from his right side. He scrambled to his left, seeing Christopher streaking down the sideline, waving his hands wildly. Matt noted Dylan covering Chris loosely but threw the pass anyway. It was a bomb, arcing high into the bright blue Irish sky. Clare crashed lightly into him, taking him gently to the ground and careful of his still-sore ribs, and they both turned to watch the perfect spiral as it floated towards Christopher. Matt thought he'd overthrown his son, but at the last second, Christopher seemed to burst forward, arms outstretched, and caught the ball with his fingertips. Dylan grabbed him, but Chris passed between the two balled-up sweatshirts they used to mark the endzone.

"Touchdown!" Chris yelled. "Touchdown!"

Everyone smiled, including Matt, who was rubbing his sore ribs. Clare was laughing as she lay on the green grass next to him. The sun was out, puffy white clouds and the fresh, salty smell of the harbor in the air, and it had turned out to be one of those fantastic Fall football days. Rory, Seamus, and Shane had been good sports and quickly picked up the rules of the game. Chris had been tossing a ball with Mick and Michael Feenan, who lived with Rosie on the farm, all week. For the past hour, they'd been playing touch football on the small soccer pitch outside Haulbowline Officer's Mess.

It was Thanksgiving day—the first holiday they had celebrated since the cataclysm began.

The Moms had originally wanted to host Thanksgiving dinner at the Spaniard Inn just above the Raffeen House in Scilly. However, as the attendance list grew, Matt felt that he didn't want everyone to visit them in Kinsale for security reasons. The Officer's Mess on Haulbowline had a beautiful restaurant with floor-to-ceiling windows situated right on the bay, overlooking Ringaskiddy and Spike Island, and easily large enough to seat a hundred guests.

Their invitation list had topped out at sixty-eight. This included the extended Sheridan clan, the Malones in Kinsale, and everyone from Haulbowline. Matt had also invited Liam, Shane, Sharon, and John, plus an additional carload of his choosing, to come down from the Sport Ireland campus in Blanchardstown.

Marvi and Molly had taken the lead in putting the huge dinner together, but it was interesting to see that Kevin and Tom both fancied themselves excellent cooks and were keen to help put the extravagant meal together. Dave had volunteered to roast a small pig from Rosie Malone's farm, and Tom and Molly had added two lambs to the feast. Unfortunately, they had not encountered any wild or domesticated turkeys, but Molly had insisted on at least roasting several chickens to provide stock for the stuffing. Obviously, plenty of potatoes were on the menu, as well as a variety of canned vegetables. Matt was most looking forward to the desserts, as more than a dozen people had volunteered to make various items.

The last week had been wholly uneventful, and Matt was truly grateful for that. He had been extremely diligent in resting his ribs and, after five days of inactivity, he'd felt appreciably better. Though still sore, he felt confident they were just bruised, and he was back to at least 90%

functionality.

In addition to the preparations for their first Thanksgiving feast in Ireland, each functional area team had made considerable progress. Dave and his security team had ventured to Kilkenny, about a ninety-minute drive northeast of Cork, to secure the armory of the 3rd Infantry Battalion. Their trip had been completed without incident, and on the way back, they had taken the scenic route to recon the city of Waterford and the coastal highway east of Cork. Kevin had accompanied Dave's team and had been able to vaccinate three small groups of survivors that they had come across on their route.

In addition to the Kilkenny trip, Kevin and Grace's community vaccination teams continued to hold ad hoc vaccination clinics in the areas where they'd posted flyers, mostly north and west of Cork City. They had ventured north to Mallow and along the southwest coast as far as Clonakilty, adding another 187 vaccinated survivors over the last week. Kevin had also made another trip back to Blanchardstown and, with the assistance of some of Liam's group, had vaccinated forty-six more individuals. Matt was quite pleased with the progress they were making in expanding the footprint of vaccinated survivors.

The most significant accomplishment of the last week belonged to Tom and Sarah, along with Pete and Liz. With help from others, the four had set up a radio repeater and amplifier at Cork Airport that extended the range of everyone's handheld radios. Anyone between Cork City and Kinsale was now completely reachable by the small walkie-talkies that they possessed in abundance. Of perhaps even greater benefit to Matt's group in Kinsale, Tom and Liz had cobbled together a wide area network surrounding Kinsale. While not linked to the internet in the traditional sense, this Wi-Fi network allowed connectivity and communication between Wi-Fi-capable devices within a kilometer's radius of Kinsale Harbor. Like what they had put together on Vinalhaven, Liz and Juliet had placed surveillance cameras on all avenues of approach to downtown Kinsale and numerous cameras throughout the town and along the harbor. The result was a command center on the Irish Rover that had day and night visibility over their entire area.

While all this was happening, Matt and Stan continued to monitor the situation in the United States through QuAI. As Stan predicted, there were indications that at least some of The Base's leadership had survived the nuclear strike. Base insurgents continued to attack and harass the paratroopers and Marines in Richmond and Philadelphia, and QuAI indicated considerable disorganization in Cheyenne Mountain. A significant portion of what remained of the federal government's leadership strongly opposed President Moravian's unilateral decisions to launch the initial invasion and the subsequent nuclear strike. QuAI had intercepted communications between Cheyenne Mountain and government officials in Hawaii, southern California, and Florida that proved a complete lack of confidence in Cheyenne Mountain's ability to govern what remained of the United States.

"Dinner, guys! Come and eat!" Dave had stepped out onto the deck of the Mess and was ringing a bell that he had found, calling everyone to come inside from the football game. Clare helped Matt to his feet, and everyone began wandering towards the open doors of the restaurant. In addition to those playing football, several other groups converged on the dinner bell—those that had wandered down to the shoreline and another large group sitting on blankets astride the football pitch and enjoying the afternoon sun.

Molly and Tom, fresh from the kitchen and still wearing aprons, stood in the wide entranceway to the mess, welcoming all the guests, many of whom were celebrating their first Thanksgiving. They greeted each person warmly, encouraging everyone to sit with someone new. Molly had been adamant that there be no assigned seating, and her goal was to get the various groups to mingle as much as possible.

Clare led Matt to a table in the corner, where he saw Kevin and Beth sitting. Liam and Kim asked if they could join them as he took his seat. Rounding out the eight-person table were Molly and Tom. Unfolding his napkin, Matt looked around the room, pride swelling in his chest. He rarely became emotional, but looking at everyone laughing and talking as they took their seats, fresh-cut flowers on every table, Matt was overcome with joy. Looking to his right, he saw Chris and Laurie sitting with a half-dozen other children at the "kids' table" under the watchful, smiling eyes of Kelsey, Kirstie, and Millie.

Matt felt his wife's hand squeeze his knee as she leaned in to whisper in his ear. "You did this, honey. We're all sitting as a family here because of you." Matt smiled, kissed her quickly, then quickly wiped his eyes before anyone could notice. He didn't trust himself to speak, so he just sat there enjoying the moment.

Ding! Ding! Ding! Someone rapped their knife against their water glass, and Matt looked around to see who it was. At the table next to Matt's, Pete stood up to the accompaniment of a chorus of people clanging knives against their glasses. Reaching down to grab the glass of water in front of him, Pete spoke in the booming voice he had perfected in both the courtroom and boardroom.

"Welcome! Welcome, everyone, to this first Thanksgiving feast here in Cork. I won't bore you with a speech, but I do think it's appropriate to give thanks for this wonderful day spent with family and new friends. In America, we traditionally celebrate Thanksgiving on the third Thursday of November, and the celebration traces its roots to the new settlers of

America sitting down to enjoy a meal with their Native American neighbors. Given today's circumstances, it seems wholly appropriate that we continue this tradition here in Ireland—all of us survivors who will need to work together to build our community, our society, so that future generations may thrive. First, I'd like to propose a toast to the wonderful people who made today happen. Molly, would you please stand up?" Molly looked around shyly, initially shaking her head before forcing herself to stand up.

"For those of you who don't know, Molly was the one who first proposed this dinner, and it is only through her diligence and hard work that we're all sitting here today. She planned this meal, organized the cooks and the food, and prepared much of what we're going to eat today." Pete raised his glass high. "To Molly!"

"Here, here!" The crowd drank and applauded as Molly quickly tried to retake her seat.

"Please stay standing, Molly. Marvi, Rosie, Kevin, Tom, and Dave. Would you all please stand as well?" Pete paused, waiting for those selected to stand. "While the rest of us have been playing football and soccer, walking along the shore, or sunning ourselves on this beautiful day, these six have been slaving away since before dawn, cooking the wonderful food we are about to feast upon. To the chefs!" Pete raised his glass again to another round of cheers. Those standing quickly took their seats as the applause died down.

"Lastly, I would be remiss if I didn't highlight one more individual. He's not one for the limelight, but I think it's important. Matt, please stand." Matt stared daggers at Pete, not wanting this attention. He sat there defiantly for a second until Clare nudged him repeatedly to stand. "Matt and I have known each other for more years than I care to recall. I know I look much younger than him, but I'm technically two years older than Matt. We met his freshman year of college and have been close friends ever since, sharing many adventures over the years. Everyone sitting here already knows that we owe our lives to this man. We each have our own tale of survival, but this man is the reason we are all sitting here today: safe, happy, surrounded by family and friends, and looking forward to what tomorrow may bring. To you, Matt Sheridan!"

Everyone began cheering loudly, and Matt tried hard to will back the tears forming in his eyes. He looked around at everyone clapping, whistling, and smiling and felt a tear slide down his left cheek. Laurie turned from her table and sprinted over to give her father a hug. Trying desperately to keep his emotions in check, Matt decided the best solution was to simply sit down and hope people would stop clapping.

"Speech! Speech! Speech!" Several people began saying, and Matt noticed Derek and Dylan leading the chant from separate tables. Clare nudged him again, urging him to stand up. Matt looked over and saw Pete and Dave laughing loudly, enjoying every moment of their friend's discomfort.

Standing up, Matt used his hands to signal quiet. "Okay, okay," he said. "Thank you, Pete. I owe you." Matt winked at his friend. "Well, look, I'm not really one for speeches. But I will say this. I am tremendously proud to be sitting here today with each and every one of you. We are the survivors. We have taken care of each other to help us through these terrible times, and because of everyone's hard work and commitment to each other, we are now seeing daylight at the end of the tunnel. And each day, that light shines just a bit brighter and the end of the tunnel seems just a bit nearer. There will undoubtedly be tough times ahead, but today is a day for celebrating not only our accomplishments but our family. We've become a family, and I feel very strongly that everything we do should be to make our family safer and stronger." Matt paused, looking around the room. "To Family!"

Another round of applause and Matt began to take his seat.

Just as he was about to sit down, he thought of one more thing he wanted to say. "I'd like to add one more thing to this first Thanksgiving tradition in Ireland. We thanked the chefs, and now they should be able to relax. In the US Army, there's a custom that the leaders always eat last. But at Thanksgiving and Christmas, the Army's leaders take this a little further. During this time of celebration, as a small symbol of appreciation for everyone's hard work, the leaders serve the meal to their soldiers. Pete, Dave, Kevin, Seamus, and Liam—would you all please follow me to the buffet line set up by our chefs? It would be our honor to serve all of you, beginning with the children first."

Matt looked down and could see tears streaming down Clare's face. Across the table, he saw that both Molly and Tom were equally emotional. Bending to kiss his wife and daughter, Matt strode over to the buffet table and donned an apron alongside his friends.

Thanksgiving dinner was served.

CHAPTER 24

November 28, 6:09 pm

The dinner had been amazing, definitely one of the best meals Matt had ever experienced. After filling himself with pork, lamb, stuffing, and mashed potatoes, Matt reached deep to find room to sample several of the delicious desserts on offer. Fully sated, Matt sat alone at the large, round table, enjoying the remaining sips of a pint glass of Harp.

Liam and Shane had taken it upon themselves to bring kegs of Guinness and Harp beer from Dublin, and with the help of Seamus and Rory, the foursome had figured out how to get the tap running in the Officer's Mess bar. Along with the full supply of hard alcohol already present at the bar, the result had been the free flow of libations to lubricate everyone's good senses.

While Matt had conservatively paced his beer drinking, the same could not be said of many of the other attendees. Dave and one of Seamus' sailors had volunteered to remain fully sober and on guard, which allowed everyone else to partake fully in the festivities. An hour ago, much to Matt's amusement, the first Thanksgiving dinner had turned into the first Thanksgiving nightclub.

Several tables had been pushed to the side to create a central dancefloor, and Matt watched as Rory stood behind a small table next to the bar, two three-foot-tall speakers on each side of him. Like every professional DJ Matt had ever seen, Rory had headphones around his neck and was fiddling with the sound system while holding a microphone. The Black-Eyed Peas "I Gotta Feeling" was blaring from the speakers, filling the room with sound to the delight of the more than forty people jumping up and down on the dancefloor. Matt smiled as he saw Clare, Tracy, and Kirstie dancing in a group with Christopher at the center showing off his dance moves. Laurie, slightly out of rhythm, bobbed up and down next to them, twirling and attempting to gain everyone's attention with her gymnastics moves. Matt laughed as he saw Molly and Tom dancing, completely entranced by the modern music, along with the much younger generation.

As the song ended and merged into the House of Pain classic "Jump Around," Matt noticed Clare extricate herself from the crowd and approach his table. Sweaty with flushed cheeks, she plopped down in the chair next to him and immediately finished the rest of his beer. *She's never looked so beautiful,* Matt thought.

"I forgot how thirsty you get dancing!" Clare said, leaning in and shouting a little to be heard above the music. Matt reached forward and pushed a full glass of water towards her, which she readily grabbed and drank half of in one gulp.

"I'm glad you're having fun," said Matt. "This is amazing. Everyone is having such a good time."

"Have you noticed everyone seems to be pairing up a bit?" Clare said, pointing to the dancefloor and giggling. "Looks like Thanksgiving might bring a bit of romance to the group."

Matt had, in fact, already noticed. He had known that several of the younger generation had been paired off for the last few weeks, including Grace and Dylan, as well as LT and Amey. However, he had noticed tonight at least two new couples that he'd previously been unaware of. "I see Kelsey and

Seamus seem to be hitting it off. They'd make a great couple. And Derek and Gianna. Am I seeing that right?"

"You most definitely are," said Clare. They both watched as Derek and Gianna jumped up and down to the song, completely focused on each other.

"That's interesting. I'm glad Derek can move on from Celeste. That was hard on him, and he keeps it all inside." Derek's college sweetheart, Celeste, had died of the Black Pox in the driveway of their farmhouse in Vermont, while Derek watched helplessly, unable to do anything for the young woman he loved.

"Yeah. I noticed he and Gianna spending a lot of time together on the voyage from Vinalhaven. They're a good fit. She's great—ridiculously smart and an amazing sense of humor. I think they both share having lost someone close during the pandemic."

"Yeah, I'm happy for them," said Matt.

"And did you see Kim and Liam?"

"What? No way!" Matt exclaimed. Clare pointed her finger to the right, and Matt saw Kim and Liam sitting at a table by themselves, completely engrossed in a conversation. "Really? You think so?"

"Oh, yeah, baby," said Clare. Matt could tell she was more than a little bit drunk.

"I see College Clare has come out to the party," Matt said, smiling at his wife. Back in Rhode Island, their friends joked that Clare reverted to her college self when she became drunk, tucking away the conservative mom personality in favor of a happy, go-lucky party girl. They called this personality "College Clare" in reference to some of the wilder stories Clare told about her days at university.

"Yep! C'mon, let's dance." Clare knew Matt absolutely hated

to dance.

"I'd love to honey, but my ribs," said Matt, pointing to his chest. "Doc says I should take it easy."

"Bullshit! C'mon. One song. The kids will love it."

Matt's resolve started to cave, and just as he was about to agree to dance, "Jump Around" ended and was replaced by a slower ballad, James Blount's "You're Beautiful." *Perfect*, Matt thought.

Rory's voice booming came over the speakers as the song changed. "We're gonna slow this craic down for a bit. C'mon everybody, grab a partner and enjoy this wonderful ballad."

"Okay, honey. I'd love to." Matt stood up and took Clare's hand, leading her to the dance floor. As they walked up, Christopher and Laurie were walking off with pouty looks on their faces. They enjoyed the fast songs but had no time for the slow ones. "Grab Chris. Let's teach them to slow dance."

Matt exchanged his wife's hand for his daughter's, leading Laurie back onto the dance floor. He put his arm around her back and held her left hand out in a classic dance pose, then began slowly turning and swaying to the beat of the music. Laurie loved it, and Matt laughed when he turned and saw Clare dancing similarly with his son. Matt twirled his daughter around, watching her giggle even louder. Around them, other couples had paired off and were dancing to the music.

The song ended, to be replaced by one of Clare's all-time favorites—"Can't Help Falling In Love" by Elvis. Laurie and Christopher had their fill of slow dancing, so Matt shooed them off and grabbed his wife's hand. It felt good to hold her and lose themselves in the music. Matt tried hard to push away all the thoughts constantly running through his head regarding security, survival, and building their community. For now, it was just the music, friends, and family.

CHAPTER 25

November 29, 8:30 am

The straight-backed wooden chairs were a bit more comfortable than they looked, and Matt sat at the table across from Stan and Dave. The yellow walls and dark wooden ceiling beams created the ambiance for the historic Spaniard Inn, and Matt admired the large model replica of what he assumed was a ship of the Spanish Armada. The clean smell of disinfectant had replaced the stale, musty smell the Spaniard had developed after two months of inactivity.

Molly had turned the Spaniard Inn's restaurant and bar area into where most of those living in Kinsale now ate their meals. Her home at the base of the hill in Scilly had many bedrooms but a very small kitchen, and Molly found it much easier to prepare and serve meals for everyone here at the Spaniard. It had become the morning gathering spot, after which everyone normally filtered out to do their assigned tasks for the day.

Being the morning after Thanksgiving, Matt assumed that almost everyone was sleeping in, as it was just the three of them at the moment. Stan had been the first to arrive and started the coffee brewing, with Dave and Matt arriving just a few minutes ago. Liam had asked for a meeting this morning before driving back to Dublin, and Matt was expecting him any moment.

Matt turned as the main door opened and watched Kim enter the dining room, closely followed by Liam.

"Morning, guys," Matt greeted them. "Grab yourself some coffee if you'd like. We just got here ourselves." Both Kim and Liam grabbed mugs of coffee from the bar and sat down at the table. Neither appeared as if they'd had much sleep, and Kim had a glow Matt had never seen before.

"Good morning, gentlemen," said Liam. "I appreciate you taking the time to meet with me this morning. And thanks again for inviting us down for Thanksgiving. It was definitely a memorable day."

"Glad you could come. I'm surprised you're up this early. Shane had the Jamesons flowing pretty freely when Clare and I left with the kids."

"Well, I'm pretty sure Shane is still lights out," said Liam.

"So, how are things at the Sport Ireland campus?" Matt asked. "Is there anything we can help you with?"

"Yeah, that's what I'd like to talk to you about," Liam replied, pausing to collect his thoughts. "As you know, we had 106 people on campus when we met you. We currently have sixty-one."

"What happened to the rest?" Dave asked. "I assume they left?"

"Yes, exactly. Fifty-five have left. Now that we're vaccinated, most of the folks want to go back to their original homes. As I think I told you, we're basically a conglomeration of people who were stranded in the Dublin area. Many are athletes, but we have quite a few foreign exchange students or university students from elsewhere in Ireland or Northern Ireland. We spent much of the last week jumpstarting vehicles and filling them with fuel so people could go home."

"I see," said Matt. "And is this good or bad for those

remaining?"

"Well, I guess it's mostly neutral. We have half as many people to do the work, but we also cut our food requirement in half."

"Good point," said Matt.

"The big issue for us now is where to rebuild. The Sport Ireland campus doesn't have any real housing accommodations. We stayed there mostly because it was so isolated. Now that we don't have to worry about the Black Pox, we all feel it'd be much better to find a proper home to rebuild. We've discussed everything from taking over a modern apartment building in Blanchardstown, to a row of flats along Phoenix Park, to even a waterfront hotel in Malahide or Dalkey along the coast."

"Those all sound like worthy locations. We'd be happy to help you scout them out if that's what you need?"

"Honestly, Matt, I asked this meeting to see if you'd be open to having some of us join you down here. I've talked with several people I've become close to over the last two months and have given this a lot of thought. I'm 22. I don't know what I'm doing, and honestly, we survived the last two months mostly on luck. I'm from the US, and while my mother is originally from Cork, she now lives with my dad in Sarasota, Florida. So, I have no geographical ties to anywhere here in Ireland. If I'm going to start fresh, I might as well start with a group of people I trust."

Liam paused, trying to gauge the reaction of Matt, Stan, and Dave, who all had their poker faces on full display. "We can be an asset to your group, Matt. I mean, most of us don't have any real skills, but we're almost all either athletes or college students, and we'd do whatever you needed us to. With so few people left alive, it makes sense to us to be part of a bigger group rather than continue forging ahead on our own." Liam stopped, this time committed to waiting for a response.

Matt looked at both Stan and Dave. He didn't need to look at Kim, as she had begun nodding her head affirmatively as soon as Liam started with his pitch. Matt didn't feel like he needed their approval, but he did notice just the slightest nod of the head from Dave and a twitch of Stan's mouth, which Matt took as a positive sign.

"Liam, we'd be happy to have as many of your group as would like to join us. I want to discuss with our leadership group and get input from your people as to the best place for you to relocate. I honestly am not sure if it would be best to have you here in Kinsale or closer to Cork, but in principle, it makes a lot of sense for you to join forces with us."

Liam smiled from ear to ear, and it did not go unnoticed by Matt that Kim's smile was just as wide. Liam reached across the table to shake Matt's hand, then proceeded to shake with Stan, Dave and Kim.

"How many of you would come to Cork?" Stan asked. "All fifty-five of you?"

"I think about thirty or so, initially," replied Liam. "But I also think maybe a dozen or more of the people who left may eventually want to come here. Most of them went to check on their families, knowing there was a 99% chance their families were dead. Some of them will stay in their towns, especially if they can find other survivors, but some will return to Blanchardstown. About half of the thirty I mentioned are foreigners, mostly exchange students."

"Where are the foreigners from?" Dave asked.

"Mmm, five are from the US, a few more from England and Scotland, two from the Philippines, one Russian, another from Sweden, from the Netherlands, and a couple more I can't think of right now. All eight of us that came down for Thanksgiving want to come to Cork."

“Shane included?”

Liam laughed. “He’s the one who brought it up first!”

“When would you want this move to occur?” Matt asked.

“As soon as possible. Shane and the others don’t mind if they never go back to Dublin.”

“Seriously?”

“Yes. We’ve survived the last two months, but it hasn’t been easy. People have had to rotate through the foraging teams, then quarantine, wondering every minute if they’ve contracted smallpox. The rest of us mostly spent our days trying to improve our living situation with the items we had. But again, every time we touched something new, we wondered if it would contaminate us. All I remember about smallpox is that it wiped out the Indians because there was often smallpox virus contained in the blankets given to them by the Army. I had no idea if this was true or if smallpox could be transmitted in fabric, but every time I opened a can of food or put up a new tent, I wondered if I had just touched something that would kill me in a few days. You not only saved our lives, but you also saved our sanity. I don’t know how people will live the rest of their lives in such fear if they’re not vaccinated.”

“We’re all ecstatic that we ran into you and your group in Blanchardstown and that it’s had such a beneficial outcome. For all of us. We obviously don’t want to force you to do anything you don’t want to, but I think it might be helpful to your group if at least you and Shane returned for a few days to help with a transition. I can talk to Kevin and Seamus, but I’m pretty confident we can send a big group up and help you move, get generators set up, or whatever you like. What do you think?”

“Yeah, I agree,” said Liam. “I think I’d like to take all eight of us back. Then, we can discuss things with our entire group and make some decisions. Those who want to relocate to Cork can do so, and for those who wish to stay in Dublin, we can help with their logistics. Then I can let you all know, which will allow you to prepare for our arrival."

"Excellent," Matt confirmed. "I'm looking forward to having you as part of our community, Liam."

Liam stood and shook everyone's hand one more time. "I'll be in touch this afternoon when we return to Dublin and I have a chance to speak with the entire group. We can then sort out the details for the move. Thanks again, gentlemen."

Kim walked out with Liam, leaving Matt sitting with Stan and Dave.

"Well, that was interesting," said Dave.

"It was indeed," replied Stan. "I never really thought about a group like that trying to survive. Everything he said makes sense. I spent some time with both Liam and Shane a bit yesterday at dinner. I admit, I was quite taken with both of them—Liam especially. I can tell you one thing: if we were back in Charlottesville, I'd hire that young man in a heartbeat for QuAI."

"Yeah, I like him a lot, too," said Matt.

"I don't think any of us like him half as much as Kim does," chided Dave. Stan and Matt laughed out loud.

"I'm happy for her," said Matt, replacing his laugh with a serious look. "After all she's been through, I'm just grateful she has an opportunity to get close to someone and maybe build a relationship."

"Agreed," said Dave. "Stan, what do you think about bringing a larger group down here. Should they set up in Cork or maybe Carrigaline, or should we move them here to Kinsale?"

"Well, my first thought was Carrigaline. It's close to

Haulbowline and on the direct path between Kinsale and Haulbowline. It's a compact town, so finding accommodations and getting some of the commercial buildings up and running would be easy enough. I also like keeping most people away from Kinsale, but maybe I'm too cautious. What do you think, Matt?"

Matt was looking out the window, lost in thought.

"Matt?" Stan repeated.

Snapping out of it, Matt looked first at Stan and then at Dave, still not saying anything.

"Did you hear Stan's answer?" Dave asked. "Or daydreaming?"

"Both, actually," Matt replied. "Stan, you bring up a good point, which we need to consider. My first reaction, like you, was to keep the new people close—but not too close. But I keep returning to something Clare mentioned the other night before bed. She said she was excited to build a community for our kids to grow up in."

Matt paused, letting his comment sink in. "We need to decide if we're all in on Ireland. If our family is all in, we should start building a community around us. If Carrigaline is the best place for the newcomers, it's also the best place for us. You asked if I was daydreaming, Dave. I was. I was thinking how—with fifty to a hundred more people—we could turn downtown Kinsale into an actual town again. We could have shops, restaurants, and even a school. I'm not saying we need to build some idealistic Utopia or anything like that, but I think if we had a larger community, we could bring some semblance of normalcy back to our lives."

Dave and Stan both looked at Matt, letting his comments sink in.

"A week ago, I would have taken a hard line about keeping a

protective barrier between our family and everyone else," said Dave. "But now, with Mick and Caroline running around our house and Michelle smiling for the first time in two months, I see Matt's point. You're right, Matt. If this is our home, we must make it a home."

"Yeah, I agree with both of you," added Stan. "But we should get Kevin's opinion as well. Seamus likely has responsibilities at Haulbowline, maybe. But Kevin will also have an opinion on building a community and may want to join us here."

"Great point," said Matt. "Why don't the three of us head up to Haulbowline and chat with him and probably Tom, Sarah, and Seamus as well? Pete's already up there, so we'll get his input too. This is a big decision for everyone."

CHAPTER 26

December 2, 11:28 am

Matt stood leaning against the side of the Cayenne parked in front of the Grand Hotel and watched the colorful hulls of the boats bobbing on the tide flowing into Malahide Estuary. This was the location that thirty-four of the Sport Ireland campus survivors had selected as the place to start fresh. As far as Matt was concerned, it was as good as any.

Malahide was a ritzy seaside village about fifteen kilometers north of Dublin's city center. Situated on a beautiful inlet off the Irish Sea, it was home to a fantastic marina, an exclusive 140-year-old lawn tennis club, and the famed Grand Hotel.

Originally built in 1835 and having undergone several rebuilds, the Grand Hotel was considered one of Ireland's top hotels. It had over 150 rooms, a couple of restaurants and bars overlooking the water, a conference center, and a fitness center. While selecting this site was not Matt's decision, having visited Malahide several times on vacation, Matt supported the choice. The place reminded him a bit of Camden, Maine.

The headcount at the Sport Ireland campus had changed a bit since their meeting with Liam after Thanksgiving three days ago, with several more people leaving and a handful of others returning. The bottom line was that twenty-seven people had chosen to relocate to Cork with Liam and Shane, while thirty-four others elected to move to the Grand Hotel in Malahide.

The meeting three days ago in Haulbowline had been interesting, and Matt was pleased that they seemed to have a collective strategy for moving their community forward. Upon initially meeting with Kevin and Pete after Liam had departed, the group consensus leaned towards having everyone settle in Carrigaline. It was nearer to Cork City and Haulbowline, and its compact layout would allow everyone to find accommodations near the town center.

Kevin and Pete pushed for everyone to live together. At the same time, Dave and Stan continued to express some security reservations and advocated keeping the Sheridan family in Kinsale with everyone else relocating to Carrigaline. Matt had remained silent for much of the conversation, knowing he would likely cast the deciding vote and wanting to hear all sides first. In the end, it came down to two critical points.

First, Matt insisted that they all live in the same community —building a new society would take everyone's effort. Second, and most importantly, Kinsale was the one place that offered everything they needed. Access to the town could be narrowed to several secure access points, the town center was dense enough to meet both the commercial and residential needs of their growing community and the deep-water harbor allowed them to keep their greatest assets, QuAI and the Irish Rover, very close by. Everyone quickly agreed with Matt's logic, and the decision was made. Liam's group would move to Kinsale.

Matt was currently waiting for Dave and Dylan to return from conducting a final clearance of the historic hotel building behind him. The two were accompanied by Rhonda, the woman who had stepped forward as the leader of those remaining, and three others from her group.

Rhonda was a handsome Irish woman in her mid-thirties,

extremely athletic, and who had been training as part of the Irish national cycling team. Very petite from the waist up, each of Rhonda's muscular thighs was the size of Matt's waist. She had served a tour in the Irish Army, and from what Matt had seen so far, she had a quiet, dominant, no-nonsense personality. While Matt had not particularly warmed up to her yet, he felt she was a good choice as leader of this group.

Yesterday, Matt and a half-dozen others had driven up to the Sport Ireland campus to help Liam and his group with the transition. Kevin and Kim had spent the afternoon assisting the Dubliners, as everyone in Kinsale had begun referring to them, preparing for their move. Matt, accompanied by Dave, LT, Derek, and Dylan, had used the time to visit Cathal Brugha Barracks and McKee Barracks in the middle of Dublin, albeit on different sides of the River Liffey.

As previously reported by QuAI and confirmed by Liam, the central business district of Dublin had been destroyed by fire. The area from the General Post Office to Trinity College and from the Docklands to Ushers Quay was nothing but charred and burned buildings. The popular areas of Temple Bar and O'Connell Street were gone. As their two vehicles approached the city center, they had still been able to smell the smoke of the charred ruins, and after one glance, they decided it was too dangerous even to venture near these areas.

Dave and his team had made short work of securing the two military barracks, and late in the afternoon, they had met up with Rhonda to check out Malahide. Matt supported her decision, although she certainly hadn't asked his opinion, and this morning, Dave and Dylan agreed to help her clear all the hotel rooms, marking any rooms with dead bodies and confirming the rest of the hotel was free of threats. LT and Derek had decided to stay on the Sport Ireland campus and ready the many vehicles the Dubliners were packing to go to Malahide or Kinsale.

As Matt watched several seagulls dive bombing into the harbor to catch fish, the satellite phone on Matt's vest began ringing. Pulling it from its pouch, Matt could see the caller was Kevin.

"Hey, Kevin, what's up?"

"Matt, we need you back here right away!" Matt could tell by the tone of Kevin's voice that he was highly energized and on the verge of panic.

"Okay. We can be there in ten minutes. Is everything okay?"

"For now, I think so," said Kevin, speaking too loudly. "Derek and LT just shot and killed two men after they opened fire on us."

Before replying to Kevin, Matt toggled his radio handset. "Dave, this is Matt. We have to go ASAP. Like right this second, it's an emergency."

Knowing that asking questions would delay him getting back to the car, Dave simply replied. "Roger. ETA thirty seconds."

"Matt? Are you there?" Kevin said into the phone.

"Yes, Kevin, I'm here. We're on our way. Is the situation secure? Anyone injured?" Matt said, keeping his voice calm. Pressing the button to put the satphone on speaker mode, he opened the driver's door, sat down, and started the Porsche. "Tell me what's happened."

"We're safe for now. Here's Kim. I need to check on the wounded." Matt could hear Kevin handing the phone to someone else, and then Kim's voice came on the line, energized but not panicked. Matt paused to put the phone in the cupholder and quickly reversed the Porsche to position it right by the entrance to the hotel.

"Matt, the situation is secure. Three of Liam's people were shot—two are dead. Derek and LT killed the shooters. They're securing the place now, and we don't see any other threats."

As Kim finished speaking, Matt heard running footsteps just before the passenger and rear door were flung open. Dave and Dylan piled into the vehicle. As soon as their doors shut, Matt floored the accelerator and rocketed out of the parking lot onto the Coast Road.

"Kim, I'm driving, and Dave just jumped in the car. Dave, there's been a shooting at Sport Ireland. I'll drive, you talk to Kim."

Letting Dave take over the conversation, Matt pushed the gas pedal to the floor and quickly sped through downtown Malahide. Three months ago, Matt would have had to crawl through town to avoid all the pedestrians window-shopping in the quaint seaside village. Today, he hit 120 kilometers per hour before slowing to make the 90-degree right-hand turn to stay on the R106. Matt knew they'd be on the M1 at this speed in less than a minute.

"Kim, listen to me," said Dave calmly and slowly. "The most important thing right now is for you to help Derek and LT with security. The three of you each have M4s, and you should be able to cover any approach to the Institute. Is that where you're at, Kim? Still on campus at the Institute?"

"Yes," replied Kim. "We're at the main building."

"Good. Now, where exactly are Derek and LT?"

"They've both moved to a position on each side of the access road, behind a stone wall on each side."

"Perfect," said Dave. "Just where they should be. Where are you, Kim? In the parking lot?"

"Yeah, Dave. The shooting happened right here in the parking lot. I'm standing here, covering the rear entrance. Kevin is about thirty meters away working on one of the wounded."

"Hold on, guys," Matt said, interrupting the call as he decelerated to take the sweeping onramp to the M50. "Kim, we're just over five minutes out."

"Okay, Matt," said Kim.

"What happened?" Dave asked. "Where did people get guns?"

"Dave, they're not our people. They just showed up. Four men in a sedan. We think they're Russian, but at least one spoke almost perfect English. He said they heard we had a vaccine and wanted to know if they could get vaccinated. After Kevin gave them each a shot, the one guy kept asking how much vaccine we had. Kevin was alarmed when the guy tried to snatch the bag where Kevin kept the vials. The other guys ran to their vehicle and came out with guns..."

Kim's voice rose as she told the story, and was getting upset. Matt and Dave both knew the trauma Kim had recently experienced in Maine and that she was likely reliving that experience as she spoke.

"It's okay, Kim," said Dave. "You can tell us more when we get there. Just stay on the line and keep an eye out. Still no threats, right?"

"Yeah," said Kim. "No threats."

Matt had been flying down the M50, getting close to 200 kilometers per hour. The exit for Blanchardstown came up quickly, the Porsche Cayenne smoothly taking the left exit and wrapping around to the N3 north. Matt stayed in the left lane, taking the first exit towards the Blanchardstown Shopping Center, and then they were quickly speeding up the hill towards the National Aquatic Center.

"Kim, we're turning into the Sport Ireland campus now. We'll slow down and check for vehicles or people who aren't supposed to be here. I want you to physically approach Derek and LT and tell them we're coming. We're in the Porsche, so don't shoot us."

All three in the Porsche kept their eyes peeled for anything unusual. They drove by the empty aquatics center parking lot, turned left towards the indoor playing fields, and saw nothing unusual. They certainly didn't see a group of armed Russians getting ready to raid the Sport Ireland Institute.

"Okay, Kim. This is us. Hold your fire."

Matt flashed his headlights, ensuring that Derek and LT knew they were friendlies. In seconds, they pulled into the Institute's parking lot. Dave reached down and hung up the satphone.

"I'll check in with Kevin. Dave, take Dylan and do what you need to secure the perimeter."

"Roger," said Dave, jumping out of the car and jogging over to where Derek and LT knelt behind a stone wall.

Matt could see Kevin kneeling and working frantically on someone on the ground. The wounded woman was lying on her back, her head cradled in Liam's lap as Liam brushed the hair from her eyes and spoke to her. As Matt approached, he could hear Liam telling her that she would be okay and not to worry.

As Matt got closer, he could clearly see that she was not okay. *About as fucking far as you can get from okay,* Matt thought. Matt laid his rifle on the ground, kneeling next to Kevin.

"What can I do, Kevin?"

Kevin looked up at Matt, nodded briefly, then went back to what he was doing. It appeared to Matt that he was preparing a needle to put into the side of the woman's ribcage. From the deep gulps of air she was trying to take, combined with the blood-soaked bandage stuck to her chest, Matt immediately deduced she likely had a pneumothorax, otherwise known as a sucking chest wound.

"Pneumothorax," Kevin said, and Matt wasn't sure if he was talking to himself or Matt. "Get a tourniquet on that thigh wound, mate. I've got the chest covered. Keep talking to her, Liam."

"You're going to be okay, Ellen," said Liam soothingly. "Trust me. Kevin here is a surgeon, and you'll be fine."

Matt pulled a combat tourniquet off his pouch and slid it expertly around Ellen's upper right thigh. Fortunately for Ellen but unfortunately for Matt, he had considerable experience putting on tourniquets over combat wounds. Within seconds, he had cinched it tightly, hating the pain he had added to Ellen as he twisted the tourniquet tight enough to stop the bleeding.

"Damn it!" hissed Kevin as he cut Ellen's fleece open, exposing her chest and abdomen. From the blood, Matt had assumed she'd been shot twice, once in the chest and once in the upper thigh. Looking down at her white skin, pale against the bright red of her blood-saturated bra, Matt could immediately see three entry wounds in her chest, from her belly button to her breast along her right side.

Ellen gulped for air, unable to get air into her lungs. Her eyes were fully open and locked onto Liam's. Moving quickly and confidently, Kevin wiped the blood from her upper chest, used two fingers to measure the right place, and then deftly slid a long needle into the side of her chest. Matt could hear the air coming out, and Ellen's breathing became less labored.

Matt sensed someone flop down beside him and turned to see Kim. "Matt, let me help Kevin. Dave needs to speak with you. I got this."

Matt looked up at her, nodding. "Hang tough, Ellen. You're gonna be okay." Matt made eye contact with Liam, who nodded back, continuing to soothe Ellen. As he stood up, he knew there was no chance Ellen could survive. She might make it through the next few minutes, but even though Kevin was a surgeon, they didn't have the facilities to perform the operations Matt knew she would need to survive. In Iraq, with the ability to get her to a combat support hospital in minutes, Matt put her survival probability with these wounds at no more than fifty percent. Here, on the grass of the Sport Institute, with no surgical theater in the country, Matt knew her odds of survival hovered at exactly zero.

Matt saw Dave walking back from where Derek and LT stood watch, so Matt decided to walk toward him and meet him halfway.

"What'd you learn?" Matt asked.

"How's it look? She gonna make it?" Dave asked, ignoring Matt's initial question.

"I don't think so. She took at least three to the chest and abdomen. Kevin's doing all he can, but unless he has a box of miracles in that medical kit, I don't think she'll make it."

As they both looked back, they could see that something had changed. Kevin stopped moving frantically and just stared down at Ellen. Kim moved up to wrap Liam in an embrace as he pressed his face into her neck. As someone who'd witnessed this scene way too many times, it was clear to Matt that Ellen had succumbed to her wounds. Without a word, Matt and Dave walked over to the Porsche, where they knew several tarps were stored. After grabbing one from the car's rear storage area, they gently covered Ellen's still body. Matt thought she looked peaceful. He shook his head slowly, thinking how unnecessary her death was. He didn't know her, but he knew that until a few minutes ago, she had been excited to move to Kinsale and start a new life in the community they were all building together.

Matt walked back over to Dave, looking around at the

carnage in the parking lot before them. Three bodies were covered with tarps, and four men lay dead where they'd fallen, uncovered, blood leaking in pools onto the asphalt.

"So what happened? What did LT and Derek have to say?" Matt asked for the second time.

"It sounds like these four guys just showed up out of the blue as everyone was loading up. All four got out of the car, none appearing to have any weapons. The one gentleman, the guy lying there closest to Ellen, asked about getting a vaccine. Kevin assumed they had seen their flyers or maybe been told by someone who'd left the campus, so he vaccinated all four of them. At that point, the main guy started asking a ton of questions about how many vials of the vaccine we had, and then he tried to grab Kevin's medical bag. When Kevin pulled back, the other three guys ran for their car and came out with AKs. They each got off a few rounds before Derek and LT, standing watch at the building's entrance, raised their M4s and dropped all four. It was over in a few seconds."

"So two friendlies died outright, and then Ellen died of wounds?"

"Yeah, that's what it appears."

"And who are these guys?" Matt asked. He turned and started walking towards the guy closest to him—the one who appeared to be the group's leader. "Dave, go check the other three for any ID."

Matt knelt next to the dead man and rolled him onto his back. The man had taken two rounds to the face and likely died before hitting the ground. He had shaggy blond hair and lifeless blue eyes and was dressed similarly to Matt in jeans and a fleece. Matt checked his pockets, which he found empty. With nothing left to search, he reached out and unzipped the zipper on the man's fleece. Underneath, the man wore a t-shirt with narrow black and white horizontal stripes. Matt was familiar with this shirt but had only seen it with bright blue stripes. *Telnyashka, I think they call it,* thought Matt. *A Russian paratrooper.*

Dave finished searching the bodies by the intruder's vehicle and came trotting back to Matt, holding several chains in his hand so that Matt could see them.

"Ever seen these before?" Dave asked.

Matt grabbed one out of Dave's outstretched hand. It looked very similar to the thin, metal dog tags Matt and Dave had worn in uniform, except these were oval while the US military's were more rectangular. On one side were stamped some letters, which Matt assumed to be Cyrillic above a seven-digit number. "Yeah, I have. Russian dog tags. Were they wearing striped t-shirts?"

"They were," answered Dave. "Two had on blue coveralls, while the third was like this guy in jeans and a fleece. They all had striped t-shirts on. White with black stripes."

"I've never seen the black stripes before. I went to the Advanced Course with a Russian guy, and he wore a blue striped t-shirt. They call it a Telnyashka. He gave one to each of us in our small group who were paratroopers. I thought it was the symbol of the Russian Airborne, but who knows?"

"QuAI will know," said Dave.

"True. Find anything else on these guys?"

"No, but I need to go search their car. Who knows what they might have."

"Okay. Do that. Their car has Northern Ireland plates, and it looks like it came from a Belfast dealer. See what else you can find. Then get Derek and Dylan to load these guys in their car. I'll get Liam and see if we can't get a move on. I want to be out of here in thirty minutes. I'd like you to drive the Russian's car south a few exits on the M50, and we'll leave it there in some out-of-the-way spot."

"Got it," said Dave.

CHAPTER 27

December 2, 8:43 pm

The pint glass full of Club Orange soda, loaded with the pellet ice Matt had always loved, was a pleasant end to an otherwise very shitty day. Matt sat back in the plush, green velour chair. He admired the room's layout: the deep violet tartan plaid carpet, the wooden tables surrounded by chairs similar to the one he occupied, an array of fake green ferns, and the dark mahogany wood paneling surrounding the bar. He was sitting in Sidneys Bar in Actons Hotel in Cork, directly facing Kinsale Harbor with a great view of the Raffeen House across the water and the Irish Rover docked out front. Around the table sat Dave, Pete, and Stan—his war council.

Since they had decided as a group that the Dubliners should reside in Kinsale, Pete had focused all his energies on readying a place to accommodate everyone. Actons Hotel had been selected for its more than 65 guest rooms and its ideal location, literally on the steps of Kinsale Harbor. Matt could throw a rock and hit the Irish Rover, and the houses on the Scilly peninsula were a thirty-second dinghy ride away.

Tom and Sarah had set up reliable electricity with two large generators, and Molly and her team had cleaned and aerated the rooms. Seamus and his sailors had provided the labor to clear some of the rooms and move whatever needed to be moved. Rory had taken it upon himself to not only set up the music in the bar area but also to make sure the bar itself was in proper working order with ice, kegs on tap, and even cans of cold soft drinks and Gatorade in the refrigerator.

The arrival of their convoy earlier this evening had not been the exciting, fun-filled atmosphere originally envisioned. Matt had called ahead to Clare and Stan, informing them of the shootout at the Sport Ireland campus and the loss of three of Liam's people. All three, including Ellen, had been part of the twenty-seven Dubliners who had chosen to accompany Liam and Shane to Kinsale.

Not only was Liam's group down to twenty-four, but they were all quite saddened and shaken from the day's events. None of the new arrivals had much in the way of clothing or supplies, so they had all been able to fit into six vehicles plus a cargo van carrying their bags and several suitcases. Everything else they had left at the campus or had given to the group moving to Malahide.

Prior to leaving, Matt had taken Rhonda aside for a serious talk. He strongly encouraged her to reconsider going to Malahide and instead to join them in Cork. Matt, Dave, and Kevin had decided to be very careful about not disclosing Kinsale as their actual base and instead simply told everyone that they were just outside Cork City. Only Liam had been made aware that their final destination would be Kinsale, and he was sworn not to mention it to anyone until their arrival. It wasn't that Matt didn't trust those going to Malahide; it was more just a matter of good operational security, or OPSEC as they called it in the US military.

Despite Matt's concerns, Rhonda was firmly committed to starting fresh in Malahide, and all thirty-three others in her group remained committed as well. Rhonda did ask if her group could keep the four AK-74s found in the Russians' vehicle, along with several loaded magazines for each weapon, and Matt was happy to oblige. Matt had also given her the satphone previously carried by Liam, with instructions on how to get in touch with him should they need anything. They had all agreed to stay in touch, and after Liam's group said their goodbyes to their fellow Sport Ireland survivors, the two groups had gone their separate ways.

Taking a long drink from his glass of ice-cold Club Orange, Matt looked at Pete across the table. "Damn, Pete, you kind of outdid yourself today, man. What you've done to this place is amazing."

"It was a team effort. Honestly, Molly and Sarah deserve most of the credit. They really brought it all together. Molly ensured all the accommodations were ready, while Sarah ensured everything else was in working order. Tom might have handled the electricity, but Sarah made sure the lights, stoves, ovens, heat, door locks, and everything else still working. She has a mile-long list of things to do, but what she's accomplished in three days is amazing. Same with the rooms. Molly made sure we had thirty rooms ready, and now, with the doubling of our labor pool, we'll be able to accomplish so much more."

"Incredible," said Dave, sipping his pint of Murphy's.

"Yeah, the teamwork has been unbelievable," agreed Stan. "Marvi was doing a lot of the work with Sarah to set up the kitchen and dining areas. All Marvi keeps saying is what a superhero Sarah is. We're very lucky to have her and Tom."

"Yeah, about that," Pete said, pausing. "We didn't discuss this the other day when we were all together with Kevin and Seamus at Haulbowline. But since I was put in charge of the Sustainability team, I made the executive decision to ask Tom and Sarah to move down here from Ringaskiddy. They each have one of the seven suites in this hotel. I've also spoken to Kevin and encouraged him and Beth to take up residence in the Charles Fort suite upstairs. I think the only people who really need to stay in Ringaskiddy are the sailors. Hope that's all right with everyone."

"Sounds like the right call to me," said Matt. "Kevin should definitely be here, and I'll talk to Seamus about his plans for keeping Haulbowline secure and operational."

"I completely agree as well," said Stan. "If this is going to be our community, everyone should have a home here."

"Speaking of that, Stan," continued Pete. "I've reserved the James Fort suite for you and Marvi. I know you want to be on the Irish Rover, but I also thought it would be nice for you to have a home on land as well. Especially seeing as how everyone else does."

"And what about you, Liz and Juliet?" asked Stan.

"Same. Although none of us need a suite. I've made sure we all have rooms. The Rover is probably where we'll stay, but it's good to have someplace a bit larger to call home."

"How many suites are there?" Matt asked.

"Seven."

"Make sure you're in a suite, Pete. It's not a perk, it's a necessity. You have a lot going on, and you may need extra room for a meeting, planning, et cetera."

Pete nodded, accepting the upgrade graciously.

"So now that we know where to put the mint on everyone's pillow, we need to discuss what we're going to do about what happened today," interjected Dave.

Matt noted the condensation on his ice-cold pint glass, taking another sip. "Agreed," he said. "Stan? Based on everything Dave and I provided to you, what do you and QuAI have for us?"

While Dave had found nothing else of intelligence value after searching the Russians' vehicle other than a single handheld VHF radio found in any electronics store, Liam had brought forth a young blonde woman named Iryna, who was a swimmer from Russia caught in Ireland on a training trip when the pandemic began. She was one of the eight who had attended their Thanksgiving feast, but with all that was happening, Matt had not had a chance to speak with her. She obviously spoke Russian fluently, and she had overheard some of what the Russians were saying to themselves during the vaccination process before the shootout. On arrival in Kinsale a few hours ago, Iryna had sat down with Stan and Liz to be interviewed thoroughly.

Stan took a drink from his mug of coffee, looking seriously at each of them around the table. "It's not good, gentlemen. I hate to start a briefing like that, but as we're all just having a drink amongst friends, I'll put that out right up front. First, I need to apologize. We learned a valuable lesson with QuAI today. As you know, with AI, sometimes it's garbage in and garbage out. When Liz, Juliet, and I have submitted prompts and queries to QuAI, especially concerning potential threats against us, we have always used the term Ireland. QuAI, in the literal sense, has interpreted this as the Republic of Ireland rather than the island of Ireland. We all know that the six northern counties of the twenty-six total counties on the island of Ireland form Northern Ireland—a part of the United Kingdom and not the Republic of Ireland. Consequently, QuAI has limited almost all of her sensor analysis to the geographical boundaries of just the Republic."

"So you're saying we missed a horde of Russians sitting on our doorstep in Northern Ireland?" Dave asked, slight frustration evident in his voice.

"The short answer," said Stan. "That's exactly what I'm saying."

"Jesus," said Dave, now getting agitated. "How many? Where'd they come from?"

Stan remained calm, the consummate professional. "Since you called us this afternoon, we've been focused on learning as much as possible. Here's what we know from QuAI. Three Russian submarines are docked at the York Dock at the port of Belfast. By the way, the blue-striped Telnyashka is worn by paratroopers; the black-striped ones are for submariners. They arrived as a group about three weeks ago - almost the same time we did. From where, we're not sure. All three ships, the *Severodvinsk*, the *Knyaz Vladimir*, and the *Yury Dolgorukiy*, belong to Russia's northern fleet. The *Severodvinsk* is a Yasen-class submarine, while the other two are Borei-class subs. They..."

"What's that mean?" Dave asked. "Yasen and Borei?"

"It means they are nuclear-powered ballistic missile submarines carrying about 130 men and dozens of cruise missiles and nuclear ICBMs."

"So bad motherfuckers is what you're saying?" Dave said.

"Yeah, you could say that."

"Well, yeah, I think we should say that. I mean, it's not every day you learn that there's 400 Russian sailors living a few hundred miles to your north. Not only can they drive down and kill us all, but they can also lob fucking cruise missiles at us. Did I miss anything? Fire-breathing dragons, maybe?"

"Calm down, man," said Pete. "Don't kill the messenger."

"Yeah, sorry, Stan. It's just a bit disconcerting that the four guys we just killed have 390 friends likely bent on finding us. And instead of motorcycles and gang tattoos, they have nukes and cruise missiles."

Dave was quiet for a second, so Stan continued with his assessment. "QuAI was able to use the Hawkeye 360 satellites to establish a pattern of their RF usage, both their handhelds and their subs maritime radios. The good news is that they appear not to be attempting to contact anyone else, as they haven't used their ship's radios in weeks. Also, good news is that their movement pattern seems contained almost exclusively to the area immediately around the port of Belfast. Until today, obviously."

"And they're not vaccinated," added Matt.

"It would appear not," agreed Stan. "I think these three subs drilled circles in the North Atlantic or the Arctic Ocean for two months, waiting out the pandemic. QuAI can't track their movements before surfacing and arriving in Belfast, but I think it's fair to assume that maybe they tried returning to Russia and found it uninhabitable. Or maybe one or more of them had engine or supply issues, and they couldn't make it home, so they selected Belfast."

"So the question for us is how much of a threat are they to us down here in Cork," said Matt. "Stan, do these subs have any ability to track us like QuAI can track them? Like, can they see our radio signals or anything like that?"

"No, nothing like that at all. Sitting along the dock, these submarines are fairly limited in what they can accomplish. They're nuclear-powered, so they will have electricity. And from what QuAI has provided in terms of satellite imagery, it appears they have established the camp in several of the warehouses along the docks and have run electricity from the subs."

"But can they still launch missiles? Even tied to the dock?" Dave asked.

"Yes, they can. However, their ability to target those missiles is pretty severely restricted. QuAI's working now to determine the current efficacy of the Russian satellite system, but otherwise, these guys are literally plotting targets using map grid coordinates."

"Yeah, well, you can have a pretty fucking fat finger when it comes to a nuke," said Dave, referring to using one's finger to point out a location on the map. In Army Ranger school, when students knew precisely where they were, they'd use a narrow pine needle to show the instructors; when they were lost, they'd use a "fat finger" hoping they were pointing somewhat near their actual location on the map. "They only need to know our general area to nuke us."

"Relax, Dave," said Matt calmly. "These guys aren't going to nuke us. Let's put ourselves in their situation. They're probably scared shitless. The world has ended while they're on a submarine. They can't go home for whatever reason—mostly because they know there is no home to go back to. So they come to the port of Belfast. They're living in a warehouse. Like Liam's group, they're probably deathly afraid of catching smallpox from anything they might touch. Maybe they've already had people get the disease and die. Right?"

"Yeah," said Dave.

"So they somehow hear about our vaccine. I'd bet money that someone from Liam's group went home to Belfast and somehow came across these guys at the port. After all, they probably stick out like a sore thumb, especially if their lights are on at night." Matt paused for a second to take a sip of Club Orange. "So anyway, they learn about Liam's group and the vaccine. And because they're deathly afraid of catching smallpox, they send four guinea pigs down to check it out—making sure one of the guys spoke English. If those guys hadn't been so aggressive, we'd probably be discussing how to give 400 Russian sailors the vaccine right now. Right?"

"Yeah," both Pete and Dave replied simultaneously.

"So, as Stan was outlining for us, these guys are definitely a potential threat, but they aren't necessarily the enemy. Not yet, anyway."

"Well said, Matt," said Stan. "Now that we know this threat

exists, we have QuAI focusing very closely on Belfast. I've also expanded her sensor monitoring to Western Europe and the North Atlantic. I don't want any more surprises."

"So what do you think, Dave?" Matt asked. "As far as security precautions? Should we be doing anything differently now?"

"We're currently monitoring the surveillance network from the bridge of the Irish Rover with a 24/7 rotation. Right now, that rotation is limited to just, quote, Sheridan family members, endquote—those from Vinalhaven. We can discuss opening it up to others, but I think we continue to maintain the secrecy around QuAI for now."

"I agree," said Stan.

"Okay," said Matt. "What else."

"Mmmm, ideally, I'd like to prioritize additional cameras on the N40 South Ring Road. That and the N28, N27, and N71, which are the three roads someone would take to get to either Kinsale or Haulbowline. I'm not sure how to do it, but if Tom and Liz could figure that out, that would give us plenty of warning should the Russians decide to venture down to Cork."

"We can work on that tomorrow," replied Pete. "I'll get with Tom in the morning and see what we can do. The cameras are the easy part. The real issue is pushing the signal back here so it can be monitored. We'll figure something out."

"The weak link is Rhonda," said Dave.

"Yeah," added Matt. "That's exactly what I've been thinking as well. If the Russians find the group in Malahide, it could get ugly."

The four of them sat looking at each other, no one having any good answer for what to do about the group up in Dublin.

"Well," said Matt. "Let's keep doing all that we're doing, and we can circle back after dinner tomorrow and see what other ideas we come up with. I'm gonna head back to Scilly and hit the rack, gentlemen. Dave, you want to head out with me?"

"Sure. Let's go see if the kids are still up."

CHAPTER 28

December 4, 9:54 am

Matt was always surprised at how green the rolling hills of Ireland remained in winter. Growing up in New England, he expected the grass to turn brown, but he knew the reality was that Ireland stayed green throughout the year. Speeding into the mouth of the River Bandon at the helm of the Hinckley, Matt inhaled the fresh scent of the sea while admiring the green hills sloping down to meet the rocks along the shore.

Matt wanted to tour the navy ships at Haulbowline and test the trip from Kinsale to Cork Harbor by sea. The chartplotter had the route at 17.05 nautical miles, and he hoped the Celtic Sea would cooperate with minimal swells. The weather was perfect: gray skies, calm winds, and the hope that the sun might show its face.

Matt sat in the captain's chair and looked to see Kim sitting beside him. Hitting thirty knots per hour in the boat, Matt always expected it to be much louder, but the incredible engineering of the Hinckley kept things very quiet in the cockpit. It was just he and Kim for this trip, as Matt felt everyone else had more important things to do today. Seamus and Rory would meet them on their arrival at Haulbowline, and he hoped to make the journey in under an hour.

As the Hinckley edged past the mouth of the River Bandon

and into the Celtic Sea, Matt turned sharply to the east and attempted to stay within a half mile of the shoreline. Kim smiled as the Hinckley knifed effortlessly through the two-foot rollers coming in from the Atlantic. As a marine biologist, Kim loved everything about the sea, and that, plus her proven seafaring skills, was why Matt had asked her to accompany him.

"How are things with Liam and his group? Everyone settling in well?" Matt asked.

"Yeah, everyone seems very excited to be part of the family. They are some exceptional people."

"I know. I've been so busy, but I want to learn more about them."

"As you suggested, Liam sat everyone down with the team leaders, and they figured out who would be best for each team. Did you know we actually have two nurses in the new group?"

"I had no idea," said Matt.

"Yeah, they're from the Philippines. They were here completing a training program so they could work in Irish hospitals when the pandemic hit. Aside from a dozen athletes and the nurses, most of the others are college students. A few of them were in graduate school."

"Hey, keep an eye out for any signs of rocks. We're pretty far offshore, and this GPS map software should be incredibly accurate, but this coast is littered with wrecks going back hundreds of years. I don't want to add to the tally."

"Roger," said Kim, reaching for the binoculars on the Hinckley's dash. The temperature hovered just below 50 degrees, but it was fairly warm in the cockpit of the Hinckley. *Nothing like driving a million-dollar boat,* thought Matt.

"Were the team leaders happy with their new recruits?" Matt asked.

"They seemed to be. Dave took Shane and several of the athletes to help with security, Kevin took the two nurses, and Pete took the grad students and one of the other students who was a computer science major. The rest were happy to be part of Molly's team, helping manage the hotel, the restaurant, and work at the farm. I actually think Kinsale is better than what we had at Vinalhaven. Don't you agree?"

"Mmmm, yeah, I think it has the potential to be much better," replied Matt.

"You don't sound terribly convincing. Is it the Russians?"

"Partly," admitted Matt. "But it's mostly sustainable energy and our lack of ability to control our environment. Vinalhaven was great in that we had reliable energy for decades. We could also completely control or monitor access to the island. Here, the upside is so much more. We can access the entire island of Ireland—including all of its resources and people. But at the same time, I'm concerned we might not be able to generate wind power in a secure location. And the Russians are just the first threat. There will likely be others—and we won't know about them until they knock on our door. Our family is already considerably outnumbered by the people we've vaccinated, and each day, we become an even smaller portion of the vaccinated survivors."

"But isn't that the point, Matt? If we vaccinate 10,000 people, we'll have the protection granted to a population of that size. Who else is out there capable of attacking us, then?

"Well, any of the 10,000 for starters?"

With that comment, Kim grew silent, and Matt knew she was thinking of her rapists at the Samoset Resort. Matt thought of trying to say something uplifting but couldn't find the words.

"You're kind of a downer this morning, Matt," Kim finally said.

"Sorry," Matt said, reaching out his hand to put it on her shoulder. "I'm actually feeling quite positive about our situation. But it's my job to look as far into the future as possible and figure out the best path for our family. A path that will protect each and every one of us. Don't want another day like the other day. Losing Ellen was such a waste. I'd rather move the entire group than risk losing one of us."

Kim looked at Matt, realizing, not for the first time, just how heavy the weight of leadership must be for Matt. Every second of every day, he worried about the future for everyone. Now it was Kim's turn to reach out and comfort Matt, rubbing her hand along the muscles of his back. "That's why we follow you, Matt. That's why we follow you."

They rode the next few minutes in silence, both scanning the sea in front of them. As the coastline turned more to the north, the small swells shifted to the rear of the boat, and Matt pushed forward on the throttle. Both engines responded immediately, and soon, the Hinckley was planning across the sea at thirty knots. They passed by several buoys just off of Roberts Head and then pushed northward towards the beach at Myrtleville, where they could see the waves crashing into the rocks.

As they progressed, admiring all of the beautiful homes and farms along the coast, Matt pointed to one building in particular, off-white in color with large bay windows along its entire frontage.

"See that place? That's a restaurant. Bunnyconnellan's. The name's hard to forget, and it was Tracy's mother's favorite restaurant."

"Interesting. Food any good?"

"I can't remember," Matt laughed. "The views were amazing, I do remember that."

Matt kept about 500 meters from the west coast as they

headed into the mouth of Cork Harbor. Roche's Point was off to their right, and as they passed Weaver's Point, Matt could see the seaward bastions of Camden Fort Meagher high up on the bluff. Fingers of rock stretched out from the fort like a long-fingered human hand, and Matt gave these a wide berth by steering the Hinckley toward the middle of the channel. Immediately passed the fort, they could see Spike Island to their north, and Matt turned slightly to the northwest to point directly at Haulbowline. Within minutes, they were rounding the north edge of Haulbowline and pulling into the narrow concrete channel that led to the main harbor of the naval base.

Amidst the several large Irish Navy patrol vessels, Seamus and Rory stood waiting for them on the dock. Matt maneuvered the Hinckley alongside while Kim helped the two naval officers secure the yacht with bow and stern lines. The Hinckley was docked right along the stern of one of the large patrol boats. Another large patrol boat, identical to the one behind the Hinckley, was docked on the far side of the concrete-lined harbor. In front of this ship were two slightly smaller ships tied side-by-side. Matt shut off the engines to the Hinckley and moved to the back of the yacht.

"Hello, Matt! Glad you could make it. How was the trip over from Kinsale?" Seamus asked.

"All good. The seas were calm, and we made great time. Just under an hour," Matt replied.

He and Kim shook hands with both Seamus and Rory, who were wearing the standard battle dress uniform, or BDUs, of the Irish Navy. Similar to the US Army's woodland camouflage pattern, the Irish BDUs were a muted mix of grays instead of greens and browns. On the left sleeve of each of their shirts was a velcroed patch with the flag of Ireland topped by the word "Ireland" lest anyone not recognize the familiar green-white-and-orange of the Irish tricolour. Seamus wore a full Lieutenant's double-stripes and star rank insignia while Rory bore the single stripe and star of an Ensign.

They began walking forward along the pier towards the larger ship, which Matt could now see was emblazoned with a "P61" in large black letters against the haze gray metal of the ship.

"This is the LE Samuel Beckett," said Seamus, leading the way. "She's the first of three offshore patrol vessels currently in service that are a significant upgrade to the Róisín-class ships we previously had. The James Joyce is across the harbor there, and the William B. Yeats was in Galway as of September. Lord knows where she is now. Two decommissioned Róisín-class ships are tied up in front of the James Joyce."

Matt looked up at the sleek vessel before him. The ship looked about 300 feet long, at least a third longer than the Irish Rover, with a low fantail raising to a tall central bridge with an even taller radar mast festooned with all sorts of electronics. The tall forecastle gave the ship a look of speed while a large domed cannon pointed forward towards the bow and proved the ship's lethality.

"Was this your ship, Seamus?" Matt asked.

"Yes. Both Rory and I were assigned to the Samuel Beckett, along with Petty Officer Cassidy and the five sailors we have remaining."

"Petty Officer Cassidy?" Kim asked. "Is that John?"

Seamus laughed. "Yeah, you know him as John. To Rory and I, he's Petty Officer Cassidy. Technically, we've all been discharged from the Naval Service, and we don't have ranks anymore, but it's just how we've always known each other."

"I understand," said Kim.

"So tell me, Seamus," said Matt. "Could the eight of you still put her to sea? How many people does it take to manage a ship like this?"

"Depending on the length of the trip, we could definitely manage it. Both Petty Officer...er, John and I have pretty much worked in every section on the ship. Rory and the others are each very well-versed in almost every component. We're a small Navy, so we get a lot of cross-training."

"What's the usual number of crew?"

"A full complement is forty-four, including seven officers. There's also ten extra bunks for trainees."

"And what kind of cannon is that on the front? Is that artillery?"

"It's an OTO Melara 76mm autocannon. Capable of firing a 12.5-kilogram shell with pinpoint accuracy up to seventeen kilometers away. The magazine holds eighty rounds and is capable of firing all eighty rounds in less than a minute."

"No shit?"

"No shit, Matt. As Dave would say—it's one badass mothafuckah." Everyone laughed as Seamus mimicked Dave's Boston accent.

"And does the gun take a large crew to operate?" Matt asked.

"No," replied Seamus. "Technically, it's a crew of three. But that's mostly for reloading and servicing. Once the magazine is loaded, the targeting and firing are completely controlled from the bridge. Here, let's go aboard, and I'll show you."

They walked up the gangway, and Matt and Kim followed the two naval officers as they wound their way through several corridors and up narrow stairs to the bridge. Matt had noticed two sailors working on the fantail while one was working on the forecastle. On the bridge stood none other than Petty Officer Cassidy or John as he was known to Matt and Kim.

"Hey, John," said Matt, shaking his hand warmly. They had shared some conversations over a pint at the Thanksgiving dinner, and Matt thought highly of the man. He was responsible for retrieving not only his wife and two children but also his neighbors Tom and Sarah, whose engineering skills were proving critically important to everyone's comfort and well-being. Kim shook John's hand as well, and the five of them stood in the spacious bridge.

The bridge itself was huge compared to the one on the Irish Rover. Matt estimated the room to be at least thirty feet wide, dominated by a dozen large windows spanning the entire width. The glass looked thick enough to be bulletproof, and it allowed a complete 180-degree view of everything forward of the bridge. Inside the room, a massive console stretched almost the entire width. Painted a very light shade of aqua blue, the console had at least a dozen large computer monitors built into it, as well as numerous other buttons, gauges, dials, switches, and joysticks. Many of the screens were currently on, and Matt could see they contained everything from maps, satellite imagery, ship diagrams, and data tables. Several leather chairs were bolted to the floor in front of various monitors, with one very large leather chair bolted high in the center of the room—clearly for the captain or officer in charge of the bridge. Rory pointed to the large monitor at the very left of the console.

"This here is the fire control system for the 76mm Melara. It's basically a video game, using this joystick right here." Matt looked and was immediately reminded of the commander's firing control on the Bradley Fighting Vehicle. "The gunner can use the radar imagery to find the target and use this camera to basically zoom in on the exact spot he'd like the shell to impact. Pressing this button, here, sends a laser to designate the exact range to target, and squeezing this other button sends the round on its way."

"17 kilometers?" Kim asked. "That's over ten miles."

"Exactly. The edge of the horizon. This can be a ship-to-ship weapon but also a ship-to-shore. There's several types of munitions, including armor-piercing and DART munitions, which offer command-line-of-sight guidance."

"Interesting. And I thought I saw a .50 cal mount on the side of the bridge, is that right? Is that the other weapon on the ship?"

"Well, yes, there are several mounts around the ship for both .50 cal and 7.62 machine guns. But we also have two Rheinmetall 20mm cannons amidships, one on each side. These require a gunner to stand and aim the cannon and are capable of firing more than 1,000 rounds per minute out to a range of 2,000 meters."

"The Samuel Beckett packs some punch," said Matt, impressed.

"That she does," replied Seamus.

"How about the engines and keeping things running? What's the cruising speed and range?" Matt asked.

"She cruises at 15 knots, with a max speed of about 23 knots. Range is 6,000 nautical miles."

"Very cool," said Matt. "I appreciate the tour."

"Thanks," said Seamus.

"We've kept her in top shape over the last two months," added Rory. "We didn't know what the future would hold for us. So, we wanted to ensure we always had this asset ready. The James Joyce is ready to go as well. We spend this morning here on the Samuel Beckett, and this afternoon, we'll go over to run systems and engine checks on the James Joyce."

"And fuel?" Matt inquired.

"Plenty of fuel. The bunkers are full, and you can see the massive storage tanks at the edge of the harbor. Those are all for us, mate," answered Seamus.

"Would you two care to join Kim and me for a cup of coffee

on the Hinckley?" Matt asked.

"We'd love to," replied Seamus. "I was going to ask for a tour. Never been on a Hinckley before."

The four said their goodbyes to John Cassidy, who was running system checks on various consoles, and made their way to the Hinckley, where Matt made everyone coffee with the Nespresso machine.

Sitting in the cockpit's lounge, Matt took a sip, then asked, "So Seamus, what would your thoughts be regarding docking the Samuel Beckett down in Kinsale?"

"Funny you should ask, Matt. Rory and I were talking about this the other night. Kinsale Harbor is definitely big and deep enough for our ship. On the one hand, it might be convenient to have it near everyone, and it certainly would provide significant security over the entire town. On the other hand, though, we'd be taking ourselves away from all of the benefits of Haulbowline. The armory, fuel, maintenance warehouse, and just the protections afforded by Haulbowline. There's a reason this is one of the oldest harbors in the world. The north-facing entrance channel completely protects everything docked inside here, no matter how bad the storm."

"Great points," agreed Matt. "I was just posing the question. I recognize that I know very little about naval capabilities, and while Stan has obviously been hugely resourceful to us, I wanted to get your thoughts as well. If you don't mind, I may ask Stan to spend a day with you both up here and learn more about what you have. He was one of the sharpest surface warfare officers in the US Navy over his twenty-year career, and I'd imagine the three of you would have a lot to talk about."

"Definitely, Matt," said Seamus. "I sat next to him at Thanksgiving and found him to be one of the most interesting people I've ever met. He knows more about naval surface warfare than I'll ever know, but I'd be honored to show him around our ships. Just tell me when."

CHAPTER 29

December 6, 12:17 pm

Matt was sitting in what had previously been called Fishers Street restaurant on the ground floor of the Actons Hotel. After a morning spent in his office aboard the Irish Rover, he was eating lunch with Clare, Marvi, and Stan, sketching out some ideas on his whiteboard. Today was pasta day, which Matt knew because yesterday was soup day. For lunches, with as many people as they now needed to feed, lunch always alternated between pasta or soup. There was plenty of both to go around; it was easy to prepare and just made sense given everyone's different schedules.

Matt had opted for the buttered egg noodles, while his other three tablemates seemed to have favored spaghetti with jarred tomato sauce. It was more nutritious than flavorful, and over the past few months, Matt had learned to eat mainly for sustenance rather than pleasure. His pint glass of Club Orange over pellet ice was the day's highlight so far.

"So, how's school going?" Matt asked Clare and Marvi. The two, along with Tracy, who had been an elementary school teacher for years, had taken the initiative to start what they termed "educational mornings" and were now holding them three days a week in one of the smaller conference rooms of the hotel. They had sixteen children, and the three moms had enlisted the help of Kirstie and Millie, aged sixteen and seventeen, respectively, to help with the classroom activities. Clare had confided in Matt that her ultimate goal was to open up the bookstore in Kinsale and encourage everyone of all ages to read.

"Very well," Marvi replied after noticing Clare had a mouthful of spaghetti. "With sixteen students and five teachers, we're really able to tailor the learning. It works out, and we have five groups of several students in each age group."

"That's great. I'm not sure even a week or two ago, I would have thought our kids would be back in any form of school. Thank you both for putting this together." Matt looked across the room to see all ten children sitting at several tables on the far side of the restaurant. They all seemed to be joking and laughing a lot more than they were eating pasta. Their carefree attitudes brought a smile to Matt's face.

The dining room was about half full, with people generally eating when it was convenient between noon and 2 pm. Matt noticed Kim and Liam sitting with a group of Dublin athletes and MIT students at the large table by the entrance and others at various other tables talking. No one sat alone.

Matt's satphone started ringing in the small bag he had set down next to his chair. While the satphone would normally ring when he was inside and somewhat close to a window, he needed to be either outside or by a window with an expansive view of the sky to get a strong connection. He grabbed the phone and thought of going to the windows, but when he saw it was Rhonda calling from Malahide, he decided to head outside. He had just spoken to her this morning, as he did most mornings, and he figured she was calling to ask another question. She was a bit rough around the edges and very direct, but he was growing to like her.

Stepping outside, he clicked the green button on the satphone to answer it. "Hey, Rhonda, how's it going."

"Hello, Matt. My name is Andrei Miskov. It is a pleasure to speak with you finally." The voice on the other end of the line was definitely not Rhonda. It was a man's voice, exuding confidence and charisma. The man spoke perfect English, but Matt detected a hint of a Slavic accent. *The Russians?*

"How'd you get Rhonda's phone, Andrei?" Matt asked, trying to keep his voice very calm and neutral. "Is she okay?"

"Rhonda was pleased to let me use her satellite phone. She's fine, of course. I was hoping we might have a conversation, you and I."

"Sure, Andrei. Is Rhonda there? I want to speak with her if I could." Matt walked over to the picture window in front of the restaurant and motioned to those inside, hoping to get Stan or Clare's attention. Stan saw him immediately, and he, Clare, and Marvi rushed outside. Liam and Kim also noticed him, and the five sprinted outside to join him. Matt covered the phone's microphone, mouthing to Liam to get Iryna, who he had noticed was having lunch at Liam's table. Liam rushed off to get her, both of them returning in seconds.

Matt looked down and punched the speaker button on his phone, allowing everyone else to hear.

"Yes, Matt. She is right here. Let me put you on loudspeaker."

"Rhonda?" Matt said, waving for everyone else to be silent.

"Yes, Matt. I'm here."

In the background, Matt heard Andrei say something in Russian. It sounded like "*selytsyav shluku*" or something like that.

"Are you okay, Rhonda?"

A slight hesitation. "Yes."

"Is everyone else safe?"

"Yes. We are all safe." The stilted and formal language

Rhonda was using was not her usual diction.

"Okay, great, Rhonda. Thanks. Andrei? Still there?"

"Yes, Matt. I am still present. Did that satisfy you? I understand that you are aware four of my men came to get vaccines four days ago. They did not return, but it is my understanding from Rhonda that they received their vaccines and left. I came to visit Rhonda, hoping that she might have more vaccines for my men. She informed me that I must speak with you to ask about the vaccine. Is this correct, Matt?"

"That's correct, Andrei. I am the one with the vaccine. Why don't you tell me a bit more about yourself? How many are in your group, and where have you been living?"

"Of course, my friend. I am happy to share. We are very many. I have almost three hundred men, including myself. We have been living in Belfast."

"You don't sound like you're from Belfast, Andrei. Where are you originally from?"

"We are from Russia. We were on a ship when the variola virus began spreading. We eventually docked at Belfast, and that is where we have been living." Matt knew the variola virus was the scientific name for smallpox.

"Are all three hundred of you there with Rhonda? Where are you calling me from, Andrei?"

"I am in the town of Malahide with Rhonda. I have a few of my men with me now, but the remainder stay in Belfast. Do you have the vaccine, Matt? It is my understanding that you are providing the vaccine to survivors. We would very much like to accept your offer and get the vaccine. Will this be possible?"

Matt looked at everyone to see their reaction to this question. He was expecting to see either nodding or shaking heads. Instead, everyone remained neutral. *Thanks guys!* Matt thought. *I guess this is why I make the big bucks.*

"Yes, of course, Andrei. We would be happy to vaccinate each of your men. I will need to speak with our doctor, who's not with me at the moment. Maybe you could stay in Malahide overnight or return in the morning, and I can have an answer for when we would be able to come to you in Belfast. It's a long trip, so it might be a few days." Matt was simply trying to buy some time and also to see how Andrei would react to the delay.

"Matt, I think receiving the vaccinations as soon as possible would be best. You can imagine our fear of the virus, and now that we know it is available, there is not a moment to waste. I am happy to come to you. I also have medically trained personnel, so if you could spare 300 doses of the vaccine, then we could vaccinate ourselves. Please let me know your location, and I am happy to drive to you now." Stan and Clare were now both emphatically shaking their heads no.

"I'm afraid that won't be possible, Andrei. I do understand your anxiety, and I promise that once I can get ahold of our doctor, we will make every possible effort to get to you as soon as possible."

"I do not think you fully understand, Matt. We would very much like the vaccinations today. By 1600 hours, please, if you will."

1600? That's not an arbitrary time. This guy knows we're in the Cork area, about three hours away.

"Andrei, I really am terribly sorry. I do not have contact with our doctor, and it will be around 1600 before I can even speak with him. It would also be irresponsible for us to travel at night. I'm sure you can understand."

There was a pause on the line.

"Okay, Matt, I am a reasonable person," Andrei said a few moments later. "I will expect you here by 1000 hours tomorrow morning. Not later than that, please. With 300 doses of vaccine."

"Rhonda?" Matt asked. "Are you still there, Rhonda?"

There was a bit of commotion on the other end of the line, and then Rhonda spoke from some distance away from the phone. "Yes. I'm still here, Matt."

"Is it okay for Andrei and his men to stay the night there with you? If you put him up two to a room, do you have enough rooms for them?" *Please get what I'm asking Rhonda. I know you're smart!*

"Yes, of course, Matt. It's only three rooms." *Yes!! Thatta girl. There are six Russians.*

"Okay, Rhonda, that's great. And please tell Ellen I have that book I promised her. Can you do that?" Another slight pause.

"Yes, Matt. I'll tell her right after this call." Stan gave Matt the thumbs up, knowing exactly what he was doing. *Good job, Rhonda!*

"Okay, see you in the morning, Rhonda. Andrei, are you still there?"

"Yes, Matt. I am here."

"I will be there by 1000 hours. Please make sure that everyone in Malahide is safe. Do we understand each other, Andrei?"

"Yes, Matt. I think we understand each other well. If you are here by 1000 hours tomorrow, everyone in Malahide will be fine, as well as everyone with you. I personally guarantee that."

"I look forward to meeting you, Andrei. I would like to hear all about what it is like in Belfast. I will bring my doctor and the vaccine."

"That is good, Matt. I will meet you tomorrow." Andrei disconnected the call.

Matt looked around at the others, his eyes settling on Iryna. "Iryna, there was one phrase in Russian in the background. Did you catch it?"

Iryna looked a bit frightened. "I think what they said would translate to 'aim at the whore's head.' Like as in, aim a gun."

"Are you sure? It's okay if you're not."

"I'm sure. They definitely used the slang word for slut or whore."

"Okay. Thanks, Iryna. That's extremely helpful." Matt looked at his watch and then made eye contact with everyone else. "Think about what you all just heard and try to remember every detail. I want to meet with the Adult Council in the dining room of the Irish Rover at 5 pm. Liam, that now includes you. I'll call Kevin, Dave and Pete. See you all in a few hours."

CHAPTER 30

December 6, 5:01 pm

"I think everyone's assembled," said Marvi, poking her head into the captain's office aboard the Irish Rover. Matt and Stan sat huddled, looking at a map on a computer monitor connected to QuAI while Liz typed away on a keyboard.

"Okay, honey," replied Stan. "We'll be right in." Stan turned to Liz. "Could you please print this screen for us, Liz? Thanks."

Matt covered his face with both hands, using the tips of his fingers to rub his eyes in an attempt to relax and release the tension. "Why do we always have to deal with fuckers like this? Huh, Stan? Is it bad luck, or is this what the world has become?"

Stan pushed his swivel chair back a few feet, looking at his friend. "I think the world has always been this way, Matt. We just used words and lawsuits, in addition to threats of violence. It's always been 'every man for themselves,' just a bit more civilized."

"Yeah, I guess you're right. I don't know why we can't all just get along. I mean, shit, we've been giving the vaccine to anyone who wants it. Now, these Russians want to force our hand."

"That's the classic security dilemma," said Stan. "If they had the vaccine, they wouldn't give it to us, so therefore they assume we wouldn't give it to them."

"I had a boss once. A great guy named General Jim Vine. He used to say that there are 6 billion Buddha-loving people in the world, and 5.8 billion of them want what we have. Many of them are willing to kill us for it."

"Sounds like a real philosopher; a truer statement has never been said."

"Okay, Stan. Let's get this party started."

Matt stood up and began walking down the narrow hallway towards the formal dining room, with Stan close behind. Liz remained monitoring QuAI. Matt could see all his closest friends arrayed around the table as he entered the room. The large table sat twelve, and all but one chair plus the seats at each end of the table were taken. Clare sat between Pete and Dave on the table's far side, along with Molly and Kevin. Seamus, Marvi, Kim, and Liam sat in the near side seats. Matt took one end while Stan sat at the other.

"Thanks for coming on such short notice, everyone. I know that each of you is doing great things in your areas, but something has happened this afternoon that impacts all of us. So I think it's important everyone has input and helps us decide as a group what we should do. As some, if not all of you, already know, I received a call from the satphone we gave to Rhonda and her group in Malahide at lunch this afternoon. On the other end of the line was a man calling himself Andrei. He informed me that he was from Russia, currently in Belfast, and had three hundred men with him. He offered to come to our location to get three hundred vaccine doses. When I said that would not be possible, he demanded that we bring him three hundred doses by ten o'clock tomorrow morning. I felt like he was conveying some veiled threats over the phone, and at one point, we overheard someone in Russian ordering someone to quote, aim at the whore's head, unquote. I told him I would be there tomorrow morning with the vaccine."

Matt paused, looking around the table. He assumed most had already heard some version of this story, but he wanted everyone to hear it directly from him.

"The other thing worth mentioning was that I was able to have a brief, coded interaction with Rhonda. I asked her to put the Russians up for the night, two to a room, and she mentioned it would be three rooms. From this, we can infer there are six Russians in Malahide. I also asked her to pass a message to Ellen, and she said she would. In my previous experience with kidnap and ransom situations, this is a tactic we use. The idea is that if the person goes along with our lie, they are confirming that we know something is amiss. Based on Rhonda's willingness to go along with what she knew to be a false statement about Ellen, I believe she was letting us know that all is not well in Malahide."

"So why give the guy the vaccine?" Dave asked.

"Great question, Dave. That's exactly the question I brought you all here to answer. In fact, there are two questions I want this meeting to focus on. First, do we give Andrei three hundred doses of vaccine? Second, what do we do about the threat Andrei and his 300 men pose to our family."

"Do you include Rhonda as part of our family?" Liam asked. "Sorry, Matt, is it okay if I just ask a question, or do I need to raise my hand?"

Matt smiled, along with several others at the table. "Liam, you're a full member of what we call the Adult Council. You can ask or say whatever you like, whenever you like."

"Okay, thank you," continued Liam. "So when you say 'family,' are you including Rhonda and the group at Malahide? Or do you mean only those of you who came over on the Irish Rover?"

"When I say family, Liam, I mean everyone in our group here in Kinsale. There are eighty-four of us here, and to me, every person is as much a part of my family as Clare, Christopher, and Laurie. That is my personal commitment to this group and this family, and I want to make sure that everyone here understands this. My goal—frankly, my only goal—is to ensure all eighty-four of us survive and have the opportunity to lead a full and productive life. That is what I wake up to as my focus each morning, and that is what I dream about each evening.

"So, to answer your question, no, I do not consider Rhonda and her group part of this family. We can't save the entire world. But I can and will do everything in my power to save everyone in this family."

Liam nodded, and Matt looked around the table. "Anyone have any thoughts on Dave's initial question? Should we give Andrei the vaccine?"

"Fuck no," said Dave, answering his own question. Matt noticed several people in the room looking at Dave sharply, including Kevin and Clare.

"Okay, Dave, let's start there. It's always easier to start our analysis from a known point rather than a fork in the road. Let's assume we do not give him the vaccine tomorrow morning. What happens then?"

"He likely starts using the Malahide people as ransom and begins killing them until we provide it, or he tortures them to try to find our location," Pete answered.

"I think you're right, Pete," said Stan. "Based on that conversation this afternoon, I agree that is likely what will happen. Andrei specifically told Matt that the people in Malahide would be safe if we brought the vaccine by 10 a.m. He definitely wanted us to infer that the Malahide folks would *not* be safe if we didn't show up."

"Is that true, Matt?" Kevin asked.

"Yeah, Kevin. There is no doubt in my mind that Andrei is holding the Malahide group hostage. He's just being nice about it for now. And honestly, let's look at it from his perspective. He sent four people to get vaccines, and they didn't return. He might think his men got vaccinated and went off to explore Ireland, but he might also think we did something nefarious to them. We don't know how much confidence he had in those men, and he wasn't giving anything away on the phone. The fact that they appeared to have a gun pointed at Rhonda, and called her a whore, leads me to believe that Andrei thinks of us as his enemy."

"Exactly," said Dave. "So if that's the case, then we should treat him the same. How about we give him vials of water and something contaminated with smallpox? That should take care of his group."

"Could we do that?" Seamus asked. "I mean, is that possible?"

"Yes, it is possible, Seamus," answered Stan. "We've kept all empty vaccine bottles and could fill them with water or saline. We could also figure out how to give him something likely contaminated with smallpox."

"I can't be a party to this," Kevin said, appearing to get upset. "I swore the Hippocratic oath, for feck's sake. We can't just go commit mass murder against three hundred people, no matter how much of a threat we think they might become."

"I agree," said Clare. "They are clearly a potential threat, but I can't condone cold-blooded murder by essentially poisoning them."

"Okay," said Dave. "Forget contaminating them. We still don't have any requirement to give them our vaccine, especially when they're attempting to obtain it through coercion and threat of violence."

"True," added Pete. "Let's look at this holistically. We've

already killed four of the Russians. By vaccinating them, are we just giving them the protection against the Black Pox that they need to travel down here and attack us? Wouldn't we then be complicit in our own destruction?"

Everyone looked around, clearly torn by the difficulty of the situation. No one wanted to be responsible for killing three hundred Russians—men who, in all likelihood, were just similar victims of the pandemic as everyone else.

"Pete makes a valid point," said Kevin. "However, I must be upfront and say that I cannot, in good conscience, be a party to administering a vaccine that I know not to be helpful. It violates my oath as a medical doctor."

"What if we give them the vaccine, and they go back to Belfast and build a productive community? What if they aren't a threat, but they become a strong neighbor to the north?" Molly asked, breaking her silence for the first time.

Matt had to smile. Molly always surprised him with her sage views on complex problems. She had completely nailed the crux of the issue. While Andrei and his group were most definitely a threat, did they have to be? Was there a path forward where Matt could turn them into allies rather than enemies?

"What do you think, Matt?" Seamus asked. "I'd be very interested in your opinion."

Matt looked around, gathering his thoughts and remembering the speech he had given Grace just before driving up to Haulbowline several weeks ago—a speech that was similar to one he had been on the receiving end from a former Army commander of his. "Well, Seamus, did you ever see the movie *Roadhouse*?"

Seamus looked at Matt blankly, but Kevin chimed in, "You mean the one with Patrick Swayze as the bouncer?"

"Exactly!" said Matt, giving Kevin a thumbs up. "Some of you have heard me use this analogy before. But basically, there's a scene in the movie when they're discussing how to handle unruly patrons. Some are advocating being aggressive, and others want to wait until a patron starts a big fight. Patrick Swayze's character has a famous line. 'Be nice til it's time not to be nice.' So, based on what I'm hearing, there seems to be some sentiment in the group that this is the stance we should take. Is that about right?"

"Yes," said Seamus. "I would agree with that."

"Yes, Matt," agreed Kevin. "I'm not sure we should label all three hundred Russians as villains just because we know four of them were bad actors."

"But do we not know that already?" Dave argued. "Four days ago, we watched three young people die needlessly at the hands of four men from this group. And remember, they weren't rapists or criminals. They weren't trying to steal things from Liam's group. They wanted one thing—the vaccine. And they were prepared to kill to get it." Dave paused to let this sink in.

"And based on what I heard with my own two ears this afternoon," contributed Stan. "This Andrei character is most definitely holding the Malahide people against their will. We have every reason to believe that Rhonda was being held at gunpoint yesterday."

"So Kevin, you'd like us just to hand over three hundred doses of vaccine and hope the Russians are satisfied with that?" Dave asked. "Hope that they'll leave us alone? Are you willing to bet the lives of all eighty-four of us on this *hope*?"

Kevin sat up straight in his chair, his face turning red. It was clear he did not appreciate Dave's question or tone. Matt decided to speak up as it was not his intention for this council to begin attacking each other.

"Okay, okay. You all have made some very good points. Does anyone have anything else they think we should consider? Any facts or assumptions that you think the group might not be aware of?" Matt paused, looking around the table to see if anyone had more to add. Seeing mostly shaking heads, he decided to press on. "I think there are two important truths that we must keep in mind when deciding how best to proceed. First, human life is precious—much more so today than before the cataclysm. As survivors, we have an obligation to attempt to preserve what little human life remains on earth, and that is why we've been so generous with the vaccine. It's not our asset to horde but rather our burden to disseminate. Can everyone agree that this should be one of our overriding principles going forward?"

Everyone around the table either nodded their head affirmatively or said "yes."

"Second," Matt continued. "We have a ruthless obligation to protect our own family at all costs. By 'we,' I specifically mean the twelve of us in this room. And when I say 'costs,' I'm not referring to money or resources. I'm referring to our own morals, our oaths, our conscience, our physical comfort, and our personal well-being. We will do what it takes to keep our family members safe and to give them the opportunity to produce future generations. Am I clear on that?"

Matt looked around again, a hard look on his face, and staring directly into the eyes of each person at the table until he knew they understood. Matt's eyes settled on Kevin before continuing. "Kevin, I have admired you from the moment we met, and your knowledge, skills, and insight are instrumental for our future. That said, your Hippocratic oath died back in September when the world decided to kill itself.

"I need to know, we all need to know, that you will always put the lives of our family above all else. And the same is true for everyone else at this table." Matt looked around the room.

"Believe me, I would like nothing more than to help three hundred sailors abandoned in Belfast who are simply trying to survive like the rest of us. But should those sailors threaten the well-being of my family, I will not hesitate one single second in killing each and every one of them in a manner, no matter how cold or ruthless, that gives my entire family the greatest chance for continued survival."

Matt paused, looking down at his hands clasped together on the table. "We've seen and done some horrific things in order to survive these past few months. Kevin, Seamus, and Liam—I'm sure you've heard stories, but you may not fully understand the depths of fear and savagery that many of us experienced or witnessed back in Vermont and Maine. Believe me when I tell you—man is a savage beast, and man's inhumanity toward his fellow man has no limits or boundaries. I am not by nature a violent man, and I will likely never sleep well at night for as long as I may live. What I have done, what I have been forced to do, haunts me. But there is never a moment that I have regretted any of the things I've done to protect my friends and family."

Looking around, Matt could see that he'd made his point. "So here is what we're going to do. Kevin, I would like you and Grace to fill eight empty vials with water or whatever substance you think will most likely pass as the vaccine. I also want you to take eight full vials of the vaccine. Find two identical small bags. Place the eight fake vials in one bag and the eight real vials in the other. Mark them discreetly and make sure I know which is which. If you'd like, mark the bottles themselves in a way that only we would know. Also, please put four hundred syringes in each bag."

"Matt, I, uh, I think..."

"Kevin, I'm not asking you to make the decision on what happens in Malahide. But I *am* asking you to support *my* decision. Please think carefully before you reply. All of you, not just Kevin. This council is important for the future of this family, to which we all belong. If you want to sit at this table, then placing the safety of this family—all eighty-four of us—above everything else in this world is a requirement for your seat at this table. This is the only oath that matters. The input of everyone in this room is important for critical moments like this, but knowing we share the same priorities is paramount to establishing the trust required by the others to accept your input."

This was something in which Matt felt he could not accept any compromise. He looked to Clare for confirmation, and as she nodded her head briefly, he knew his speech had resonated. Everyone at the table seemed to be watching Kevin's reaction, so Matt followed suit. Kevin looked around the table, casting his eyes downward as he seemed to make an internal decision.

Locking eyes with Matt, Kevin said, "You'll always have my full support, Matt. I'll put those bags together right now."

"Thank you, Kevin. Everyone else in agreement?"

Seamus and Dave each immediately said "Yes," followed quickly by everyone else nodding their heads. The unseen tension that had built up seemed to immediately dissipate from the room.

"So here's my plan, and if anyone has a comment, I'm listening. At this point, we don't know the extent of the threat posed by Andrei. I'm willing to give him every benefit of the doubt until the time, to paraphrase Patrick Swayze, that we deem him a threat and need to be ruthless. The two bags of vaccine, one real and one fake, provide me with options in dealing with Andrei on the ground tomorrow. I'm going to sit with Dave, Pete, and Stan after this meeting and come up with a plan that gives us as much flexibility as possible while also completely protecting ourselves. If all goes well, Andrei will be vaccinated and leave with enough doses to protect his entire group of three hundred. If Andrei proves to be a threat to our family, he and his team will be buried in Malahide by noon tomorrow. Any questions?"

Liam looked around, then tentatively raised his hand. Matt nodded and motioned for him to ask his question.

"What can I can do to help?"

CHAPTER 31

December 7, 9:50 am

Today's the anniversary of Pearl Harbor, Matt thought, as he parked the Porsche at the edge of the parking lot, in the specific parking space offering full view to the rooftop snipers. Matt and Dave had spent last evening finalizing the plan and notifying the team of volunteers that would travel to Dublin. Early this morning, they rehearsed everything over and over before departing for Dublin, arriving thirty minutes early to make sure everyone was in place and had proper lines of fire.

Now that they had identified their threat, QuAI had provided a plethora of information about the three hundred Russians, their submarines, their activities over the last thirty days, and even a small dossier on Captain Andrei Miskov himself. Stan, Liz, and Juliet had spent the evening querying and prompting QuAI over and over until they had built a full picture of what the team faced today, as well as the capabilities of the Russian submariners.

By narrowing down the RF frequencies used by the Russians in Belfast, QuAI pinpointed four separate radios being used by Andrei and his team in Malahide. QuAI also confirmed that there did not appear to be any means of communication between the Malahide group and the main force at the port of Belfast.

With QuAI's new information, Matt had developed a healthy respect for Andrei. Andrei, a fast-rising star in the Russian Navy, commanded the most advanced nuclear-powered attack submarine in the Russian fleet, the Yasen-class *Severodvinsk*. He had performed well enough to be selected to attend the Frunze Higher Naval School, a sign of likely promotion to Admiral, but the pandemic had derailed those plans.

As Matt and Dave put their plan together, Matt's first decision was to not meet Andrei at the Grand Hotel in Malahide. There was no way Matt was going to drive straight into the lion's den, especially knowing that Andrei and his men had all night to prepare an ambush. QuAI was able to determine that Andrei was as cautious as Matt. While Rhonda indicated that Andrei's team consisted of six men, she was unaware that Andrei had positioned a team a mile east of Malahide's town center and another team at the junction of the M50 and M1 motorways just southwest of Malahide and near the Dublin airport. These flanking elements were almost exactly where Matt would have placed his surveillance and security teams if he had been in Andrei's position.

Matt's final plan consisted of himself and twelve others and offered flexibility as well as overwhelming firepower to neutralize Andrei's team instantly should the situation warrant that. Like any plan, Matt knew it was unlikely to survive the first contact with the enemy—so he and Dave had purposely kept it simple and versatile.

The parking lot where he now stood belonged to the Tesco supermarket in Swords, the town just west of Malahide best known for being home to Dublin International Airport. It was about three miles from the Grand Hotel in Malahide and directly along the main route one would take from Malahide to get to the M1 motorway heading south. Drive five miles south on the M1, and you'd be in the heart of Dublin, while a hundred miles due north would put you at the port of Belfast with three hundred Russian sailors. In addition to being directly off the road, the Tesco was unique in that it was surrounded on two sides by a field several hundred meters across. Matt had specifically parked so that his back was to the fields, making it virtually impossible for anyone to sneak up on them from behind.

Directly to Matt's front, exactly seventy-eight meters from where he had parked his Porsche Cayenne, was the entrance to the Tesco supermarket. Built as a large box building shaped like an L, this particular Tesco offered something particularly helpful for this mission—a three-foot parapet along its entire roof length. Dave and the four most reliable marksmen in the family currently sat on the roof, including Clare, Pete, Dylan, and Liz. Their backs against the parapet and invisible to anyone on the ground, armed with both Remington 700s and HK417 7.62mm automatic rifles, these five were Matt's first secret weapon.

Matt's second secret weapon, which he sincerely hoped would not be necessary, was positioned on a warehouse rooftop directly to his right across the R125 road and exactly 146 meters away. Derek and LT had both the M240B machine gun as well as two M320 grenade launchers. From their position, the support element could lay devastating, precision fire on anyone in the Tesco parking lot while simultaneously covering every approach to the area.

Now, all that was left was for Captain Andrei Miskov of the Russian North Fleet to ruin his plan.

Matt stood in front of the Porsche with Kim, Liam and Iryna. Kevin had volunteered to accompany Matt, now fully supportive of Matt's plan, but Matt had insisted both Kevin and Grace remain in Cork. If this plan went sideways, the four of them standing in the parking lot had the highest risk of becoming casualties. Kim, Liam, and Iryna all had one thing in common—they did not have a specific skill set critical to the family's survival, whereas Kevin and Grace's medical skills were irreplaceable. Iryna was selected for this mission for her understanding of Russian, and Matt felt it was important to have at least two others on the ground with him. Kim and Liam both volunteered. While not especially important to the plan, Matt hoped that with four people, Andrei might believe this was their full team. All four were wearing tactical vests with level IV armored plates and carrying an M4 or HK416 assault rifle attached to a single-point sling and hanging to their front.

Knowing that Andrei had a surveillance team with a radio overlooking the M1 motorway, Matt's Porsche was the only vehicle that arrived at the Tesco via the M1. Dave and LT's teams wound along back roads through the business parks and horse pastures north of the M50 between Blanchardstown and St. Margaret's, skirted the airport to the north, and arrived at the Tesco without the possibility of being seen by Andrei's surveillance teams.

Looking at his watch, Matt saw it was 0955. *Go Time!*

Matt had already received radio calls letting him know everyone was set and in position. He toggled the mic on the radio stuffed into a pouch on his vest. "Dave, LT, this is Matt. I'm turning on my other radio and making the call."

"Roger," they both replied instantly. Matt had a second handheld VHF radio stuffed into one of the pouches on his vest. He planned to tape down the transmit button on this radio, allowing both Dave and Pete, who also had a second radio tuned to the same alternate frequency as this one, to listen in on his conversation. This alleviated any need for Matt to call them or signal with his hands.

After ensuring his alternate radio was transmitting, Matt pulled out his satphone, placed it on the speakerphone setting, and pressed the speed dial for Rhonda. Rhonda's answering would set his mind at ease, but he knew Andrei would answer.

Sure enough, after one ring, it was Andrei who answered.

"Good morning, Matt. I trust you are almost here?"

"Hello, Andrei. Good morning to you as well. Of course, Andrei, I told you I would be here by 1000 hours and always keep my word. We've already arrived. We're in the parking lot of the Tesco Superstore in Swords, maybe five kilometers from you at most. It's right on the R125. Rhonda and her folks know where it is because I've been here with them. Is Rhonda there?"

While Matt's tone was friendly and calm, Andrei's reply had an icy tension. "That was not the plan, Matt. You were to come to the Grand Hotel."

"Well, Andrei, I can see where there's a bit of confusion. I'm sure Rhonda has told you what a nice guy I am and how I'm always willing to go out of my way to help people. Like bringing enough vaccine for all of your people. But I think maybe the confusion is you thinking we're doing this according to *your* plan. Let's get one thing straight, Andrei, so that we never have to address this again. We do exactly what I say from here on out. And you and your men coming to the Tesco Superstore on the R125 in the next ten minutes is exactly the plan. *My plan.* Do you understand, Andrei? Please speak up now, as I do not want any misunderstanding."

While Andrei paused before replying, Matt looked at Liam and Kim, who were both smiling despite the severity of the situation.

"I think it would be best for everyone, especially Rhonda and her lovely friends here if you were to bring the vaccine to me at the Grand Hotel in Malahide as we discussed yesterday. Now!"

"I guess we still do have a misunderstanding, Andrei, and I feel I must take some responsibility for that. My apologies, sir."

"So you're saying you will come to the Grand Hotel?" Andrei

asked.

“No, Andrei. I’m saying that I guess I wasn’t clear a second ago. I *do not* care what you think is best! Is that clear enough for you? I’m willing to wait ten minutes for you and your men to arrive, at which point I will happily shake your hand, have my nurse vaccinate your men, and provide you with vaccine for all of your men in Belfast. If you are not here in ten minutes, I will assume you no longer wish to be vaccinated.” Matt pausd, enjoying the silence on the other end. “I imagine the only question you have at this point is how to get to the Tesco Superstore. If you would kindly hand Rhonda the phone, I’ll make sure she knows how to direct you. I look forward to meeting you in person.”

Matt knew that Andrei must be scrambling right now, his mind racing and trying to figure out the best thing to do. If Andrei were planning to ambush Matt on arrival, he would never come to Tesco as he’d realize Rhonda would at some point tell Matt of his nefarious intentions. It’s one thing to threaten verbally, it’s another to plot to kill someone.

“I really must insist that you come to the Grand Hotel, Matt. Immediately! It would be very bad for Rhonda and her people if you did not come here. Now it is I who is asking you if that is clear. Is that clear, Matt?"

“Crystal,” said Matt, smiling. He’d always loved the movie A Few Good Men, but never in his life did he ever think he’d have an opportunity to use Lieutenant Kaffee’s line in real life. He knew that both Pete and Dave must be chuckling to themselves. “It’s been a pleasure speaking with you, Andrei, and I’m disappointed that we’ll never get a chance to meet in person. Please give my best to Rhonda. Goodbye.” Matt pressed the End Call button on the satphone, terminating the connection. Kim and Liam had a look of astonishment on their face, while Iryna looked like she might cry.

The radio crackled. “You need me on that wall!” Dave said

over the radio, laughing as he said it. “You’re a fucking piece of work, Sheridan.”

“I couldn’t help myself,” replied Matt into the radio. “My bet is 90 seconds. What do you guys think?”

“Two minutes,” said Pete over the radio.

“No more than sixty seconds. This guy’s smart,” said Dave.

“We’ll see,” said Matt.

“That was quite a bluff,” said Liam.

“What bluff?” Matt replied. “We don’t need him, and he can’t survive without us. I’m not bluffing.”

“You would...you would let him harm everyone in Malahide?” Iryna asked.

“It’s not our fight, Iryna. I’m happy to help, but Rhonda and her people each decided where they wanted to live. I won’t unnecessarily put our lives in danger, nor would I ever expect anyone else to do that for me."

Matt’s satellite phone began ringing. He looked at his watch, noting that it had been just under sixty seconds. He let it ring a second time.

“Looks like you win, Dave,” Matt said into the radio. “Fifty-five seconds or so.” The satphone rang for a third time. Looking at the phone, Matt pressed the green button to answer.

“Hello, Andrei. Should I expect you here at the Tesco?”

“Yes, Matt. We will be there in less than ten minutes.”

“Thank you, Andrei. Oh, one more thing. Feel free to bring someone from Rhonda’s group to help with directions, but leave Rhonda at the Grand Hotel. With this satellite phone. I expect her to call me in two minutes, without any of your people present. We will not be here when you arrive if she doesn’t call. I’ll see you in ten minutes, Andrei.” Matt disconnected the call without waiting for a reply.

"Holy shit," said Liam. "That worked."

"We'll see," said Matt.

"Which bag are you giving him, Matt?" Kim asked.

"I haven't decided yet."

Matt keyed his radio. "Game time, boys. We can expect his two vehicles in five minutes or so. Seamus, keep an eye on their recon element and let Dave know if they move." Dave had placed Seamus and Petty Officer Cassidy in position by the airport to keep an eye on Andrei's motorway surveillance team using binoculars.

"Will do," replied Seamus.

"Matt," came Dave's voice through his radio earpiece. "Stan just called. The Hawkeye 360 has RF signals moving west along the R106 from the Grand Hotel. Looks like two vehicles talking on the radio as they drive. They are talking to their surveillance on the M1 as he's also getting RF hits from those locations."

"Roger," said Matt. "All as expected. Keep me posted."

Matt's satellite phone began ringing in his hand. "Rhonda?" Matt said, keeping the phone on speaker so everyone could hear.

"Yes, Matt! It's me. What did you say to him? He seemed extremely upset, but he said many things in Russian, and they all got in their vehicles and left."

"How many, Rhonda? Six?"

"Yes, six, including Andrei."

"Did they hurt any of you? Did they threaten you?"

"No, Matt. I mean, they were scary as hell. Really had us nervous all night long. They were polite but stared at the women to the point of embarrassment. Very creepy! Only Andrei spoke English well, two others had passable English. They stuck to themselves but were courteous and helpful. They even helped clean up after dinner last night."

"Okay, Rhonda. Were you able to give Ellen that message for me?" Matt knew this was a way for Rhonda to tell him if she was under duress. Matt knew there was a distinct possibility that Andrei could have left men there to keep Rhonda at gunpoint.

"Ellen's dead, Matt. I was hoping yesterday that by saying that you'd get that I felt threatened. Wasn't that why you asked?"

"Yeah, Rhonda. You did good. I'm just asking now in case you're under any duress. Did they ask anything more about their four men?"

"Yes, they did. But we told them that they were vaccinated and didn't return. I'm certain no one said anything other than that."

"Okay, great. Thanks, Rhonda."

"No, thank you, Matt. They aren't coming back, are they?"

"Hopefully not, Rhonda. Thanks for your info. I'll call you soon." Matt disconnected without waiting for a goodbye.

"Everyone hear that?"

"Roger," replied both Dave and Pete over the radio. They both knew better than to discuss anything more over the open air. What would happen now was going to be entirely up to Matt. *I actually can't fault Andrei one bit for insisting on the place of the meeting. He isn't vaccinated, and I am an entirely unknown quantity to him. Additionally, four of his men have disappeared, and he doesn't know what happened to them. I'd be a little threatening, too, if I were in his shoes.*

CHAPTER 32

December 7, 10:06 am

Matt stood silently in front of the Cayenne in the Tesco parking lot, waiting patiently for the arrival of Andrei and his team while the other three fidgeted nervously. The automatic doors to the Tesco stood wide open, and Matt could smell the sour, fetid stench of rotting food on the easterly breeze. Matt found his mind wandering to the bedtime conversation he'd had the previous evening as he tucked Christopher and Laurie in before heading back out to continue planning for today's events.

His son had told him that Mick was now his best friend, and young Christopher wanted to thank Matt for not shooting him even though Mick had shot Matt with an arrow. His son's comment hadn't meant anything to Matt last night, as he had known from the moment he saw the boy knocking another arrow that Mick was just trying to protect his sister and survive in this crazy world in which they all found themselves. *We're all just doing what we need to in order to survive*, Matt thought.

"Heads up. They're twenty seconds out. Two SUVs," came Dave's voice through his earpiece. "Turning in now. I count six men. Say again, six men."

Matt looked up and watched as the two vehicles turned into the parking lot along the open side of the L formed by the building. The arrows on the pavement directed traffic to head first toward the back of the lot, turn left, then choose a lane marked with a one-way arrow heading toward the store. Andrei's vehicle either didn't see these arrows or intentionally disregarded them, for the lead SUV entered through the marked exit, cutting in front of the Tesco building and headed directly toward where Matt stood. Both vehicles stopped side-by-side about fifteen meters in front of Matt. *Perfect,* Matt thought. *I couldn't have scripted this any better. Their backs will be to the snipers on the roof, with the angle ensuring we'll stay out of the line of fire.*

All four doors of the lead vehicle opened, while the second vehicle's doors remained closed. Matt could see a driver and passenger in the second SUV, but his attention was drawn to the man getting out of the lead vehicle's front passenger seat. Matt's mental picture of Andrei was that of Hans Gruber from the Die Hard movies, but this image couldn't have been farther from reality. The man was neither tall nor short, maybe 5'10", but appeared exceptionally fit. He was clean-shaven with hair cut military short—white-walled sides and a flattop of blond hair on top. It was the first military haircut Matt had seen since the pandemic began. He wore cargo pants and a zipped-up navy-colored fleece. The man was not visibly carrying a weapon and strode around the front of the vehicle towards where Matt stood. He moved with cat-like grace and confidence, walking right up to Matt with his hand extended in greeting. He had piercing blue eyes and a wide smile that never reached his eyes.

Matt heard Dave speaking in his earpiece. "AKs are in the vehicles, but no one is holding a weapon."

"Matt? It is a pleasure to meet you finally. Please, I am Andrei."

Matt clasped Andrei's hand and shook it warmly. Matt was expecting Andrei to attempt an overpowering grip for some reason, but he found the handshake nothing but friendly. "Good morning, Andrei. Thank you for meeting us here. Let me introduce you to Kim, Liam, and Iryna." Everyone waved as Andrei replied by introducing the three gentlemen standing in the open doors of their vehicle. He did not acknowledge the second vehicle, and Matt decided not to bring it up.

"In normal circumstances, I would prefer small talk, but obviously, we all know why we are here," said Andrei. "Would it be possible to see that vaccine?"

"Absolutely," answered Matt. "Let me grab it. I propose first that Kim administer the vaccine to your team here. Then, we can give you instructions on vaccinating the rest of your group. You mentioned three hundred, but I brought four hundred doses. I hope you will vaccinate any survivors in your area of Belfast."

"Thank you, Matt. Would you mind if I reviewed the vaccine bottle? It is not a matter of trust; it is just that I would like to see the label."

Of course, it's a matter of trust! But I don't blame you in the least. I'd do the same thing.

"Not a problem. Let me get it from the vehicle," said Matt. Matt turned and went to open the rear hatchback where he had placed both bags of vaccine vials and syringes. Matt grabbed a bag, ensuring he had the correct one, and brought it to the front of the vehicle. He took out a vial and handed it to Andrei for him to read. "Kim, would you mind injecting Andrei and his folks?"

This was all part of their plan, and Kim stepped forward as they had rehearsed. While she knew there were two bags, she did not know the markings indicating the real vaccine from the placebo.

"If I may ask, Matt. How did you acquire this vaccine? It looks directly from the manufacturer in the United States and was produced in late September, so I assume this is the most updated vaccine."

"Yes, Andrei. My family was in the United States then, and we lived in a location that received a major vaccine shipment. I was able to keep some, and I brought it with me when we came to Ireland."

"Are things as bad in the United States as here and in Europe?"

"Yes. Maybe worse. There's a lot of violence, which we haven't seen in Ireland. And we sincerely hope Ireland remains that way." At this last comment, Matt looked directly into Andrei's eyes, ensuring Andrei understood what he was trying to communicate.

"Yes, yes, of course. We all must do what we need to to survive, but I see no reason why everyone can't live together peacefully. How many doses of the vaccine do you have?"

"Well, we've been vaccinating every survivor we've encountered since we arrived. By giving you four hundred doses, we have some remaining but not a very large amount."

"I see," said Andrei. Andrei turned toward Kim. "Kim, is it? I would be pleased if you vaccinated me first and then the rest of my men. Normally, I would let the men go first, but I want them to know I am confident in the vaccine." Andrei unzipped his fleece to reveal a long-sleeved black t-shirt underneath. Unlike the four Russians at the Sport Ireland campus, he was not wearing the black-and-white striped Telnyashka. He was, however, carrying a semi-automatic pistol tucked into the waistband of his cargo pants. Matt recognized the pistol instantly as a Grach, standard issue across the Russian military.

Kim grabbed the bag from Matt and removed one of the eight vials and six syringes. Andrei rolled up his left sleeve to allow Kim to inject him. Matt couldn't help but notice a prominent tattoo on Andrei's muscular forearm depicting a red scorpion on top of a green frog. After quickly vaccinating Andrei, the three other Russians from the first SUV moved forward to get their injections. When they were vaccinated and standing back by their vehicle, Andrei motioned for the two men sitting in the second SUV to exit and receive their shot. At no point did anyone other than Andrei appear to be armed, but Matt knew from Dave's radio call that the vehicles contained automatic rifles.

As Kim rezipped the bag, Andrei turned to Matt, his fleece now back on and zipped. "How much more of the vaccine would it be possible to get, Matt? Did you bring more with you today?"

Matt looked at Andrei guardedly. "Well, that depends entirely on how much you need, Andrei. You asked for three hundred, and Kim will hand you eight vials of fifty doses each. Minus the six doses she just administered, of course. That's almost four hundred doses, and I hope you'll share the extra with survivors in Belfast. I'll also give you a satellite phone with my number programmed into it." Matt reached into a small assault pack he had placed on the vehicle hood and handed Andrei a satphone. "This will allow us to communicate going forward. As you encounter more survivors, please let us know, and we'll send a team up with more vaccine."

"Yes, thank you, Matt. We greatly appreciate this. But I am still very curious." Andrei's tone of voice seemed to harden a bit, and the intensity of his strikingly blue eyes seemed to want to penetrate Matt's skull. "How much more vaccine do you have with you now? And how much do you have in total?"

As Matt thought of the best reply, his thoughts were interrupted by Dave speaking quietly into his earpiece. "The Russians have edged closer to the AKs in their vehicles. Two of them are gripping the pistol grips. We have everyone covered should they make a move." Matt casually looked at Kim, and as he looked back to Andrei, he let his viewpoint widen to see Dave and the entire sniper element propped on the Tesco roof's parapet, weapons pointed directly at the Russians who had their backs to the Tesco.

"Andrei, you keep asking about the amount of vaccine, so I think it's important that I be very forthright and honest with you."

"Yes," said Andrei. "I think that would be best."

"First, I think it's very important that I tell you—you are not in a position of strength here. I'd like you to tell your men to step away from their vehicles and leave their weapons inside."

Andrei stiffened and attempted a laugh. "What do you mean, Matt? Are you accusing me of something?"

"Andrei, please. Let's drop the pretense, okay? We don't know each other well, but we can at least show each other the respect each of us deserves. Do you really think I would meet you in this location without ensuring my safety?"

"Matt!" Dave's voice hissed in his ear. "They're edging closer to the weapons. They look about to pounce."

"Now, Andrei," Matt ordered. "Tell your men to step away now, or you can watch them die where they stand." Matt looked hard at Andrei, then moved his eyes to the Tesco rooftop. Andrei followed Matt's gaze, seeing the five rifle barrels aimed at them. Seventy-eight meters appears much closer when the rifle barrel is pointed at you.

Andrei hesitated slightly, then hissed a word that sounded like "*Vsayuh Uspokoilis*" to his men, followed by a quick "*Shag Nazad*" or something similar. The effect was immediate. The men moved their hands away from their bodies and took a step backward. Several glanced up at the rooftop and raised their hands slightly, not in surrender but in the universal expression of meaning no harm.

"Now that we better understand each other, the second thing I was going to say is that we both know the vaccine is a tremendously important commodity. We've been very willing to provide it to every unvaccinated survivor we've encountered. That said, how much or how little I have is irrelevant to you. Unless, of course, you're planning to take it from me. Is that your plan, Andrei?"

It was now Andrei's turn to take a long, hard look at Matt. Matt could imagine that many a young Russian sailor had withered under Andrei's menacing gaze. Andrei allowed a brief smile, but as before, the smile never reached his eyes. "I like your honesty, Matt. Truly, I do. So let me be honest with you, please. While your goal is to protect your commodity and keep your safety, you also understand that learning as much about you and the vaccine is in my best interest. You can oppose me, but you cannot fault me."

"I don't fault you, Andrei. Which is why I'm being so direct with you now. You want what we have. And I'm telling you, not only can't you have it, but you don't have the power to take it from me. Let's not make this a pissing contest to see who has the bigger dick. I'm confident we can learn to be friends and help each other. We're all sharing this big island. Working together is in our best interests. Do you agree?"

Matt could tell Andrei was trying to absorb everything he had just said. This was not how the Russian thought this morning's meeting would go. Calculating quickly, Andrei appeared to make a decision. Matt could imagine that quick decision-making was a skill required of all submarine commanders, and by all accounts, Andrei was one of the best in the Russian Navy.

"Yes, Matt. I agree. We will be friends. I will return to Belfast and vaccinate my men; then, we will begin rebuilding Belfast. I will remain in contact with you, and as we need additional vaccine, I will call you."

"Excellent," replied Matt, extending his hand to shake on it, which Andrei immediately reciprocated. "And honesty, Andrei. If you have a question, please ask. If I do not feel comfortable answering you, I will tell you. But please, no more threats or deceit. We'll get along well if we're honest with each other."

"Yes, Matt. Thank you again. You have been most gracious with your vaccine, and on behalf of myself and my men, I sincerely thank you. We must go now to vaccinate our men. Goodbye." Andrei waved quickly to Kim and Liam, then raised his hand to wave at the snipers on the roof.

Andrei gave his men several brief commands in Russian, then got into the front passenger seat of his SUV. In seconds, the Russians had driven out of the parking lot.

After several seconds of silence, Matt realized he was holding his breath. Taking several deep breaths and noting the rancid-smelling air emanating from Tesco, Matt reached up to toggle his radio mic.

"All clear, Dave? Did they head toward the M1?"

"Roger, Matt," replied Dave. "They paused for a sec on the R125 just outside your view, but they are now proceeding east to the roundabout for the M1. This is a southbound onramp only, so they'll either have to do a U-turn on the M1 to head north or go south to link up with their guys at the M50 exchange."

"Matt, this is Seamus. We have the M1 in sight. We'll see if they approach. We still have eyes on the Russian vehicle at the M50. So far, they've not moved." The Russian surveillance team was parked in plain sight and normally would go unnoticed as simply an abandoned vehicle. However, with the QuAI and the Hawkeye 360 satellites, QuAI could pinpoint their specific location so Seamus could identify them.

"Roger, Seamus," Matt replied into his radio mic. "Keep

us posted. Dave, bring your sniper team down. LT and Derek remain in position until we confirm the Russians are northbound."

As Matt waited for Dave to bring his team down from the roof, Iryna walked up to him.

"Matt, I heard something, but I'm not sure it all makes sense," Iryna said.

"What? Was it something Andrei said to his team?"

"Yes. I'm sure he said: Radio Oleg and tell him to follow them. Let's go to Severodvinsk."

"Okay. What doesn't make sense?"

"Severodvinsk. It's a small city in northwestern Russia. I only know it because my grandparents are from Archangelsk, a larger city nearby."

"That's okay, Iryna. I know what it means. Thank you so much for translating what he said. It's very important."

By this time, Dave and the others came trotting from the front doors of the Tesco. Clare ran up and hugged Matt. Everyone mingled in the parking lot for a minute while Dave communicated over the radio with Seamus to see which direction the Russians drove on the M1 motorway.

Pete sidled up next to Matt and Clare. "Which bag did you give him?" Pete asked.

Matt looked at both of them, not sure he wanted to tell them but knowing he should. It had not been a difficult decision for Matt, but he knew he might regret it. "I gave him the real vaccine," Matt said. "I wasn't going to condemn 300 men so quickly just because their boss might be too aggressive."

Clare leaned up and gave him a quick peck on the cheek. "You did the right thing, honey."

"Yeah," seconded Pete. "You did. It's one thing to have to deal with them as a threat. It's another to sign their death warrants just because their boss is an asshole."

Liam and Kim had also wandered over and began nodding approvingly when they heard of Matt's choice.

"It was the right thing to do," said Kim.

"I know, but I can't help feeling I made the wrong choice."

CHAPTER 33

December 7, 1:12 pm

Behind the wheel of the Porsche and approaching the town of Glanmire, Matt pressed his foot down on the accelerator and watched the speedometer slide smoothly upwards from the steady 120 kilometers per hour they'd been maintaining for the past two hours to hover around 160 kilometers per hour. Matt could see Pete's SUV receding quickly in the rearview mirror. Clare sat next to him with Liz and Dylan in the backseat.

A few minutes after Andrei departed the Tesco parking lot, it became clear that Andrei had indeed headed north back to Belfast. The Russian surveillance team remained parked by the M1/M50 junction under Seamus' watchful eye. This was a contingency they had planned for last night.

LT and Derek immediately descended from their rooftop support position. Dave, wearing his assault vest and body armor and carrying an HK417, jogged out to the main road, where LT and Derek picked him up in their vehicle. They planned to use the backroads north of the airport to circumvent the Russian surveillance team and get ahead of them on the highway back to Cork.

Matt and the remainder of the team loaded their two vehicles and gave Dave a ten-minute head start. They then drove as a two-vehicle convoy south on the M1, directly past the "hidden" Russian surveillance team, and counter-clockwise onto the M50 beltway around Cork. They maintained a steady 120 kilometers per hour, with Matt leading them onto the M7 southbound, following the signs to Limerick, Cork, and Waterford. They followed the M7 southwest for just over a hundred kilometers, then turned due south onto the M8 headed directly for Cork.

For the entire journey, the Russian follow car attempted to maintain some visual contact while remaining out of site as much as possible. Matt had to give them credit—they were smart and well-trained. They clearly had a map with them, paper or electronic, Matt didn't know, for they would fall back out of sight along the highway where there were no exits. As soon as Matt's convoy got within two kilometers of an exit, the Russians would creep back up just close enough to see if Matt's convoy exited the motorway. The Russians fell back out of sight when it was clear Matt was continuing straight. Matt had to admit that if he and Pete hadn't been looking for them, they might have gone the entire trip not noticing.

Glanmire was a small town approximately ten kilometers northeast of Cork City and alongside the M8 motorway. This part of the motorway had two distinctions, both of which Matt planned to take advantage of. First, the motorway curved fairly sharply, creating several undulating S-curves. As Matt accelerated away from Pete, he quickly lost sight of him. Second, this part of the M8 was just north of where the motorway crossed Lough Mahon, which was a widening of the River Lee between Haulbowline and Cork's city center. While most motorways crossed a body of water via a bridge, in this case, the M8 had been tunneled to run underneath the 500-meter-wide lake.

"Stan, this is Matt, we're approaching the tunnel."

"Roger," replied Stan instantly. They had communicated several times via satphone while en route, and Matt knew that

Stan had supervised Rory and a small team of sailors set up the obstacle as they had planned.

As they approached the tunnel entrance, Matt noticed that the right tunnel, which was designated for northbound traffic, was closed to traffic, with several large signs and a couple of stationary vehicles blocking it. The Porsche's headlights immediately turned on as they entered the southbound tunnel, and after a few hundred meters, Matt began braking. They could all see the light at the end of the tunnel. Matt continued driving, and with the enlarging aperture of the tunnel's end, Matt could see stationary vehicles and a couple of orange caution signs blocking the right lane.

Matt slowed to ten kilometers per hour as the vehicle entered daylight again, the sunlight a sharp contrast to the tunnel's darkness. Suddenly, Dave and Stan were standing on the road next to the last stationary vehicle, waving for Matt to stop. Matt braked and left the Porsche in the middle of the road, turning to put the nose right up against the twenty-foot tall vertical steel wall that formed both sides of the funnel leading into and out of the tunnel. With the rear of the Porsche sticking into the travel lane, there was perhaps just enough room for a single car to pass.

"Everybody out!" Matt said. "Quickly! We have less than a minute to get into positions. You all know your roles."

Dylan, Liz, and Clare grabbed their Remington 700s and sprinted southbound, heading for where the steel retaining wall sloped down to meet the road. A few feet up that hill waited one of Rory's men, waving to them. Matt sprinted around the rear of the Porsche and took up a position behind the cars closest to the tunnel exit, sitting down next to Dave, LT, and Rory to form what they were referring to as the close-in assault team. Stan remained at the head of the line of parked cars, immediately adjacent to the small gap left between the rear of the Porsche and the last parked car, maybe thirty meters into the sunlight from the actual tunnel entrance.

"Hey, man. All set?" Matt asked Dave, putting out his fist, which Dave promptly bumped with his own.

"All good, brother. These fuckers aren't gonna know what hit them."

Thirty seconds later, they could hear Pete's SUV throttling into the tunnel from the north. Matt had been specific in telling Pete to keep his speed up to at least 100 kilometers per hour. He wanted to increase the gap as much as possible between Pete's vehicle and the Russians. With the power out, the tunnel was pitch black. He was betting that the Russians would intentionally slow their pace rather than turn on their headlights for fear of giving themselves away.

Matt watched as Pete's SUV glided past, rapidly decelerating. Stan jumped up and guided Pete's vehicle into a position behind the Porsche Cayenne so that it completely blocked all traffic heading south. The Russians were, in essence, driving right into an artificial cul-de-sac created by the row of parked cars. Everyone in Pete's vehicle bailed out with their kit and weapons, taking up a position in groups of two behind the engine blocks of each parked car. Pete and Stan were behind one vehicle, while Kim and Liam were positioned at another. Each group aimed their assault rifles across the hood of their vehicles and directly at the opening of the tunnel. Iryna, the odd person out, had been given strict instructions to hide behind a vehicle's front wheel and keep her head down. She seemed all too happy to comply. In the middle of all of them was Derek, standing behind the M240B machine gun propped up on its front bipod legs on the hood of an SUV.

With everyone in place, the result was a perfect L-shaped ambush. At the base of the L stood the 'base of fire' element of Stan and Pete's group, with Clare and Dylan acting as snipers from their elevated position and able to fire directly over Stan and Pete's heads into the oncoming vehicle. The goal here was not to kill the Russians outright but rather to force them to a screeching halt when they realized they were looking down the barrels of a half-dozen automatic rifles.

"Here they come," said Dave on the radio net. "Hold your fire. I'll be the first to fire if necessary." They waited and could hear the noise of an approaching vehicle engine echo through the tunnel, marking its approach. Kneeling on the ground at the rear bumper of a vehicle, Matt waited, ready to spring forward. The engine noise grew louder, and the sound of tires on the pavement added to the symphony of the approaching car.

A gray sedan, Matt thought maybe a Mercedes, rushed out of the tunnel and immediately slammed on its brakes—hard. The anti-lock braking system kicked in, and the vehicle bucked forward and backward quickly.

"Now, now, now!" Dave yelled. He screamed as he ran out from his covered position, and Matt jumped to his feet to follow him. LT and Rory followed suit, all four yelling at the top of their lungs, along with everyone in the base of fire element.

"Stop! Stop! Stop!"

"Hands up! Hands up!"

The key to success for any ambush is what's called 'violence of action.' Surprise, shock, and overwhelming fire superiority are what win ambushes. In this case, as their intention was not to kill the Russians if possible, the shock and awe factor was Dave, Matt, LT, and Rory running full speed up to the side of the Russian vehicle. Dave and Matt were aggressively banging the barrels of their rifles into the passenger windows of the vehicle.

"Get out of the fucking car!" Dave screamed. "Open the fucking door! Open it now!" He kept screaming over and over. Matt was similarly screaming while simultaneously watching the reactions of the Russians. Should any of them attempt to bring a weapon to bear, Matt and Dave were going to put bullets into them from point-blank range.

The Russians had no earthly idea what was happening. One minute, they were driving into the bright light after riding through the tunnel, and the next moment, the two Russians were thrown forward into their seatbelts, and men with guns were screaming at them and banging on the window.

The Russians did what any sane person in their situation would do: they raised their hands high in the air.

Things calmed down immediately when everyone stopped yelling. So far, so good. The ambush had been a success.

"Get out of the car!" Dave yelled, tapping the barrel of his M4 against the driver's window and motioning for him to get out of the car.

"You two go around and pull the other guy out," Matt said to LT and Rory. Matt stood where he was and covered both Russians with his rifle. In seconds, both men were out and kneeling on the ground in front of their sedan, hands laced behind their necks. LT stood behind one while Dave stood behind the other, their M4s held at the low ready. Dave quickly leaned over and frisked each man, ensuring neither was carrying a weapon.

Matt let his M4 fall to hang by its sling and strode forward to stand directly in front of the Russians, taking deep breaths to reduce the adrenalin flowing through his body. "Do either of you speak English?" Matt asked, his voice calm and clear.

Both men looked up at him. Matt saw that each man wore the black-and-white striped Telnyashka t-shirt common to Russian submariners.

"Gentlemen? This will be so much easier if you admit you speak English. If you don't, I will find a tablet that can translate, but it means you will both spend an awfully long time on your knees kneeling on this hard pavement."

By this time, Stan, Pete, and Iryna had gathered around the Russians, standing behind them. Matt could tell Iryna was willing to translate, but he wanted to keep her knowledge of Russian a secret. It had already helped them twice. Who knows how many more times her fluency in Russian would come in handy?

"I'm finding it difficult to believe Andrei sent two trusted sailors to spy on us without having any knowledge of English. Is that possible?"

"Da," said one of the Russians, the man they had pulled out of the passenger seat. "I mean, yes, I do speak English." His accent was significant, but he seemed fairly fluent.

"Excellent," said Matt. "Let's get right to the point. Why are you following us?"

Both men remained silent.

"Did you not understand the question? What's your name?"

"Oleg," the man said. "My name is Oleg."

"And your friend?" Matt asked. "What's his name?"

"My name is Gregor," the second man said proudly. His accent was even more severe, and Matt made the snap assumption that Gregor probably understood a good deal more English than he could speak.

"Okay, gentlemen. My name is Matt, but something tells me you already knew that. Why are you following us?"

Silence.

"Listen carefully, Oleg and Gregor. I just finished meeting with your boss, Andrei. You unfortunately weren't present for that meeting, so you likely aren't aware of the foundation we established for the relationship to continue between our groups. As I told Andrei, I am a straightforward person. I don't threaten, and I keep my word." Matt paused to let his words sink in with both men. "Andrei and I also agreed to be honest and to refrain from deceit. Do you understand the word 'deceit'?"

"Yes," said Oleg, but Gregor didn't seem so sure.

"It's means sneaky, Gregor. Like hiding things. Or maybe following us on the road in a way that we don't know. Do you understand now?"

Both men nodded affirmatively.

"So I'll ask again, why are you following us?"

Continued silence.

"Okay," said Matt. "I guess there is one other thing that you may not understand, as you weren't present at the meeting between me and your boss. I am not a patient man. At all. Please nod that you understand that." Both men nodded. "So I will ask you one final time, as I have other things to do with my day. If you do not answer me, I will simply assume that you are following us with the plan to kill me and my family. I will nod to the two gentlemen standing behind you, and they will put a 5.56-millimeter bullet in each of your brains. We will leave you lying here on the road and continue on our journey." Matt looked at his watch for effect. "I have quite a few things to do today, gentlemen. So, for the last time, why are you following us?"

"We were told to follow you to see where you went," Oleg spoke quickly. "We were then to return back to Belfast. We were told not to harm any of you. We are not vaccinated yet. So we do not want any interaction. Please. I tell you the truth."

"Excellent," said Matt, smiling. "That wasn't so difficult now, was it? Please, stand up. Both of you." Matt reached down and helped the men to their feet. "You are both free to return to

Belfast. And I urge you to go directly to Belfast, both so that you may receive your vaccination but also so that you may pass a message to Andrei. Tell him that I will forgive this first breach of our trust. The next time, I will take it as a personal attack and be forced to deal with it ruthlessly. And by ruthlessly, think Josef Stalin. Do you understand?"

"Yes," stammered Oleg, fear evident in his eyes.

"Great," Matt continued, still smiling. "I look forward to seeing both of you under better circumstances next time. Have a safe trip back to Belfast."

When both men realized the conversation was over, they turned around and returned to their car. Gregor immediately put the Mercedes in gear and executed a three-point turn to reverse direction. They sped off into the tunnel.

CHAPTER 34

December 7, 7:39 pm

The meeting with the family's Adult Council had just ended, and Matt couldn't sit in the chair any longer. It wasn't that the plush leather chairs of the Irish Rover's dining room were uncomfortable; it was simply that he was sick of meetings and just wanted to relax. Clare and most of the others had just departed, and she and Michelle were heading to Scilly to get the kids ready for bed. Matt and Dave promised they'd be over within an hour to give the children a good night kiss and maybe read them a story or two before they turned out the lights.

Matt approached the birch-paneled bar and grabbed two beers from the refrigerator. *Huh, Stella Artois,* he read to himself. Matt really couldn't care what brand it was as long as it was cold. He had always enjoyed an Irish stout, but nothing beat a crisp, cold lager or pilsner.

"Grab two more, would you?" Stan said as he and Pete walked into the room. They had previously left the Adult Council meeting a bit early to do some work with QuAI.

The Adult Council meeting went as expected, although it took longer than Matt had hoped. He felt it was extremely important to keep everyone informed, starting with the Adult Council. From there, he felt confident the information would flow out quickly and informally to each member of their extended family.

The first question everyone had asked once assembled was which version of the vaccine Matt had given Andrei. *And by everyone, I mean Kevin,* Matt thought. At first, Matt considered not telling them, but in the end, he decided that while it was his decision to make, it was everyone's right to know.

"I gave him the full vaccine. All four hundred doses." This comment was met by smiles around the table. Even Dave had expressed to him after the ambush at the tunnel that he felt giving Andrei the full vaccine was the right call. *Not because they deserve it,* Dave had said. *But because you don't deserve that on your conscience.*

Once Matt and Dave had recounted the details of the morning's and afternoon's events, the focus shifted to the future. Winter was coming, and with eighty-four members of the family, they had a tremendous amount of work yet to do, but at the same time, they now had a significant number of people to accomplish the work. Kevin's community teams also continued to push westward and provide vaccinations to survivors. They had pushed as far west as Bantry, Kenmare, and Killarney. The result was the vaccination of another 368 survivors vaccinated since December 2nd.

Matt paid particular attention to an interesting side note to this part of the meeting. Thirteen of these new survivors had asked to move to Kinsale and become part of the extended family. These included a mother with four teenage daughters from Dunmanway, three children around ten years old who had survived on their own outside Kenmare, and six soldiers of the 1st Cavalry Squadron. These soldiers, similar to the situation Seamus and Rory had found themselves in, were tasked with guarding the Kilworth Camp outside Fermoy. All thirteen were now being accommodated at Actons Hotel.

As Clare referred to them affectionately, the 3 M's, or Molly, Marvi, and Michelle, had focused considerable effort on revitalizing parts of downtown Kinsale. They had targeted several buildings at the corner of Pier Road and Market Quay, including the Commercial Hall and Temperance Hall. They'd organized a team from Liam's group to clean them out and gather useful merchandise everyone needed. One group with a panel truck had begun going to all SuperValue grocery stores to collect non-perishable food items. Another group scavenged pharmacies and medical clinics for items coveted by Kevin and Grace's medical team. A third group gathered winter clothing, while a fourth sought fuel and batteries. Overall, they had revitalized Kinsale to the point where people walked around during the day, playing at the playground. Matt had even seen several people jogging and doing calisthenics in the park.

The Irish on the council had assured everyone that despite getting dark before 4 pm in the afternoon, the winters were mild compared to New England. It was unlikely to snow enough to accumulate on the ground, and if it did, they'd all have a laugh, and it would be melted by noon the next day.

With most of the Adult Council departed Matt tipped his beer towards Stan, Dave, and Pete—his war council.

"Whadda ya got for us, Stan?" Matt asked. "You and Pete seemed all fired up to get to something on QuAI. I hope it's something good."

"Yeah, we've got several things I think you'll enjoy hearing about. First, though, I need everyone to know how much of the credit belongs to Liz and Juliet. Those girls put in twenty-hour days every day and never say a word. When I tell them to take a break, they take a thirty-minute nap and are right back at the computer."

"Yeah. I can't remember being in the captain's office without one or both of them there. I'll make a point of saying something, as I know it's different coming from someone other than their father. So what amazing AI function have we added today?" Matt said, rubbing his hands together in anticipation.

“First, as we discussed yesterday,” Stan began. “We’re spending considerable time focusing QuAI on monitoring the Russians in Belfast. We’ve established what I think are some very advanced protocols that should also identify any additional threats or anomalies anywhere in Ireland, north or south. We have a monitor dedicated solely to providing real-time coverage of all RF frequencies within one hundred kilometers of Belfast. We’re also tracking the location of the satphone you gave Andrei. If he keeps that phone with him, as you feel confident he will, we’ll know exactly where he is at all times.”

“Have we noticed any major changes to their RF patterns or locations since receiving the vaccine this morning?” Dave asked.

“Not yet, Dave. But the beauty of QuAI is that she’s all about patterns and anomalies. She’ll know exactly when something is out of the ordinary and will alert us immediately.” Not seeing any more questions, Stan pushed on. “The second thing is something I think you all will get a kick out of. QuAI, in her infinite wisdom, has spent the last several weeks slowly tweaking various satellite systems that she has access to. These include US government satellites as well as commercial ones. When we were forced to leave Vinalhaven, Juliet and I spent a lot of time during the voyage working with QuAI to have her minimize the ability of Cheyenne Mountain to detect her existence while maximizing her access across every sensor platform possible. A month later, the result is that we now have access to several satellite systems that give us almost 24/7 live satellite imagery over the entire island of Ireland.

“You’re shitting me,” said Matt. “That’s unbelievable, isn’t it?”

“I’m not shitting you, Matt,” replied Stan. “And yes, I do think this could be a game-changer. I’ll caveat that we have varying capabilities depending on the time of day and even which day of the week. Still, QuAI's made it seem to Cheyenne Mountain that these satellite systems have stopped working, and she can now redirect them. It's almost impossible to keep static coverage over Ireland due to various orbital issues, but QuAI's been able to patchwork a system of sensors that give us an amazing capability."

"So we could zoom in and see what Andrei is doing on the docks in Belfast right now?" Dave asked.

"Mmmm, sort of," replied Stan, hesitatingly. "These aren't all Keyhole satellites where we can read license plates. But we have very close to real-time capability to see many things, just maybe not as zoomed in as some of the intel imagery you've seen in the military. However, with AI, even a birdseye view can often allow us to see even the smallest things."

"Outstanding," said Matt. "This is something I'm going to want to get more involved in tomorrow. There's a lot I want to look at."

"That's what I figured. Juliet has become the imagery guru, and she's available anytime."

"Stan, would this be helpful for our energy assessments? I'm thinking maybe looking at wind farms around the country and seeing which remain operational and how well they seem to be performing?" Pete asked.

"Yeah, Pete. I think QuAI would be excellent in doing some of that analysis for us. Remember, guys, QuAI has almost unlimited bandwidth. Rather than us pouring over imagery, we simply need to ask her questions. She can analyze and provide answers faster than we could ever do ourselves."

"I'm impressed," said Matt, sitting back and drinking from his beer. "This day is ending much better than it began."

"I have more," said Stan.

“Do tell,” encouraged Matt.

“The last thing I have regards satphones. We have about a dozen of them, but we often find ourselves out of radio range with all the different teams moving around Cork. I asked QuAI for a solution, and I believe she has one. Like how she’s been able to control various imagery satellites, she’s also gained access to the Iridium network. While the business servers are undoubtedly down due to the pandemic, QuAI informed us she’s been able to alter some of the code to allow us to introduce new satphones into the system. This means Pete can go to the local electronics store and grab a handful of brand-new satphones. We can give QuAI the relevant info from the phone, and she can ensure the phone is registered and will work.”

“Wow,” said Pete. “So basically, almost everyone could have a satphone?”

“Something like that,” said Stan. “I think there may be some restrictions on the phone brand, but in general, we should be able to increase our number of working satellite phones significantly.”

“That’s amazing, Stan,” concluded Matt, standing up and walking towards the bar. “You deserve at least one more beer after that briefing. Can I get you one? Anyone else?” Everyone nodded affirmatively, and Matt retrieved four cold Stellas. “Okay, Dave, it’s your turn. What’re your thoughts on security given this new threat?”

Dave took a second to take a long swig from his beer, collecting his thoughts. “Well, some of what Stan just briefed changes what I was gonna say, so I’m improvising a bit here. Our current focus needs to be maintaining surveillance and increasing our defensive capabilities. I was gonna pitch you all a plan for maintaining a network of scouts in an outer ring around Cork to identify threats and provide early warning. But if I heard correctly, QuAI should be able to do that on her own with the new satellite access and coverage. Is that correct?"

"Yes," said Stan unequivocally. "QuAI will not only be a better perimeter security than human scouts could ever be, but we can also extend that perimeter to Belfast. Not only will she detect anything approaching us here in Cork, but we can also establish criteria for her to warn us should any movement happen anywhere else, like around Belfast."

"Awesome," said Dave. "Actually, wicked awesome, as we used to say growing up in Maine." Dave took another sip from his beer. "So what that does is allow us to focus on building up our defensive measures. I had a chance to grab a cup of coffee with Sergeant Jimmy Laffan of the 1st Cavalry Squadron. He's a pretty interesting character, and I instantly liked him. He's a squad leader tasked with guarding an ammunition supply point at Camp Kilworth, about 45 kilometers northeast of Cork City between Fermoy and Mitchelstown. The most interesting thing was that the Army only sent six of them because they were deployed with two Mowag Piranhas. For you Navy guys, the Piranha is like the LAV used by the Marines or the Army's Stryker vehicles. It has eight wheels and a 30mm Bushmaster autocannon. For reference, Matt, it's basically the same gun as used on the Bradley Fighting Vehicle, except in 30mm instead of 25mm. It can reach out and put a hurt on someone out to 3,000 meters and is one bad motherfucker."

"Damn," said Pete.

"Yeah, damn is right," added Dave. "Collins Barracks has a squadron of these bad boys. I plan to bring six of them to Kinsale and six more to Haulbowline. They require a three-person crew, so we can't man them all. But I'd like to have some pre-positioned for point defense and more in reserve. I'd also like to start identifying people in our group to serve as crew members and have SGT Laffan train them up. Whadda you guys think?"

"I like it," said Stan.

"Love it," added Pete, looking to Matt to complete the circle.

"Yeah, I love it as well, Dave. Great idea. Let's talk in the morning about who we think some of those crews should be, and then we can discuss with the team leaders a plan to carve them out for training. We can train Seamus and his sailors on the Piranhas staged at Haulbowline, but I don't want that to be their priority. I have something else in mind for them. What else you got for us, Dave? We need to get to the house in a few minutes to tuck the kids in."

"That's it for me, Matt, what about you?"

"I have two things, very briefly. I still need to flush out the plan for both, but I want to get you all thinking about them. First, I want to make Collins Barracks appear to be lived in. Pete, that's mostly you. Figure out how to get electricity in some of the buildings so we have lights on at night. Second, I'm considering moving one of the Irish offshore patrol ships down here to Kinsale."

At this last comment, everyone sat up a little straighter.

"Wow," said Stan. "I hadn't thought of that. I can definitely see the merit in it."

"I love it," said Dave. "Our own fucking naval artillery. You just trumped my Piranhas."

CHAPTER 35

December 9, 11:22 am

Matt sat staring at his whiteboard, now jammed with different bulleted lists and a few diagrams, while Dave poured over satellite imagery of Kinsale and Cork City. They were sitting in the opposing desk chairs of the owner's office aboard the Irish Rover, separated by the expansive mahogany desk. Steady rain continued to soak everything outside, and not for the first time, Matt was glad they sat within the luxury megayacht's luxurious comforts.

Now numbering 97 people, the extended family was making considerable progress across all functional teams. The military men, Seamus' section of sailors, and Sergeant Laffan's squad of cavalry troopers were proving to be the workhorses of the family. Yesterday, they had moved six Piranha armored vehicles to Haulbowline and Kinsale, along with considerable ammunition stores. Matt had spoken with Seamus about readying one of the offshore patrol vessels to move to Kinsale, but they had both agreed to hold off on making the actual move.

Matt's mind wandered to watch rain droplets carve paths downward along the tinted floor-to-ceiling windows of the Irish Rover's office. *I wonder what we're having for lunch?* Matt thought. *Is it a pasta day or a soup day? I missed lunch the last two days, so can't remember which day of the rotation we're on.*

Unable to concentrate, Matt stood up to stretch and considered making a fresh pot of coffee. "This guy, Andrei, he's up to something, Dave. I can feel it in my bones. I told you about his tattoo, didn't I? The scorpion on the frog?"

"Yeah," replied Dave. "It's in his nature, you said."

"Exactly! It's in his goddamn nature." Matt stretched again, looking out at the rainy harbor. "Hey, you want some more coffee?"

"Hey, you two! You still up there?" Stan's booming voice echoed through the small office. He was standing at the foot of the stairs on the main level below, calling up to them. Matt walked out of the office to hear him better.

"Yeah, Stan. We're here."

"Come on down to my office. You're going to want to see this."

Matt and Dave rushed out of the office and down the Irish Rover's central staircase to the deck below. They strode past the formal dining room, juked through the galley, and reached the captain's office just short of the yacht's bridge. Stan was sitting in front of a large computer monitor, with Liz and Juliet off to his left, typing away on keyboards linked to QuAI's vast stack of servers. Matt and Dave crowded in behind Stan to view what was on his screen.

"What're we looking at, Stan?" Matt asked. On the monitor, they could see what appeared to be a video taken from a satellite.

"On this monitor is a live feed of Northern Ireland, zoomed in to an area just north of the small city of Lisburn, a little over ten kilometers southwest of Belfast. The Hawkeye 360 system is being displayed on the smaller monitor to my left. That one shows the RF signals and tracks Andrei's satphone."

"What's the bugger up to? I knew he'd be up to something."

"So look here, at these four vehicles driving toward Lisburn. QuAI is highlighting them in red. D'you see?" Stan pointed to the monitor where four vehicles, each overlayed with a tiny red diamond, drove in a convoy. The view was unlike the Predator drone footage often seen on television or YouTube, with an angled view zoomed in to see individual people walking on the ground. The view on this monitor was from a much higher angle, like riding in a plane several thousand feet in the air. The four vehicles were noticeable because they were the only thing moving on the screen. Otherwise, it was too high to note any distinguishing characteristics of the vehicles.

"Yeah, we see," said Matt. "Who are they?"

"It's Andrei. If you look at the Hawkeye 360 monitor, you'll see the yellow satphone tag is currently in the same place as this convoy. You'll also note the flow of RF signals along this route—the guys in each of the four vehicles are talking on handheld VHF radios. According to QuAI, the convoy left the port where the Russian subs are docked approximately fifteen minutes ago."

"Where're they headed? To the green dot labeled Thiepval?" Matt asked.

"Exactly. QuAI's been kind enough to identify where she thinks this convoy is headed, and so far, she appears to be correct."

"Okay," said Dave. "I'll bite. What or who is Thiepval?"

"It's most definitely a what, Dave," replied Stan. "Better known as Thiepval Barracks. Home to the 38th Brigade and the 2nd battalion of the Royal Irish Infantry Regiment also called the Rifles."

"Oh, shit," said Dave. "That motherfucker!"

"Andrei the Scorpion," Matt said.

"Huh?" Stan looked at him oddly, unaware of the story of

Andrei's tattoo.

"I'll tell you later, Stan. Andrei is doing what we did. He's securing his area by tapping the local Army bases. Smart."

"Yeah, I thought you'd want to see this. The satphone is in the lead vehicle, so we can assume Andrei is leading the convoy himself."

"Has QuAI given any indications of anyone heading our way?"

"No," replied Stan. "Nothing so far."

"He's coming. He will most definitely be coming. It's in his nature."

The three men watched the monitor for the next ten minutes, noting the arrival of Andrei's column at Thiepval Barracks.

"Okay, Stan. I have a meeting with Molly at the restaurant which I am now late for. Keep an eye on these guys. They didn't bring any trucks, so I'm guessing they're scouting the place rather than loading up on arms and munitions. But let's see what we can learn. I'll have my radio with me if you need anything."

CHAPTER 36

December 9, 3:48 pm

The skies had cleared after lunch, and Christopher had been begging to toss the football in the park in front of Actons and the marina. Soon after Matt started playing catch with Chris and Mick, several others joined them. Before long, there were fifteen adults, teenagers, and children running around the wet green grass, playing with a multitude of balls. Shane was attempting to show Chris and Dylan the nuances of Gaelic football, using a ball that looked to Matt to be similar to a heavy soccer ball. Liam, Sharon, and Iryna were kicking a real soccer ball around with Laurie, Caroline, and several other children under ten, with a small goal set up where Liam was a simply awful goalkeeper, letting the young kids score kick after kick. Matt, whose first love had always been football, was tossing the pigskin back and forth with Mick, who had quickly learned to throw a nice tight spiral.

Mick's problem was that he couldn't catch.

"I'm calling you 'Stone Hands' Mick, from now on!" Matt joked. Like Christopher, Mick was a natural athlete, and the two boys got along like peas in a pod.

"I'm going deep, Matt. Throw it, and I'll catch it this time." Matt dropped back while Mick ran as fast as he could towards the park's far end. Matt tossed a perfect spiral, lobbed high in the air. Several onlookers stopped to see if Mick would catch it, jumping for joy as the ball landed softly in the boy's outstretched hands.

"Touchdown!" Yelled Mick. "That's what you say, right Matt?"

"That's right," said Matt. "That looked just like a Tom Brady to Randy Moss pass."

"Who's Tom Brady?" Mick asked.

Matt stopped in his tracks, staring at the young boy trotting back towards him with the ball. "Are you serious? Please, please tell me you did not just ask that question."

"Nope. Who is he?"

Matt looked at him, astonished. Others had stopped to watch the exchange, wry smiles on the faces of the Americans. "Chris!" Matt yelled. "I'm sorry, son, but we're going to have to take Mick back to Curragh Camp. I can't have you associating with someone who doesn't know who Tom Brady is." Everyone in the park started laughing, joining in the fun. Mick knew it was in jest, but he still didn't know who Tom Brady was. "Seriously, Mick, Tom Brady is simply the best quarterback ever to play the game of football. He's the GOAT—the greatest of all time. Mick, I'm not joking when I say this. Even at my advanced age, I dream of being Tom Brady when I go to sleep."

"You're funny, Matt," said Mick, laughing along with everyone. "Throw me another. Just like Tim Brady would." Mick winked at him, smiling.

"Chris! Go get your Tom Brady jersey. Mick is going to wear number 12 for a week!"

Just as Matt was about to toss another bomb to Mick, streaking down the field, Molly rushed out of the front of the Actons Hotel and called to Matt. "Matt! Matt! It's Stan on the radio. He says he needs to see you urgently on the Irish Rover."

Shit! Matt thought. *I left my radio with my gear inside the hotel. I wonder what he needs.*

"Okay, Molly. I grab my stuff and head over."

"He said urgent as in 'tell him to run as fast as he can."

Matt took a deep breath and began sprinting across the park toward the Irish Rover without saying a word. It was docked less than a hundred yards away, and Matt was there in no time. *It's very unlike Stan to panic. This can't be good.*

Matt bounded up the gangway, ran through the main salon, and took the stairs two at a time. Out of breath, he bolted into the captain's office, where he knew he'd find Stan, Liz, and Juliet staring at their computer monitors.

"What's up, Stan? What're we looking at?"

"The *Severodvinsk* just cast off her lines and is moving into the Belfast Lough heading towards the Irish Sea."

The blood drained from Matt's face. *This can't be! This is the one contingency we never even contemplated.* Matt took several deep breaths, his mind racing.

"Any indication where he's going?" Matt asked.

"None," said Stan. "QuAI just alerted us when she noticed the submarine hull begin to move."

"Were we able to get any indication of what they took from Thiepval Barracks?"

"I'm not sure they took much of anything. They were only there for thirty minutes. Juliet and Liz have both reviewed the footage several times, zooming in much more than the view I showed you earlier. Combined with a lot of radio communications while they were onsite, our best estimate is that they could not get into any of the arms rooms or didn't find whatever it was they were looking for."

"Interesting," said Matt. "I guess we need to remember that Dave and I have an intimate knowledge and understanding of how the Army operates. It would be extremely difficult to break into those arms rooms, but we knew where they would likely maintain the keys. Maybe the Brits took the keys with them?"

"Yeah," said Stan.

"One thing I thought of, Dad," said Juliet to Stan, the first time Matt could recall her speaking in this office without being directly asked a question. "I wonder if they were looking for information about us? Maybe they assumed we would be housed at an Irish military base, and they were searching for maps or other information. Especially given all of the military equipment and weapons we displayed."

"That's a great point," admitted Stan. "Russians might not understand the intricacies of Irish politics, thinking the north and south have the same military." Thiepval Barracks and the Royal Irish Rangers were a part of the United Kingdom's military and not affiliated with the Irish military in any way.

"Yeah, especially as a submariner," added Matt. "That's really good insight, Juliet. I think you might be on to something there." Matt paused, studying the satellite video of Belfast harbor. "That's a very large submarine. How big is that thing?"

"The *Severodvinsk* Yasen-class submarine is 456 feet long," answered Liz. "That's about 80 feet longer than our equivalent Los Angeles-class submarines. The other two subs, the *Yury Dolgorukiy* and the *Knyaz Vladimir* are even bigger. They're 557 feet long and a hundred feet longer than the *Severodvinsk*."

"Jesus. That's twice the size of the Irish Rover. He's still above the water," said Matt. "How deep does it have to be for him to submerge? And will QuAI be able to track him underwater?"

"That sub drafts almost thirty feet of water. I'm guessing they barely make it through into the channels of Belfast harbor, which are only about ten meters deep. Submarines normally operate in water at least 600 feet deep, or two hundred meters. Periscope depth is about sixty-five feet, but they'd want at least a hundred feet of water beneath them. So quick answer—he could submerge in 100 feet of water, but I wouldn't expect him to submerge until he has at least two hundred feet or more."

"Here, Matt," said Juliet, anticipating Matt's next question. "Here's a map of the Irish and Celtic Seas and their water depth. The numbers are in meters." Matt shifted his gaze over to the monitor in front of Juliet. The land mass of Ireland was colored yellow, while the seas were white. Dozens and dozens of numbers were spaced haphazardly across the screen along with contour lines similar to those found on the topographical maps Matt often used in the Army.

"Okay. So it's plenty deep in the middle between Ireland and the UK. 100-200 meters in most areas. But it appears much shallower along the coast. Am I reading that right?"

"Yeah, Matt, you are," Juliet replied. "The coast has a shelf that brings the water depth to about 20-30 meters in most places. There are areas a submerged sub could get to within several miles off the coast, but any closer than that, and they would likely need to surface."

"And to answer your second question, Matt," interjected Liz, who'd been sitting quietly until then. "The satellites QuAI is tapped into can probably track the sub if it's submerged down to about thirty meters, depending on the clarity of the water. It would also depend on if we had a good idea where to look."

"You know my next question, right, Stan?" Matt asked.

"Yes, I do. Worst case—twelve hours."

"Seriously? That sub can get here in twelve fucking hours from Belfast? It's almost four hours to drive it going as fast as we can."

"That submarine is considered the fastest nuclear submarine on earth, faster than ours. It's estimated to have a top speed of 35-40 knots. That's faster than the Hinckley going all out."

Matt felt truly afraid for the first time in a very long time. He realized he had almost no idea of the full capabilities of Andrei and his submarines.

"Is Andrei on the *Severod*...whatever it's called? Is he on the sub?"

"We can't be 100% sure, but we believe so. The last ping from the satphone came while it was located in the vicinity of the sub's conning tower just before being cast off. If the phone is inside the submarine's hull, there is no way to track it."

"Okay," said Matt. "I need to think for a few minutes. Please call Pete and Dave on the radio and get them down here ASAP. The four of us need to meet as soon as they can get here. Would you also put the word out—I'd like everyone to come to Actons if they're not already here. The only exceptions are Rory, Petty Officer Cassidy, and their five sailors. I'd like them at Haulbowline, standing by the radio. We'll have a meeting of the Adult Council after dinner. Thanks. Oh, and keep an eye on that sub, and let me know if QuAI predicts where it's heading. Maybe he's heading back to Russia now that he's vaccinated."

Matt walked out of the office without waiting for an acknowledgment or reply, his mind still echoing with thoughts of a submarine traveling over forty miles per hour *underwater*.

Finding himself in the upstairs salon of the owner's deck, Matt sat down in one of the overstuffed leather recliners. He pushed the button to extend the footrest, leaned back in the chair to look at the ceiling, and mentally put on his thinking cap. *Okay, motherfucker, what are you trying to do here with your trip to Thiepval Barracks and now your cruise around the harbor in your fancy submarine?*

Matt closed his eyes and mentally attempted to run through all the possible scenarios, discarding those that he felt were most unlikely and moving to the top of the list those most dangerous to his family. As he imagined QuAI could do billions of times per second, Matt tried to think through each course of action and decide how best he should prepare and respond. Fairly quickly, these various responses merged to form several distinct groups of options. It was now his job to decide which option was best for his family while preserving his ability to shift to other options should he choose wrong the first time.

After five minutes, Matt opened his eyes.

He had the makings of a solid plan firmly in his mind. Now, it was time to bounce it off his most trusted advisors and let them poke holes in it.

He grabbed the radio clipped to his belt and turned the volume back up. "Seamus, this is Matt. Come in, Seamus."

After about five seconds, Seamus's voice came over the radio, albeit weak. The repeater system worked, but it wasn't perfect. "Go ahead, Matt. This is Seamus."

"Remember what we talked about the other day on the tour you gave me? How long would it take to get started? And how long to get here?"

"We keep both ready to go, Matt, so we could realistically depart with an hour's notice. We could be there in one hour, but I'd plan for two."

"Roger. Have Rory and the men prepare to do just that. I'd like to see you here for the Adult Council meeting, and we can all decide together."

"Will do, Matt. However, if I may, I would like to stay here as my place is on the bridge."

"No worries, Rory. I'd like you here for the meeting, but

you'll have plenty of time to drive back. Trust me. I want you on the bridge. Matt, out."

Matt heard a commotion downstairs at the stern of the ship. Seconds later, Pete, Dave, and Kim entered the salon and took seats. Kim was not technically part of his war council, but he didn't mind if she sat in. He had often found that she approached problems much differently than the four military men and welcomed her novel ideas. She had also proven adept at finding gaps in their plans.

"What's up, Matt?" Pete asked. "Stan said it was urgent. He should be up in a sec." Stan walked into the salon from the foyer, several papers in one hand. "Speak of the devil."

With his war council around him, Matt asked Stan to give everyone an overview of the situation. Stan briefly outlined the Russians' activities earlier in the day and ended with the recent revelation of the submarine departing the port of Belfast. At the current time, the *Severodvinsk* was motoring slowly through the Belfast Lough towards the Irish Sea, making about ten knots and giving no indications of planning to submerge.

"Thanks, Stan," said Matt. "As you can see, this changes our security situation significantly. Before I get into my thoughts on a plan, I'd like to tell everyone a quick story. An old Russian fable—The Scorpion and the Frog. Some of you have undoubtedly heard it before, so I'll keep it short.

"According to this Russian fable, a frog and a scorpion are on the bank of a river and want to cross. The scorpion, unable to swim, asks the frog if he can ride on his back across the river. The frog turns him down, stating that the scorpion is too dangerous and would likely sting him as he swam. The scorpion scoffed at the frog, telling him that it would make no sense to sting him as surely the scorpion would himself drown should anything happen to the frog midstream. This made sense to the frog, who agreed to ferry the scorpion. Halfway across, the scorpion fatally stings the frog. Dying, with both of them about to drown, the frog asks the scorpion why he stung him despite knowing it would also be the scorpion's death. The scorpion replied: I'm a scorpion; it's my nature to sting."

Matt looked to make sure everyone was paying attention.

"Andrei, the Russian submarine commander, had a tattoo of a scorpion riding atop a frog on his forearm."

Matt let that fact settle in with those who didn't already know.

"So what he's doing is in his nature," said Kim somberly.

"Yes, that's exactly what I believe," said Matt. "Let's look at this in simplified terms. Andrei's actions fit into one of three boxes. First, they have absolutely nothing to do with us, and he's pursuing an agenda that's irrelevant to us. Second, he's fucking with us—either in an attempt to intimidate us or to pin down our location. Third, he's en route to destroy us." Matt looked around the room. "Can anyone come up with another reason? One that doesn't fit into these three boxes?"

Silence as everyone gave this thought.

"We can immediately discount the first box. Not that it's not plausible, but it would be negligent of us to wish this problem away. We'll know soon if he's heading to Russia or somewhere else. However, my gut tells me this is not the case. If they were leaving, all three subs would have stayed together. Correct me if I'm wrong, Stan, but QuAI has not alerted to any activity to indicate the other subs are preparing to depart, right?"

"That is correct," replied Stan.

"I think that box number three is equally unlikely," continued Matt. "First, I don't believe he knows exactly where we are. Second, if he wants to destroy us, he's sitting on a couple dozen nuclear missiles between the three subs. He could vaporize us and never think twice about it. He doesn't need to leave Belfast harbor to destroy us."

"So that leaves box number two," said Pete. "He's fucking with us."

"Exactly," said Matt. "Remember, he's a scorpion, and this is his nature. Stan, what access does Andrei have to sensors like QuAI does? Can he tap into satellite imagery? Or RF signals? Things that have been so useful for us?"

"Nothing like that," Stan said. "Liz and I just went through those same questions with QuAI. The *Severodvinsk* most definitely does not have access to satellite imagery. These subs are used to operating at the bottom of the ocean. All their systems are built to receive a dump of intelligence information from their headquarters when they near the surface. Everything needs to be pushed to them, and none of their capabilities allow them to pull it directly. Remember, the Russian leadership doesn't generally trust its military officers, so they keep a close hold on most information. As no one in Russia is alive to push it to them, they can't access these sensors, even if they do exist. As for RF signals, they have some sensitive collection sensors onboard, but these are almost exclusively geared for underwater collection. They have limited ability to collect data from above the sea, and they are especially adept at interpreting sounds, such as airplanes and helicopters, to determine the range and bearing of the threat."

"Good, that's what I'd hoped," said Matt. "He's a scorpion. He's spent his entire career in nuclear attack submarines. What do attack submarines do? They stalk and then toy with their prey before killing them silently and without notice."

"And we're his prey?" Kim asked.

"No, Kim, we're not."

"We're the frog," whispered Dave, just loud enough for everyone to hear.

"Exactly!" Matt exclaimed. "We are the motherfuckin' frog!" He looked at the four others around him. "The motherfucking frog, folks. That's who we are to this guy; we can never forget that. Cuz' he sure as shit never will."

Everyone looked at Matt, a bit stunned by his outburst.

"So, to complete the analogy," continued Matt, his voice calm and soothing. "He needs us to get across the river. In this case, the vaccine. But unlike the Russian fable, Andrei the Scorpion has a greater agenda. Our interactions the other day show that he desperately wants to get his hands on the remaining vaccine. He doesn't know how much, but I think it's safe to assume he believes it's in the thousands of doses simply because we didn't blink at giving him four hundred doses. Regardless of his long-term survival plans, acquiring thousands of doses of vaccine is equivalent to him crossing the river. During our conversations, he couldn't keep himself from asking about the remaining vaccine. Over and over.

"So what's his goal in fucking with us, Matt?" asked Pete. "Intimidation? Fear?"

"Yes, Pete, both. Understanding this situation requires us to put ourselves in his shoes. If I were him, there would be only one solid option for obtaining that vaccine. Anyone care to take a guess?"

"Come get it from us," said Dave.

"Nnnnhhhhh! Wrong, Dave. That's what an Army Ranger would do. But Andrei the Scorpion isn't an Army Ranger; he's a Russian nuclear attack submarine captain."

"Get us to give him the vaccine," said Stan.

"Bingo! You failed to phrase your answer in the form of a question, Stan, but I'll give it to you anyway. You've just won Final Jeopardy!" Everyone chuckled, although mostly to humor Matt and not because they found him amusing. "He's sitting in Belfast with three hundred men and these hulking submarines that are only good at sinking ships or lobbing missiles. He knows we have the vaccine but doesn't know where we are. He thinks we're somewhere near Cork because I'm sure one of Rhonda's gang told him as much, and maybe he can assume we're near the coast because we did recently arrive here from the US, which was likely by boat rather than plane. But other than that, we could be in one of a hundred towns along the coast in County Cork. With me so far?"

Everyone nodded affirmatively, so Matt decided to charge on.

"He can also probably narrow it down to the vicinity of Cork City, as that's where we made our stand with Oleg and Gregor at the tunnel along the M8 motorway. We had an ambush waiting, so if I'm Andrei, I'm likely figuring that my base is within thirty minutes or so of that location. Far enough to keep Oleg away from the hive but close enough to be able to move my warrior bees into ambush position. Whadda ya know, folks, Cork Harbor meets all those criteria. It's the second-largest natural harbor in the world and would be a great spot for us to establish our home base.

Matt stood up to grab himself a bottle of water from the bar. "Anyone want one?" He asked the group, but none were thirsty. Gulping water, Matt continued. "He needs us to give him the vaccine. To bring it to him voluntarily and without conflict. What better way to intimidate us than to show us his trump card: a 500-foot, hulking black nuclear submarine manned by real fucking Russian sailors and carrying real fucking cruise missiles. I believe Andrei intends to sail the *Severodvinsk* into Cork Harbor, on the surface, and for all of us to piss our pants the minute we see it."

Everyone stared at Matt, thinking about all he had just said. Stan put his palms together as if praying and began tapping them against his lips, carefully examining each aspect of Matt's assessment. Pete sat staring out the window, thinking. Dave stood up and got himself a bottle of water.

"You had me at fable," said Dave, laughing and standing up to get a cup of water. He looked around to see if anyone else had got his joke. "C'mon guys. Jerry McGuire? Really? 'You had me at hello'?"

"Oh, we got it, Dave," said Pete, deadpanned. "It just wasn't funny."

Matt couldn't hold back any longer and burst out laughing. "I thought it was pretty good, Dave."

"Yeah, I'm teasing," said Pete, chuckling himself. "You and your movie quotes."

"I think your analysis is sound, Matt," said Stan, getting the conversation back on track. "He's either gone for a joyride or some other purpose, or he's headed for Cork Harbor. At least that's what we should plan for."

"Agreed," said Matt. "And I think there's only two courses of action for us as I see it. We plan as if he's going to Cork, and he's come to intimidate us. And we plan as if we're wrong, and he's coming to Kinsale to kill us. Either way, we can't lose. Let's discuss some details, then brief everyone at the Adult Council meeting."

CHAPTER 37

December 10, 04:53 am

"We have positive satellite confirmation that the *Severodvinsk* has just surfaced two miles off the mouth of Cork Harbor in the Celtic Sea," Stan's voice boomed through Matt's earpiece. He had turned the volume up on the off chance that he fell asleep. Matt had been sitting along with Dylan in the windowless stone room at Camden Fort Meagher, wrapped in a heavy quilt and poncho since just after the witching hour of 3 am. Despite the thermal underwear and waterproof outgarments, his teeth were chattering.

"Dave, I'll keep you updated, but let us know when you have eyes on."

"Roger," replied Dave. Matt figured Dave was just as cold as he and Dylan were, situated on a bluff about two kilometers south of Matt and Dylan's hide site in Church Bay. Matt would have been wrong, as Dave felt his and LT's hide position was cozy.

He had planned ahead, bringing several dark tarps, thin air mattresses, and heavy quilts. To ensure they remained hidden from the approaching submarine, Dave laid the air mattresses down on the tarp, then covered him and LT with a space blanket, the heavy quilts, and another dark green tarp. They would be invisible to binoculars, infrared, or thermals—plus, they were pretty warm tucked in their cocoon.

Their defensive plan was fairly straightforward, and everyone at the Adult Council, although quite alarmed, fully agreed with their steps. First, Matt gave Seamus the green light to bring the Samuel Beckett offshore patrol vessel from Haulbowline to Kinsale. The plan was to moor it in the interior of the Kinsale Harbor, a few hundred meters south of where the Irish Rover was docked. While the Samuel Beckett would be protected from view by the rising bluffs of Castlepark and James Fort, its 76mm autocannon could shred the *Severodvinsk* as soon as it attempted to enter the River Bandon en route to Kinsale's harbor.

Second, while the Irish sailors were repositioning to Kinsale, Matt had SGT Laffan send three men to Haulbowline to man one of the Pirhanas staged there. This would be a last-ditch point defense weapon to keep the Russians on the *Severodvinsk* from attempting to disembark at Haulbowline and steal or sabotage the Irish ships.

Third, Matt had put in place a small ruse, although he was sure it would be unnecessary. Pete and Kim, along with Liam and Shane, had gone to Collins Barracks high on the hill above Cork City and turned on as many lights as were hooked up to the generators Tom had put in place there. He doubted the *Severodvinsk* could see this light from the lower reaches of Cork Harbor, but just in case, Matt wanted to present the illusion that Collins Barracks was occupied.

Matt didn't believe the *Severodvinsk* would get past the lower entrance to Cork Harbor because he and Dylan were sitting in one of the old bunkers built hundreds of years ago to repel invaders from the sea. While he didn't have a massive battery of coastal artillery, he did have something he felt would make the *Severodvinsk* turn around.

"Update?" Matt said over the radio.

"Russians on a bearing of 342, 2,400 meters south of Line Alpha, speed 10 knots. Dave, QuAI estimates you will have a visual when it reaches 1,500 meters south of Alpha. That's in 3 minutes."

"Roger," replied Dave. Line Alpha was their designated line that crossed the open mouth of the entrance to Cork Harbor. Dave's position was approximately 400 meters north of this line. They had designated Line Bravo as a point 1,000 meters north of Line Alpha, just under 1,400 meters south of Matt's position. According to the charts, the water depth at Line Bravo was 67 feet, which would ensure the sub was surfaced and put the *Severodvinsk* within range of Matt's surprise.

Matt waited anxiously, his foot tapping up and down, refusing to look at his watch.

"We're missing something, Stan," Matt said. "I can feel it. Have Liz and Juliet monitor everything with QuAI. I feel it, Stan."

"We have eyes on," Dave said. His voice was incredibly calm for someone staring at a Russian submarine directly approaching him.

"Matt, this is Stan. Not sure what to make of this. The satphone you gave Andrei just pinged the satellite. It's on the dock in Belfast." Matt looked at his watch; it read 5:01 am.

"Stan, get another monitor showing the live feed of Belfast. Or query QuAI. See what's happening there." Matt could only think of two reasons why the satphone was in Belfast. One, Andrei had given it to one of his men. Two, Andrei was not on the *Severodvinsk*.

"Stan, will the subs in Belfast have radio communication with the *Severodvinsk*?"

"Yes," replied Stan. They should have long-distance UHF radio communications if they're on the surface, or at least have their periscopes up."

"Line Alpha," Stan relayed over the radio net. "Just over three minutes to Line Bravo."

Something was going on. Matt could feel it.

"Matt, there's a convoy of vehicles leaving the port of Belfast. Four cars and what appears to be a school bus."

What the fuck are you up to, Andrei? Matt thought.

"The sub appears to be slowing down," Dave radioed. "Its wake has virtually disappeared."

"Roger, Dave," confirmed Stan. "Speed has reduced to two knots. She's barely making way, still heading north."

"This guy's playing chess, Stan," Matt said into his mic. "I think we're right that the sub is to intimidate us. But I also think it's to keep us occupied. Follow that convoy. That's his main effort this morning."

"We're on it."

They all waited as the *Severodvinsk* made its way slowly towards Line Bravo.

"Convoy is getting on the A1 motorway. Heading south toward Dublin. The satphone is with the convoy." Matt knew the A1 turned into the M1, which would take the convoy to Dublin. They could juke onto the M50, then take the M7 and head towards Cork. They could be here in less than four hours. Three cars and a bus could equal as many as fifty Russians.

You sneaky bastard. If you get on the M7 motorway, I will cut your fucking balls off, Andrei.

They waited. The *Severodvinsk* had come to a complete stop just north of Line Alpha. It floated just off Roches Point under the watchful gaze of Dave and LT.

Ten minutes.

Twenty minutes.

Forty minutes.

After forty-three minutes, the *Severodvinsk* surged forward back to her original ten-knot forward speed. "She's moving," called Dave. "Halfway between Alpha and Bravo. You should see her any second, Matt."

"Stan," Matt radioed. "Where's the convoy?"

"Just north of Swords, Matt. Maybe five klicks north of the Dublin Airport."

"Roger, keep an eye on it." Matt and Dylan both peered through their night vision binoculars. They could see the bow of the *Severodvinsk* in the dead center of the channel, heading north towards their position. It was an ominous sight through their long-range night vision optics. The water surging off the bow and the churning froth of the wake gave off a fiery luminescence in stark contrast to the sleek, dark hull of the submarine itself. The sub was now just over 1,500 meters away.

"Matt, the convoy just exited the M1."

"Onto the R132, right, Stan?" Matt answered, immediately knowing what Andrei was up to.

"Yes," replied Stan. "How'd you know that?" *Fuck!* Thought Matt. *You crazy, Scorpion mother-fucker.*

"Malahide, Stan. He's heading for Rhonda. I'm calling him." Matt's initial reaction was to warn Rhonda, but he realized it was too late. At this hour, she wouldn't likely be able to evacuate in time, and it was almost certain to get back to Andrei that Matt had called. This would give up a distinct advantage of knowing the satphone's location.

Matt pressed the speed dial for Andrei's phone and put the call on speaker so Dylan could hear. Matt wondered who would answer it if anyone. After the second ring, the phone connected.

"Hello, Matt. How are you this wonderful morning?" It was Andrei. He was in the convoy heading to Malahide. Matt motioned with his hand for Dylan to tell Stan over the radio.

"I'm hoping you can help me, Andrei. There is a large, black submarine entering Cork Harbor as we speak. Would you happen to know anything about that?"

"Why would you think that I would have any knowledge of that, Matt?" Andrei paused, and Matt willed himself to remain silent until Andrei spoke again. "It just so happens, Matt, that I do know a little about submarines. I would say that the fact you can see it is a very bad thing. They have extremely dangerous capabilities. You definitely wouldn't want to tangle with a submarine."

The guy's a scorpion, Matt thought. *What's his endgame? Is he willing to sacrifice a submarine? Matt had gambled that Andrei wouldn't take that loss, but that was when everyone thought Andrei was commanding the submarine. The fable, Matt, remember the fable!*

Matt hit the Mute button on his satphone. Toggling his radio, he calmly said, "Pineapple, Pineapple, Pineapple." This was the family's pre-established codeword for everyone to hunker down and prepare to evacuate. The submarine in the area made it too dangerous to move the Samuel Beckett or the Irish Rover. However, everyone in Kinsale was to gather at Actons and prepare to evacuate on command—Pete's group at Collins Barracks and SGT Laffan's three men on Haulbowline were to head directly back to Kinsale immediately. Any nuclear or cruise missile strike were most likely to be focused against targets in Cork City. Everyone in Kinsale should be safe. Looking at Dylan, Matt said, "Tell SGT Laffan to prepare to fire on my command."

Turning the Mute function off, Matt said into the phone,

"You mean I shouldn't assume that they are fellow survivors and welcome them with open arms, giving them the vaccine, like I did with your group?" On the other end of the line, Andrei said nothing. "Last chance, Andrei. Do you know anything about this submarine?"

"What do you mean, last chance?" Andrei asked over the phone. "Is that a threat, Matt?"

"It's only a threat if you know something about this submarine. If the submarine does not turn around in ten seconds, it will be full of holes and sink right to the bottom of Cork Harbor."

"What?" Andrei's tone had turned from icy confidence to alarm. "What are you talking about?"

"Ten seconds, Andrei. I don't bluff." Matt paused, listening to the commotion on the other end of the line. He could hear Andrei yelling at someone in Russian. "Ten...nine...eight..."

"Wait! Wait! Stop counting!" More furiously spoken Russian in the background.

"Six...Five...Prepare to fire on my command." Matt purposely said the last comment directly into the phone but also signaled Dylan to relay that to SGT Laffan. Twenty meters to Matt's left, SGT Laffan sat in the turret of a Piranha, the 30mm autocannon's barrel pointed downward at a slight angle and lined up directly with the submarine approximately 1,000 meters away. Matt had previously given SGT Laffan instructions that when Matt gave the command, the Piranha's gunner was to stitch the hull of the *Severodvinsk* right at the waterline. The Piranha was to keep firing until Matt told them to stop. They would only get one chance to defeat the submarine, and they needed to put as many of the armored-piercing 30mm rounds as possible into her steel hull. "Three... Two..."

"Stop! The *Severodvinsk* is stopping! It is not a threat." Matt held up his hand, signaling to Dylan and SGT Laffan to hold fire. Dylan held up eight fingers, signaling that *Severodvinsk* was now only 800 meters away. Matt could hear Andrei's muffled voice spouting off instructions in Russian. *I should have brought Iryna to translate, but it was too dangerous for her,* Matt thought. "Matt? Are you there, Matt?"

Matt looked through his night vision binoculars and could see that the wake behind the *Severodvinsk* had disappeared, and the submarine seemed to be floating in the middle of the channel without forward progress. The close distance worked significantly to Matt's advantage. Unlike the models of World War II, modern submarines no longer carried deck guns or anything that could harm Matt's team high up on this bluff. While they carried variants of anti-ship missiles, these hugged the surface of the water and would not be able to arc up to reach him on the bluff. Similarly, the cruise missiles carried by submarines such as the *Severodvinsk* had a minimum range, normally around ten miles, within which they couldn't be targeted.

"Yes, Andrei. I'm here. What're you trying to prove with this stunt?"

"What stunt, Matt? The submarine in Cork Harbor is not meant to harm you. Now that my men are vaccinated, we felt it appropriate to explore more of Ireland. I am sorry that we did not seek your permission first. I was unaware that you felt you were in charge of the entire country. And I am shocked that you would threaten harm to a vessel that has shown no hostile intent towards you."

You're a scorpion, Andrei. That's all the proof I need. Matt thought this, but Andrei's comments had him beginning to second-guess himself for a moment. *Could I have been wrong? No! He's at Rhonda's right now, and there's no way he's just stopping by for tea and biscuits.*

"Matt!" Stan's voice came through Matt's earpiece loudly.

For the first time Matt could remember, Stan's voice seemed somewhat alarmed. "Matt. QuAI has just detected a launch signature from the port of Belfast. She estimates it to be two cruise missiles heading southwest towards Cork, bearing 115 degrees, speed 650 miles per hour. If Cork is the target, time to target is just over thirty minutes."

Matt quickly jammed the Mute button on his phone, simultaneously toggling his radio mic. "Nuclear, Stan?"

"Not likely. The nuclear missiles on Russian submarines are supersonic ballistic missiles, normally multiple-warhead reentry vehicles. This is a cruise missile. Probably a 1,000 pound conventional warhead," Stan replied immediately.

"Roger," Matt replied. "Evacuate Kinsale to the fallback position just in case. Keep it orderly. They have plenty of time."

Matt paused for a second, staring towards the submarine floating in the channel below him, knowing that two missiles were inbound towards his location. *If I were Andrei, what would be my game plan? It must all be about the vaccine, and nuking us doesn't get him the vaccine. He needs us to give it to him.* Matt took several deep breaths, organizing how he wanted to play this. He couldn't inform Andrei that he was aware of either the impending missile attack or Andrei's move on Rhonda's group in Malahide. *How best to react in a way a scorpion will understand?*

Matt pressed the Mute button again, allowing his voice to be heard by Andrei on the satphone.

"Andrei, still with me?" Matt said into the phone.

"Yes, Matt. I have never left. It is you who, I think, put me in silence."

"I'm tired of playing games with you, Andrei. You say you want to be friends, but then you always do something to push the limits. You've been all about issuing veiled threats and demands from our first interaction. I told you in the parking lot that I would not tolerate threats or deceit. And I assume Oleg briefed you on our encounter, did he not?" As Matt spoke, he walked along a gravel path over to where SGT Laffan and his crew manned the idling Piranha. His head poking out of the commander's hatch on the Piranha's cupola, Laffan noticed Matt's approach and stood up in the hatch.

"Yes, Matt. Oleg and I discussed what happened. I have not yet threatened you, Matt. But if that is something you wish, I could arrange it."

"You see, Andrei. You can't help yourself. That comment in and of itself constitutes a threat." Standing next to the idling Piranha, Matt motioned for SGT Laffan to lean down so he could hear Matt. "Oh, Andrei. Please excuse me for one moment. I apologize, but I must give instructions to one of my men. I won't put you on Mute, as maybe hearing my instructions will be helpful for our ongoing relationship."

"Matt, I don't..." Matt stopped listening and held the phone at his waist. Dylan now stood next to him, and Matt looked up to SGT Laffan in the commander's hatch. "You're cleared hot, SGT Laffan. But instead of the waterline, I want you to place ten rounds spaced along the entire length of the hull, maybe six feet above the water line. Take your time. Make each shot count. I also want you to put ten rounds through the sail. Fire when ready." SGT Laffan gave him the thumbs up, and Matt quickly sprinted back to the cover of the stone room he had previously been in, with Dylan following close behind. Matt knew how loud the 30mm autocannon would be and wanted to put some space between him and the armored vehicle. He also wanted to watch the rounds impact the *Severodvinsk*. "Dylan, get eyes on and count the hits."

Matt put the phone back to his ear. All he could hear was Andrei screaming commands in Russian. "Andrei, are you still there?"

"Fuck you, Matt!" Andrei hissed, then disconnected the call.

Matt put his binoculars to his eyes just in time to see a huge wake appear behind the *Severodvinsk,* as it turned sharply to port, toward the bluff Matt was on. Smart, thought Matt. He's hoping whatever gun we have can't depress far enough to shoot downward. Unfortunately, he'd be wrong.

Bang!! The first round from the 30mm was much louder than even Matt anticipated. Dylan jumped sideways and almost lost his balance. Through the binoculars, Matt saw the impact two seconds later near the nose of the sub.

Bang!! Pause. **Bang!!** Pause. **Bang!!** Pause. **Bang!!** Pause. **Bang!!**

Bang!! Pause. **Bang!!** Pause. **Bang!!** Pause. **Bang!!** Pause. **Bang!!**

The gunner on the Piranha was taking his time, lining up each shot through his eyepiece and methodically firing single shots. While the 30mm Bushmaster was capable of firing almost two hundred rounds per minute, the truly amazing aspect of the weapon was its laser targeting system. It was so accurate that the gunner could easily put 30mm rounds through the same hole should he want to. However, the armor-piercing rounds currently loaded in the Mowag Piranha would slice through the sub's outer shell and pierce right through the much-thicker inner pressure hull of the submarine.

Matt and Dylan watched all ten rounds stitch the side of the *Severodvinsk* from bow to stern.

Bang! Bang! Bang! Bang! Bang! Bang! Bang! Bang! Bang! Bang!

Ten more rounds turned the conning tower into Swiss cheese.

"Matt, this is Dave, sitrep." Matt heard over the radio. *Shit!* In all the excitement, Matt hadn't kept Dave and everyone else informed. Dave could see the rounds hitting the *Severodvinsk,* but Matt had failed to tell everyone else.

"Sorry, Dave. Things got a bit hectic here for a second. Everyone, listen up. We have just disabled the approaching submarine. I intentionally did not sink it, but we have significantly damaged the pressure hull. It should be able to move under its own power, but it will never again be able to submerge. Its danger to us was its stealth, which it no longer has. There are no doubt casualties on board, but I think it should be able to make its way back to Belfast on the surface. Stan, how much time to impact?

"Twenty-six minutes, Matt. We've been thinking, and so has QuAI. We think the target is your location. Andrei knew you had to be on the western bluff overlooking the channel. QuAI thinks this was possibly his plan to locate us. By calling him and knowing where his sub was when you called, he could extrapolate the few locations where you could have eyes on his submarine. It's a tactic submariners often use to flush their opponents out of hiding."

"Roger," replied Matt. "I was thinking the same thing. Either my location or Dave's. His goal with those missiles is to prove a point and possibly eliminate me as an adversary. He can't risk destroying the vaccine, but he would enjoy destroying me."

"Agreed," said Stan. "You should both evacuate ASAP. QuAI has eyes on the submarine, so we no longer need to take the risk of having you on those bluffs."

"Roger," replied Dave. "Heading back to base now."

"Same here," replied Matt.

CHAPTER 38

December 10, 08:04 am

Matt's war council had expanded now that they were at war. Again.

They set up in the salon on the owner's deck, where Matt often sought refuge and relaxation. There were two large televisions, and Liz could quickly connect these wirelessly to the QuAI network to display satellite feeds and various maps. There was seating for all seven, as Matt added Kim, Liam, and Seamus to the informal war council.

The extended family had evacuated Kinsale, except for the sailors and volunteers crewing the Samuel Beckett and the dozen participating in the offensive plan. These twelve, consisting of Liam, LT, Derek, Dylan, Grace, Shane, and SGT Laffan and his five troopers sat in the bar of Actons, having a hot breakfast they prepared themselves. The rest of the family had loaded SUVs and passenger vans to drive fifteen kilometers west of Kinsale to Coolmain Castle. The historic castle, owned by Disney, had been renovated into a luxury accommodation and was situated on a small inlet a hundred meters back from the coast just south of the village of Kilbrittain. It was easy to get to by road. It was also an alternate location to move the Irish Rover and the Samuel Beckett if needed.

Matt sipped hot coffee, still feeling the chill of sitting atop

Camden Fort Meagher most of the night. *Although the chill could be because I just started a shooting war with the goddamn Russian Navy*, Matt thought to himself.

The widescreen television to his front showed a split-screen. On the left, the *Severodvinsk* limped along Ireland's south coast just east of Cork harbor. It was able to make ten knots and appeared headed back to Belfast. The right screen showed a zoomed-in picture of the port of Belfast, with the large black humps of two submarines nestled bow to stern along a concrete dock. Several large warehouses sat opposite the dock, separated by a paved apron about eighty meters wide on which more than a dozen vehicles and three school buses were parked amidst several stacks of shipping containers. This was where Andrei and his men now called home.

The two Russian cruise missiles had impacted near where QuAI had predicted. The first was centered on the parking lot at Camden Fort Meagher, while the second exploded about three hundred meters south. With a 990-pound warhead, the explosion would have devastated anyone within 150 meters of impact. Unlike in the movies, no one saw or heard the missiles or their explosions. They came in low from the northeast at over 600 miles per hour, hugging the contour of the earth as they navigated toward their target, bursting to supersonic speed a mile or so out, rising high into the air, and then slamming down to destroy a bunch of dirt and rocks on an Irish hillside. It was a tough morning for the parking lot at Camden Fort Meagher, but other than that, the missiles had proven harmless.

Unless you factor in that they'd started a war. A war that would require all of Matt's war council's skills to bring to a rapid and violent conclusion.

"Okay, folks, let's get started," Matt said to his assembled team. "We were forced to go a bit off-script this morning, but everyone is safe, so that's what matters. Also, we confirmed that Andrei is, in fact, a scorpion. Stan, Liz, and Juliet—you did an amazing job putting together all the intel to develop the variables we needed to put our plan in motion last night. We now have a much better read on Andrei's priorities and decision-making, which will allow us to be victorious.

"I just want to bring you all up to speed on a couple of things. First, Rhonda did not answer the satphone when I called her. The phone is turned on, and we are tracking its location. Currently, her phone is in a warehouse and is in close proximity to the satphone we gave to Andrei. The satellite feed shows that Andrei and his crew rounded up most people at the Malahide house. Counting the exact number being loaded onto the bus was impossible, but our best estimate is about forty people. We think Rhonda had about sixty folks staying at the Grand Hotel, so we don't know what's happened to the other twenty." Matt paused, letting that sink in with everyone sitting around him. Despite sitting in the plush couches and chairs of the Irish Rover's salon after being up all night, everyone was laser-focused on everything Matt said.

"Stan, would you mind giving us an update on the submarine we shot up and what's happening in Belfast?"

Stan glanced at several sheets of paper he had in his hand before speaking. "The Russian attack submarine is currently nine miles east of Roches Point. Ten minutes ago, she increased her speed to sixteen knots, which is just a bit slower than her max surface cruising speed of twenty knots per hour. We know that she must have sustained significant damage, but it appears her propulsion system remains intact, which is good. Otherwise, we'd be forced to deal with ninety Russian sailors abandoning ship in Cork Harbor. At her current rate of speed, it will take approximately 18-20 hours to return to Belfast's port.

"We believe that Andrei has kidnapped all of the women from Malahide. It's somewhat difficult to tell, but based on several indicators, QuAI believes all people who boarded the bus in Malahide and exited in Belfast are female."

"Sorry to interrupt," interjected Liam. "But what happened to the men?"

"We don't know, Liam," answered Stan. "We've reviewed satellite footage from the Grand Hotel over the last hour. We've seen no activity outside, and there have been no RF signals from that area since the Russians departed." Stan could see the pain on Liam's face, as these people were his friends. "I'm sorry."

"Are you saying they're dead? The Russians killed them?" Liam continued, getting agitated.

"I'm saying we don't know," replied Stan calmly. Liam sat back on the couch, wanting to ask more but knowing there weren't any answers.

"So what's going on in Belfast?" Dave asked, trying to steer the conversation toward something Stan might have more information.

"Both ballistic missile submarines remain docked in place at the York Dock in the heart of the port of Belfast. The Russians have set up their base in this area. We estimate all three hundred Russians live in the warehouses or aboard the submarines. The forty women were led into the warehouse upon arrival this morning, and based on the array of Russians around them, they were led at gunpoint."

"So they're there against their will?" Liam asked.

"We don't believe there's any other conclusion," Stan offered.

"What about the submarine this morning?" Dave asked. "Do you or QuAI have any thoughts on why Andrei would sacrifice his own attack submarine? Why not use one of the other subs? And why trust it to another captain?"

"First, we don't believe he planned to sacrifice his

submarine. We strongly believe his goal was to intimidate us and did not think we posed any threat to his vessel. Remember, everyone, we know a heck of a lot more about the Russians than they know about us. At best, we think Andrei believes we are capable fighters armed with small arms: rifles, pistols, etc. Until two hours ago, he had no earthly idea that we possessed large-caliber autocannons capable of puncturing his submarine. It's the only reason we believe would allow him to put his submarine into such a vulnerable position."

"So we think he thought we'd see this big, black submarine and shit our pants? Then we'd surrender and hand over the vaccine?"

"Yes, to the first part, Dave. And no, to your second question," said Stan.

"What do you mean?"

"I mean, yes, I think Andrei thought the sight of his sub in our harbor would scare the bejesus out of us. But he also has a healthy respect for us, especially Matt, after what transpired in Malahide and with Oleg at the tunnel on the M8 motorway. Given Andrei's cunning and proven strategic mindset, our best estimate is that he's living by the quote Matt often uses from Teddy Roosevelt: speak softly and carry a big stick."

"So if the submarine is his big stick, in that analogy," said Kim. "How is he speaking softly?"

"Rhonda," replied Matt, answering for Stan. "He's kidnapped all the women from Malahide. Andrei can't possibly know that we're fully aware that he's taken them to Belfast, but he knows we tried calling Rhonda this morning and that she didn't answer. That's him 'speaking softly.' I think he believes we'll start to worry and maybe send a team to Malahide to check on her. We'll capitulate when we see what we see there, which I believe will be all the men slaughtered and the women forcibly kidnapped—sorry, Liam, but that's what I think's happened." Matt paused, taking another sip of coffee. "Look, the submarine this morning was Andrei the Chess Player's attempt at Check. Kidnapping Rhonda and killing the men—that's him putting us in CheckMate."

"So did he?" Seamus asked, speaking for the first time.

"Did he what?" Stan asked back.

"Did he put us in CheckMate? I mean, for fuck's sake, we're staring down a man armed with two dozen nuclear Sea-Launched Ballistic Missiles and another couple dozen non-nuclear cruise missiles. If we're not in Check Mate, where the feck are we?"

"We're in the 'it's time not to be nice' time, Seamus. Unfortunately, we've dealt with guys like this before." Matt's mind flashed back to the leader of the Nomad bicycle gang in Vermont. "We're all in survival mode, but this guy is wired to think it's a zero-sum game, and his survival requires our destruction. There's no negotiating. There's no middle ground. We have two choices. We can run and hide—meaning we flee Ireland and hope he doesn't chase us with his submarines, or we can devise a strategy to remove Andrei and his nuclear-armed submarines as a threat forever."

"And I suppose you have a plan for that?" Seamus asked.

"Seamus," replied Dave before Matt could answer. "The one thing you are about to discover—our man Matt, here, *always* has a plan." Everyone chuckled despite the seriousness of the situation.

"I'm not sure if that makes me feel better or worse," said Seamus.

"Me either," said Dave with a completely straight face. With Dave's sense of humor, no one could tell if he was joking.

"Well, smartass, it just so happens that I do have a plan. A pretty good one, I believe," said Matt. "And for the record,

Seamus, I think you'll like it. Dave? Not so much."

CHAPTER 39

December 11, 1:41 pm

"It's bad, Matt."

Dave, Derek, and LT had driven up to inspect the Grand Hotel in Malahide, and Dave was now calling Matt to brief him.

"How bad?" Matt asked. "Is it what we thought."

"Yeah, exactly as we thought. It looks like all of them—at least twenty. The Russians gunned down most of them either in the hallway or in their rooms. A few look like they were executed with a shot to the back of the head."

"All males?"

"Yep. All males. One dead female in the lobby. Looks like maybe she was trying to make a run for it."

"That motherfucker," Matt said, mostly talking to himself. "Okay, man, you know the drill. I'll see you in a few hours. You should be able to radio Shane once you're on the M50 and do the handoff just as you practiced this morning. Call me when you're at Position Bravo."

"Roger," said Dave. "I'm going to enjoy fucking this guy up. He needs to go, Matt. Whatever we do, Andrei the Scorpion needs to die."

"And you guys were all dressed alike, wearing body armor,

baseball caps, and sunglasses?"

"Yeah, Matt. The entire time. Anyone watching wouldn't be able to recognize us individually, and you and LT have pretty similar builds."

"Thanks, Dave. Just wanted to make sure. I'll talk to you soon."

Matt disconnected the call with Dave and immediately phoned Stan onboard the Irish Rover. "Dave just called. It's just as we thought. The Russians killed all the males and took the females."

"Okay," replied Stan. "This is a good plan, Matt. It's complicated, but it's also extremely simple. It'll work."

"It needs to, Stan. Or we're all done. Best case, our wives end up slaves of the Russians. Worst case, we're all vaporized in a big mushroom cloud."

"It'll work, Matt."

"Yeah, it will. What's your status? Seamus in position?" Matt asked.

"We're all set. We moored the Irish Rover about a mile up the Arigideen River after we checked on everyone at Coolmain Castle. Clare and Marvi are holding down the fort, and all is well. We found a protected spot to moor the yacht and can remain here indefinitely. Seamus is tucked in and needs two hours heads up to be in position."

"Okay. Excellent. How about the Hawkeye 360? Did the Russians bite?

"Yes, it looks like they just did. QuAI just alerted to two handheld RF signals transmitting between a position just north of the Grand Hotel to one out by the M1. Looks like maybe they have someone in overwatch of the hotel and someone else on the road—just as you said they would."

"Okay," said Matt. "This guy's nothing if not predictable. So far, anyway. Dave knows what to do, and so does Shane."

"How about you guys? Any issues?"

"Nothing we couldn't figure out. The car park was not accessible as the entrance was in view of their pier. I found a nice spot to tuck in the SUVs between the hotel and the museum, and Dylan and Liam are now lugging everything up to the roof. I've told them to be slow and methodical, and we should have everything moved up to the roof here in the next thirty minutes. Kim and I have eyes on target. I haven't seen Andrei yet, but we should know where he is when I call him in a minute. I know you can see this through the satellites, but they've docked the damaged sub exactly where you predicted. Where they have it tethered in the narrow part of the channel, it's essentially parked in the other two submarines, which is perfect for us. All set to monitor the call?"

"Yeah, Matt. That's the next step in the plan. We'll be monitoring."

"Okay, standby." Matt disconnected the call with Stan and took a deep breath, collecting his thoughts. Once he made this next call, there was no going back. The plan they had spent yesterday morning refining and most of the night rehearsing would be put in motion as soon as he spoke with Andrei. The next few hours would very likely determine whether his family continued to live safely or not, and it would almost certainly determine if Matt himself lived or died. *C'mon, Andrei,* Matt thought. *I need you to be two things today: a naval submarine captain and a goddamn scorpion. Please! Let these be your nature.*

Matt pressed the speed dial for Rhonda's phone. He wasn't sure if Andrei would answer, but the plan called for him to try Rhonda's phone three times before calling Andrei's satphone. Rhonda's phone picked up after the second ring, but the person answering made no sound.

"Hello?" Matt spoke into the phone. "Rhonda? Are you there, Rhonda?" Matt didn't need to try too hard to make his voice sound worried.

"Hello, Matt," responded Andrei the Scorpion, his voice as icy and lifeless as his eyes had been when Matt had first met him.

"Andrei? What have you done with Rhonda and the women?"

"At this point, Matt, that is none of your concern."

"This is all so unnecessary."

"What was unnecessary, *Mudak*, is you attacking my submarine yesterday. As you say in your movies, you drew first blood. Did you enjoy the present I sent you?" Matt knew Andrei was referring to the cruise missiles and made a mental note to ask Stan what Mudak meant in Russian. From the tone, Matt was pretty sure it meant asshole.

"Yeah, you missed."

"I won't miss next time. The one thing they taught us in the staff college is that it's pretty difficult to miss with a 100-kiloton nuclear warhead. What do you think a 100-kiloton warhead would do to your home in Cork? Or maybe your lovely town of Kinsale?"

Matt's blood ran cold, and he couldn't breathe. *Andrei knew about Kinsale!* Panic set in, and he wondered if their entire plan was about to literally be blown out of the water.

"What's the matter, Matt? Cat got your tongue?"

Matt's mouth instantly became so dry he wasn't sure he could speak.

"Listen, Andrei, I'm not sure what…"

"No, you listen and listen carefully. I am done playing with you. I tried to be nice, and now it's time not to be nice." *Are you fucking kidding me*, Matt thought. *This guy just quoted Patrick Swayze!* "Are you familiar with *Roadhouse*, Matt? I grew up on American movies. It's how I first learned English. All we had were many of your movies from the 1980s. Patrick Swayze, Sylvester Stallone, Tom Cruise, Arnold. I loved the Terminator movies. Did you watch those movies, Matt?"

"I'm familiar," Matt replied. His mind was racing 1,000 miles per hour. Andrei seemed to know much more than Matt had given him credit. *How could he know about Kinsale? Did he have eyes on us? If he did, he knows about the Samuel Beckett and the Irish Rover. He might even know about our evacuation to Coolmain Castle. Is he playing me the way I thought I was playing him?* All these thoughts were racing through Matt's mind as he tried to concentrate on his conversation with Andrei.

"What do you want, Andrei?" Matt asked in resignation.

"How much vaccine do you have remaining?" Andrei asked. *Of course, this has always been all about the vaccine.*

"About two thousand doses," replied Matt, purposely offering a number that was a fraction of what they had.

"I don't believe you," said Andrei.

"I don't know what to tell you, Andrei. We have just under 2,000 doses left." Matt was confident Andrei had no clue about the real number, as only a trusted few of their original group from Woodstock knew the true amount. "Is that what you want? The vaccine?"

"Yes. What I want is for you to bring me all 2,000 doses. And I want you to bring them right now. I will give you four hours to get to Belfast, and I want you to deliver them personally."

"That's impossible, Andrei."

"Matt, do you know how long a nuclear-tipped ballistic missile will take to travel from Belfast to Cork? Less than a handful of minutes. I suggest you leave now."

"I'm not in Cork, Andrei. And I don't have the vaccine with me. I just left Malahide, which is why I called Rhonda."

"Ah, yes, of course," Andrei replied, seemingly amused. "I'll tell you what, Matt. I'm feeling generous today, seeing as how I'm now surrounded by all these lovely ladies with Rhonda. I will give you until midnight to get the vaccines to me at the port of Belfast. Do you need directions? You can't miss us. You will see our lights from the highway bridge across the River Lagan."

"You better not lay a finger on Rhonda or those women, Andrei," Matt said.

"Or what, Matt? What are you going to do about that? Three hundred sailors have needs, you know." Andrei replied, ice returning to his voice. "I've changed my mind. Your deadline is now 2200 hours. If you are not here with 2,000 vaccine doses, Cork will be vaporized. Game over, man, as they said in Aliens. Game over."

"I'll be there, Andrei."

"Don't do anything foolish, Matt. You never know who is watching." Andrei disconnected the call.

Fuck, Matt thought, willing himself not to panic. *Andrei knows too much. He's going to be on alert.* Instead of calling Stan, Matt made a quick call to Dave.

"Hey, man," Matt said when Dave answered. "Did you make the switch?"

"Roger, smooth as silk. Shane and two guys were waiting on the M50 at the Blanchardstown exit in the same model and color SUV we're in. We pulled off the exit just as he got up to speed. The Russian tail never saw it and is now following Shane back to Cork.

"Excellent," replied Matt. "I think we have a problem, though."

"What's that?" Dave asked, and Matt quickly filled him in on the conversation with Andrei and the mention of Kinsale.

"He got it from one of Rhonda's group," said Dave. "He must have. There's no way the Russians had eyes on us at any point. I'd stake my life on it, Matt."

"That's the point, Dave. We are staking our lives on it. Are you sure?"

"Yeah, definitely. We didn't have any OPSEC between Liam's group and Rhonda's. They used the satphone and talked to each other a bit. It never crossed my mind, Matt. I fucked up. But that's where he got it. He didn't have people watching us."

"Okay, what's your ETA?"

"Ninety minutes. We'll be at Bravo in ninety minutes."

"Okay, Dave. Call me when you get there." Matt disconnected and called Stan, who had been monitoring the satphone conversation with Andrei and the one with Dave.

"I agree with Dave," said Matt. "Andrei's fishing a bit. He's trying to intimidate you. It's what he does, remember?"

"Yeah," replied Matt. "He's doing a decent job of it. When he quoted Roadhouse, I almost shit myself, Stan." Matt chuckled at the thought. "Seriously, what kind of psychopath quotes fucking Patrick Swayze?"

Now it was Stan's turn to laugh. "You, Matt."

"Oh yeah," said Matt, smiling. "Well, to paraphrase Marcellus Wallace from Pulp Fiction: I'ma get medieval on his ass."

"The plans a good one, Matt. Juliet and I are monitoring everything, and it's lining up exactly as we sketched it out. There's a lot of moving pieces, but everyone knows their job, and it's going to work."

"Okay, Stan. Last chance, though. We could still deliver him

2,000 doses of vaccine and walk away."

"That's the point, Matt: the Scorpion and the Frog fable. There's no walking away. He's going to sting us no matter what. It's in his nature."

"Yeah. You're right, Stan. You're right. EENT is 5:33 pm, and we're still on track to kick things off at 6." EENT was the end of evening nautical twilight—the time of day when full darkness descended after the sun went down.

"Roger, we'll be standing by."

Matt disconnected and sat back against the roof's wall. As it had been most of December, the sun was hiding, and he felt chilled. He wasn't sure whether it was from the temperature or his call with Andrei. Taking a couple of slow, deep breaths, Matt nodded his head a few times, thinking to himself that this plan was going to work.

He looked to his left, where Dylan lay prone on a foam mat, his eye glued to a spotting scope. The two of them were on the roof of the Titanic Museum. Kim and Liam rested inside the roof's stairwell after an hour of shuttling all their equipment and supplies up five flights of stairs. Matt had smiled when studying the maps and satellite imagery of the port, noticing the large silver, star-shaped building immediately across the man-made channel from the York Dock, where the three submarines were tethered. Five stories high and just over 300 meters from the subs, the Titanic Museum's rooftop offered the perfect vantage. The view was so good Matt was at first cautious that Andrei may have placed a sentry there. However, Andrei was a submarine commander, not an Army general, and thankfully, his instincts had not been to assign a person as lookout across the harbor.

After selecting the vantage point of the Titanic Museum from the satellite imagery yesterday morning, Matt took a moment to savor the irony of launching the destruction of the

Russian submarines from such an aptly named building. He then worked with Dave, Stan, and Pete to refine the plan he had formed in his mind.

Matt's plan had four steps to success: deceive, divert, fix in place, and destroy. These identical elements could be found in almost every successful attack plan going back thousands of years of military history. An attacker should first make his enemy believe that an attack is not imminent. Second, when possible, the enemy should be oriented in the wrong direction from which the attack will occur. Third, the enemy must be stationary to allow the destroying force to bring down the hammer. Lastly, overwhelming violence of action should be unleashed to destroy the enemy's capability and will to resist.

This plan had three objectives—two of which Matt felt certain they would either succeed in or die trying. These two were the destruction of the Russian submarines and the death of their commanding officer. Matt hoped they could also achieve the third objective—the safe liberation of Rhonda's group—but was less certain of their ability to do so. He was unwilling to trade the lives of his family members for hers, and he hoped that killing Andrei and many of the Russians would allow Rhonda and her friends to escape.

The war council finalized the plan yesterday morning and immediately launched several moving pieces. The Samuel Beckett was the first to move out, with Seamus, all his sailors, and those from Liam's group who had volunteered to assist on the offshore patrol vessel. In addition, they had two additional special passengers, Pete and Liz. Those remaining in Kinsale had been broken down into their assigned teams for the upcoming mission and spent the day preparing and rehearsing.

Before first light this morning, those heading north had departed up the M8 motorway in a convoy of vehicles, including SUVs, two Piranha armored vehicles, and a panel truck. They made a quick detour to stop at Curragh Camp in Kildare and load up on some special items Matt had identified for the mission, and then the teams split up to go their separate ways.

All the moving pieces would come together shortly—at 6 o'clock this evening, to be precise.

CHAPTER 40

December 11, 5:55 pm

F*ive minutes until GO time!*

Matt looked through his night vision binoculars to confirm nothing had changed since he had last looked two minutes prior. They had spent the last few hours watching the Russians across the channel and mapping the dock to identify key targets. There were only so many places for the Russians to hide on the concrete pier, and Matt's team planned to target all of them.

The roof of the Titanic Museum had proven to be the perfect overwatch position. The building was constructed in the shape of a diamond, with a triangle jutting from each of its four sides. The result was an eight-sided star shape, with the points of the four triangles extending much farther out from the main diamond-shaped building. It reminded Matt of the bastions of an old military fort.

What proved extremely beneficial for Matt's team was that these bastions allowed him to establish separate firing positions for the four of them, each of which converged on the same area of the York Dock where the Russians were situated. While less than four hundred meters away from the Russians, the real beauty of Matt's position was that the 100-meter-wide River Lagan separated him from the Russians as it flowed from the heart of Northern Ireland into Lough Belfast. This made it virtually impossible for the Russians to launch any counter-attack against his team on top of the Titanic Museum.

The Port of Belfast was shaped like a three-tined fork with its long handle pointed to the northeast and the tines pointed southwest like the devil's pitchfork pointed downward when viewed on a map. The middle tine of the fork was the River Lagan, flowing northeast into the three-mile wide Lough Belfast, which opened into the North Sea. The west and east tines were each almost a mile long but only 150-200 meters wide. The land between the tines consisted almost entirely of concrete piers, container storage lots, and warehouse after warehouse. The western tine, a mile-long inlet for ships to dock along, was called Pollock Dock. The eastern tine was labeled the BP Dock, and as one could guess, it had dozens of immense oil storage tanks adjacent to the water.

The Port of Belfast was most famous for its shipyards, several spread across the three tines forming the port. The most famous of these shipyards, Harland & Wolff, was where the Titanic had been built before her doomed maiden voyage in 1912. It was at this location, between the River Lagan and the BP Dock on the east side of the port, where the Titanic Museum was located.

The York Dock, where the Russian submarines were tethered, was a small offshoot on the west side of the central tine, only about five hundred meters long. The result was that the warehouses where the Russians were living were on a narrow peninsula of land with water to its front and rear. When the shooting commenced, the Russians would only have one direction to flee unless they planned to swim.

This geography made it simple for Matt to plan his attack: place a fixing element at the head of the peninsula, labeled Position Bravo, and a support element with defilade fire across the breadth of the Russian submarines and warehouses, labeled Position Alpha. Position Alpha was where Matt, Dylan,

Liam, and Kim sat atop the roof of the Titanic Museum, while Position Bravo was where Dave waited with his team. The decisive element in Matt's plan, what he referred to as Thor's Hammer, would come from neither of these two positions. Thor's Hammer would strike from the sea.

Matt looked at his watch. It was time to get this party started.

Not knowing whether the Russian subs could detect RF radio signals, Matt had insisted that all communications before the attack be restricted to satellite phones. Likewise, Matt had forced the Samuel Beckett to move into her final staging position with all of its radar turned off to not alert the Russians.

Matt had just had his final call with Stan to confirm that all elements were in position. The Russians seemed to be helping things, as Dylan and Kim noted that most Russian sailors seemed to be staying in either the large northern warehouse or on one of the submarines. From what they had seen, their best estimate was that the southern warehouse was where Rhonda and the other hostages were being held. The Russians had not been idle since their arrival in Belfast and had established power cables between the submarines and the warehouses. The buildings were lit up like Christmas trees, along with a dozen site lights illuminating the 200-meter by 100-meter concrete pier between the warehouses and the subs. This illuminated pier would transform into a killing zone in exactly sixty seconds.

Matt hit the speed dial for Dave, who picked up instantly. "All set, man?" Matt asked him.

"Roger, we're all good. We'll switch to radio once the first round goes off."

"Yeah, that's still the plan. Everyone has a radio, including the bridge of the Samuel Beckett and Pete. It'll be much easier to communicate. I plan to leave my satphone on so that Stan and Juliet can hear everything, as they won't be able to monitor our radio comms. You're cleared hot, Dave. Get those first rounds close."

"Will do. It's been a while since I've used a mortar, but SGT Laffan seems to know what he's doing. Happy hunting! See you on the flip side."

Their call disconnected, and Matt took a moment to breathe deeply and collect his thoughts. The next few minutes would be the most hectic of his life. There was also a very real possibility that they would be the last few minutes of his life. He was about to attack 300 Russians armed with AK-74s and nuclear missiles. What could go wrong?

Matt looked to his right and gave the thumbs up to Kim and Liam. They were sitting about ten meters away from him, making final adjustments to the Command Launch Unit, otherwise known as the CLU, attached to two Javelin anti-tank missiles. Next to Liam, a .50 caliber machine gun sat menacingly on its tripod, set back a few feet from the roof's parapet, with the barrel pointed over Matt's head. When the shooting began, the plan was for Kim and Liam to fire their anti-tank missiles into the submarines. A fire-and-forget weapon, at 350 meters, the armor-piercing missile should easily penetrate the submarine's pressure hull, but to Matt's knowledge, no one had ever been dumb enough to shoot a Javelin at a submarine. Stan had carefully instructed them where to aim, to penetrate the hull near the sub's combat information center and thereby disrupt any ability to launch a missile. Once the missiles had been fired, Liam was to man the .50 caliber machine gun, with Kim as his assistant gunner to keep the gun loaded with ammunition and to spot targets.

Another ten meters to their right, Dylan remained in the prone position. However, he had swapped his spotting scope for a Remington 700 with its attached night vision optics.

Dylan and Matt were the designated snipers for this mission, with the objective of dropping any Russians attempting to board the submarines and anyone who looked like a Russian officer. While Matt still had his trusty M4 by his side, he had elected to exchange his Remington 700 for one of the Accuracy International .50 caliber sniper rifles they had liberated from the Army Ranger Wing's armory.

Matt heard a launching mortar's distinctive, hollow pop, followed rapidly by five more pops. It was second only to the whistling of incoming artillery in terms of sounds Matt never wanted to hear again in his lifetime. This time, Matt at least knew the incoming mortar rounds were not targeted at him, and he hoped Dave's aim was true. The 60-millimeter mortar was one of the items they had stopped at Curragh Camp to retrieve, and Matt had taken two of them. Half the length of the ones employed by the US Army, the South African-made Denel Vektor M1 60mm mortar allowed a three-person team to put accurate indirect fire onto targets up to 1,500 meters away.

Dave's team was located at Position Bravo: Buoy Park adjacent to St. Anne's Cathedral, approximately nine hundred meters southwest of the submarines at the York Dock. This part of the city had been decimated during World War II, with almost 1,000 people killed in a single night of German Luftwaffe bombing in April 1941. Tonight, the bombs were outgoing from Buoy Park and not incoming.

The high-angle flight of a 60-millimeter mortar takes approximately ten seconds to impact from the time it is launched. It can be the longest ten seconds of your life.

Interestingly enough, the Russian submariners appeared unfamiliar with the popping sound of a launching mortar. Matt looked through his night vision scope atop the AI .50 cal and noticed all the Russians standing in front of the warehouse stop in their tracks upon initially hearing the sound. Instead of dashing for cover as Matt would have done, they pointed towards where the sound came from and appeared to be discussing it. Quite a few Russians ran out of the warehouse to see if they could identify the sound. The Russians stood their ground for ten seconds, discussing the six loud, strange popping sounds across the city.

Everything changed when the first round impacted. Everything.

Dave's aim and distance were spot on, as the first two mortars exploded dead center on the concrete pier between the submarines and the warehouse. Unlike movies where bodies fly from impacting artillery, these explosions were accompanied by a tremendous *Whump!* followed by spraying shrapnel and bits of concrete in all directions. The Russians standing within twenty meters of impact dropped like marionettes with their strings cut. Many lay still, but most rolled in pain or tried to stand back up to run away. Additional mortar rounds continued to explode across the pier.

Matt turned and yelled "Fire!" at Kim and Liam but saw they were already aiming their Javelins' CLU and pressing the trigger. Likewise, Matt could hear Dylan firing methodically from his position across the rooftop. Matt reached up to toggle his radio mic. "Execute, Execute, Execute. Let's go, Seamus! We need rounds on target!"

Matt heard the soft whoosh of the soft launching Javelin, followed a moment later by the ignition of its rocket engines. Matt could smell the chemical afterburners of the rockets. As Matt put his eye back to the .50 cal's scope, he noticed the two large explosions along the sides of the largest Russian submarines, the Borei-class ballistic missile subs. Matt quickly found a target for his rifle, a Russian standing alongside the lead sub. A gentle trigger squeeze preceded a tremendous kick to Matt's shoulder as the rifle recoiled. At this range, there was no doubt that the Russian had just been torn in half by the large caliber bullet.

Matt shifted his aim to the open door of the left warehouse, where he knew Rhonda and Andrei's satphones had been. The first man to run out the door was blown backward by another of Matt's .50 cal rounds. Matt thought of shooting into the building, knowing his rounds would slice through the thin aluminum siding like a hot knife through butter, but he was distracted by the call on the radio.

"On the way, Matt. Firing now," came Seamu's Irish accent over the radio. Seconds later, supersonic 76mm high-explosive rounds began impacting along the hulls of the submarines. The LE Samuel Beckett had arrived at the party!

Having departed Kinsale yesterday afternoon, Seamus, Rory, and their crew had sailed up the eastern coast of Ireland, careful to remain at least a hundred miles behind the *Severodvinsk* limping back to Belfast. They had spent most of today anchored just offshore the Ards Peninsula, waiting to be called forward and serve as Thor's Hammer for Matt's plan. They had inched around Copeland Island earlier that afternoon and then, an hour ago, pulled up just short of Helen's Bay, around the corner, out of sight and about ten kilometers from the entrance to the concrete piers of Belfast's Port. Ten minutes ago, they had crept slowly towards the port, and when the first mortars were launched, Seamus had gone flank speed ahead to get the Samuel Beckett into position as quickly as possible.

Now floating five kilometers from the mouth of the port, Rory zeroed in the Beckett's fire control system onto the heat signatures of the two Javelin explosions in the side of the Russian submarines. The state-of-the-art computer-enhanced optics mounted high on the Beckett's mast allowed Rory to literally zoom directly in on the submarines, press a button to activate the laser rangefinder, and then squeeze the trigger to launch a 12.5-kilogram 76mm shell at supersonic speeds towards the target. The supersonic round of the OTO Melara

76mm gun allowed for a flat trajectory similar to a rifle round. At this range, the SAPOM armor-piercing projectile tore into the hull of the lead submarine, the *Knyaz Vladimir*. These rounds tore gaping holes in the vessel's side, and from Matt's viewpoint, he wondered at the level of destruction the shell must be causing within the ship's bowels.

The night erupted in a mass of confusion as dozens of 76mm shells continued to pummel the hulls of all three submarines. Rory was instructed not to stop firing until the initial magazine was empty. With eighty rounds in the magazine and a rate of fire of one hundred rounds a minute, it didn't take long for Rory to put eighty rounds into the Russian subs.

If this doesn't disable them, I don't know what will, Matt thought. When they put together their plan, Stan had assured them there was virtually no risk of detonating one of the nuclear warheads aboard the submarines. However, he did caution them that there was a real risk of radiation leaking from the vessels, more likely from their core reactors than from the smaller warheads.

"Shift Fire, Seamus! Shift Fire!" The Samuel Beckett's autocannon had an automated reloading system that allowed two crew members to quickly and continually keep the 76mm gun supplied with fresh rounds. They switched to high-explosive shells rather than the armor-piercing ones for the reload. Matt watched as the Beckett shifted its considerable firepower to focus on the larger Russian warehouse containing most Russians. This was Matt's cue to embark on the next phase of his plan, and he got up to run back to the stairwell.

"Look out!" Kim yelled. Matt wasn't sure who she was yelling at, but he instinctively dove to the rooftop just as an explosion washed over him, covering him with debris blown from the roof's parapet. Matt felt searing pain along the back of his left shoulder but was pretty sure it was just some minor shrapnel. "RPG!" Kim yelled, slapping Liam on the back and pointing to the left of where the machine gun had been firing. Matt sat up and watched as Liam shifted fires to decimate four Russians attempting to employ several RPG launchers against Matt's team atop the Titanic Museum.

"Phase Two!" Matt yelled into his radio. "Phase Two, Phase Two," he said again to make sure. Picking himself up, Matt dashed for the stairwell. He had less than a minute to get into position for his pickup. As he ran, he flexed his left arm and, while painful, noted there didn't appear to be any significant damage to his limb.

"Assault team at Positions Charlie and Delta," Dave's voice said clearly and calmly over the radio net. "Moving forward now."

"Good copy," replied Matt, rushing down the five flights of stairs. Positions Charlie and Delta were located on Garmoyle Street and Corry Road. About two hundred meters south and west of the Russian warehouses, the assault team assured that no Russians could flee to the south or west without being cut down by their withering fire.

The intensity of the battle continued to rage outside the Titanic Museum, and to Matt's attuned ears, he was thankful that most of the rounds appeared outgoing rather than incoming. Of greatest importance, there had been no missile launch from the submarines, nor even the opening of any launch tubes. At the bottom of the stairs, Matt grabbed a pre-positioned cut-down ballistic helmet mounted with a night-vision monocular and infrared light along with a bandolier of 30-round 5.56 magazines. He slapped the helmet on his head and slung the bandolier over his shoulder as he sprinted out the museum's door and headed north.

Matt could see the 76mm high-explosive shells streaking before him and impacting the warehouse. Matt ran north from the museum, across an open 150-meter stretch of flat concrete pier, at the end of which was Matt's destination. As he ran, it occurred to Matt that this concrete was where the Titanic's keel had first been laid. Matt knew he was exposed during this run but felt confident he would be aided by darkness and the fact the Russians had bigger things to worry about than a single person sprinting away from them.

Out of breath, Matt tried talking into the radio, "Pete, this is Matt. I'm ten seconds out."

"We're here," replied Pete instantly. "You'll see us when you get to the end of the pier."

Matt continued to run and saw the dark silhouette of a sleek RHIB bobbing at the end of the pier. Even in the darkness, Matt could distinguish Liz at the helm of the 24-foot rigid-hull inflatable boat's center console. Pete stood amidships, one hand holding one of the aluminum guardrails positioned around the RHIB while the other held onto the aged metal ladder built into the side of the pier. Matt began lowering himself down the ladder and felt Pete's hands grab his vest and haul him on board. The RHIB's inboard-outboard engines were whisper quiet, but Matt knew from Seamus that the boat could reach speeds exceeding 45 miles per hour. The Samuel Beckett had three MST 800 RHIBs, using them as life rafts and assault boarding vessels.

"Welcome aboard," said Pete, who was dressed identically to Matt with a magazine-festooned assault vest, Level IV armor plates, helmet, night vision goggles, and M4 hanging from a two-point sling. "Everything going as planned?"

"So far, so good," replied Matt. "Hit it, Liz. We need to get over there now."

Liz pushed the throttles forward and expertly steered the craft across the narrow channel of the River Lagan. Bringing the sleek boat quickly onto a plane, Liz accelerated northeast to the point a few hundred meters away where the ports 3-tines separated into individual channels. She swung the boat hard to port, making a U-turn and zooming into the channel for the York Dock. The night was extremely dark, but they could all see clearly with night vision goggles. Explosions still rocked the warehouses about 600 meters to their front, and Matt could see .50 caliber tracer rounds zipping across the channel from atop the Titanic Museum, as well as muzzle flashes and infrared beams from laser pointers from where he knew Dave's assault element was encroaching towards the Russian warehouses. The three Russian submarines lay dead in the water directly to their front, fire, steam, and clouds of smoke visible through the dozens of holes punched in their hulls. Through Matt's night vision lens, the emergency lighting inside the submarines shown brightly through the dozens of jagged holes in their hulls, making Matt think of Swiss cheese. 76mm rounds from the Samuel Beckett continued to explode into the closest Russian warehouse.

Matt toggled his radio mic. "Seamus, Rory, ceasefire. Ceasefire from the ship." The RHIBs route was taking them directly underneath the line of fire from the Irish ship to the warehouse. Matt had little interest in being that close to the high explosives screaming overhead at supersonic speeds. Matt knew that Rory was now shifting his aim back to the submarines and would use the computer-enhanced zoom capabilities of his fire control system to see if the Russian vessels posed any threat.

"Right up there, Liz," Matt yelled. "See the ladder?" Matt pointed to another ancient metal ladder built into the side of the concrete pier. The ladder fronted a point just before the York Dock, where a slot had been built into the pier for single ships to dock and unload. Matt could see large mounds of aggregate, what looked like sand or maybe crushed stone, in 5-meter-high piles beyond the pier's concrete apron.

Liz deftly maneuvered the RHIB against the pier's ladder,

and Matt clamored up the rungs, followed close behind by Pete. Standing atop the pier, Matt could see they were now less than eighty meters due north of the Russian's main warehouse. As he and Pete began slowly walking towards the warehouse, the night suddenly seemed to become much quieter. The firefight to their front continued to rage, but all around them was silent.

Matt was now on the hunt. A Scorpion hunt.

He and Pete moved about ten meters apart and walked slowly towards the cover of some scrap metal about fifty meters north of the Russian warehouse. They could hear over the radio the two elements of Dave's assault team maneuvering up to the southern warehouse, the one they believed Rhonda and her group were being held hostage. The hostages were Dave's priority. Matt's priority was Captain Andrei Miskov.

When Matt put the plan together, he knew Andrei would be in one of four places at this point in the battle. He could be dead or trapped aboard one of the submarines, dead or fighting from the open tarmac of the concrete pier, or in one of the two warehouses.

"Dave, this is Matt. We're north of the warehouse. What's your status?"

Matt could still hear a significant amount of fire from where Dave's assault elements were approaching the southern warehouse. The goal of Dave's element was two-fold. First, assaulting the southern warehouse offered the best chance of freeing Rhonda and her fellow hostages. Second, he would flush the Russians, particularly Andrei, directly towards Matt and Pete. Given the level of pure destruction wrought by the Irish warship, Matt wasn't sure how many Russians remained alive. Those who were alive would likely be cowering on the ground and crying like babies. Matt had never been on the receiving end of a weapon like the 76mm autocannon, and after watching its destructive capabilities, he hoped he never would.

"My close support element is in place, and I'm with my breaching team. We're on the south side of the southern warehouse and about to breach," said Dave over the radio. While calm, he sounded out of breath.

"Roger. We're continuing to press towards the northern warehouse. Still no sign of Andrei."

"Good copy, Matt. We'll keep our eye out for him."

Matt and Pete continued to move forward cautiously, taking up a position on each side of a six-foot-high stack of what appeared to be steel I-beams, less than thirty meters from the north warehouse. To their right, closest to where Matt was kneeling, was a line of a half dozen port-a-potties. A breeze blew, and Matt was overwhelmed by the smell of feces, almost causing him to gag.

"Jesus, Pete. Did you just shit yourself?" Matt whispered.

"Now's really not the time for jokes, Matt," Pete said. Matt forgot that Pete was a Navy lawyer, and his sense of humor seemed to disappear in the midst of close-quarters combat.

"Sorry, buddy," Matt whispered back. "Stay frosty. As soon as Dave breaches, we're gonna have some action.

All of a sudden, the southern warehouse flashed brightly as if struck by lightning. A split second later, Matt heard the near-simultaneous crack of four flash-bang grenades detonating. Not knowing exactly how big the interior of the warehouse was, Dave had erred on the safe side and used four flashbangs instead of one to temporarily immobilize anyone in the front part of the building. While Matt was too far away to see it, he knew that Dave's assault element, consisting of Derek, LT, and Grace, were now sprinting into the warehouse, shooting anyone who looked like a Russian sailor.

Matt and Pete kept their eyes focused on the corners of the

northern warehouse. Based on their position, Pete watched the corner closest to the submarines while Matt concentrated on the back corner. Matt sensed movement to his right and watched as six figures darted out from the rear corner. They were heading almost directly at Matt's position. The two figures at the front and rear of the single file were armed with assault rifles, while the two men in the middle carried only pistols. They were not wearing any combat gear and appeared to only be wearing pants, shirts, and shoes.

Having no time to warn Pete, Matt simply placed the infrared beam of his PEQ-15 aiming laser on the lead Russian, and rapidly squeezed the trigger twice. He immediately shifted his aim to the second person and placed two bullets into his torso before the man had time to react. The other four dropped to the ground, with the two men in the rear spraying Matt's position with automatic fire. Having ducked back behind the stack of I-beams, Matt quickly leaned out and loosed off a half dozen rounds at the area where he saw the Russian's muzzle flashes. The Russians responded in kind with massive bursts of automatic fire in an attempt to suppress Matt.

Pete, taking the initiative, crept around the left side of the I-beam stack as soon as he heard Matt shooting. This put him in the blind spot of the two Russians at the rear of their column, and as they focused their fires on Matt's position, Pete took careful aim and fired several rounds into each of the Russians.

The two men in the middle of their single file immediately popped up to their knees and placed their hands in the air.

"Don't shoot! Don't shoot!" Yelled the Russian in the lead. "There is a mistake! Don't shoot!"

Matt recognized the voice. Andrei.

"Cover them, Pete," Matt yelled. "Both of you! Keep your hands in the air and walk slowly towards me. Any sudden move and you will be shot. Do it now!"

Both Russians, their hands held high in the air, began walking slowly towards where Matt kneeled by the corner of the stack of steel. When they were five meters away, Matt instructed them to keep their hands high and get on their knees.

"You're a fucking piece of shit, Andrei," Matt hissed at him. "I should fucking shoot you right now."

"This is all a mistake, Matt. I should never have threatened you. You know I would never have launched a missile. To be honest, we do not have the full code anyway. We can launch missiles, but we can't arm the nuclear component without a code from General Headquarters."

"Shut the fuck up. Who's your partner there next to you?"

"This? This is Captain Gusev. He is the captain of *Knyaz Vladimir*. He will tell you. We cannot utilize our nuclear weapons. We have only done what we need to survive. You cannot fault me for that."

"You just couldn't help yourself, could you, Andrei? I saw the tattoo on your forearm. The scorpion and the frog. It's in your nature, isn't it?"

"I won't apologize, Matt, if that's what you're asking. Yes, it is in my nature. I did what I needed to do to protect my men, the same as you would." Matt kept his rifle's laser directly on Andrei's chest. At five meters away, Matt wanted to step forward and butt-stroke the conceited Russian.

"Let me zip tie them, Matt," said Pete on the side of the I-beam pile. "We need to secure them. Others might be coming, and we need to round up the rest of the Russians. Cover me." Without waiting for Matt to reply, Pete dashed forward to secure the two Russian officers. Pete knew Matt was getting angry, and he wanted to prevent him from doing anything rash. Pete sprinted to a position behind Andrei and roughly pushed the Russian forward onto his face, grabbing the man's hands and zipping them in the plasticuffs they had brought for just such an occasion. Within seconds, Pete had also placed zip ties on the other Russian officer. Pete left both Russian submarine commanders kneeling on the ground, with Andrei twisting his body in an attempt to look at Matt through the darkness.

"I'm not gonna lecture you, Andrei, but clearly you didn't do what you needed to keep your men safe. Look where they are now. This is all of your doing. Your instinct is to sting, to lash out and intimidate. To be a scorpion. Remind me someday to tell you the story of my old Special Forces unit's nickname. You'll enjoy it." Matt looked over to Pete. "Whadda you think, Pete?

"Break, break," Dave's voice broke into the radio net. "Matt, this is Dave."

Matt knew instantly from Dave's tone that something was wrong. Very wrong. "What's wrong, Dave? Do you have casualties?" Matt's heart began racing at the thought of one of his family members being wounded or killed, especially now that Andrei was no longer a threat.

"They killed them, Matt. They fucking massacred all of them!" Dave said rapidly and without pause, very unlike Dave's normal demeanor under stress.

"Calm down, Dave. What do you mean? Who killed who?" Matt asked, keeping his voice calm and steady.

"Rhonda, Matt. The Russians shot them all as soon as our attack started."

"Are you sure, Dave?"

"Every woman here is dead, Matt. We don't know how many hostages there were; some may have escaped, but there's at least thirty dead women in this warehouse. Rhonda included. A lot of them are naked, and I assume they've been raped."

"Wait one, Dave." Matt looked at Pete through his NODs. Pete was shaking his head. Matt then looked down at Andrei and Captain Gusev. Neither man had heard Dave's transmission as Matt and Pete wore earpieces connected to their radios.

Matt could envision Rhonda and the rest of the women lying on the dirty floor of the warehouse; their bodies contorted unnaturally in death. Matt stood up and walked up to Andrei.

"I would like to hear your story, Matt. I think there is much for us to discuss."

Matt looked down at the man kneeling, his hands zipped behind his back. Andrei the Scorpion. The man who had threatened to kill his family had now just killed two dozen innocent women. Women who had done nothing whatsoever to harm or threaten Andrei and his men.

"Don't," said Pete.

Matt was no longer listening. Matt flipped up his NODs, pointing the rifle directly at Andrei's forehead. "You stupid, motherfucker. Those women did nothing to you."

"Don't, Matt," Pete said again.

"Please, Matt. Wait! I can explain," Andrei pleaded.

Matt slowly began squeezing his trigger finger, the barrel of his M4 three feet away, and pointed directly at Andrei's forehead. Matt suddenly relaxed his finger, deciding not to shoot Andrei in the forehead. Lowering the barrel several degrees, Matt quickly pulled the trigger, sending a bullet right through Andrei's Adam's apple and exploding out the back of his neck. Andrei toppled forward, blood spraying from his throat as he desperately tried to breathe.

Matt adjusted his aim to the left and fired a round into Captain Gusev's forehead, killing the Russian officer instantly.

Matt could hear Andrei gurgling at his feet, his eyes staring up at Matt, knowing the man was drowning in his own blood. It looked incredibly painful, and Matt brought this pain to eternity with him when he died in a few seconds. Matt thought of saying something, maybe some line from a 1980s movie, but this wasn't a movie. Instead, he reached up slowly and toggled his radio mic.

"Dave, this is Matt," he said calmly.

"Go, Matt," Dave replied instantly.

"Kill them all. Every. Fucking. One. Of. Them. Take no quarter."

CHAPTER 41

December 13, 10:00 pm

Matt was propped up on several king-sized pillows on his bed in the Raffeen House. Clare snored quietly next to him, sound asleep. The bedside light was on, and Matt had just started rereading one of his favorite books, the 13th Valley, which Clare had found at a Kinsale bookstore.

The last two days had been a concerted effort to get things back to normal for everyone in the extended family. Seamus and his crew had returned the Samuel Beckett to Haulbowline. Clare and the Moms had returned to Kinsale from Coolmain Castle. Dave, Matt, and the rest of the team had returned from Belfast after conducting a thorough walk-through of the York Dock.

After killing Andrei, Matt assisted Dave's assault team in clearing the York Dock of Russians. By this point, almost all Russians were either dead or had fled. A quick count of bodies tallied more than 180 dead Russians, most of whom were inside the northern warehouse decimated by more than a hundred 76mm rounds from the Samuel Beckett or on the concrete apron that had borne the brunt of the mortar rounds and whithering .50 cal fire. There was some disagreement, but the consensus was that at least twenty Russians were likely killed on each of the two Borei-class submarines, possibly as many as forty, as it seemed the Russians preferred sleeping on the subs.

Undoubtedly, a dozen or two Russians may have escaped their cordon and were now on their own in Belfast.

Fearful of potential radiation, Matt forbade anyone from inspecting the insides of the Russian submarines. The visible damage to the vessels was evident from the outside, but Matt elected to be doubly sure. Using premade satchel charges containing sixty pounds of C4 explosive, Matt dropped two satchels into the main hatch of each Russian submarine. Using time fuse, the satchels detonated when the team was several miles away, en route back to Kinsale. The blasts were easily heard, and Matt knew that the insides of each submarine would no longer be useful to anyone, possibly for a million years.

Matt hated potentially creating a dirty bomb and releasing radioactive material into the area. But he hated even more the possibility that someone could access these weapons and use them to harm his family.

Upon returning, Matt was concerned for the emotional and mental well-being of those who went to Belfast. Combat was never easy, and close combat was even more difficult. Matt knew from experience that the most difficult part often occurred in the days and weeks after the action. Miraculously, no one on either Matt or Dave's team suffered anything more than cuts and bruises and some minor shrapnel. However, the internal realization would set in that their actions had led to the deaths of more almost three hundred Russians, some of whom had done nothing wrong and were simply victims of their commander's greed and hubris. Kevin was spending a lot of time with all the participants, and so far, no one seemed to be showing any signs of PTSD.

Everyone was working hard to get back to their normal routine, and Molly and Clare were planning a large celebration for Christmas in a couple of weeks. The fact that Matt was lying in his bed, his wife and children sleeping soundly under the same roof, was a testament that things were returning to normal.

Matt looked at Clare sleeping peacefully next to him. She was wearing one of his old unit t-shirts as a nightgown, and he could see the cartoon figure on the front. Matt's Special Forces team had gone by the nickname Mongoose, and the cartoon on the t-shirt depicted a large mongoose, wearing sunglasses and carrying an M4 in one hand and a grenade in the other. A large green snake was in the mongoose's teeth, harking to the euphemism of "snake-eaters" often used to refer to Special Forces. Matt smiled as he looked at the shirt, knowing the true reason why his unit had chosen the mongoose as their moniker. Mongoose were impervious to snake venom, which allowed them to attack even the most deadly snake without fear. Matt also knew, in addition to snake venom, that mongoose were impervious to the neurotoxin of other creatures—specifically scorpions.

Matt focused on his book, John Del Vecchio's seminal novel following several fictional soldiers through their combat experience during the Vietnam War.

Ring, Ring

Ring, Ring

Matt's head snapped to look at the satellite phone ringing on his nightstand. The ringing roused Clare from her sleep, and she sat up in bed beside him. Similar to their setup on the Irish Rover, Tom had installed an external antenna on the outer wall of the Raffeen House, routing a wire inside so that the satphone could receive its signal and operate indoors.

Ring, Ring

Matt looked over and did not recognize the phone number calling him. The only people calling who had this number were Seamus at Haulbowline or his close friend Rob, who was rebuilding his life in South Africa after surviving the cataclysm. For a second, Matt wondered if this could be one of the Russians using Andrei's or Rhonda's sat phones, but Matt remembered they had confiscated both of them while searching the southern warehouse.

Who could be calling me? Matt thought.

"Who is it?" Clare asked.

"I don't know," said Matt, reaching over to pick up the phone, his thumb hovering over the green button that would connect the call.

"Well, the only way to find out is to answer it, Matt. Answer it before they hang up."

Matt clicked the button and connected the call. "Hello, this is Matt," he said into the phone.

"Matt Sheridan?" A man's voice replied. "This is President Todd Moravian. There's a lot you and I need to talk about."

THANK YOU

If you've made it this far, it likely means you've read the first three Matt Sheridan novels. I sincerely appreciate the time you've invested in my novels and hope they have provided some entertainment.

If you enjoyed Standing Ground, it would mean a lot to me if you would take the time to leave a review on Amazon. The goal of any author is to increase the readership of their books, and leaving a quick 5-star review on Amazon greatly impacts the algorithms that allow new readers to find this book. So, I would like to personally thank all of you in advance for taking the time to leave a quick rating. I read every single review and they mean a lot.

If you're considering leaving a 1-star review (or even a 2- or 3-star one), why not let me know directly instead by emailing me at Robert@OfficialRobertCole.com? I personally read every email and always welcome feedback from readers. If any of you have specific comments or questions, please don't hesitate to reach out.

Best regards,
Robert Cole

ACKNOWLEDGEMENT

When I published the first novel in this series, I did it more for a sense of accomplishment without much thought as to whether anyone would enjoy reading it. I have been overwhelmed by the positive responses from those who've enjoyed Matt Sheridan and his post-cataclysmic adventures. It has been an honor and a privilege to know I've provided you with enjoyable entertainment.

I would like to personally thank all of you who have left a review on Amazon.

While I have attempted to make this work of fiction seem as real as possible, any factual errors are entirely mine. In some cases, the errors are intentional, while others are likely due to ignorance - but in all cases, the fault lies entirely with me.

As with Matt Sheridan, Ireland holds a special place in my heart. The places you read about in Ireland are entirely real—I'd encourage all of you to have a pint at the Spaniard Inn or sample the chicken wings at Captain America's. I have taken some liberty in describing various buildings and establishments to protect the privacy of the owners. Likewise, the descriptions and layout of the Irish military bases are generally accurate, but the specific details of where and how weapons are stored have been modified for obvious reasons. The Irish and Russian naval ships described in the novel are actual vessels, and I have taken care to remain as true as possible to their real-life characteristics and capabilities. For those readers who like to argue the nuances of the process for launching a Russian nuclear missile or the gauge of needle used for a pneumothorax—you win.

A special thank you to Donald, Tracy, Kelsey, Derek, Dylan, Kirstie, Dave and Michelle for being characters in yet another Matt Sheridan novel. My apologies to Donald, who, unfortunately, was sacrificed due to the needs of the story!
Another huge thank you to all my extended family and friends who have encouraged and supported me on this journey as a novelist. I have attempted to weave bits and pieces of your personalities into the various characters, and I hope you have enjoyed some of these special moments.

Butch, Matt, Bob - thanks for your friendship, encouragement, and story ideas. A special shout out to the Lambda Iota fraternity at the University of Vermont - a group of extremely wise individuals dating back to 1836.

Thank you to my parents for their encouragement and for passing on their love of reading.

Thank you most of all to my wife and children. My daughter is the one who strongly encouraged me to finish my first novel, and my son has become my most valuable editor. Your love and support are what make everything worthwhile.

ABOUT THE AUTHOR

Robert Cole

Robert Cole is a former infantry officer in the U.S. Army who has worked as a consultant on classified government projects similar to those outlined in this novel. In addition to having served with some of the Army's most elite units, Robert is also a successful entrepreneur and college professor. He's currently working on a 4th Matt Sheridan novel in addition to another novel that readers of the Matt Sheridan series will enjoy.

To learn more about Robert, please visit his website at www.officialrobertcole.com.

Made in United States
North Haven, CT
08 June 2024

53371648R00225